'Fresh and vibrant. Miller has built on her previous triumphs and has shouted from the rooftops that she will broker no compromise with anyone, least of all her readers' *Irish Independent*

'Blends passion, drama, glamour and intrigue' *The Bookseller*

'Zoë Miller's done it again… a hot page-turner with a shiver of sensuality' *Evening Herald*

'Intriguing and fun… contains a great cast of characters, a beautiful setting and a storyline that will keep you guessing' *Chloe's Chick Lit Reviews*

'A good, solid story with romance, glamour and deep emotion' *Chick Lit Club*

Zoë Miller was born in Dublin, where she now lives with her husband. She began writing stories at an early age. Her writing career has also included freelance journalism and prize-winning short fiction. She has three children.

Also by Zoë Miller

Guilty Secrets
Sinful Deceptions
Rival Passions
A Family Scandal
The Compromise
A Husband's Confession

www.zoemillerauthor.com
Twitter:@zoemillerauthor
Facebook.com/zoemillerauthor

Zoë MILLER

A Question of Betrayal

HACHETTE
BOOKS
IRELAND

A CIP catalogue record for this title is available from the British Library

ISBN 978 1 473607231

Printed and bound by Clays Ltd, St Ives plc

Hachette Books Ireland policy is to use papers that are natural, renewable and recyclable products and made from wood grown in sustainable forests. The logging and manufacturing processes are expected to conform to the environmental regulations of the country of origin.

Hachette Books Ireland
8 Castlecourt Centre
Castleknock
Dublin 15, Ireland

A division of Hachette UK Ltd.
338 Euston Road
London NW1 3BH

www.hachette.ie

Dedicated with lots of love to the three bright stars who light up my life so much –

Cruz, Tom and Lexi

May you always shine brightly

Chapter One

September 1980

She doesn't set out to save anyone's life that evening. She's twenty-four years of age and she's far too busy saving herself, but she ends up rescuing both of them.

The private cove nestled between two headlands is her secret escape. She slips out every evening when the intensity of the bright afternoon has softened and there is a kind of lull, like the world holding its breath, before the day slides into the mellow evening, and sits in a secluded spot in the sand dunes. She hides her heartache behind a mask, and looks at the breadth of the sea frilling in and out from the far-off horizon, the immensity of a sky stretching on forever and the breeze teasing the marram grass so that it dances along the sand dunes.

Then there is the music. Up behind the sand dunes, there are a few bungalows and mobile homes scattered along the low headland overlooking the private cove. Most are occupied by families during the summer months but now, with the children back in school, they are closed up. Apart from one. Someone is still living in the big house down at the end of the track. The house that's rumoured to be owned by a foreigner. It's situated a little away from the rest overlooking the sea, and she knows it's occupied because she has heard the sound of piano music floating on the air for the past three evenings. The music is like water dancing over stones. It's alive, fluid and clear, the sparkling notes streaming out like bubbles into the calm, still air. It soothes her heart and fills her with something she'd never expected to feel again – hope. Listening to it, it's easy to imagine her life could come good again and she could be anyone she wanted to be.

She could sit there forever listening to it, but she can't. Sitting in the dunes is a secret luxury, helping her break away from the mess her life has become.

She usually has the cove to herself, so she is surprised to see the shoes. They are sitting in the sand dunes up beyond the line of seaweed and driftwood that indicates the tide mark. A man's casual shoes; grey sneakers with white laces. When she gets closer, she sees the folded note stuck into one of them. It's caught between tied laces to ensure it won't blow away. It's meant to be found. Her gut instinct tightens as cold fear slams into her head, pushing her own troubles into the background.

She plucks out the note with shaky fingers and opens it. It is a single sheet of white notepaper. There is a signature in black ink scrawled across the bottom of the sheet: Luis. Above that, three short sentences in a spidery writing that crawls across the page, in a language she guesses is French. She doesn't understand it, except for the words scrawled just above the signature: *Pardonnez-moi.*

Pardon? For what? She looks up, her eyes scanning the horizon, hairs rising on the nape of her neck. At first, she is unable to focus and then she spots a lone figure, almost blending into the grey-silk movement of the sea, a figure walking out to the vast horizon, as purposefully as is possible against the tide.

She catches her breath. Panic surges through her, and then she is running, as fast as she can, across the strand, into the shallows, the water cold as it swirls around her feet. It splashes up, soaking the bottom of her jeans, weighing them down. She ploughs on as best she can. He is tall and blond and wearing a grey T-shirt. The water is up to his waist and any minute now, he could fall forward into it. Now it is up to her hips, the weight of water slowing her.

'Hey, wait!' she calls out, her words caught on the breeze. 'Wait! Stop!' She flaps her hands futilely, her breath heaving in her chest.

He doesn't falter. The sea is up to his chest now. Chilled by the water and sick with anxiety, she makes a supreme effort. 'Help, help,' she screams. 'Help me, please.'

Her heart skips a beat when he stops, alert, his head tilted. 'Help, help,' she cries again. 'Help me.'

He turns around. He's a slight distance away but she can gather by his expressionless face that he's not really seeing her. He's lost in a world of his own.

'Over here,' she shouts, 'Luis?'

He doesn't move and she's terrified he'll turn around again and be lost to her. He's not far from where the beach shelves steeply, another few feet and he'll be gone. If he turns in another direction, he could be caught by the rip tide. She pushes through the body of cold water, as the waves slap onto her chest, the tide almost lifting her off her feet.

'Stop! I'm here,' she calls out.

'Go away,' he shouts.

'I can't. I need help. Come back, please.'

'No. Go away.'

'Please, help me,' she calls out. A wave lifts her off her feet. She screams at him as she falls backwards, the water closing over her head. She gets to her feet, her mouth full of salt water making her splutter for breath, and her arms flailing and splashing as her wet clothes weigh her down. As she lifts her head, she sees that he's retracing his steps, cleaving back through the waves.

'Where are you?' he shouts in an accented voice. 'Make noise, I must hear you.'

She splashes and shouts back. 'Hurry, for God's sake.'

3

He turns towards her, and it's only then that she realises his eyes are fixed unseeingly in her direction. He is blind. She shouts some more, splashing as hard as she can, and all the while edging back closer to the shore to bring him in a little safer. He eventually reaches her, his arms out to grasp her and she grabs on to him, putting her arm around his waist, holding him tightly.

'Are you okay?' He pats the top of her head.

'Yes, thank you. Oh, thank you.' Her teeth are chattering so much with cold and shock that she can hardly put the words together. They stand there, his body anchoring hers against the swell of the sea, the waves flurrying against them.

'What do you think you're doing?' she asks, raising her voice against the roar of the tide.

'What do you think it looks like?' he says.

She can't place his accent. Not quite German, though certainly European. Questions teem through her. What's he doing in southern Cork? How did he manage to find his way to this cove? It's a little off the beaten track, a quiet spot outside Kinsale.

'You were foolish to walk out so far,' she says. 'There's a dangerous current out there.'

'That's what I wanted. To be sucked away by the tide.'

'You don't mean that.'

The difference between the tall, vital-looking young man with the sensitive, clever face and wavy blond hair standing beside her, and the ice-cold reality of the lifeless image he puts in her head, clutches at her chest. What has driven him to this? She has dark hours herself – empty days when she struggles to keep a smile on her face, so that no one knows that she's crying inside, not even her husband, and the long nights when she chokes back oceans of tears – but she has never considered ending it all. How could she? She has seen how implacable death looks and has tasted the cruel finality it brings.

'How do you know what I want?' he says. 'You don't know me. You don't know anything at all about me.'

There is something in his taut face that strikes a chord in her heart. 'You're right,' she says, 'I don't. But thanks for helping me.' She hooks her fingers into the loop of his jeans, linking him to her, hoping it might stop him from heading back towards the tide.

'You were the foolish one to come after me,' he says.

'I was trying to save you,' she says. 'Instead you rescued me.'

She tilts her face and looks up at him in time to see him shaking his head. 'You left me with no choice,' he says. 'I would have kept going but for you, and it would have been over by now. So you're to blame that I'm still here.'

'Good,' she says. 'I think everyone's life is precious. And because you came back to help me, you must think that too.'

There is a silence filled only with the clamour of the sea, the slap of the waves and the cry of the gulls.

'We can't stand here forever,' she says, clutching his arm. 'Come on. We have to get out of this cold sea.'

'No,' he says, the angles on his face tightening further. 'I shouldn't be here now. You should have left me alone.'

'Aren't you the lucky one that I did come along?' she says, trying a different tack with him, hiding the fear gnawing at her insides. 'Come back for my sake – or I'll follow you again.'

'There's nothing to go back to,' he says.

'Of course there is. How can you say that?' It is on the tip of her tongue to ask him to look around. There is something soothing in the haziness of the approaching evening, the slow wheel of the gulls floating overhead against a striated, pink-grey sky, the symmetry of the fluttering birds that skim the surface of the sea so low their shadows flash across the surface of the puckered grey silk. She realises how futile her words would be. He is locked into a dark world in every sense. She stands there, trembling with cold and the shock of it all, gulping for breath, holding fast to him as cold water swirls around them. She tries to think.

'Luis? You are Luis, aren't you?'

He nods.

'Maybe I'm saying all the wrong things, I'm useless in these situations,' she says. She's had moments of drama in her life, especially recently, but nothing like this. 'I can't imagine how desperate you must feel right now,' she says, as gently as possible despite her chattering teeth.

'Don't dare tell me how I feel.'

'Okay. But, look, things change, feelings come and go. We all have dark moments but if you wait, they will pass.'

'What if they don't pass?'

'They do. Everything changes. Nothing ever stays the same. There's always something to hope for if you look for it, something to live for, no matter how small.'

She was finding that out for herself, wasn't she? No matter how bad she thinks things are, or how many of her hopes and dreams are soured, there is always a little voice inside her head that whispers to her to hang on in there, that her life will turn around. Each day, she makes sure to find something small that makes her smile, something to sustain her and smooth her frazzled heart, even if it's just the sight of the last summer rose. Each evening, she sits in the sand dunes, soaking up the beauty of the landscape, the music that floats out across the air an added blessing.

'No, there isn't.'

'Have you nothing at all to go back to? Who would miss you if you were gone?' She looks around, across to the headlands and back to the sheltered cove, desperate to find someone who might be able to help, but there's no one about and it's all very quiet, which is the main reason she's here. She thinks of the things that get her through the dark of the night, but they might not work for Luis; after all, she doesn't know what demons he's running from.

'Even if you've nobody at all in the world, don't you ever want to feel the sun on your face again or the wind in your hair?' she says. 'Or taste a salty breeze, a juicy fat strawberry ... or woman's kiss? Or smell a flower or freshly cut grass?'

Then he says something that surprises her. 'You have a nice voice.'

'Have I?' She's still so overcome by the magnitude of how close he came to ending it all that she's shocked he has noticed her voice.

'Yes, it's soft and Irish. Except when you're yelling at me.'

'I am Irish, from Cork. And I yelled at you because I'm freezing cold and very cross with you. It's lovely here, it's beautiful, yet you want to do something that would hurt other people.'

'Go slowly. You speak too fast.'

He wants her to speak. He hasn't shrugged off her arm or plunged back towards the rip tide. She hopes he's finding a crumb of comfort in the touch of her arm, as well as the sound of her voice, even if she's saying all the wrong things.

'What will I talk about?'

'Tell me ... tell me what it looks like. The sea. Tell me so I can picture it.'

'It's very beautiful,' she says, knowing instinctively not to patronise him by diminishing the spectacular landscape just because he can't see it. She begins to describe it: the colours, the immensity of it all, the way the streaky sky is reflected in the crumpled water, the circling gulls and rush of birds skimming the surface of the sea. He is still while she talks, and she imagines him picturing it in his mind.

There is a silence when she's finished, and then, 'Thank you,' he says. 'You make it sound ... very lovely.'

'It is. I come here every evening, to sit in the sand dunes and listen to the music.'

He turns his face towards her, suddenly attentive. 'What music?'

'The piano music.' Her voice is shaking with the cold. She can hardly form the words, but she is aware that he is listening to her closely. 'It comes from one of the houses up on the headland. It's beautiful. As beautiful as the sea and the sky,' she gabbles. 'It makes me feel full of hope. You should listen to it, Luis. It would make you feel good.'

He is silent for a moment. Then he says, 'You're freezing.'

'What have I been trying to tell you? I'm also soaking. So are you. Can we go back now? Please, Luis?'

'What's your name?'

'My *name*?'

'Don't sound so surprised. You know my name, so why shouldn't I know yours?'

'It's ...' She hesitates. *As you said, I don't know much about you and I'd prefer if you didn't know anything at all about me.* She takes a quick breath. 'If you really must know, it's Sylvie.'

'What a lovely name. You should be proud of it and not hiding it away. Tell me more about this music, Sylvie, and how it makes you feel.'

She talks as cheerfully as she can, despite her chattering teeth and saturated clothes. She tells him how it sounds, how it helps her to feel happy and full of joy. To her relief, he comes with her as she begins to wade in the direction of the beach, but she still clings to him, terrified he might change his mind.

She'd love to tell him the truth and loosen the ache in her chest. But she puts on the mask of a happy, smiling face, even if he can't see it. She can't tell him that the music floods into the sore corners of her heart like lifesaving water into a parched desert, it helps her forget for a while all the troubled moments that disturb her sleep and, most of all, it stops her from feeling afraid at the dark turn her life has taken.

Chapter Two

As she stared down at the tiny sleeping face of Lucy, her new little god-daughter, Carrie Cassidy was amazed how peaceful it was to simply sit and cuddle a tiny baby. In the same way that she could just be herself in the safe confines of her home on Faith Crescent, and didn't have to answer to anyone, tiny babies didn't expect you to be clever or funny or explain yourself in any way. They put their complete trust in you and all you had to do was sit and cuddle them, and feel the warm weight of the infant in your arms and stroke the unbearably soft skin of their face. They didn't know that you felt all washed up at thirty years of age.

'You look like you're getting your hand in practice,' a voice shattered her fragile calm.

Carrie's grip on her new god-daughter tightened. The baby's tiny hand opened on reflex, silky, matchstick fingers unfurling in the shape of a five-pointed star. Carrie looked up, just in time to see her Aunt Evelyn's face cloud with anxiety.

Evelyn Sullivan fidgeted with the string of pearls around her neck. She looked very stylish in a taffeta aquamarine dress that Carrie had sourced for her at Jade, the high-end, luxury clothing company that Carrie worked for.

'Sorry, Carrie,' she said, 'I forgot for a moment … me and my big mouth …'

'It's okay.' Carrie shrugged and forced a smile.

Her aunt leaned in a little closer in a conspiratorial way and touched her lightly on the arm. 'How have you been? Really, I mean, since Mark?'

The hotel room stilled around Carrie as his name slammed into her head, bringing an avalanche of images that made her ache all over. Carrie's heart lurched as her aunt sat down on a vacant chair beside her and turned a kind, attentive face to her. How had she been? There was no way to put into words the blank reality she was living through every day, going in and out to her job in a kind of vacuum. Sometimes she felt dizzy, when the ground beneath her seemed to sway, whether it was the lunch-hour, city-centre streets or the carpeted office floor. The only thing that seemed solid and purposeful to her right now was the reality of the warm bundle resting with supreme trust in her arms. Even if she could articulate how she felt, here and now on this April afternoon was the wrong time and place to try. The Sullivan clan were gathered en masse in a Dublin south city hotel to welcome Lucy, Evelyn Sullivan's new grandchild, into the world and celebrate her christening.

'I've been okay,' she lied, clutching Lucy to her as though she was a warm, comforting pillow. 'I think I've had a narrow escape. I'm not cut out for marriage and babies.'

Her aunt smiled. 'Don't dismiss yourself, Carrie, you'd make a wonderful mother.' Then she spoke hurriedly as if to temper her words in case they caused further upset. 'But it would have to be with the right man. Marriage and parenthood is wonderful, but even with the most loving couples, there are times when all hell can break loose – so you need to be very sure of your man.'

'I know,' Carrie said. Funny that Evelyn had inadvertently put her finger on the heart of Carrie's problem. Sure of her man? Equally so, the man would have to be very sure of his woman. Her aunt's glance momentarily dropped to Carrie's left, ringless hand. Carrie became aware again how painfully light her third finger felt without its diamond cluster. Like a phantom limb, sometimes she thought it was still there and checked for it with her thumb. Sometimes she forgot that it was buried in a black velvet box in the bottom of her bedside table.

'What's for you won't pass you by. I'd like to think you're happy, whatever you decide. I know it's all your mother would have hoped for you … and your dad …' Once again Evelyn's voice trailed away. 'Sometimes I wish … if only Sylvie was still here, and John, they'd be so proud of you. And there I go again with my big mouth.'

Carrie gave her aunt a quirky smile, the one she always used to hide her sadness behind when it came to her parents. 'Hey, this is a good day for you and the family. We're celebrating new life. You can't change anything that has happened.'

'No, none of us can – but I love you, Carrie. We all love you, you're family and never forget you're important to us all. You're my daughter as much as Fiona. So don't ever feel you're on your own.'

Carrie grinned. 'How could I feel alone with this gang keeping me firmly in my place?' She looked beyond her aunt to the lively gathering in the room, the white and pink balloons drifting in the perfume-laden air, the tables scattered with wine glasses and remains of dessert after their meal. She was in the bosom of her extended family. Uncles, aunts, cousins. She was lucky to be related to this noisy, loveable gang, taking them for granted sometimes, letting them annoy her other times, even if she was a little on the edge of them all.

The Sullivans.

The name alone was a force to be reckoned with. Jack Sullivan, her Cork-born grandfather, had set up his construction supply empire in the 1960s, now managed by his two sons, Sean and Andrew. Along with their wives, Evelyn and Clare, they had settled down on lands adjacent to Willow Hill, the large, rambling house that was home to the Sullivan family in Cork, and between them had produced seven children in less than ten years, Carrie's lively, boisterous cousins. Carrie was the only child of Jack Sullivan's precious daughter, Sylvie, who had settled in Dublin with her husband, John Cassidy. She might have been reared in leafy Dublin suburbs, but Carrie had spent many a childhood holiday running free in the fields around her cherished grandmother's big, rambling home, surrounded by her gang of noisy cousins. Her grandparents had died when Carrie was a teenager, and her cousins were now scattered between Cork, Dublin, London and America, but the family unit was still as close-knit as ever and they had all come together to celebrate baby Lucy's christening.

'Here's Fiona now,' Evelyn said, as her daughter crossed the room towards them.

Carrie watched Fiona weaving through the jumble of young children, and couldn't help admiring the glow of new motherhood that lit up her cousin's face like a beacon. She, too, was dressed in an outfit from Jade, a blush pink swirling dress that Carrie had suggested. She saw Fiona pass an involuntary hand across her stomach, as if self-conscious that it hadn't yet returned to its trim, pre-baby shape, and Carrie wanted to hug her and berate her and tell her she was more beautiful than ever.

'How's my little sweetheart?' Fiona asked, stroking Lucy's tiny cheek.

'She's great,' Carrie said. 'I could sit here all day with her.'

'Now that's an offer!' Fiona laughed.

'I'll leave you pair to discuss babysitting duties,' Evelyn laughed as she got to her feet.

Fiona perched on the edge of Carrie's armchair. 'Thanks for being Lucy's godmother,' she said. 'I really appreciate it.'

'Nonsense. It was an honour,' Carrie said. 'And I fully expected you'd ask me, I was your chief bridesmaid after all.'

She fell silent for a moment, trying to push away the memory of Sam and Fiona's wedding. It had been the first time she'd seen Mark, coming face to face with him as she'd reached the altar ahead of Fiona, finding out later that the tall, lean groomsman with the jet-black hair and light-grey eyes fringed with thick, dark lashes was a good friend of Sam's, home from Singapore and back working in Dublin.

Finding out all sorts of other, even more delicious things later again …

Carrie blinked.

'What I meant,' Fiona said gently, 'was that I appreciate how good-humoured you've been today, considering everything.'

There was no need to be ultra-brave in front of Fiona. Carrie gave her a lopsided smile. 'Yes, well, today was special, and I love my little god-daughter to bits, she's so beautiful. And so perfect and relaxed, so that you can help feeling relaxed with her.'

Together they stared down at the sleeping baby. 'Besides,' Carrie grinned, 'do you think any of my Sullivan cousins would let me get away with wearing a self-pitying mask?'

'Nope,' Fiona grinned back. 'It would soon be wiped off your face by my brothers for starters.'

A year older than Carrie, Fiona had three younger brothers, and she regarded Carrie as the next best thing to a sister. During those long, childhood holidays in Cork, they'd staunchly supported each other against the combined might of the Sullivan boys. Their deep friendship had continued into adulthood and during the years that Carrie had stumbled through life in the aftermath of her parents' death, Fiona had always been there for her.

'We have to be out of the room by seven o'clock,' Fiona went on. 'Sam and I will be going straight home with Lucy, but I think some of the gang are heading to the bar for a few drinks if you're interested.'

'I'll see.'

Sam and I. Carrie noticed the way the words were dropped into the conversation casually and unthinkingly by Fiona. It was something she took for granted, that she and Sam were a double act, a unit all to themselves, enriched now by the arrival of baby Lucy. Carrie was beginning to think she'd never be the other half of a couple.

'I'm going to take this little pet off you now,' Fiona said, reaching for the baby. 'She needs a feed and a change.'

Carrie held up the baby and Fiona scooped Lucy out of her arms, leaving a cold, empty spot where the soft, trusting warmth of her had nestled. A feeling of being bereft swept over Carrie and, in an effort to fill the vacuum, she took her mobile out of her bag, logged on to Twitter and tweeted about the wonderful family day she was enjoying. At least she'd had no fear of Mark stalking her on Twitter or any social media site after their breakup. Even though he worked for Bizz, a global internet company, he'd always been adamant that he'd never regurgitate the minutiae of his daily life for anyone else's vicarious consumption.

She heard Mark's amused voice as though he was sitting on the sofa beside her. 'You're addicted to that stuff. I trust you're not putting out anything about us.'

'Oh, yeah,' she'd teased. 'Our sex life has gone viral. It's so hot I'm making everyone else jealous and upsetting all my followers.'

'I can't abide all that social media crap,' he'd said, reaching for her and taking her mobile out of her fingers, putting it out of her reach before gathering her in his arms. 'But I like what you said about the hot sex life.'

In an unguarded moment, she'd been tempted to confide that she'd found social media a very convenient way of connecting with the world at a basic level after her parents' death. Even if it was just silly comments about television, or opening a bottle of good wine, responses to her tweets had been a connection of sorts, a kind of lifeline, making her feel less alone. And it had been easy to pretend to be happy-go-lucky Carrie behind the anonymity of a Twitter feed, even if she felt blank and empty and had strange, dark circles under her eyes when she looked in the mirror. But she'd let the moment pass and instead of confiding in him, she'd closed her eyes and kissed him back, folding her body tightly into his.

Later, she watched Fiona and Sam laughing together as they gathered up all the baby paraphernalia, the gift bags and christening cards, and took them out to the car. They returned to say their goodbyes, then Sam lifted the tiny, sleeping Lucy, secure in her car seat, and with his other hand in the small of Fiona's back, they left. Carrie felt curiously empty after they had gone and decided to join her cousins in the bar.

But that turned out to be not such a good idea after all. They'd all heard, of course, of her broken engagement. Fiona's brothers were there, two of them with their girlfriends, along with more cousins, taking up a roomy booth in a corner of the bar. They smiled almost too brightly at her, before promptly moving around the banquette to make room, shifting coats and bags, taking her jacket and placing it carefully over the pile of coats. Shane, home from London for the weekend, went to the bar to order her a mojito, telling her she looked far too sober.

'I am the godmother,' she said.

'All the more reason to let your hair down now. Godmothers are supposed to have all the fun and none of the work,' he said, giving her a wink.

Later, Shane walked with her to a taxi. 'He was awful careless not to hang on to you,' he said to her quietly. 'I thought Mark was a sound enough guy.'

'He was,' she said, the chilly spring breeze cold on her face after the heat of the hotel. 'I didn't give him much of a choice, though. It was my decision to call it all off.'

'We all want a happy ever after for you, Carrie,' he said, 'whatever that might be. After everything you've been through you deserve it.'

'Thanks, Shane,' she said, getting into the taxi.

The Sullivans were the only people in the world who got away with talking to her like that. Anyone else who demonstrated the slight degree of sympathy towards her was treated to Carrie's merciless glare and a toss of her dark, wavy hair.

As the taxi swung out of the car park towards the south city, she thought of the empty house ahead of her. It would be exactly as she'd left it that morning, cold and silent, undisturbed. There would be no Mark to share a nightcap with, never mind a laugh and a joke, or to look at the photographs she had taken on her mobile of Lucy. No Mark to say Carrie was beautiful as he peeled off her cream silk dress and matching jacket, or to free her hair, which was caught to one side and clasped in a glittering Swarovski slide so that it cascaded in a dark, glossy wave over her left shoulder. No Mark to cuddle up to in bed or wrap her long legs around or make long, slow and very satisfying love to … to have a friendly, sleepy tiff with over who'd cook brunch the next day, and go out for fresh milk and crusty bread and the Sunday papers. It was amazing how the daily incidentals of a life you shared with someone else could be taken for granted, and how keenly they could be missed.

Carrie's house was tucked into the middle of a semi-circular cul de sac of terraced houses. 'Bijou' is how the auctioneer had described it. This had translated as cramped, but the minute Carrie had walked into it, she knew the house was for her – even if her bookcase had to be squeezed into the hall and the cloakroom was a cubbyhole under the stairs. The sturdy, red-bricked walls seemed to wrap around her, holding her safely in their embrace. The house backed onto the grounds of a big, hundred-year-old church, which could be seen rising up above the six-foot-high wall that ran across the end of her back garden. She got used to the sound of bells echoing out from the church tower at regular intervals. She got used to the birds as well, who were regular visitors to the bird table in the middle of her small patch of a lawn.

As the taxi turned the corner into Faith Crescent, everything was quiet and shadowy, lights glowing here and there from curtained windows. Only her cosy little sanctuary wasn't just the same as she had left it that morning. The blue light in her alarm box under the eaves was flashing soundlessly. The alarm box that was hanging askew after a late-winter gale. *What was the point in turning on an alarm if it didn't make a sound? Typical of my half-arsed approach to life right now.* She'd meant to have it serviced. It was one of the last things Mark had advised her to do before he'd left, but it was something else she'd neglected in the upset of the past few weeks.

'This your house, love?' the taxi driver said.

'Yep,' she said, checking her bag for her mobile, a sick feeling starting in the pit of her stomach and rising up to her chest.

'Looks like your alarm's going off, only I can't hear it.'

'The bell is broken,' she said. 'I meant to have it fixed.'

'I'll wait here until you check the house,' he said, cutting off the engine.

'Thank you,' she said gratefully, wondering if she could ask him to accompany her inside, but that was probably against company health-and-safety regulations or protocol or something. She was thankful when he stepped out from the driver's seat and waited at the kerb, ready to respond if needed. She left the door wide open as she walked down the short hall and punched in the code for the alarm, extinguishing the flashing blue light. She checked her front room, then her kitchen-cum-dining room, checking the back door.

All was neat and tidy. It didn't look like anything had been disturbed.

She went back to the hall door. 'I'm just going upstairs,' she called out to the taxi man, thinking it was some kind of advance warning in case anyone was prowling about up there.

'Right you be, love, I'll wait until you give the all clear,' he said in a loud voice, obviously on the same wavelength as she was.

Again, all was quiet. Eerily quiet. She scanned her bed with its smooth coverlet, she opened the wardrobes and the dressing-table drawers, but there was nothing out of place. She stood there for a moment trying to pinpoint why she felt uneasy, but nothing jumped out at her. Carrie went back downstairs, out to the pavement, and told the taxi driver it was a false alarm.

'Glad to hear it, but you'd best get that thing fixed,' he said good-naturedly as he got back into the driver's seat. She closed the door and went into the front room, switching on lamps and putting on the television to help break the silence in the house, passing by the framed photograph of her parents on the mantelpiece. Carrie most resembled her mother, but at the moment, she felt like a pale image of the vivacious, dark-haired Sylvie with the beautiful blue eyes smiling out at the world. Beside Sylvie was Carrie's father, John, the gentle giant with his warm, intelligent eyes, looking happy and contented, his hair flecked with a distinguished-looking silvery grey.

The photo had been taken on their twenty-ninth wedding anniversary, which the three of them had celebrated together, sipping champagne in a Michelin-starred restaurant in the city centre. After that, Sylvie and John had gone on the holiday of a lifetime to continue the anniversary celebrations, but less than a month after the photograph had been taken, they'd perished in a plane crash in South America.

Sometimes Carrie couldn't help recalling one of the final, fateful conversations she'd had with her mother, a couple of days before her parents had left on their trip – a conversation that she'd puzzled over, wondering what her mother might have meant, telling herself that she was attaching too much significance to it because it happened so close to the accident.

'We've made our will,' Mum had said. 'It's all signed and sealed and with our solicitor. I've put a copy with all our papers in the filing cabinet in Dad's den.'

'Your *will*? Come on, Mum, you and Dad will see eighty or ninety. What are you telling me this for?'

'I fully expect we'll get to eighty or ninety, and we'll be flying around on Zimmer frames, driving you mad with our crotchety demands,' her mum had laughed. 'But it's just common sense to have a will made, it saves a lot of red tape, and we should have done it before now.'

'Yeah, okay,' Carrie had said. 'But talk of a will is freaky.'

Her mother smiled and touched her arm lightly. 'Carrie, relax. It has to be done. There's something else I must talk to you about, a private matter, but it'll wait until we're home.'

'Oooh – sounds very secretive.'

Her mother's blue eyes had clouded over, and most unusually for her vivacious mum she'd looked, Carrie remembered, a little sad.

'It's rather sensitive and confidential, but you need to know ... just in case ... something ever happens.' Her mother had blinked and pulled herself together. 'It's history now – in a way, so it'll keep until we're home again. Now, does that convince you that I know we'll be back?'

Carrie couldn't help recalling the day they'd left – a busy day, full of last-minute packing and preparations, the new suitcases lined up to attention in the hallway, her mum counting down the hours and bubbling over with nervous excitement as she checked things off her list. Cool, confident, know-it-all Carrie, saying they'd be back before they knew it. Then the last smiles, and the final – final – farewell kisses as they'd tumbled out the door of Waldron Avenue into the waiting taxi, in a flurry of anticipation and uncool, brand-new luggage. Carrie on the doorstep, and then her mother's hand, waving out the taxi window, all the way down Waldron Avenue. Sometimes she still thought of the last sight of her mother's hand. She wished she could go back in time and run after the taxi and hold it again, press it tightly to her face, and kiss it to bits.

Carrie was the one who'd bought them travel vouchers for their wedding anniversary. She was heading off herself, on a gap year with Fiona, between completing her master's degree and getting a job. She was the one who'd urged them to take a leaf out of her book, spread their wings, and do something adventurous for once before they were curtailed by the restrictions of their Zimmer frames.

So was it any wonder she felt partly to blame for the way their lives were cut short?

Chapter Three

September 1980

She doesn't set out to become involved in someone else's heartache, she has enough to cope with herself, but she finds herself drawn in to his poignant story.

By the time they get back to the shore, Luis is shaking and the cold has gone through to her bones. Even though it is a mellow September evening, the sea breeze heightens the chill of their wet clothes. Still clinging together, she guides him across to the sand dune where she found his shoes. They are now covered by a light dusting of sand. She also sees the collapsible white cane lying beside them, half buried in the sand. She thinks of the items being found by someone searching in vain for Luis, and her heart clenches.

'Are you okay?' she asks.

'No,' he says.

'How can I help?' she asks, unsure what to do next. 'Tell me what to do, how I can help you. Can I get someone for you?'

The shock that she'd caught Luis moments from taking his life is a trauma that's beginning to overwhelm her, like icy liquid spreading out from her stomach through all the capillaries into her heart and her limbs. She fights down sudden panic, taking several deep breaths to steady herself. Luis seems to be doing the same, breathing heavily and slouched forward as though he's just completed a marathon. She doesn't know how he arrived here or how he'll find his way back to wherever he came from. She doesn't know if she should escort him home safely to make sure he gets there. Has he been missed by anyone already? She's terrified he might head back into the sea if she leaves him. She releases her grip of him long enough to squeeze drops of seawater from her damp hair and put it into a knot and she pulls her dripping top away from her body.

He sits down on the sand and rests his elbows on his knees, dropping his face into his hands. 'No, there's no one.'

She sits down beside him and risks putting her arm around his waist. He doesn't brush it off and she tightens her hold.

'Were you really going to slip away from everyone like that?'

'Yes. Until I heard you calling for help, and ...' He shakes his head. 'Can we just sit like this for a few minutes?'

'Of course,' she says. She's doing something right, and a rush of gratitude fills her chest.

'Tell me about you,' he asks. 'The girl with the soft voice.'

'Except for when I'm yelling at you,' she says, risking a joke. 'What do you want to know?'

'Who you are? Where you live? What you do?'

She tries to think of what is safe to tell him. She takes a deep breath. 'I'm Sylvie Cassidy, from Willow Hill, a couple of miles from here. I've been living in Dublin for the past two years. What do I do? I'm a school teacher, but I'm staying back home for a while because I'm helping to look after my mother, who has had an operation.'

'You must have a kind heart to match your kind voice.'

'She's my mother. I'm happy to help out.'

'Yes, mothers are special.' There is a long silence; he fidgets with his hands, clenching and unclenching his fists, and she senses he is waging some kind of internal battle. She waits, leaning against him, her arm brushing his, letting him know she is there by his side.

Then he lifts his head. 'I've lost my mother.'

She's not exactly sure how fluent his English is. She's half-hoping that he means he has lost contact with his mother or that she is no longer talking to him. That way, there would be some hope of reconciliation. He sounds so sad that she guesses the worst has happened and his mother has died.

'I'm sorry,' she says. 'That must be hard.'

'I was with her in the car when it happened. I don't remember anything. I woke up in hospital four days later – and I could no longer see.'

His blunt words outlining the scale of his personal tragedy take her breath away for a minute. 'Luis.' She reaches out, grasps his hand and holds it tightly. 'How sad. When did this happen?'

'Early last year. I cannot ... the time, it is nothing.' He grips her hand in return, holding so tightly she thinks he might break her fingers. 'I don't want you to feel sorry for me, I could not stand that.'

'Have you anyone else in your family?' Surely he had other family and friends? And surely someone would have noticed his distress?

'Just my father. His heart is broken. I will not talk to him either. I am sometimes very angry. Some days I shout and throw things. Some days I do not get out of bed. I shut out my friends because it is easier. Some of them ... ignore me, they don't know what to say. They are embarrassed. My father is now very busy with his work, to distract him. He should have been with us and there might have been no accident if he'd been driving.'

Two men, raw with grief, unable to open their hearts.

'You don't know what might have happened had your father been there. At least you still have each other. I know some of what you're going through.'

'How could you?' he asks angrily.

'I've lost loved ones too. People who were close to me. I know what it's like to have your heart broken into tiny pieces,' she says, her voice thick with emotion. 'Does your father know you wanted to end it all?' she asks, changing the subject before she says too much.

'No, if he did he would try to stop me.'

'Then he must love you. So you are worth something. And I'm here for you,' she says. 'How old are you?'

'I'm nineteen.'

'Do you want to talk about your mother?'

'No.'

'Where are you from? You're not Irish.'

'I'm from Switzerland. Geneva originally, but we live in Lucerne now.'

'You speak very good English.'

His accent is very attractive, sexy almost, but she isn't about to tell him that.

'My grandmother was English. We speak English as well as French and German.'

'How come you're here, in Cork?' she asks, feeling her way cautiously.

'I'm with my father. He's a scientist and he's helping with research and giving some lectures in the hospital in Cork.'

'It is just the two of you?'

'Yes, most days my father goes to the hospital. We have a housekeeper who comes every day until the afternoon. She cooks and cleans and makes sure I have everything, and then my father is home at six. We've been here for two weeks already, and will be staying almost another two weeks. My father thought it would be good for us to be near the sea, with the fresh air and the sound of the waves.'

He falls silent. Is he thinking about his father arriving home to an empty house?

'So you must be staying close to the beach?'

'Yes, it's just a short walk.'

'It's not the big house up behind us? At the end of the track?'

'It's very near because I can hear the sea through the windows and it was easy to find my way to the beach.'

'Then you ...' she hesitates, a little puzzled. 'Is that the house the music comes from?'

He lets go of her hand and rubs his face.

'Yes.'

'Then you must have heard it?'

'I have. It's me.'

'I don't understand.'

'I play the music.'

'You?' She stares at him, disbelief clouding her mind, finding it hard to equate the uplifting sound with the downcast, bedraggled man sitting beside her. 'You mean you're the pianist?'

'Yes.'

'I don't believe you,' she splutters. 'How dare you.'

'How dare I what?' He lowers his hands and straightens up, alert, clearly surprised by the tone of her voice.

She's unable to curb her anger. 'How dare you throw all that away. Have you any idea how good you are? Or the difference you were making? For God's sake, I can't believe you were about to ... end all that. And me, the big eejit, asking you if you had anything to live for or anything to go back to? What could be better than that? I'm raging with you.'

'Raging?'

'Furious. Cross. Very, very angry.'

She tries to swallow back tears but they are pooling in her eyes. 'I know it's terrible that you lost your mother and can no longer see. But there are people who can help you when you're feeling down, if you let them. You're still alive. You can smell and touch and hear, and you still have a heart and can feel things, and there's no reason why you can't love.'

'Maybe I don't want to be alive like this ... it's frightening.'

Her heart is heavy, but instead of commiserating with him, she rounds on him. 'That's great, Luis. Are you telling me I risked my life to get you out of the sea for nothing? And at a funeral, say, you'd prefer to be the one lying cold and stiff in the coffin instead of being the person helping everyone else by playing some wonderful music?'

Suddenly she is bawling her eyes out, overcome with all the emotion of the evening.

'Sylvie – don't.' Luis reaches out his arm and she feels it curving around her shaking shoulders.

'Leave me alone,' she says.

'Sylvie–'

'Stop.'

'You don't understand–'

'No, I don't. People die all the time, Luis. In car crashes like your mum, in all sorts of other accidents. They die of sickness and old age. They die young of cancer. They leave behind broken-hearted families. Have you ever seen anyone fighting for their life? Struggling to breathe, hoping to live, praying there might be a cure? Bargaining with God that the call from the doctor or the specialist won't bring bad news. Knowing helplessly there is nothing they can do while their precious life ebbs away. And you – someone who is mostly whole and healthy and can play music that's sparkling and wonderful and brilliant and beautiful – want to throw that life away? Sorry, but no, I don't understand. So I'm furious and annoyed and very, very cross with you. And I don't care if that's not what you want to hear.'

She sits there on the sand in her wet clothes, hugging her knees, crying freely. He leaves his arm curled around her. After a while, she calms a little, hiccups, falls silent. Her hair is ruffling in the breeze, she tastes salt on her lips. Then Luis takes his arm away and says, 'Sylvie, I need you to do something.'

'What?' she asks, her voice sounding hoarse. He feels around for his sports shoes and scrabbles in the sand for something. He picks up a collapsible white cane.

'I need you to guide me home. Please.'

She knows by his tone of voice there is a hidden meaning in his words.

'Sure,' she says, standing up in her stiff, damp clothes, wiping her eyes. She links her arm through his and they walk across the dunes and down the track to the house at the end. It's far bigger than any of the other holiday homes, surrounded by landscaped gardens, and with a generous balcony wrapping around the upper storey, which must, she guesses, have fantastic views of the sea. They go in through the back gate and when they reach the back door, she pauses.

'It's open,' he says.

She opens the door and Luis folds up his cane and uses the tips of his fingers to guide his way through.

'Thank you,' he says, turning back to her. 'Are you still angry with me?'

She feels deflated now, wiped out after the drama and emotion. 'No, not angry, just annoyed and sad that, well, you're wasting something so good. Please talk to someone, your father ... anyone. When will he be home?'

'Soon enough.'

'You'd better change out of those clothes and so should I. Have a hot bath or something.'

'Can we talk? Tomorrow? We could meet on the beach.'

She thinks quickly. It wasn't part of her plan. Meeting Luis today was a huge distraction and she needs the solitude of the beach. But neither can she leave him like this. 'My mother goes for a rest every evening, so I have a little time to myself and I often come out for some fresh air but is the beach a good idea?'

'I won't do anything stupid.'

'I don't know that for sure.'

'You have my promise. You have made me stop and think. But I'd like to talk to you some more.'

'I'll meet you on one condition. Don't tell anyone about me, okay?'

'Who is there to tell?'

'I mean it, Luis. Nobody must know ... not a soul.'

'Agreed. You can be my mystery lady. There was something else you said, when we were out in the sea. You talked about something to live for ... like a woman's kiss. So I'd be very happy if you kissed me, Sylvie Cassidy.'

A kiss. Just a kiss. Is it okay for a married woman to kiss a younger man in these exceptional circumstances? She wonders when he was last kissed. She tries not to think about the last time she was kissed. She blots it out of her head and leans into him, resting her hands on the tautness of his waist to balance herself. He puts a hand on her shoulder and slides it tenderly up to her face. Their mouths come together in a kiss that surprises her, for it is gentle and sensual all at once, and it fills her up in a way no kiss has ever done before.

Even though she is shivering, she waits at the end of the back garden until she hears a car approach along the headland and pull in to the driveway at the front of the house. His father is home.

Chapter Four

'I want to hear your side of the story,' Carrie said to Tara, the sales assistant sitting in front of her.

Tara took a sip of water from the glass Carrie had left out. It was a Wednesday afternoon and they had the office in Jade's city centre HQ to themselves as her colleagues Shelley and Elena were out at a trade event with Steve Boyle, Jade's CEO. They would be suitably wined and dined, Shelley had said with glee. As a marketing executive in charge of the North Dublin region, where Jade's chic boutiques and glitzy concessions were dotted in prime shopping locations, Shelley saw herself as Carrie's main rival – and treated her job as if her life depended on it. She looked adoringly at Steve, peppering her conversations with a range of enthusiastic sound bites, such as mission statement, results-driven, synergy on the ground. What Shelley didn't know was that Carrie simply struggled to get through the days sometimes. Carrie had watched Shelley prancing out of the office before lunch and tried not to think about the quarter bottle of white wine loitering in the fridge and the frozen chicken curry she'd be microwaving that evening, never mind the reason why her name hadn't been on the invitation list.

'Sometimes, Carrie, we feel you're not as dedicated to your role as you could be,' Steve had said to her after a recent meeting. 'You might need to re-invigorate your personal vision statement.'

Carrie had felt her eyes glazing over. 'Absolutely, Steve.'

His lips had formed a thin line. 'You're obviously very clever, to judge by your qualifications, but we'd like to see you breaking out of that – um – detached shell you sometimes wear and engaging with the core business values of Jade in a more committed way.'

Committed? Hadn't Steve realised who he was talking to? The safe, detached, engagement-free and very risk-averse Carrie Cassidy.

Mark …

'I haven't done anything wrong,' Tara said belligerently, bringing Carrie back to the present. 'The customer came in on Monday morning looking for a refund for a luxury gown that I know she'd already worn. The Diane model. One of our more expensive.'

Carrie nodded her head. The Diane dress retailed for four hundred and fifty euro. An intricate mix of raw silk and cotton, it was one of their key statement pieces in the spring-summer catalogue.

'She had a receipt,' Tara said, 'but the tags were missing and the dress was stained with makeup around the neckline, *and* there were splashes of drink on the skirt. I pointed this out to her and explained our refund policy, then all hell broke loose.'

Carrie made some squiggles on her pad and looked back at Tara. 'What do you mean by "all hell broke loose"?'

'The customer began to shout and roar at me,' Tara said, her cheeks reddening. 'She threatened to report me to head office …' Her eyes darted to the printed email on Carrie's desk. 'Which she did, obviously. I stayed calm and repeated the company's refund policy as politely as I could. Look, Carrie, you get to know after a while who's genuine and who's trying it on, and she certainly was – trying it on. She probably wore that dress to a wedding at the weekend and decided she didn't want to wear the same dress twice. And she wanted the refund back in her credit card account before the bill came in … I've seen it all before.'

Carrie made a few desultory notes on her pad. She knew that Tara was probably right, but what she wanted to ask Tara was why she cared so much. Another assistant might have just turned a blind eye to the stains, handed over the refund and saved themselves all this angst.

'So what happened next?' Carrie asked.

Tara sat up straighter, gathering her dignity about her. 'I said there was nothing we could do for her, it was company policy, the dress was not in a saleable condition, and she demanded to see the supervisor.' Tara's eyes darkened. 'After a while Niamh came along and handed over the refund, and, well, we had words.'

'Words?' Carrie raised an eyebrow.

Tara shrugged. 'I was completely undermined, Carrie.'

Carrie pretended to be making more notes. Her job as an area manager for the South Dublin region was supposed to be about initiating strategies to grow the company's luxury reputation and ramp it up, but all too often she found herself embroiled in the fallout of customer complaints, where they had been escalated to head office. *I don't need this*, Carrie decided. It certainly wasn't adding any benefit to her life, but she couldn't walk out of another job. She'd been careful with her parents' legacy but it wouldn't support her indefinitely. Besides, even if her job irritated her at times, she needed the distraction it provided, the basic requirement to get out of bed each day, have a shower, button herself into a suit, and leave her house on Faith Crescent to face the world and be part of the human race. Otherwise she'd probably spend her time slobbing around the safe confines of her small terraced home in a three-year-old grey tracksuit or, on really bad days, her comfy chain-store PJs and shabby rabbit slippers, beans on toast her main meal of the day.

'Tara, you know the best thing is for you and Niamh to come to a workable solution. I don't want to have to pass this up the line or you could be looking at suspension without pay.'

Tara smiled ruefully. 'I knew you'd be on their side. The management. Those beautiful people in their ivory towers.'

Carrie ignored her comment. Tara was probably right, but she didn't have the heart to tell her that some of the management just didn't want to be there. 'From now on, if you're in any doubt, or if you think the customer is going to give you hassle, call the supervisor first. Let them take the heat.'

'Sure, Carrie, that'll be every ten minutes. You're going to be very popular with the supervisors if you spread that message around.'

'Let me deal with that,' Carrie said. Steve Boyle would love her even more.

'Still, I need my job to pay the bills,' Tara said as she rose to her feet. 'But how do you think I feel about Niamh making a fool of me?'

'I can only deal with the facts of the case,' Carrie said, ignoring her slight discomfort that she *wasn't* depending on her job to pay the bills. 'Feelings can get in the way and you have to sidestep them.'

Carrie was tempted to tell Tara that feelings can be dangerous, they can suck you dry and leach through to your bones, making you feel frozen and immobile, so they were better off buried and forgotten about. *That's something I* am *a pro at*, Carrie thought ruefully as Tara left the office. She stared across the room, out through the window. It had started to rain, April showers misting the window, distorting the view she had of the tree outside that was fuzzed with tiny leaf buds. John and Sylvie Cassidy would surely be proud of their daughter, sitting at her pale-ash desk in Jade HQ, her trim figure in a charcoal-grey suit, her dark hair caught in a clasp at the back of her head, looking the picture of professionalism. No one knew better than she did how far she'd sidestepped the sadness that could have engulfed her. By now, Carrie's heart was toughened enough to withstand anything. After all, she'd learned the hard way.

* * *

When her parents died so unexpectedly, one of the things Carrie found most difficult to accept was that they'd only travelled so far away because she had decided to take a year out and head off backpacking with Fiona, who'd just been made redundant from her executive job in a pharmaceutical company. 'I'm twenty-five,' she said. 'You'll be relieved to hear I'm finally growing up and cutting the apron strings. It's about time I saw the world before I settle down to the daily grind of earning a living.'

'At last,' her dad joked. 'Thought we'd never be rid of you.'

All through college, Carrie had lived in the roomy family home on Waldron Avenue, south County Dublin, studying for her degree and then her master's qualification in Business and Marketing, working in a city-centre boutique at the weekends and college holidays.

'You should follow my example and spread your wings this year,' she said.

'We'll think about it,' her mother replied.

'Do you mean you might go as far as another continent?' Carrie laughed. It was a standing joke between them that her parents had always played safe when it came to holidays. All of Carrie's childhood holidays had been spent in Cork, her schoolteacher mother off during the summer months and coming down with her senior civil-servant father, joining them at weekends. Then when she was fifteen or sixteen, they started holidaying abroad, sticking close to home, mostly mainland Europe, always bringing Carrie and Fiona along with them.

'Freebie for you,' her dad would say. 'You might as well take it while you can get it.'

'Surely I'm a bit too old for parental freebies?' she would answer, as one year rolled into the next. She was twenty ... twenty-one ... twenty-two ...

'We'll call a halt soon enough and kick you into touch,' her dad would say.

'But if we keep out of each other's hair …?' Carrie would reply.

'I think that's a given,' her dad would answer with a laugh in his voice.

Another of their standing jokes was that booking one bedroom between them would have been enough as they could have taken it in shifts. Carrie and Fiona were usually heading out for a night's partying while her parents were arriving home to go to bed. Then her parents were heading out for a walk on the beach or a day trip somewhere when Carrie and Fiona were falling into bed.

She'd never guessed how swiftly those holidays would come to an end.

Nobody outside the family quite understood how close-knit Carrie and her parents were. Years earlier, when her dad had been helping with her maths homework, and she'd been wrestling with Venn diagrams, he'd taken a page of her copybook and drawn a large circle.

'This is me and your mum,' he'd said. 'There's no beginning and no ending. No part of us that exists outside of the other. Well, maybe just a bit when Mum goes out with her friends and I go golfing … but this is all of us.' Then he had drawn a slightly smaller circle inside the big circle. 'And this is you, Carrie,' he'd said. 'You're part of us, and always with us.'

She'd never understood the rebellious phases some of her school mates had gone through because she'd never felt the need to behave like that. 'The three musketeers,' her dad called them. 'The three amigos,' her mum had said. So lots of summers during those student years, while her college mates went to America on J1s or headed off to save the whales, Carrie was happy to relax on the beaches of France or Spain, her parents in the background and Fiona with her to party the night away. Until that final, fatal trip.

At first it was great. Two days after her parents left on their holiday of a lifetime, Carrie and Fiona flew out from Dublin to

Heathrow and on to Kuala Lumpur on the first leg of their journey. Full of excitement, Carrie emailed photos to them and Sylvie and John emailed photos of their adventures. But then, the apron strings had been severed for good in a way Carrie never expected.

Carrie and Fiona were in New Zealand when the call came through from Fiona's father, Sean. To this day, Carrie pulled a veil over what happened over the next few months. But certain things stood out like beacons in her mind's eye – Sean and Evelyn coming out to New Zealand to be with her and to help her and Fiona make the difficult journey back to Ireland and the overriding feeling that she was moving around under thick, heavy water the whole time, her movements so slow and lethargic, her responses muffled by the weight of that smothering water. After they returned to Ireland, Sean and Evelyn had gone out to South America, while Carrie stayed in their house in Cork, not moving, not talking, not crying. Fiona and her cousins stepping delicately around her, terrified of meeting her eyes.

The unreality of standing in the airport chapel, when the remains of whatever was left of her parents were eventually flown home to Cork. She dug her nails into her palm while the priest local to Willow Hill said prayers over the closed caskets. Remains? Her parents? No way. Not the John and Sylvie Cassidy who had breezed through life in Waldron Avenue. It was all a massive joke and they were just hiding somewhere. The caskets stayed closed, but Sean told her that Sylvie and John had looked peaceful when he'd identified them in the mortuary in Brazil. He was only being kind, she knew. How could there have been anything left to identify?

She watched dispassionately, as though she was watching a movie in a foreign language, as the caskets were lowered into the earth in a graveyard close to Willow Hill with a view of the sea, where the breeze came in small, lively flurries and ruffled the tips of the far-off waves as well as the funeral wreaths. Funnily enough, the sight of the flowers turned a knife in Carrie's chest. Her dad had bought her mother flowers every birthday and anniversary. Her mum had always looked surprised and delighted. It was inconceivable to think her mum would never get flowers again.

She stayed in Cork while Sean and Evelyn went up to Waldron Avenue and put it to rights, sorting out the paperwork. They dealt with red tape, the accountants and solicitors, and brought back clothes for Carrie and things for her to sign. After a few months, when Sean and Evelyn were finally convinced that Carrie would never return to Waldron Avenue, and when Carrie agreed that there was no point in leaving it empty, they went back to Dublin and spent a few days locking family belongings safely away in a small room in Waldron Avenue, bringing more important documents back to their house in Cork for safekeeping. Then they arranged to let the house. A young professional family, they told Carrie, who wanted a long lease. It just meant more things for her to sign. She couldn't even bear to look at the address at the top of the documents. She just scribbled her name on the bottom line.

She moved back to Dublin with Fiona, sharing an apartment as close to the city centre as possible, so that she wouldn't have to be near the neighbourhood of the family home.

Carrie got a job as a receptionist in a building supplies firm, thanks to Sean putting in a word for her. It was far below what she was qualified to do, but all she could handle at the time and jobs were scarce. She told herself she could be worse off, that she was lucky to have had her wonderful parents for as long as she had. In the evenings, Fiona tempted her out – salsa classes, yoga, Spanish for beginners, wine tasting. When Carrie didn't see the point of her job any more, and got fed up with customers quibbling about the shade of their fireplace paint or the thickness of their kitchen worktop or the finished glaze on their bathroom floor tiles, she left.

'You do realise we're in the middle of a recession?' her manager said, looking at her as though she had two heads when she handed in her notice.

She held his gaze and resisted telling him that lots of people were stony broke, they could hardly put food on the table, and it seemed ridiculous to be arguing over the degree of gloss on a bathroom tile. She resisted telling him she didn't really need that much money, that her parents had left her well provided for.

Eventually, she got a job as a medical receptionist in a busy, city-centre practice. Carrie had continued to shun any kind of relationship, but Fiona met Sam. The medical receptionist job lasted six months. Carrie was fired when she snapped at a woman who was demanding an immediate appointment because she was dying of the flu.

'What exactly did you say?' Fiona had asked when Carrie came home from work in high dudgeon and pulled the cork out of a bottle of wine, sloshing some into a glass.

'I told her she couldn't really be dying of the flu. If she was, she'd be too weak to call the doctor. You should have heard her, Fi, she wanted me to push other people – genuinely sick people – aside, just so she could jump the queue. Besides, all she needed was bed rest and hot fluids. I told her that but she was having none of it.'

She went on the dole for a while. Queuing up once a month to sign on didn't bother her: she had too much time on her hands, and spent a lot of that in bed. Until Fiona dragged her out of bed one morning, telling her she'd made an appointment for Carrie to get her hair done and that she wasn't to come back to the apartment until she'd looked for a job.

'I know you don't really need the money,' Fiona said, 'but I'm being cruel to be kind – I'm a bit fed up seeing you moping around.'

'Moping? As in sorry for myself? I've never moped in my life. I'm just …' she searched for words, 'trying to decide where my talents lie.'

'Maybe it's time you talked to someone? Someone like a trained professional? It could be a help,' Fiona said gently.

Carrie raised her eyebrows. She must be in a bad place for Fiona to make that suggestion. 'I'm fine,' she said. 'I don't need to talk to anyone at all. I certainly don't need to pay good money to talk to a total stranger.'

'I worry about you.'

'Don't. Far worse things have happened to much nicer people than me.'

At this stage, Sylvie and John had been gone three years. To Carrie, it could have been three minutes or three days since she'd watched her mother's hand waving farewell. Sometimes, she pretended it was just three hours and they were still laughing and sipping champagne as they flew through sunny blue skies en route to Machu Picchu or the Iguazú Falls. It was better than thinking of them rotting away in the cold, hard earth.

Then Fiona said, very tentatively, that she was moving in with Sam, if Carrie was okay with it. Carrie had seen it coming. She'd watched, week by week, as Fiona fell in love with Sam, and he with her.

'Great. That's the best news I've heard all week. I'm very happy for you both. Just make sure I'm chief bridesmaid – or else,' she grinned.

It was Fiona who suggested that Carrie should buy rather than rent, given that property prices were on the floor, especially if she wasn't going to live at Waldron Avenue again. Carrie thought it was a great idea – she had no intention of returning to Waldron Avenue and buying her own place announced in the best way possible that she was moving on.

She found the house in Faith Crescent herself, and immediately liked the way its warm, cosy atmosphere wrapped around her as she walked down the hall. She even liked the name, Faith Crescent, although she doubted if she'd soak up any particles of faith in her future from living there, let alone any slivers of belief in an afterlife of sorts. Her parents were gone, leaving her with a cold, hard emptiness; there was nothing soft or spiritual about it, nothing to encourage her to believe that they still existed in another room somewhere beyond her sight.

She spent some time settling in to Faith Crescent, but after a while, she needed to find something purposeful to fill her days. So she had her hair done again, got a new suit and killer heels, updated her CV to reflect her experience in the most attractive light possible and, at Fiona's insistence, put up her profile on LinkedIn. Her new image worked and she got a job as an area manager in Jade, looking after the eastern sector. It was far from the fulfilment of her life's purpose, whatever that might be, but she was determined to make it work and at least her job ensured she had some kind of life.

Soon after that, just sixteen months ago, she met Mark O'Neill at Fiona and Sam's Christmas wedding. It was one thing when Mark began to chip away at the defences around her toughened heart, stealing through them with his sexy grey eyes and warm, amused smile, as well as his very thorough love-making that swept her away, but left her scarily vulnerable.

But when it came to lifelong commitment, she panicked. How could she promise to love someone for the rest of her life? She could never live up to the kind of strong, powerful love her parents had shared; the warm, enduring love that had started in adolescence and lasted until it had perished along with them on the stricken flight.

'Your mum and I were childhood sweethearts,' her dad had said many times, fondly recounting stories of their past, bringing it alive for Carrie. 'We met in school. If she was in a good mood with me, she let me carry her schoolbag home and she made me feel like a king. I knew I was going to marry her on the night of her sixteenth birthday party …'

Chapter Five

May 1972

Sylvie Sullivan's heart was bubbling over as she half-waltzed, half-danced into the kitchen in Willow Hill in her flared Levi jeans, checked top and cork-soled platform sandals. It was the first day of May and her sixteenth birthday. The sun was shining, the kitchen was full of the warm aroma of baking and large picture windows framed the long back garden bordered by apple blossom trees, beyond which a countryside glimmered with the fresh green of early summer, fields and valleys undulating down to the thin blue rim of the sea in the distance. Later that evening, she was having a party for her friends. Her dress was hanging up in her bedroom, an A-line floral print dress with a wide collar and bow trim that she'd bought in Dublin on a recent trip there with her mother.

'I feel happy,' she sang, circling around the flagged floor, 'Oh so happeee ...'

'Good,' her mum said, smiling at her as she turned from the kitchen cupboard. 'That's the way you should be today.'

'It's not every day you can be sweet sixteen,' the housekeeper Molly McCann said. 'And never been kissed,' she added, chuckling, as she wiped her flour-dusted hands on her apron.

'Maybe tonight's the night,' Sylvie said, feeling giddy.

'Lucky for some,' Molly said, winking at her.

Sylvie's heart thumped as she twirled strands of her long, dark hair. John Cassidy was coming to her party with some of his friends. Even though she was just sixteen, she knew she was in love with him. Sixteen wasn't too young to know who you wanted to be with for the rest of your life, was it? He was a year older than she was, tall and with a broad chest that was lovely for snuggling into, and he had a wide, generous mouth and friendly green eyes that were always joking at the world. She thought about him first thing every morning and last thing at night and a hundred times during the day. They were fast becoming best friends – they both loved books and music, they talked about everything and kept no secrets from each other. Because they were both still in school and had little money, they spent their time together walking hand in hand around the banks of the nearby river, listening to music and the occasional outing to the pictures in Cork. When he looked at her a certain way with those green eyes, she felt a thrill that went right down to her toes. Sometimes, she felt as though a kind of aura surrounded the two of them. She wondered if he felt it too.

She helped herself to one of the cupcakes that Molly had just taken out of the oven. The soft concoction melted in her mouth. 'Delicious. You're a star, Molly, but you'd better keep these away from Dad and the boys or there'll be none left by tonight.'

'There are lots more where they came from,' Molly said, 'as well as cream sponges, apple tarts and fruit flans.'

'Then we'll have finger food as well,' her mother said, 'cocktail sausages and chicken wings.'

Sylvie hugged her. 'You're going to a lot of trouble for me.'

'No bother,' Kathleen Sullivan said, hugging her back. 'You're growing up so fast anyhow. You'll be gone in no time.'

'Not for a while,' Sylvie said. 'I have another whole year and a bit before I finish school.'

'That'll fly by,' her mum said.

Sylvie didn't agree with her mother. She loved English and History, but didn't like having to study the rest of her subjects all that much, especially Maths and Biology. She was impatient for that time to be over. To her, a year felt interminably long. Her dad had sometimes said that life went by in a flash, but she didn't believe him.

'Then after I finish school, I'll still have three, maybe four years in college. Hopefully Cork, so I'll still be around to torment you!'

'And after college the world will be your oyster,' Molly said.

She'd heard that talk before from teachers, as though college would be a golden ticket to new adventures and a wonderful life. Ireland was changing, the world was changing, the youth had more energy and education than ever before, and Sylvie appreciated that the teenagers of her generation would be among the first to enjoy all the new freedoms – but all she wanted to do after college was get a teaching job and marry John. The thoughts of it all filled her with happiness and contentment.

'Willow Hill is my oyster,' Molly went on. 'I'll have it spick and span by this evening in honour of the great occasion.'

'I'll help,' Beth, Molly's daughter said, as she came into the kitchen with a basket of fresh herbs from the kitchen garden.

'You're not allowed to help, Beth,' Sylvie said, waggling her finger. 'You're one of my special guests tonight and you're to relax and enjoy getting ready. John's bringing some friends from his football team, so you never know, I might be able to fix you up with one of them, but only if I think he's good enough for you,' Sylvie grinned.

Beth's cheeks flamed. Sylvie knew it was partly on account of John's name being mentioned. It was no secret to her that shy, retiring Beth had developed a crush on John Cassidy – she couldn't blame Beth, as he was gorgeous – but it would be good to see Beth with a boyfriend of her own. 'I still haven't decided what to wear,' Beth said.

'Whatever you pick, you'll be gorgeous,' Sylvie said.

Beth was in the same year at school as Sylvie, but she wouldn't be going to college. She planned to leave school next month on her sixteenth birthday and get a job in the village supermarket. There was little spare cash in the McCann home. Molly had raised her two daughters, Anna and Beth, single-handedly when she'd come home from England, minus their father, and she depended on her job with the Sullivans to pay the rent on her council house and look after the bills. Molly's eldest daughter Anna had died several years earlier, but it wasn't something that was spoken about. All Sylvie knew was that she and Beth were both around six years of age when Kathleen Sullivan had given Molly a housekeeping job in Willow Hill after Anna's death, and they had been like sisters ever since.

'Sylvie's right,' Kathleen said. 'Go off home, Beth, and enjoy getting ready for the party. 'Besides, Molly, there's no point in cleaning much, as it'll all have to be done again tomorrow after the party.'

'I can help out then,' Beth said.

'Have you seen Sean anywhere?' Sylvie asked her.

'He's gone off on his bike,' Beth told her.

'I hope he's back soon, I need to talk to him about the music for tonight.'

'He said something about getting more records from his friends.'

'That's what I'm afraid of,' Sylvie grumbled. 'He'll be in charge of the record player and I don't want Jimi Hendrix or Mungo Jerry taking over the night.'

It was only a gentle grumble. Sean was a year younger than her but already a head taller, and was proud to be helping out at her party tonight.

'And who would you like, pet?' Molly asked. 'What are your special requests? The Beatles? Joe Dolan?'

'Yes, and there's that guy called Elton John,' Sylvie said. John liked him too. She'd scraped up to buy him *Tumbleweed Connection* the previous Christmas. They listened to a lot of music together, begging and borrowing LPs and tuning into Radio Luxembourg in the evenings. Then there was Andy Williams with the theme song from *Love Story*. They'd been to see the film, she'd wept buckets, and tonight she wanted nothing more than to wrap herself in John's arms while this song echoed around the sitting room. Sean would probably gag, so she wanted to make sure he wasn't going to make a mess of it. Her younger brother Andrew was only twelve, so he was allowed to take part on condition that he helped to pass around the food. Her parents had agreed to stay in the kitchen all night, leaving the party people alone in the big sitting room that ran the length of the house.

Before the party got going, her dad produced his camera and they posed for photographs, Sylvie with her parents, then Sylvie and Beth with Sean and Andrew, grouped behind the laden table in Willow Hill.

'Hey, Molly, get in to a photograph,' Sylvie urged.

'Yes, come on, Molly,' Kathleen Sullivan said.

Molly smiled and patted her hair. Smoothing down her apron, she joined the tightly formed group in front of the camera. They moved to make room for her.

'Cheese,' her dad said.

'Sausages,' Sean said in a deadpan voice.

Everyone laughed and her dad pressed the shutter and half a dozen of them were frozen in a black and white photograph in that innocent moment in time.

It is great being sixteen, Sylvie thought, smiling at the camera. She was over the gawky, awkward teenage stage and knew how to use makeup and do her hair, even if she'd had to practice for hours using the tips from a *Jackie* magazine. But what made it even better was that she was in love with the most wonderful boyfriend, her whole life lay ahead of her like a dazzling-white clean sheet, waiting to be filled with wonderful things.

Chapter Six

On Friday morning, Carrie found herself staring out the window at the soft spring sunshine, wondering how much longer she could stick her job. She'd lasted in Jade a lot longer than her previous jobs, but she still wasn't committed enough; she just flitted on the surface of it all, doing enough to get by. What was she going to do with the rest of her life? How would she find something of substance to do with her time? She wanted a job that gave her purpose and satisfied her. But how would she do that given her, to quote Steve, 'lack of engagement skills'?

'There was a call for you while you were away from your desk,' Shelley said to her before coffee break. 'But she didn't leave a name or a message, and I didn't recognise the number.'

'It can't have been urgent so.' At least it wasn't Steve or an angry supervisor asking to open a dialogue about her future direction or otherwise, because Shelley surely knew their numbers off by heart.

'There was a lot of noise in the background, like a shopping centre. She sounded a bit – I dunno – stressed or something.'

'Great,' Carrie said, logging back on to her computer. Probably a Jade supervisor out for her blood.

'When I said you'd be in the office for the rest of the day, she said she'd catch you later.'

'Something to look forward to,' Carrie said, bringing up her work emails.

Carrie was relieved it was Friday. Jade's HQ was closed at the weekends, when all the branches were at their busiest. Headquarters staff got to go home and have a weekend, so Carrie could legitimately hibernate in Faith Crescent and slob around for the whole two days. Having spent the week engaging on some level with the world, she deserved it. She'd three microwaveable meals in the freezer, indeterminate varieties of chicken, and two bottles of a decent white wine chilling in the fridge. And there was chocolate, and her favourite Ben & Jerry's ice cream.

When she went into the ladies before going home, Shelley was already there, in front of the mirror.

'Anything exciting lined up for the weekend?' Shelley asked as Carrie plonked her bag on the shelf and glanced at their reflections. She was taller than Shelley. As she looked at the difference in height between them, she remembered the way she'd fitted in halfway between her petite mother and six-foot-something Dad. He'd fondly called them steps of stairs. Carrie blinked away the sudden mist in front of her eyes and smiled brightly at Shelley.

'Oh, I've lots of *very* exciting things on,' she lied, in what she hoped was a voice that sounded suitably enigmatic.

'Well … er … enjoy.' Shelley looked surprised at her megawatt smile. 'Are you too busy to join the gang in the pub?'

Some of the office crowd usually went to the nearby pub on a Friday evening. The invitation to join them was said in such a slightly patronising way that Carrie knew Shelley was dying to hear all the gossip on her split with Mark and was probably sour that Carrie hadn't let down her guard enough to utter one word about it. Carrie knew that in a city the size of Dublin, rumours about why she had split with Mark and the fact that he was now free and available would have gone around like wildfire.

'Thanks but I can't tonight,' Carrie said. 'I have other plans.' She leaned into the mirror and applied her lip gloss. She fluffed up her dark, wavy hair and sprayed on her perfume, deriving a ridiculous pleasure out of the fact that it looked as if she was readying herself for a night on the town instead of lazing in front of the telly, spooning ice-cream out of the tub.

'Very hot date,' she mouthed to Shelley in the mirror, as she fluttered her mascara wand and bigged up her dark-blue eyes. Shelley gave her an uneasy grin in return. No doubt Carrie's comments would be all around the Jade crowd in the pub tonight.

Carrie took the stairs down to the ground floor and hoisted her bag onto her shoulders as she marched across the tiled foyer towards the glass entrance doors.

'Hey, Carrie,' Bill, the security guy called her, from his desk across the lobby.

'Yes?' She paused, turning to face him.

'There's a visitor here to see you,' he said. He indicated a woman waiting in one of the deep, leather armchairs to the side of the foyer. Carrie had never seen her before in her life. She was middle-aged and beautifully groomed, with smooth, ash-blonde hair that was cut in a bob and gleamed like a shell. She sat erect, her carriage perfect, hands resting precisely on her soft-leather handbag.

'To see *me*? What for?'

'Search me,' Bill shrugged. 'She didn't want me to call you or disturb your work. She asked if she could wait here until you were finished for the evening.' Bill looked uncertain. 'Is that okay? I can run her off if you like.'

Too late. The woman had obviously heard their discussion. She looked across at Carrie and rose to her feet. She was quite petite. After a minute, she began to walk towards her, her movements as elegant and graceful as a ballerina. She was elegantly dressed in a cashmere coat and silk scarf.

'It's fine, Bill,' Carrie said. 'I'll sort this out.'

'I'm here if you need me,' Bill winked at her.

She met the woman in the middle of the foyer.

'You are Carrie? Ms Cassidy?' Her accent was foreign and Carrie couldn't place it. 'Please accept my apologies for the intrusion, but I need to talk to you.'

'To me?'

'Yes. You are Carrie Cassidy, the daughter of Sylvie Cassidy?'

The woman seemed calm and in control, not the least bit threatening or intimidating, but Carrie's hackles rose at the mention of her mother. 'What's my mother got to do with anything?'

'That's what I need to talk to you about.'

Carrie tilted her chin. 'Who are you?'

The woman held her gaze, her eyes respectful. 'I'm Maria Meyer – from Switzerland. I found your contact details on LinkedIn after a Google search.'

'Google.' No doubt Maria had also come across online newspaper reports of her parents' accident in her internet trawl of Carrie Cassidy. Several reports on various news sites had included a reference to Carrie as the surviving daughter of John and Sylvie Cassidy.

'It was the only way I could find you,' Maria said, her face full of apology. 'I flew into Dublin today to try and see you face to face. It's urgent.'

Carrie was too thrown by everything to fully acknowledge the efforts this woman had made in order to talk to her. 'I'm very sorry you've wasted your time,' she said as smoothly as she could, 'but I'm not about to discuss my mother with a perfect stranger.'

'Please. I understand, but I can explain. Just give me fifteen minutes.' Maria was elegant and gracious, but a hint of sadness lurked in the depths of her grey eyes.

Carrie shook her head, conscious of Bill hovering in the background. Behind her the lift door pinged and Shelley and some of the HR gang spilled out and swept towards the doors in a wave of perfume, bubbly chatter and Friday-night anticipation. From their sidelong glances and the embarrassed, half-smiles darted in her direction, Carrie knew immediately that she'd been the subject of their conversation. She waited until they had left the building, watching their progress as they click-clacked through the entrance doors, knowing from a couple of backward glances that they felt her eyes upon them. Maria, too, seemed content to wait until they were out of earshot.

'I even called your office this morning to make sure you were in before I booked my flight,' Maria pressed on.

'You've gone to a lot of trouble to see me,' Carrie acknowledged finally.

'It's a personal and private matter. I wanted to see you face to face.'

'Personal and private?' Carrie echoed, a cold blankness creeping over her.

Her mother smiled and touched her arm lightly. 'There's something else I must talk to you about, a private matter, but it'll wait until we're home.'

'It's something that happened a long time ago. I know it might be difficult for you, but it's about your mother, and it's rather sensitive,' Maria said gently.

Carrie was rooted to the spot.

'Does the name Luis mean anything to you?' Maria went on.

'Luis?'

'Luis Meyer? The concert pianist?'

Something rose inside her; another filament of memory … a holiday on the Costa Brava.

'You're hardly going all the way to Barcelona for just a classical concert?' Her eighteen-year-old voice, dripping with mock indulgence.

'No, we're not,' her mum had said calmly. 'We're going to do some cultural sightseeing as well, but we know you and Fiona would rather stay here by the beach.'

'Too right. I'm not wasting a moment of precious sunshine traipsing around museums or spending the evening in a concert hall.'

'Good, so, we'll leave you and Fiona to it. We're just staying one night, in a hotel off Las Ramblas.'

'What's this concert about anyhow?'

'Like I said, he's a classical pianist. Nobody you'd have heard about ... or be interested in ...' Something in the forced casual tone of her mother's voice had rung an odd note. But the sun was climbing high in a cloudless sky, and Carrie had stretched her limbs and reached for her glass of cold white wine and dismissed it.

Now she shrugged as she faced Maria. 'I've never heard of Luis,' she said.

Maria gave her a gentle smile. 'That's more or less what we expected, in the circumstances.'

'What circumstances?' *And who was 'we'?*

'Luis is my husband,' Maria continued, as though she'd registered Carrie's unspoken question. 'His connection to your mother is what I want to talk to you about. Fifteen minutes?'

What flipping connection? 'You expect me to believe that you flew in from Switzerland today just to talk to me for fifteen minutes? About some connection your husband had with my mother?' This was absurd.

'I'm sorry, Carrie, it's not what you might think. I need to explain it properly and I hope that when I start to talk, you might listen to me for a little longer than fifteen minutes.' She waited quietly, giving Carrie some space. 'I have a suite at the Merrion Hotel. Perhaps we could go there?'

Carrie thought of the empty house waiting for her, of Maria claiming to know something sensitive about her mother, of a concert long ago that her mother had mentioned, deflecting Carrie's curiosity with a studied casualness. She also thought about how, before she'd left for the airport, her mother had wanted to talk to her about something private that was supposed to be history. Those words still puzzled her. Was it possible that Maria held the answer? She'd be kicking herself tomorrow if she sent Maria back to Switzerland without at least talking to her, wouldn't she?

'Okay,' she said, surprising herself. 'Fifteen minutes. Then we'll see.'

Maria smiled and drew on a pair of thin leather gloves. 'Thank you.'

Chapter Seven

'So, Carrie. You don't know anything about me at all? Or Luis, my husband?' Maria Meyer said, watching her closely.

'Absolutely nothing,' Carrie said.

They were sitting in comfortable armchairs drawn up to a small table in a corner of one of the elegant drawing rooms in the Merrion. Maria had been ushered to the table as soon as she announced herself, and Carrie guessed she'd reserved it in advance. Even though it was coming up to six o'clock and they were late for the slot, after a nod from Maria, afternoon tea was served with a delicious-looking concoction of sandwiches, cakes and pastries arriving on the table, along with tea for both of them.

'I took the liberty.' Maria glanced at her with a hint of apology. 'They said there was sure to be something to suit both of us. If it's not to your liking I can order something else …'

'No, it looks delicious, thank you,' Carrie said, selecting a slice of brown soda bread with salmon. Not that she felt the least bit hungry. It was more to keep her hands occupied.

'I appreciate you have time pressures. A woman like yourself is bound to have weekend engagements.'

'Yes, lots,' Carrie said, thinking too late that Maria wouldn't appreciate the irony in her voice.

'This won't take too long.'

'Supposing I hadn't agreed to come?' Carrie said, trying to delay the inevitable moment when Maria Meyer told her whatever it was she knew about her mother. Carrie had a strong premonition that she wasn't going to want to hear it.

'I would have cancelled the table and had something to eat in my suite.'

'Is Luis – your husband – here with you?'

A shadow fell across Maria's beautiful face. 'No, unfortunately, he's at home, as he can't travel. My husband is dying.'

'Oh, I'm sorry.' Carrie could have kicked herself. She fell silent, empathising completely, but not knowing what to say. She knew how wretched it had been to lose her parents suddenly and it helped her to appreciate how awful it must be to know in advance that your loved one was dying.

'We live in Switzerland, on Lake Lucerne,' Maria went on, her voice low and calm as though she hadn't imparted distressing news; only the slight shake of her hand as she lifted her tea cup betrayed her undercurrent of anxiety.

'So why do you want to talk to me?'

'It's … rather delicate.' She glanced at Carrie as if to check her use of the word. 'I'm here at the wishes of my husband. He was … he … knew your mother many years ago.'

Carrie's gut clenched. 'I don't ever remember my mother talking about Switzerland.' *Never mind someone called Luis.*

'Luis came to Ireland in September 1980 when he was nineteen. His father was a scientist, assisting with a research project in Cork University Hospital for a few weeks, and that was when Luis met Sylvie.'

'My mother was married by then, my parents were married in June 1980, so he must have known my father as well.'

'Your father?' Maria's face clouded with uncertainty. 'As far as I know, Luis didn't think that Sylvie was married at the time.'

'How well did Luis know my mother?' She had to ask, to find out the truth.

'Very well,' Maria said, the implication clear in her tone of voice.

Every cell in Carrie's body rebelled against this inference. She wanted to get up and walk away but she had to find out more.

'It was a few years before I met him,' Maria went on. 'Sylvie meant a lot to Luis. She changed his life around. After he returned to Switzerland, there was no contact between them. Nothing at all. It was Sylvie's decision. They knew their ... relationship ... was only going to be temporary, as they lived in different worlds. Luis trusted she was happy, so he got on with his own life. Then, a few months ago, Luis was diagnosed with quite an aggressive cancer. When he realised he was dying, he began to take stock of his life. He couldn't help remembering the time he'd spent with Sylvie and some of the things she'd said. He decided to find out how Sylvie was, discreetly of course.' Maria paused.

Carrie took a sip of her tea, bracing herself for what was coming next. The china cup was so delicate that she thought the handle might snap off in her clenched grip.

'I helped him and, thanks to the internet, it didn't take us long to find out Sylvie had died in a plane crash, along with her husband, a few years ago, and that they were survived by their only child, their daughter Carrie. It was very sad.'

Maria shook her head slowly, as if to acknowledge the distress this must have caused and she looked at Carrie with a mixture of empathy and respect. 'I can't imagine how hard it was for you. Luis was ... quite upset. All along, he'd hoped she was living happily, raising her family ... He found it hard to believe she had been gone for five years ... It was a difficult time for him. He felt he should have known somehow. He checked his appointments to see what he'd been doing that day and found out he'd been playing in a concert in Vienna around the time of the crash. He thought that Sylvie might have been happy with that.'

Carrie's head was reeling. Something else she'd tortured herself with since the plane crash was what she'd been doing at the moment her parents had died – she'd been partying with Fiona and some Scottish guys in an apartment in Christchurch. Knocking back some lurid-looking punch and laughing her head off about the credentials that lurked beneath a Scottish kilt, while the Black Eyed Peas had boomed out from a speaker somewhere. 'I don't get this,' Carrie said. 'Luis and my mother? Having some kind of affair? It couldn't have happened.' The words tumbled out of her. 'Why did you want to see me, really? And by what right has a stranger called Luis got permission to feel upset about *my* mother?'

One of the things she'd hated most in the aftermath of her parents' death was having to share her grief with so many strangers – people who felt at liberty to touch her arm and hug her and kiss her cheek, people she'd never met before intruding on her private hell, wanting a piece of her, when all she wanted to do was to hold the pain to herself, tightly, curl up with it, and hide somewhere so she could absorb it in private. Instead, she'd moved through the days, weeks and months afterwards like an automaton. It had, eventually, become a habit, a convenient way of getting through her life.

Maria stayed calm in the face of Carrie's outburst. 'I'm here because Luis has three months, at the very most … we don't know. One of his last wishes is to meet you and talk to you, Sylvie's daughter. I love my husband,' Maria added simply. 'I would do anything to fulfil his final wishes. When I called your office this morning and was told you were in, I decided to take my chances.'

'What difference would meeting me make to Luis?'

'It would bring him some little spark of happiness near the end of his life. Sylvie meant a lot to Luis. She brought him back to life and gave him a reason to live at a time when he felt there was nothing to live for. She has stayed in his heart ever since. So he thought it would be wonderful to meet you, her daughter. As well as that, he has something he wants to say only to you.'

Carrie put up her hands. 'Sorry, Maria, but I can't accept any of this. There's no way my mother would have … been involved with another man. You have the wrong Sylvie.'

Problem solved. Why hadn't she thought of this earlier? Somewhere out there lived another Sylvie Cassidy, who had been in a relationship with a Swiss guy years ago. Her parents had worshipped each other. Her big, gentle bear of a dad had been great at telling stories about their romance, including the story about how he'd known Sylvie was the girl he'd marry from the time of her sixteenth birthday party. Then there was the story of their engagement, their wedding day, the wonderful time when they'd discovered they were expecting a baby and, the icing on the cake, the day Carrie had come into the world. How they'd sat up the first few nights they'd brought her home, terrified in case she stopped breathing. The stories had been trotted out year on year, marking the anniversaries of those dates, added to and embellished with extra little details since Carrie had been old enough to understand.

Maria Meyer opened her bag and took out a small notebook. 'I have some details here that Luis gave me to check with you.' There was the ghost of a smile on her face. 'He anticipated that you might find this a little unusual, and he also wanted to make sure he had the right person.'

'Go ahead.' Carrie felt a ripple of nerves at the sight of Maria's notebook. She took a small tart off the plate. On any other occasion she would have enjoyed it, as it looked so beautiful and tempting, it would be a pleasure to bite into it. Her head was starting to pound. She was going to jump into a taxi, go straight home and get into her PJs; she would skip the frozen chicken-whatever, go straight to the Chardonnay, put her feet up on the comfy sofa and turn on Friday-evening mindless TV.

She used to relax on the sofa with Mark, sitting back against the cushions, her shoes kicked off and feet tucked into his lap. Sometimes he stroked them automatically as they watched the TV or listened to music. Sometimes he tickled them, and she tickled him back, until they were laughing so much that they fell, collapsing together across the cushions, or onto the rug in front of the fire and … she blinked hard in order to shut down the succession of warm images flooding her mind.

Maria Meyer put on a pair of reading glasses and checked her notes. Sylvie's father owned a building supply firm. She had two brothers, who were over in Canada on work experience, before joining the family business. Sylvie had gone to university and she was now a secondary-school teacher in a girl's college in Dublin. She was back home in Cork for a few weeks taking care of her mother.

As Carrie listened, the room spun around her. 'I still think you're mistaken,' she said doggedly. 'There's no way my mother would have had a relationship with anyone other than my father. They were crazy about each other and they had the perfect marriage.'

'I understand this must be a shock to you,' Maria said. 'Luis had no idea your mother was married at the time.'

'And you were hoping I'd go to Switzerland to meet him?'

'Yes, at your convenience, of course. Luis would love to talk to you, although there isn't much time—' Her face dropped. 'All your expenses would be paid. We could book you into a hotel, although Luis was hoping … that you might stay with us, and be our guest in our home on the shores of Lake Lucerne.'

Switzerland. She'd never been there. Then again, she hadn't flown anywhere since her parents had died – except Paris, with Mark. After he'd done everything possible to make it easy for her to get on the plane. Even now, the memory of that had the power to shake her.

'I'm sorry to disappoint you, but I don't accept any of this,' Carrie said. 'You'll have to go back and tell Luis he was mistaken. Whatever fond memories he has of his romance with an Irish girl, it wasn't my mother. She would never have betrayed my father.'

'It wasn't just a romance,' Maria said. 'It was bigger … it was more than that. Carrie, she saved his life. She rescued him. Luis was in a very dark place when he met Sylvie. He was …' She hesitated, her eyes pained.

'He was what?' Carrie asked, her voice soft, some premonition telling her it wasn't going to be good.

Maria gave her a sad smile. 'He was trying to end it all when she stopped him.'

'Oh.' Carrie felt humbled by what Maria had to say, and the simple and dignified way she spoke. It wasn't difficult to visualise her mother in this light. Sylvie had always been a warm, positive person, full of lively good humour. In love with life. In love with her husband.

'Sylvie saved him from his dark side. They talked … a lot. Nearly every day. Their relationship lasted less than two weeks, but he never forgot her.'

Carrie's gut instinct rebelled.

Maria was still speaking. 'Thanks to Sylvie, he went back to Switzerland a different person, and went on to make a great success of his life. I met him about five years later, so I owe Sylvie a debt as well, for saving him for me. We've been very happy.'

'That's all very life-affirming, but I'm sorry I can't help you,' Carrie said, feeling curiously empty and flat as she picked up her bag and readied herself to leave. Maria Meyer had been so gracious, it was hard to disappoint her. 'I'm glad things worked out for Luis, and I'm really sorry to hear he's so ill. I hope you're successful in your search and please give your husband my warmest regards. I hope the next few months are …' she paused; what did you say to someone

whose husband was dying? What could you say? This was crap, '…
as smooth and peaceful as they can be.' *Smooth and peaceful when
you're dying of cancer? Top marks, Carrie, for your consolation skills.*
'And now, if you'll excuse me, I don't think I'll take up any more of
your time.'

Maria sat still, her previously erect carriage somehow collapsed.
'Can I email you?' she asked. 'In case Luis thinks of anything else?'

'Yes,' Carrie tried to sound non-committal. 'If there's anything
at all I can help you with at this end, let me know,' Carrie said. 'I
might be able to save you coming over from Switzerland on a wild
goose chase. I might even be able to reunite you with the real Sylvie.'
She smiled.

Maria shook her head. 'It was never Luis' intention to contact
Sylvie if she was still alive and married. He wouldn't want to interfere
or cause any complications. After he knew about her accident, and
in view of the time that has elapsed since then, he thought it would
have been safe enough to talk to you and help enrich your memory
of your mother with whatever he had to say. And maybe humour
him a little at the end of his days … but I see we were wrong. It was
selfish of him to think you would have reason enough to visit him,
and of course, the question of your father changes the picture. Luis
believed that Sylvie was unattached at the time they met. I apologise
if we have upset you.'

'It's fine, Maria, I'm okay about it.'

Carrie got up and put on her coat, conscious that Maria seemed
so deflated she was unable to move. She bent down and, on impulse,
kissed Maria on the cheek, catching her expensive perfume, noting
the discreet diamonds at her neck and on her ears. She wondered
what Maria was going to do for the rest of her evening, alone in
Dublin after her aborted mission or how she was going to feel
returning to Switzerland to her dying husband without any answers
and minus the possibility of a visit from Carrie.

'What's he like, your Luis?' she asked, surprising herself at the way she was suddenly reluctant to leave Maria on her own.

Maria smiled, her face becoming luminous as she spoke of her husband. 'He's the most beautiful person I know. He's a concert pianist, a composer and incredibly gifted.'

'Really?'

'His music is … out of this world. He has an almost spiritual approach and plays from the depths of his feelings. He has won many awards. That's why I thought you might have heard of him.'

Despite herself, Carrie sat back into her chair. 'No, I haven't, he sounds wonderful and now I don't know what to say,' she said, lost for words. 'I like music, but not classical music particularly.'

'Luis has brought great joy to many people. They, too, should be thankful to Sylvie. Without her, his music would have been lost.'

And now his brilliant spark was about to be extinguished, Carrie thought. Life really sucked. Although she knew that already. 'You must be finding it hard to come to terms with his … illness.'

'That is another bridge to be crossed,' Maria smiled sadly. She took out her mobile, her slim fingers flying across the screen. 'I'll show you a photograph of him.' She handed the mobile to Carrie, who studied the photo of the handsome man in the white jacket with the shock of thick hair that looked like it had been blond once, but was now faded and speckled with silver. But there was something odd about the picture. She looked at his face, fearful of voicing her suspicions in case she was wrong.

'He reminds me of …'

'Yes?' Maria prompted.

'Except for his hair, he reminds me a little of … Andrea Bocelli. Is Luis …?'

Maria smiled, anticipating her question. 'Yes, Luis lost his sight when he was eighteen, in a car crash that killed his mother.'

'Oh gosh.' She chided herself for the inane words, knowing there was nothing she could say.

'The following year he was in Cork for a few weeks ... that's when he met Sylvie.'

Carrie chatted some more, reluctant to leave Maria. More and more, she felt her heart going out to the other woman, who seemed to be honest and truthful – but who was surely on the wrong track as far as Sylvie was concerned. Eventually Carrie said her goodbyes. Yet, in the taxi taking her home to Faith Crescent, Carrie couldn't help feeling a spasm of uncertainty as she went over everything Maria had said. Except for her father, the details added up, and Maria sounded so genuine and sure of herself. Carrie tried to recall every detail of what her mother had said to her in Waldron Avenue before her departure – 'a private matter ... history now ... but something you needed to know just in case ... something ever happens'. *In case what happens?*

Was it possible there was any truth in what Maria had said?

And if so, what exactly had Sylvie been up to?

Chapter Eight

September 1980

She doesn't set out to fall in love with someone who is not her husband, but that is what happens. She knows from the outset that their time together will be limited, that whatever they have will be short-lived. The bubble of time they are caught in is coloured by the heightened emotions they both feel as well as the fraught circumstances of their first and very fated meeting. It's a slice of borrowed time suspended between his life back in Switzerland and her life in Dublin, and charged with a breathtaking intensity.

On the second evening, Luis is already waiting for her, his elbows resting on his knees, his folded white cane on the sand beside him. He is wearing denim jeans and a matching denim jacket over a grey top.

'Open your mouth,' she says to him.

'Open – *what*?'

'Go on. Trust me. Open your mouth.'

He is smiling as he turns towards her, his mouth a little open.

She takes a napkin out of her bag and, opening it, she picks up a strawberry and feeds it to him.

His face brightens. 'That tastes like nectar.'

'There's more,' she says, feeding him again. When the juice runs down his chin she mops it up with her finger, placing it against his lips so he can lick it off – which he does, giving her an electric charge as he sucks the tip of her finger.

'That's – thank you. No one has ever done that for me before.'

'That's because you've probably never allowed anyone to do it.'

'Where did you get those? They're delicious.'

'I robbed them from an orchard. Now I want you to take a deep breath,' she goes on, holding a rose close to his face.

'Ah, I know what you are up to,' he says, taking the bloom from her and pressing his nose into it. 'It's beautiful.'

He is quiet for a while before he speaks again. 'Tell me what you look like, Sylvie, so I can picture you.'

'Um, what do I look like? Let me think ...' she hesitates. She hasn't expected this and a hard pellet of anxiety forms in her stomach.

'What would I see if I was looking at a photograph of you? It can't be that hard.'

A photograph. All she has to do is picture a photograph and describe what she sees. 'I'm not that tall,' she says. 'About five foot three.'

'Well, I guessed that much. I could tuck you into my chest very easily.'

Her head swims as she imagines being tucked into his chest.

'I have long hair.'

'I guessed that much too. What colour is it?'

'It's kind of dark brown. And I have blue eyes.' As she speaks, she realises it says nothing at all about her, but this is one time when a lie is far better than the truth.

He lifts his hand towards her face. 'May I?'

Something sparks inside her. She knows she is on dangerous ground, but she still tilts her face towards him. 'Okay.'

His touch is feather light, his fingers tracing her profile as gentle as thistledown. He circles her forehead, around her eyes and nose, along the angle of her cheek to her jaw, and then around her mouth. She is stilled by the delicacy of his hand. He traces the contours as though her face is a precious object and he is committing every inch of it to a picture in his mind. She feels peculiarly bereft when he takes his hand away. Then he sifts through her hair, again with a slow, deliberate stroke that sends little shivers down to her toes.

'Thank you, but you didn't tell me the truth,' he says, catching her by surprise.

'*What?*'

'That you are beautiful,' he says.

If he could see her, if he knew what she was really like, he might not think she was all that attractive. But his words, coming on top of the tender touch of his hand, make her feel beautiful on the inside and cause her throat to swell. A bubble of heat rises inside her; with a touch like his, Luis could be a very sensual lover.

'You're not that bad yourself,' she tells him, trying to lighten the sudden and dangerous shift in her mood. Dangerous because she can't go here, can't give these alarming thoughts space in her head. Still, there's no harm in finding him attractive, is there? It means she is still alive somewhere under the mess her marriage has become. Alive to a man's touch, her nerve endings responding to a sensual stroke, a flood of heat sweeping through her. It doesn't mean she has to do anything about it.

'What do you see?' he asks.

'I see a man who is tall and well built, with strong shoulders. Your hair is wavy and a little long, but ... attractive like that.' She almost says 'sexy', but swallows the word at the last minute. 'You have an honourable face, like a proud Roman god or a fearless Greek warrior. You have a generous mouth that is made for fun. When you smile, your whole face brightens.'

She thinks of all the girlfriends he must have had running after him before the accident. She wonders if any of them have stuck around, or if he pushed them away and shut them out, along with everyone else, not wanting any sympathy.

'You flatter me,' he says.

'I'm just telling you what I see. How do you feel today?' she asks.

'I don't know. Different to yesterday. Less dark. A little calmer. I was in a bad place yesterday but, as you said, it passed. You were right.'

'What caused it? Anything in particular? You can tell me.' She slides her hand into his and he begins to talk.

'I've been playing the piano since I was three. I've won scholarships and prizes. My mother was very proud of me, as was my father. After she died, I was so angry with life that I refused to play anymore. I couldn't bear to listen to anything. But here ...'

'Here what?' she prompts softly.

'There's a piano in the house and one evening in the time between the housekeeper leaving and my father coming home, I was alone and I found my fingers running across the keys, thinking no one could hear me. I played it the next evening and the next ... but then, in the middle of a Chopin sonata, it made me remember my mother and her happy face when she came to listen to me in the concert hall or at home in Switzerland, where she would sit looking out to the lake as I played ... The pain was ... indescribable. All my insides felt dark. What is the point of that? Why suffer in pain if you can get rid of it for good?'

He turns his face to her and her throat is suddenly dry. She has often heard the saying that the eyes are the window of the soul. Maybe they are to a large extent. But looking at Luis, she realises that an expressive face can tell a thousand stories. Luis' face is lit with something vulnerable and raw and totally unguarded in the way it reaches out to her.

'The pain will ease in time,' she says. 'Nothing ever stays the same.'

'You have helped, with your soft Irish voice and talk of hope – and your kiss.'

She stares at his face for a long time, feeling drawn to him. 'Good. I'm different today as well,' she says. She attempts to lighten the mood a little. 'I'm not as wet or cold, for a start. Neither am I scared half to death.'

'Scared? What were you frightened of?'

She is silent for a short while, knowing she can't tell him about the thing she is most frightened of. 'I was afraid of what you might do,' she says quietly. 'And that I might not have been able to stop you in time.'

He interlaces her fingers in his, tightening his hold. 'I'm sorry if I upset you.'

'It's okay, I forgive you. But you have to make it worth my while. You owe me.'

'How can I make it worth your while?'

'I'll think about that. Did you talk to your father yet, about how you feel?'

'No.' His face is set.

'He loves you, he would want to know.'

'It's easier to talk to you.'

'Why?'

'You saw me when I was at my worst, a stranger, and still you were kind to me. You were honest and truthful. Very few people are honest with me anymore. They pretend. They think I can't see that they are lying, but I know, inside. It's easier to talk over things with someone you've never met before.'

'We've met again today,' she points out.

'Yes, but you're different. I know by your voice I can trust you, Sylvie.'

Trust her? She's relieved he can't see her face.

'Can we go for a walk?' he asks. 'I'd like to go for a walk along the beach, without this.' He pushes his cane away. 'I want it to be just you and me.'

'We can walk down by the water's edge if you like.'

As soon as she speaks, she wonders if it is such a good idea, bringing him back to the water, but he seems calmer today. They both take off their shoes and roll up their jeans. She feels a little awkward at first, but then it seems perfectly natural to allow him to put his hand through her arm, linking her, as they stroll down to the water's edge, laughing at the rush of cold water swirling over their feet. She forgets he can't see as they saunter along the quiet cove in the cool of the early evening. The air is bracing and vibrant, carrying with it the cry of the gulls and the constant clamour of the sea. Up close, the water looks like frilly lace as it whispers and fizzes across the strand, and farther out, where the water is deeper, the waves crash and splatter as they roll on in the tide. Luis matches his pace to hers and she is conscious of his body, their hips touching, their arms entwined. Her pulse beats more quickly than normal, a heightened excitement clutching hold of her at the simple pleasure of being here with him like this.

'Tell me what it looks like,' he says.

She describes everything she can see in the panorama around them. She tells him to take deep breaths of the air and to notice how the sun feels on his face. To her surprise, it is cathartic for her too; it fills her with a sort of peace and it fixes her in that moment with him. There is just this now, being on the beach with Luis. Nothing else matters, not the wedding day that was perfect and felt like a dream until things started to go wrong, nor the sickening fear that's been slithering through her veins telling her she is totally inadequate.

He is waiting for her the following evening, and the next, and she knows he likes to make sure he is there first so she won't see him approaching with his cane. Sitting in the sand dunes, he could just be an attractive young man in a pair of jeans and a light jacket, waiting for his girlfriend to join him.

His *girlfriend*? She laughs at herself. She brings along titbits for him to taste, popping them into his mouth – cubes of full Irish cheese, fresh pieces of soda bread, raspberries and blackcurrants. She presses a big conch shell to his ears, and holds a spray of lavender and a piece of pine bark to his nose.

They talk about their childhoods, laughing while they compare the vast difference between them. Luis had a privileged and affluent upbringing; private school, piano lessons as soon as he was old enough, classical piano training in the conservatoire, trips to Zurich, Salzburg and Vienna for concerts; a life steeped in culture and full of expectation of a brilliant future in the concert arenas of Europe, if not the world.

It is scary, she thinks, how easily such an advantaged life can fall apart in the space of a moment on a Swiss motorway, like pulling the pin out of a grenade and demolishing all the secure structures around you.

'It all sounds very different to Willow Hill,' she says. 'It was very ordinary, with no money for extravagances. We went to the local school, then after school we all had to help out and had our chores to do. Holidays were spent helping out with my father's business, then after school it was straight to college and after that, into a teaching job. And, well, here I am ...' She picks up a small piece of driftwood and draws patterns in the sand, deciding not to complicate anything by talking about her marriage.

'You're not happy,' he says.

'Says who?'

'Says the sound of your voice.'

He's good at picking out the subtle clues from her tone. Truth is, she had forgotten what happiness was, or how it felt, fizzing in her stomach, until she met him. She'd been happy on her wedding day, over the moon, ecstatic. She wasn't foolish enough to expect that heightened level of emotion to continue, but neither had she expected to pitch into a downward spiral of fear and anxiety, where peace of mind seemed far away.

'You're right,' she says, wanting to be honest with him. 'There are a few problems I need to sort out, now that I'm away from Dublin for a while.'

'What kind of problems?'

She stares out to where the sea is rolling in, today a gun-metal grey mirroring the clouds. 'Things that are making me ... quite unhappy.'

Compared to Luis, who has a mountain to climb, her troubles are molehills, she had reasoned with herself in the dark of the previous night. Nobody has died or is incurably ill, there just aren't any safe, secure or impregnable structures in life, not even within a marriage. There are no guarantees of perfect happiness either, she has discovered the hard way that it's a fairy-tale illusion.

She takes a deep gulp of the salt-laden air and continues. 'I can't really talk about it, it's rather ... complicated, but I want you to know that being here with you is great. It's giving me breathing space and taking me away from my own troubles.'

'I'm glad to help.'

'You'd help more if you played some music for me,' she says.

'Sorry, but no.'

'I've already heard you, remember?'

'I didn't think anyone was listening.'

She tries a different approach, keeping her voice light to take any sting out of her words, wondering if he'll fully understand what she's trying to say without taking offence. 'Luis, I hope you're not one of those precious artists who always has to be coaxed to perform? Like a spoiled child.'

'Spoiled?'

'Indulged. Pampered.'

'Stop trying to shame me into playing. I can't face it again.'

'I know it made you sad, but you can't keep your gift away from the world.'

He stays silent.

'What kind of a life do you think your mother would have wanted for you?' she says, her voice firm. 'What did she hope for when you were growing up? That you'd waste your life?'

'You're annoyed with me now.'

'I'm not annoyed with you,' she says. 'I ... I like you too much. I'd prefer to fill you up with the confidence and daring you need to get on top of the tough things life has thrown at you. The courage to sit down at the piano and be the master of it – but I don't know what to say or how to make you strong, the way you should feel inside.'

She wants to fill herself with those qualities too, the qualities she thinks she most lacks in her marriage. The courage to speak out about the silent things that crackle like invisible electricity between herself and her husband, the confidence to stand up for herself. She has the wild hope that, in trying to instil them in Luis, she might find a way to improve them in herself.

'Sylvie?'

She doesn't answer at first.

'Sylvie, you are with me?'

She jumps. 'Yes, I'm here.'

'I thought you had forgotten your name,' he jokes.

'I was thinking.' *Don't think. Just be here on the beach with Luis.*

'I wanted to ask you, how much do you like me?'

He sounds nervous and unsure. There are girlfriends who have no doubt turned away from him, embarrassed by the depth of the tragedy that has hit him, girlfriends who were probably throwing themselves at him before it all happened. In spite of her gnawing insecurities, she leans into him and kisses his mouth. He hasn't been expecting her kiss and he jumps.

'I like you that much,' she says.

She sees the smile flit across his mouth. 'I'm not sure what you meant, could you do that again?' She leans into him again and he puts both his arms around her and holds her close. They are silent and still for a moment, both a little hesitant, their foreheads touching, and the anticipation of his mouth on hers is already tingling inside her.

I am married, a voice whispers in her head. *This is wrong.* It doesn't feel wrong. His breath on her cheek is filling her with excitement. Her senses are humming with the whole, wonderful nearness of him, and her body is liquid where it touches his. *It feels so right.* Something outside of her says that if she wants to become more daring and confident, where better to start than here? Whatever happens in the sand dunes this evening has nothing to do with her marriage or the impasse that's lying between herself and her husband. She wants to kiss Luis and keep on kissing him because she can't remember the last time she was so quivery with need that she felt she was dissolving.

She gives a little sigh and their mouths come together in a slow, deep kiss. His lips are hungry for her, his arms around her tighten until they are locked together. She puts her hand up to touch the curve of his jaw, as if to secure him to her even more, and all her worries and concerns fall away, vanishing into a white void, until there is nothing but the heat of this man's body against hers, their mouths crushed together, speaking a language without words, and sending a fever right through her, so that she is giddy and dizzy and something inside her is whirling around with joy.

Chapter Nine

As soon as Carrie reached home that night she poured a generous glass of white wine. Then she settled herself on the sofa, opened her iPad and googled Luis Meyer.

There was no shortage of information about him – biography notes, lists of books about him, glowing reviews of his concerts and DVDs, all of it bearing out what Maria had said about him and his talent. His composition was eloquent, his expression inspirational and visionary, and he infused his playing with a pure and simple beauty. He was too young to die, just like her parents. There were photographs of him stepping off planes – in Rome, in Paris, in Berlin for concerts – in which he was always smiling. And he was always with Maria. They made a beautiful and distinguished couple. There were photographs of him on stage in huge arenas in front of vast audiences. There was even a photograph of him with his elderly father, who had passed away just two years earlier at the age of eighty-five.

There was a link to a newspaper article announcing that his summer tour of Italy had been cancelled on account of illness. It didn't give any details, but the implication that it was terminal was clear. The article said Luis would be spending the next few months quietly at his home on Lake Lucerne with his wife while he attended to some personal matters. He trusted his privacy would be respected.

There were YouTube clips of his performances, and Carrie watched those as well, putting on headphones, finding herself entranced by the powerful music and transported to a different world, so that she was surprised when one clip ended and she found herself in her front room in Faith Crescent, hunched over her iPad, blinking her eyes in the sudden silence.

Her mind was still teeming with the unbelievable idea that there could be a connection between her mother and Luis when Maria Meyer emailed her on Saturday evening:

Dear Carrie

Thank you for taking the time to speak to me yesterday evening. I enjoyed meeting you and talking to you even if my visit was not entirely successful. I have passed on your regards to Luis, who fully understands how you feel, and he realises that it must have been painful to have the subject of your parents raised, particularly your mother, in the circumstances I described. I also talked to Luis about you, and he considers that you sound just like the kind of lovely daughter that Sylvie deserved; warm, caring and loyal.

He does not recall any word of Sylvie's husband, so he hopes it was not distressing for you to hear me speak.

Another detail Luis recalled in case it's any help to you, was that the name of the house in Cork where Sylvie grew up was called Willow Hill, that there was a gardener and handyman named – he thinks – Seamus who came in regularly ...'

Something thudded into Carrie's chest and she ignored the rest of the email. She saw it in her mind's eye: the wooden sign on one of the big gate posts that marked the entrance to the curving driveway that led up to her grandparents' rambling house situated on an elevated site outside Kinsale: Willow Hill. A reel of memories swamped her.

Sitting in her cosy terraced house, with a view of the church over the high back wall, Carrie was transported back in time. She recalled summers in Willow Hill: the excitement of arriving in early July, her grandparents coming out to welcome them as soon as her mother pulled up on the gravel after the long journey from Dublin; Fiona coming running through the adjacent field and throwing her arms around both Carrie and her mother; the scent of freshly mown grass on the spacious meadow that was a pungent backdrop to those summers; the tang of the sea carried on a stiff breeze when the cousins trouped down to the cove and nothing but weeks unrolling ahead in which to run free.

Christmases were extra special, travelling down from Dublin in all sorts of weather with her parents, wiping condensation off the car window and peering out at a darkened countryside; lights blazing at Willow Hill and more warm welcomes, but this time laced with the excitement of Christmas and the evocative smell of big turf fires smouldering in huge grates as well as the aroma of pine needles from the beautifully decorated noble fir tree in the hallway. The snow blanketing the Willow Hill meadow and her mother running out the door to be the first to make some footprints in the thick layer of white drift … turning to laugh with Carrie when her boots got stuck, her laughter echoing in the clear air.

As Carrie sat there, a wave of nostalgia tinged with loss washed over her.

She remembered Seamus, although Carrie wasn't sure how proficient a gardener he was. She had a recollection of a wizened countryman who knew everything there was to know about the weather and the turn of the seasons, someone who made himself useful by cutting the meadow grass, repairing the roof of the barn, and chopping up logs and turf for the big winter fires.

The sign was still there, marking the entrance to Willow Hill. It had been cleaned and polished up. After her grandparents had died, the house had been renovated and was now a successful Spa and Wellness centre, the business co-managed by her aunts Evelyn and Clare, who lived close by.

Carrie took a deep breath and scanned the rest of the email.

'... but we will not annoy you with any more of this talk, Carrie. We will leave it be. However, the offer of a visit to us in Switzerland is still extended to you, if you'd care to fly over for a couple of days, all expenses paid. Luis sees very few people but he would enjoy talking to an Irish girl like you, as Ireland holds a special place in his heart. Please know that nothing at all is expected of you in return. You are most welcome any time.
Yours sincerely,
Maria.

It would have been hard to read such an email and not be moved. Even harder to reply and refuse the invitation, which was what she'd be doing. The boat and train to Switzerland wasn't an option for a few days and Carrie didn't fly. She didn't do air travel, full stop. Maria was sure to understand her reasons. Mark had managed to persuade her to fly once – and only once – and even that had taken a long time, buckets of love, gentle coaxing and, in the end, some downright dirty tactics.

* * *

'So you're going to spend the rest of your life on terra firma?' he'd asked, on one of those lazy, summery Sunday mornings about four months after he'd moved in with her.

'Yep,' she'd said, wiggling away from him in bed. 'You'll never catch me getting on a plane. Ever.'

His hand had reached across and stroked her face. 'That's knocked my great idea on the head.'

'What great idea?'

'I want to make you fly, Carrie Cassidy. In every sense of the word.'

'Nope. Never.'

You do make me fly, she could have said. *In bed, where you make me soar. So high that sometimes it frightens me.*

'That's going to be a pain in the ass. I had lots of adventures in mind for us.'

'Like what?'

'Lots of exciting things, um, white-water rafting in the Grand Canyon, an African safari, a hot-air balloon ride over the Hunter Valley in Australia, the Northern Lights off Norway, a cruise around the Galapagos islands.' As he spoke, he turned around in bed, straightened the duvet so it was tucked around both of them, and then gathered her close under its warmth.

'It would take a lifetime to fit all that in.'

'Hey, didn't you guess?' He flicked her hair. 'That's part of the plan too.'

What plan? He was rushing her. 'I didn't know you could white-water raft in the Grand Canyon.'

'You can.'

'But you don't have to go to Norway to see the Northern Lights.'

'No, but that's where they are the most spectacular.'

'What a pity I'm going to miss all those exciting adventures.'

'You don't have to, you know. All you have to do is agree to come with me.'

'All I have to do is get on a plane again.' She untangled her legs from his, moved away from the heat of his body and stared at the angle of the sun slicing across the ceiling. It was going to be another lovely summery day. 'No, thanks. Look, Mark, it's only fair to warn you that I'm never flying again. The boat and the Eurostar will bring me to France and on to Europe, but if you want someone to join you in all your wild and wonderful adventures, it won't be me. I'm not the adventurous type whatsoever. I'm not into risk-taking of any kind.'

'Not even if I promise to keep you safe?'

'Nope.' No one could promise her that. She only felt truly safe between the solid walls of Faith Crescent.

'Promise with my whole heart?'

'Mark, please. Try and understand … your parents didn't plummet down from the sky.'

'How can I understand when you won't talk about them?'

'What's the point? It's history.'

'Okay, you don't want to talk, I can live with that for now, but I'm making it my mission to bring you somewhere nice, somewhere romantic, maybe not too far away for our European city break, to which we will be flying.'

'That'll be mission impossible.'

'That'll be happening sooner than you think.' He laughed and pulled her into a hug.

He took it on as his pet project over the next few weeks. During the week, he sent her texts and at weekends she found post-its stuck around the house.

Carrie is sitting in the departure lounge, looking forward to her flight …
Carrie feels good as she walks up the steps to the plane …

Carrie is calm and relaxed boarding the plane …

He left pictures of holiday destinations in strategic locations, pinning them to the fridge with a magnet, sticking them up at eye level along her bookcase, even putting one in the dishwasher. He emailed her links to travel articles in which tourists were enthusing about the wonderful time they'd had.

'You're mad, you know that?' she said to him one Saturday after she'd lifted a post-it from the fridge door. 'You're not in work today, trying to do whatever you get up to in that playroom of yours in Bizz.'

'It's not a play room, it helps the team to come up with lots of good ideas.'

'Sitting around on primary-colour beanbags. Lying in hammocks or … or sliding down chutes. I'd call that lots of fun.'

'You sound jealous. Don't you enjoy your job?'

'Not really. It's a means to an end, but I don't get a lot of satisfaction out of it.'

'Then you should look for a different job, one that really interests you.'

'I'll see,' she said half-heartedly. 'Anyway, you rarely go up steps to planes anymore. So that one is misleading. It would probably confuse me.'

'You do on some flights. But I can change it to gangway … or jet bridge.' He leaned against the doorjamb and folded his arms. He was wearing a soft denim shirt and she knew how it would smell if she went over and put her arms around him. It was the small intimacies of living with him – like knowing how he organised his laundry, the way he zoomed around a supermarket forgetting half his stuff – that had taken her by surprise.

'It won't work anyway,' she said airily. 'I don't believe in any of that mumbo jumbo.'

'So what does Carrie Cassidy believe in?' His head to one side, appearing mildly curious, but she knew by his eyes that her answer interested him.

She took a carton of milk out of the fridge and pretended to be checking the best before date while she answered as honestly as she could. 'Not much, to be honest. So don't be under any illusions as far as I'm concerned.'

He raised an eyebrow. His mouth curved in a smile as he came over to her and took the carton out of her hands, putting it on the counter. 'I'm under no illusions, Carrie darling. I know I've an uphill battle on my hands but I like a challenge.' He took her hands and linked his fingers through hers. 'Repeat after me: Mark holds Carrie's hands at thirty thousand feet up in the sky.'

'Hmmm. I hope you're a good sport about losing. You'll never find me at thirty thousand feet. And I don't think I'll be your "darling" by the time you've given up,' she said, loosening her fingers and flouncing past him.

Then, he started talking about Paris ... the quaint cafés, the tempting brasseries, the wide, clean boulevards, the Louvre, the Eiffel Tower at night.

'Paris! You can get there by train,' she scoffed.

'I've thought of that,' he said. 'It's just a ninety-minute flight, but if you really found it all that impossibly scary on the way over, I'd promise to bring you home the long way around. I've even put together a playlist for you, and it takes exactly ninety minutes.'

'A playlist?'

'All your favourites, the most relaxing music. I just need to load it onto your mobile.'

'Ah, here, you're really serious, aren't you?'

'Have you ever been to Paris?'

'No.'

'If, as you say, you don't need to talk about your parents' death and you're fine with it, this is one way of proving it to me.'

'That's gross manipulation. Underhand tactics. Dirty tricks. Of *course* I've moved on, I'm over it, it's been more than four years. It's all ancient history now.' *Why are you doing this to me,* she wanted to say. *Let's just leave things as they are.*

'I don't actually buy in to the whole "moving on" trip, or "getting over it" stuff when it comes to certain things.' He paused. 'And, yes, lots of people have been dealt worse blows in life … I know that's the next thing you usually say when you're trying to dismiss it.'

She didn't reply.

'Thing is, I hope you're okay about it all, deep down. See, Carrie, if everything about it really is history, you should have no problem getting on a plane. I'd hate to see you going through the rest of your life without taking the opportunity to travel around the world. You'd miss out on so much.'

'I can if I want to.'

'Will you at least come to Paris with me? I'll hold your hand all the way. All you have to do is sit there, close your eyes and listen to your music. It should help you from panicking too much.'

'Panicking when, exactly?' she asked softly.

'Well … this, you see …' He stood up and plucked a sheet of paper out of his jeans pocket and handed it to her. A copy of flight confirmations. To Paris, in both their names. For the end of August, which was just two weeks away. She looked at it in silence, shocked at the feeling that someone was picking at a painful scab over her heart. How could that be? Now, over four years later? She was fine, wasn't she?

'Look, maybe this wasn't a good idea,' he said, taking the sheet off her. 'Forget it. I jumped the gun a little. I can see you're upset.'

She watched his long fingers folding the page over, then she plucked it back out of his hand. It was the one sure-fire way to convince Mark she was fine. That she had no scars left. And maybe this lovely man deserved a break.

'Just this once,' she said. 'And in recognition of your very clever but totally underhand tactics, you're on.'

* * *

He'd held her hand during the flights all the way over and back. She'd managed it, but only because he was with her. It didn't mean she had the guts to get on a plane again, Carrie told herself as she read Maria's email for the second time. Maria and Luis were going to be disappointed. Then again, if she didn't go, she'd never hear whatever it was that Luis wanted to say to her …

Chapter Ten

Meyer. Luis Meyer. As he waited for his flight to take off, Adam scanned the French newspaper article again, trying to translate more details, and breathed a little easier. It was just a familiar name that reminded him of the past. It posed no threat to him. There was no way ancient history could catch up with him after all these years.

He'd just spent a week in Marseilles. There was nowhere quite like it to blend with the crowds, to be another thrill-seeking, anonymous tourist. The only currency that counted there was the thickness of his wallet, which he'd filled before he'd left home. His credit card had been tucked away in the safe in his hotel room, but that was only for emergencies, he didn't want to leave a trail of transactions. His mobile was not traceable back to him, and was a cheap version of his state-of-the-art mobile that he'd left in the safe back home. He'd learned his lesson after he'd sailed a little too close to the wind in Morocco two years earlier, when the house he'd thought secure had been raided by an Interpol vice squad. He'd escaped. Most of the young, female occupants hadn't. Then again, he'd reasoned, they'd simply be exchanging one form of imprisonment for another.

He shoved the newspaper into the seat pocket in front of him as the aircraft thundered into the darkened skies over Marseilles and set course for Dublin. A peculiar feeling of foreboding gripped him.

Old names writhed up from long-buried memories and their ghosts danced eerily in front of his vision, thrusting him back to Willow Hill, Sylvie and Beth, and to the time it had all started, the first day he'd seen her in the bank.

* * *

It was 1979 and she was standing in front of him in the Xerox room, waiting for a stencil to be copied. Her long blonde hair was held back with a pink hairband. She wore a cream blouse and neat navy skirt and she had nice legs. Above the acrid smell of stencil corrective fluid, he caught the clean scent of her hair. He tipped her on the shoulder and she turned around. She looked about sixteen, with that innocent expression in her eyes, but he knew she had to be older than that.

'You must be the new girl,' he said. He was rewarded when her pale face turned brick red.

'Y—yes, I'm fairly new, I suppose,' she said a little breathlessly. 'I'm just here three weeks.'

'I've been on holiday. That's why I haven't seen you. You're very welcome to the Mutual Banking Corporation. Is this your first job?'

'It's my first job in Dublin.'

'And are you settling in here okay?'

Her smile was nervous. 'Well, everyone in the typing pool seems very nice.'

She was letting him know her position, although he'd already guessed. 'And what about the managers?' he asked a little cheekily. 'Are they treating you all right?'

'Well …' She gave an embarrassed laugh and backed away slightly. 'I don't really know any of the managers.'

'Oh, I'll have to see what I can do to change that. I'm Adam.'

'And I'm Beth.'

Beth. It suited her. It was a soft, placid name.

In the next few weeks, whenever he met her in the corridors of the bank or passed through the typing pool and paused by her desk, she flushed. He noticed that she didn't seem to join in the gossip with the other typists and, mostly, she went to lunch alone. A couple of times he even 'happened' to pop into the same café as her for his lunch, and asked her very nicely if he could share her table. He knew by the flustered look on her face that she guessed he had deliberately followed her in.

He found out she was virtually all alone in the world, and that her mother had died of cancer three years earlier.

'No other family?' he asked, after he sympathised.

'My mother was from Cork, and she had a brother, but he emigrated to Australia in the 1950s and she lost touch with him. Then, you see ...' Beth paused. She stirred her tea slowly and he knew she wasn't sure what to say next.

'Then what?'

'My mother went to England to live with her aunt in Manchester. She got married over there and my sister was born, but then when she was expecting me, my father ...' She hesitated, and, lowering her eyes, she looked away.

He was proud of the fact that his eyes never faltered. His voice was very soft. 'It's okay, you can tell me, is your father no longer around as well?'

She glanced at him from under her lashes, a little relief evident in her expression. 'Well, yes, he went off to work on the oil rigs and unfortunately he went missing ... after an accident ...'

He knew she was glossing over something. Oil rigs? Missing? Her father had probably done a runner, only she was too nervous or ashamed to admit it.

'So my mother came home to Cork,' she said, 'where I was born, but then my sister died a few years later.'

'That's sad, Beth. Your mother was very brave and courageous. It must have been difficult for her.'

'It was.'

Two weeks later, he asked her out on a date. He kissed her softly at the end of the night and felt her trembling in his arms. Sweet, biddable Beth. He couldn't have asked for anyone more suitable in his life right then. They dated for a few weeks and it was all going fine, but then their cosy little twosome was threatened by none other than Beth's good friend, Sylvie, and the look in her steady blue eyes.

* * *

Sylvie! He shifted in the narrow confines of his aircraft seat as he remembered the deliberate way she had watched him. He shouldn't have let a newspaper article unsettle him so much. He had nothing to worry about, least of all old ghosts. That's all they were – ghosts, with no power on earth to harm him, let alone disrupt his secure life. He'd be glad to get home to the comfort of his apartment, part of his penthouse stronghold, with the deep leather chairs and views over the city, and relax with a whiskey before he retired for the night. He would have to get used to an empty bed once more, after the very pleasurable temptations he'd enjoyed on his holiday. He went abroad four or five times a year to indulge his appetites, but it wasn't nearly enough.

Still, when his flight landed behind schedule in Dublin on Saturday night, he felt the city closing in on him a little. As usual, when he returned from his holidays abroad, he was edgy as he queued in passport control, thinking of his illicit activities. This evening, added to that, an old spark of guilt at the memory of Beth and Willow Hill that was buried deep in his conscience stirred long enough to make him wonder what it would be like, really, to have the arm of the law landing on his shoulder, ready to haul him off for questioning. To have to call his solicitor. What would it be like to be incarcerated in an interview room or a prison cell in Mountjoy, with no way of escape.

He slid his passport under the counter, a minuscule lift of relief surprising him when the veteran guard on duty seemed to recognise his name and paused for a fraction before waving him through deferentially. If anything went wrong, he'd miss all this – the respect and attention granted to him by virtue of his status as one of Ireland's foremost financiers, never mind his comfortable lifestyle, something he'd worked and aimed for all his life.

He waited in baggage reclaim, observing the tourists milling around him. He liked to think he looked just like them, blending with them namelessly in his casual jeans. Apart from his name on the passport, there was nothing in his face to indicate that he was anyone other than a rather ordinary man returning from an early holiday abroad. Nothing to indicate he could once have afforded a private jet when his fortunes had been on the rise, or that he was replete with sexual pleasure, the physical side of which was over until his next trip abroad.

Ireland was too small to take any chances. And the good times would come again, he just had to be patient.

On a screen by the luggage belt, news headlines and the weather forecast played out on a continuous loop. Nobody was paying it much attention, as the travellers who weren't craning their necks to see if there was any sign of the luggage emerging were scrolling through their mobile phones, staring at their screens as though they'd been parted from them for a week instead of a couple of hours. The addiction to mobile media distraction almost ranked up there with alcohol or nicotine dependence. Then again, social media and mobile phones had their uses. There were very few people in Dublin who didn't have some kind of online presence, which was all the better to keep track of things. Track of people. That was why the mobile now switched off and secreted in the end of his carry-on baggage would be consigned to the depths of his safe as soon as he reached home. The mobile with enough illegal videos and images, never mind valuable contact details of his circle of acquaintances – more than enough to ensure a stretch in Mountjoy. He strolled through Customs, reminding himself that it was untraceable to him.

Just as well mobiles hadn't been around all those years ago, he thought, annoyed that he was back there once more, albeit fleetingly. Instant communication and the ability to keep track could have prevented him from getting away with it. And that, he determined, as he strolled out into the chilly night, wasn't going to change. He'd just have to keep a closer eye on the only person who could possibly find out the truth about what had happened – Carrie Cassidy. She was the last remaining link to Willow Hill and Sylvie.

Chapter Eleven

Carrie spent the weekend with the defeated expression on Maria's elegant face nibbling at her conscience and the look of Luis on those YouTube clips – beautiful, proud, smiling Luis – arousing her curiosity. By the time Fiona called her on Sunday evening, she was glad of the sound of her cousin's voice.

'You seem a bit down,' Fiona said cheerfully. 'When was the last time you were out, as in "out"? And I don't mean work or food shopping.'

Standing in the kitchen in Faith Crescent, mobile to her ear, Carrie cast her mind back. She couldn't remember, apart from Lucy's christening and meeting Maria Meyer. 'What's this?' she asked defensively. 'Ways to get Carrie back in action?' She slid a container into the microwave and switched it on.

'Hey, relax, there's no need to be jumpy with me,' Fiona said. 'I understand if you're still, well, on a bit of a downer after Mark. I'm just trying to help if I can.'

She'd never let Fiona in on the whole sorry mess of what happened with Mark, the only thing she admitted was that she was the one who had called off the engagement.

'Thanks, Fiona, it's not just Mark,' she said. 'Something happened last week that I'm still trying to get my head around. This is going to sound weird,' Carrie said, as she took a plate and cutlery out of the press. She told Fiona about Maria's visit and Luis wanting to see her, though she left out the supposed love affair.

'So? What's weird about that? The poor guy has obviously made out a bucket list and your name is on it. It's sad that he's dying. How long did you say he has?'

'Three months … ish.'

'Ah, Carrie, the least you can do is humour him.'

'He's not exactly a bus ride away. It's Switzerland. Lake Lucerne.'

'Even better. That's supposed to be really beautiful. What's the problem? Or do you think you're being lured over there for some slutty reason? Sex trafficking or drug stuff. Or, even worse, your fabulous body parts.'

'No, Maria seems to be totally up front and genuine and Luis is a famous musician, a pianist and composer. I've googled him … but you know I can't do flights.'

'Not even for someone who's dying? Look, I know where you're coming from, more than anyone else, but you know you've a far greater chance of getting knocked down by a bus. Or winning the Lotto.' Fiona delivered this in her no-nonsense voice.

The microwave pinged and, still holding her mobile, Carrie went over to open it.

'Is that your dinner?' Fiona asked.

'Yep.' Carrie lifted out the plastic container of chicken supreme that consisted mostly of sauce and rice. To be accompanied by a bottle of beer she'd found rolling around in the bottom of the fridge.

'Ah, here, hon, you owe it to yourself to break out of the mouldy pit you're stuck in.'

* * *

She hadn't actually made a decision but, on Monday, Carrie found herself asking Steve Boyle about getting some time off the week after next. He agreed with such alacrity that Carrie was mildly insulted.

'It'll do you good to have a break and recharge the batteries,' he said, raising an eyebrow as though he wasn't sure if even a week's break would be enough to re-invigorate Carrie and refresh her vision. He sat back in his leather chair, splaying his legs, and he clasped his hands behind his head as he swivelled slightly. 'Going anywhere nice?'

'I'm not sure yet,' she said.

He pursed his lips. 'Once you're out of this place?'

'I haven't actually decided, Steve,' she said stiffly.

'Hey, relax, Carrie, don't look so serious, that's supposed to be a joke.'

She felt his gaze pinned between her shoulder blades as she left his office. She went back to her desk and tried to rise above Steve and his comments. The first hurdle had been cleared and it scared her a little. There was nothing to stop her from going to Switzerland, except herself.

* * *

She pinned the first sign to her fridge; it was typed out in size 18 font to make sure it was sufficiently eye-catching.

Carrie is relaxed as she boards the flight to Zurich.

Then she put another one on the side of her bookcase in the hall, so she'd see it every time she walked out of the kitchen.

Carrie is happy to travel to Switzerland.

And a third one on the mantelpiece in her sitting room.

Carrie feels good as she checks in at the airport.

Then, on Thursday evening, she wasn't home from work long when the doorbell rang, and it was Mark.

He was facing away from her, distracted by some kids playing football in the cul de sac. It didn't matter what way he stood, she still felt a punch landing in her stomach at the sight of his back, his shoulders covered by a navy coat specked with drops of rain. She knew how the muscles in those shoulders rippled when he pulled off his shirt in one easy movement, how hard they felt under the touch of her fingers. She knew how it felt when he sat on the edge of the bed and she knelt behind him, running her hands across the contours of his body, skin touching skin as she teased him with her nakedness.

She swallowed back a wave of dizziness.

'Mark?' Her voice felt rusty.

He turned around to face her, and the closeness of him on her doorstep winded her afresh.

'Sorry to disturb you, Carrie, but I might have left something behind … when I moved out, I mean,' he said, discomfort etched on his face.

Carrie. She hated the warm, sexy way he said her name almost as much as she used to love it. No one had ever said it quite like him. Then again, no one else she knew had such a warm, sexy voice.

'Left something behind?' she echoed, unable to summon much clarity of thought.

'Yes, I think I stuck it in a book … somewhere.'

'Stuck what?'

'My car insurance certificate.' His face was sheepish. And embarrassed. And endearing. How dare he turn up on her doorstep like this, upsetting her fragile calm.

'Your car insurance certificate?' For a moment, she couldn't grasp what he meant.

He looked beyond her, down the hall, into the kitchen. 'I think I tucked it into a book, and I forgot to take it with me. Thing is, I need it.'

There was a soft glitter in his eyes as he spoke. Was he glad he had a valid excuse to call or was she imagining it? They stood in silence, staring at each other. Carrie's skin prickled with anxiety. It was the kind of thing she would have laughed at just a few short weeks ago, but now his forgetfulness was full of foreboding. Because it meant he would have to come in and invade the relative calm of her home.

'Aren't you going to let me in?' he said. 'I'll be as quick as I can. I think I know where it is.'

Wordlessly, she stood aside, her limbs heavy. He gave her a little nod of gratitude, along with a quick, tight smile, and then he filled the narrow hallway with his lean, angular presence and reached the kitchen with three easy strides.

She followed behind him slowly and stood in the doorway, watching him go straight to a corner shelf where she had stacked a couple of cookery books, his movements relaxed as though he was very familiar with her kitchen. She wrapped her arms around her chest, hugging herself, because it was the best way to stop herself from crying at his unexpected arrival. He lifted down a Jamie Oliver cookbook, flicked through the pages with long, thin fingers that were painfully familiar, and an envelope fell out.

She saw herself, in another life, handing him some post as he cooked an evening meal. He had one eye on the pots simmering on the hob and another checking the instructions in the cookbook. She saw him taking a spoonful of sauce mixture out of the pot, waving it in the air to cool it a little; then he fed it to her, laughing as she opened her mouth to his offering. Their eyes locked as she savoured the spoonful in her mouth and licked her lips, his thumb gently wiping a residue from the corner of her mouth. Then, lifting his slender hands, he cupped her face in his palms before kissing her.

A different life.

She felt a pang in her stomach as Mark swiftly checked the contents of the envelope before folding it and putting it into the inside pocket of his coat. She recalled with a stab of pain how some mornings she used to slip her arms around his waist under that coat, rest her head on his chest, and tell him not to go to work. He would secure her there for a few moments before kissing her goodbye. A long, lingering, tender kiss. Her face flamed at the memory.

'Carrie?'

'Yes?'

'Thanks for that, and sorry for bothering you.' He gave her a half-smile and his eyes were kind. She'd done her best to forget the impact of those eyes and the way the effect of them spiralled all the way down to her toes. He'd be gone in a minute and she, almost instinctively, took a step towards him, as if her body was recalling the movement in a blueprint of some kind, but she checked herself in time. Instead, she moved back as he walked towards the kitchen door, sucking all the energy with him, every fibre of her senses heightened as he passed her by. Then he saw it as he passed it by – just as she realised they were there, too late to do anything about them, too late to think up a reasonable story while her brain was fried to pieces and her thoughts whirled like confetti.

Carrie is relaxed as she boards the flight to Zurich.

He froze for a second or two and she saw his gaze travel out into the hallway where a similar sign was hanging from the side of the bookcase facing the kitchen.

Carrie is happy to travel to Switzerland.

He stopped, looked at her, puzzled. 'Going somewhere?'

She shrugged. 'What's it to you?'

His face closed. 'You're right. None of my business.'

The slight snub in his voice, coupled with the ridiculous feeling that she'd been caught red-handed, sparked the anxiety inside her that had simmered since he'd knocked at the door. 'I might be going to Switzerland.'

Incredulity rippled across his face. 'Are you serious?'

'Yes, that's right. I'm thinking of flying out on Sunday.' She tried to sound nonchalant, as though she flew to Switzerland on a regular basis, but she wondered if he could hear her heart hammering loudly in her chest.

'Flying,' he said. 'On Sunday.'

'Yep.' She deliberately jutted out her chin and gave him a cheeky look.

Right in front of her, and before he had a chance to hide it, a light dulled in his eyes, as though he was disappointed about something. 'Well, fair play, Carrie. To quote your own words, you've really "moved on", haven't you?' he said, in a smooth voice. 'Flying to Switzerland says it more than anything else. I'm very impressed.'

'Thanks. So am I. Impressed with myself, I mean.'

It was better this way, she reminded herself as they went to the hall door and she opened it. She saw his car parked farther around the crescent.

'Whoever is bringing you over there,' he said, 'must be very special.'

She thought of Luis. Of his wish to talk to her before he died. She thought of Maria's beautiful, honest face. 'He is, actually.'

'Well done,' he said, moving past her. 'Ten out of ten for your new-found ability to grab life by the balls.'

'Hold on,' she said, realising too late how her words had sounded. 'It's not what you think.'

'No?'

He halted on her doorstep and looked at her, his face pale. In the intensity of the moment, all the barriers between them dissolved. Everything they'd ever been to each other was there in his light-grey eyes. Everything they'd meant to each other as they came together in a kiss, everything they'd whispered about in the small hours of the night or laughed about on a lazy Sunday morning or shared across her kitchen table over a pizza and a bottle of wine. Her senses reeled.

'I'm going to visit,' she gulped, 'an old friend of my mother.'

He was still looking at her intently. 'A friend … of your mother's. In Switzerland.'

'Yes. He wants to see me, to talk about her.'

A muscle moved in his jaw. His eyes narrowed for a moment, as he absorbed this information. Then the expression on his face closed over, and the barriers were back in place.

'Thanks, Carrie,' he said, moving away from the door, 'I think this, more than anything, tells me how utterly dispensable I am. Enjoy your trip. And by the way,' he tossed, 'you forgot to get your alarm fixed.'

Really, he had done her a huge favour. Because after he'd left, it was relatively easy to call Maria to say she'd visit, although she'd prefer to stay in a hotel. After that, it was relatively easy to book her flight for Sunday evening, and go to the airport and tailgate the person in front of her through the check-in and security desks, right through to the boarding gate. And shuffle on board and take a seat next to a loved-up couple, grateful she had her playlist to distract her. Mark's playlist.

After the roller-coaster shock his unexpected visit had caused, getting on a plane seemed like child's play.

Chapter Twelve

September 1979

In the ladies' powder room in the Shelbourne Hotel, Sylvie Sullivan lifted her left hand and tilted it so that her engagement ring gleamed in the light. She slid it off her finger and handed it to Beth.

'There you go, you turn it three times in the direction of your heart as you make a wish,' she said.

'Gosh, thanks, Sylvie, it's beautiful. I thought we'd never escape out here so I could have a good look at it.'

Sylvie watched as Beth put her solitaire engagement ring on her small finger and twirled it around, Beth's eyes as big as saucers as they admired her ring.

'It's gorgeous. And you look great yourself. What did you do with your hair?'

Sylvie shook her head so that her dark hair flowed around it. 'It's called the gypsy look. I like experimenting.'

'And when's the big day?'

'John and I are planning a June wedding next year, down in Willow Hill,' Sylvie said.

'You must be so happy.'

'I am,' Sylvie said. 'Very much.' She couldn't find the words to explain to Beth that she was finding out that happiness wasn't so much a big spark of fireworks bursting excitedly over her head, it was more a deep and assured contentment, a glow that ran through her veins like warm sunshine and was there all the time, steadily thrumming along with her heartbeat.

'I know what I want to wish for,' Beth said, looking at her friend's reflection in the mirror.

Sylvie raised her hand. 'Don't tell me, or it mightn't come true.'

'Oooh, I couldn't risk that,' Beth giggled, handing Sylvie back her ring.

'You look very happy yourself.'

'Do I? Sometimes I don't know what way I feel,' Beth said. 'Excited, nervous, panicky ...'

'Why should you be nervous?'

Beth's glance darted around the powder room, her face reflected over and over in the line of mirrors. They had the area to themselves. 'See, Sylvie,' she said, 'I can't believe this is really happening, that we're out tonight as a foursome, you and John with me and Adam.'

'Why not?'

Beth's words came out in a rush. 'It's Adam! Why should he be interested in me?' She looked appealingly at Sylvie. 'We're going out together over a month now. What does he see in me? I left school at sixteen. There are other, prettier girls in the bank, who are far more confident than I am. He's a junior manager. What does he find interesting about me? So, sometimes it's brilliant, I feel I'm in a dream; other times I come down to earth and I feel panicky.'

Sylvie grabbed Beth's arm. 'Beth McCann, I could give you a good shake. Stop putting yourself down. Don't you realise how lovely you are? If you ask me, Adam should be the one who's thanking his lucky stars that *you've* agreed to go out with *him*.' She regretted her tone of voice as soon as she'd uttered those last few words.

'Why?' Beth asked, her forehead wrinkling. 'Don't you – don't you like Adam? I thought it was a good idea for the four of us to meet to celebrate your engagement. I thought the evening was going well. John and Adam seem to have lots to talk about.'

'Football and more football,' Sylvie said. 'Typical men. But, absolutely, it was a good idea,' she hurriedly reassured her friend. 'Even if it's just for me to check him out and see if he's good enough for you.'

'And?'

'I'll have to think about that,' Sylvie said, smiling and squeezing Beth's arm again as she looked at her anxious face.

'Don't you think my mother would have been proud of me?' Beth said. Sylvie's heart snagged at the entreaty obvious in her eyes. 'Still, I have you to thank for all this …' Beth went on, throwing out her hands. 'I never thought I'd even set foot in the Shelbourne, never mind meet someone like Adam.'

It was Sylvie who had picked up the pieces of Beth's life after Molly McCann had died within six months of a cancer diagnosis. During the hot summer of 1976, Beth had hid her heartache, left her job in the village supermarket, and quite easily slotted into the space her mother had left so that everything in Willow Hill ran as seamlessly as it ever had. Besides, Beth had said, it was far better spending her days in the warmth of the Sullivan homestead than standing behind a cash register or putting in hours in the small council house her mother had still been renting when she'd died.

Then Sylvie had taken her aside the following year. 'You're very welcome to stay on here for as long as you want,' she'd said, as she sat with Beth at the kitchen table. 'We all love you, you're part of us. But, Beth, I'm sure you don't want to spend your life running after this family.'

'I don't know what else to do.'

'What would you *like* to do?' Sylvie asked.

'I really want to get married and have a big family. Lot of kids. That's my biggest dream.'

'There's nothing wrong with that, it's what I want for me and John, but you have to get out there and live a little. Don't stay here because it's convenient. There's so much more out there for women nowadays. Get out and get working and mixing with people our age. Have some fun. That's the best way to find someone to love.'

'What could I do, Sylvie? I'm not bright like you.'

'You *are* bright, in different ways. I can't cook half as well as you, for starters. I'm going to be in real trouble when I move to Dublin. God help John,' Sylvie had laughed.

'You're definitely going?'

'I'll be starting a teaching job in September and I can't wait. John's getting on great in the civil service. He loves working on St Stephen's Green. Why don't you think about doing a commercial course? Then you could get a job in Cork or even Dublin. It'd be fun, meeting up with you in Dublin.'

It had taken Beth a further six months to decide to move on from Willow Hill and do a commercial course, after which she'd got a secretarial job in a Cork nursing home. Then Sylvie had seen the advertisement for the Dublin bank and had encouraged Beth to apply, helping her with the application form and exam preparation. It would open up a whole new world for her, she'd said. When she'd landed the job, Beth had been full of excitement at the prospect of her new life.

Sylvie's own words came back to haunt her as Beth checked her lipstick in the powder-room mirror. 'Beth, your mother would have been very proud of the way you've turned your life around,' she said.

'But …' Their eyes met in the mirror.

Sylvie shrugged. 'I don't have any "but". However, I think you need a big dose of confidence. You're every bit as good as the Adams of this world, if not more – and never forget that. Don't let the fact that he's a junior manager turn your head. He's your first real boyfriend, isn't he?' Then she continued, her tone softer. 'You might want to meet a few different men before you know who's the right one for you.'

'Like you did with John?'

Sylvie grinned. 'You're right. Who am I to talk! But take it easy with Adam. Please don't rush into anything. Seriously, Beth, I'm not happy with the way you feel anxious or think you're not good enough for him.'

When it should be the other way around, Sylvie wanted to say. He might be full of charm and have ambitions for a very successful career, but she didn't like Adam, and she felt he was totally wrong for the innocent, guileless Beth. There was something about Adam that she found darkly compelling, almost predatory, apart from the fact that – and she hoped she was only imagining it – from time to time when she caught him glancing at her, it was as if he was slowly undressing her with his hooded blue eyes.

Chapter Thirteen

It was late Sunday evening in Zurich when the plane started its descent. Carrie looked out the cabin window, keeping her fright at bay long enough to appreciate how beautiful the night-time city panorama looked from the sky, jewelled with millions of tiny lights, before they were dropping down to the harshly lit airport tarmac.

She turned off her stream of music and breathed out. She'd done it. She'd got here. A wave of immense relief was followed by something she hadn't felt in such a long time – a little nugget of accomplishment.

Outside in the arrivals hall, Christophe, Luis and Maria's driver, was waiting for her. She knew who to look out for as Maria had already emailed a photo of him, and Carrie spotted the tall man in his fifties immediately, even before she saw the cardboard sign he held with her name on it. Gripped with sudden anxiety, for a moment Carrie was tempted to walk on by, forget all this and get the next flight home. Surely if ever she'd been on a wild-goose chase, this was it.

She put her feelings to one side, second nature to her now, and went over to Christophe, introducing herself. He introduced himself in good English, took her bag and ushered her outside to a shiny black Mercedes. While he chatted to her during the drive to Lucerne, Carrie was unable to stop herself sinking back into the soft, creamy leather. From what she gathered, Luis and Maria seemed to have quite a backup team, managing Luis himself, his career, the house, publicity – a lot of which had now been scaled back.

'You know Luis is ill?' His eyes met hers in the rear-view mirror as the Mercedes glided through the night.

'I do.'

'He's in good humour and looking forward to meeting you. You must be very special because he does not have visitors now. I'll drop you to your hotel and collect you tomorrow afternoon to bring you out to the villa.'

She'd have four days in Lucerne, more than enough time to talk to Luis and try to work out what had been going on during his visit to Cork. Maria had booked her into a hotel in the town of Lucerne and Luis' villa was a fifteen-minute drive away around the lake.

The hotel was magnificent, the wide foyer gleaming with marble, and there were huge floral bouquets and a sweeping, gilded staircase. Her room on the fourth floor was pure luxury, with a wide, king-sized bed and a beautifully appointed bathroom with thick fluffy towels. There was also a sitting area and a balcony with a view of the lake – which, at that moment, was a dark silk ripple, stretching away into the distance and bordered by the lights of Lucerne. There was a bouquet of flowers on the table, a welcome from Maria, along with a bottle of champagne. Carrie lay down on the bed and stretched out, relaxing. She picked up her mobile and texted Fiona to let her know she had arrived, sending her a couple of photos of her room for good measure.

Fiona replied.

Wow – looks fab, would love to be there with Sam, sipping bubbly and having a second honeymoon.

Suddenly she missed Mark. He could be here with her, having fun, drinking champagne and making the most of the wide bed with the luxury sheets and plump pillows. Coming with her to meet Luis, soothing her frizzing nerves. She had no one but herself to blame, Carrie realised, as she curled into a ball and logged on to Twitter, sending off a few tweets about the luxury of the Lucerne hotel and her fabulous room.

* * *

When Carrie pulled back the drapes the following morning, she caught her breath, spellbound with the beauty of the panorama in front of her, glowing in the April sunlight. The lake was a living thing, like a big splodge of blue paint on a canvas, studded with inlets and harbours. It was calm and still near the foreshore in front of the hotel, but farther out there were cruise boats, steamers and yachts plying between the villages and the houses clustered here and there around the shore. Some parts of the lake were bordered by valleys and thick green forests, plunging down to the water's edge. Other parts were rimmed by steep mountain ranges, the far-off slopes and summits sugar-coated with snow. All of this was shimmering with crystal clarity under a bright-blue sky.

She soaked up the view for a while, watching the swans gliding by on the near side of the lake, and walkers and joggers moving along the promenade outside the hotel. She managed to tear herself away long enough to have a shower, and then went down to breakfast in the dining room overlooking the lake.

After breakfast, she walked into the centre of the town, delighting in the quaint, medieval feel of it all, the picturesque squares and towers, the cobbled streets, the beautiful bridge over the river. She stopped for hot chocolate, sitting out in the pleasant sunshine so that she'd have a view of the lake and the encircling mountains. It was the best hot chocolate she'd ever tasted.

Then at two o'clock precisely, Christophe was outside the hotel, waiting for her.

Her stomach lurched as she sat back into the comfort of the Mercedes.

'Is it far?' she asked. Maria had already told her it was a fifteen-minute drive, but she needed to say something to stop her throat from closing over with sudden apprehension. She was dressed in black trousers and a soft pink jumper, with high-heeled ankle boots and a black jacket. Conservative. Semi-formal. She hadn't known what to wear for this meeting, which felt more like an interview to her. She held on to the straps of her bag, because it stopped her from twisting her hands in her lap, hands that felt suddenly cold.

'We'll be there soon,' Christophe said. 'Your hotel, it is comfortable?'

'Yes, lovely,' she said, swallowing back a nervous giggle at the understatement. The hotel was the last word in luxury. She'd had fun, in one sense, trying not to stare too much, and to look as though she was used to staying in five-star, high-class hotels, every time she passed through the foyer. She could have done with a whole new wardrobe, however, just for walking through the lobby alone.

Christophe slowed down when he approached a pair of high, wrought-iron gates, which opened silently. Then the car glided through, towards a spacious two-storey villa, the gravelled drive crunching under the tyres. Carrie saw landscaped grounds, well-kept shrubs and red-and-yellow flowers in huge containers, a garage with rooms overhead to one side, and, beyond that, down past sloping lawns by the side of the house, a view to the shimmering lake.

Christophe stopped the car by a flagstone path and opened the door for her. Carrie stepped out to feel the sun on her face and a slight breeze stroking her hair. The hall door opened and Maria stood there, smiling as she waited for her at the top of the entrance steps. In the middle of the splendour and beauty and luxury of the past few hours, she was suddenly a familiar image to Carrie, so it was easy to walk up the steps and allow herself to be embraced.

'Carrie, you are most welcome!'

Maria drew her inside, to a wide hall that was almost a miniature of the hotel foyer, but more homely. Side tables held photographs in crystal frames, and vases of flowers threw out a heady scent. There were more framed photographs on the wall along the curved staircase leading to the next floor.

'Luis is up and he's waiting for you,' Maria said. 'I'll bring you to him. Can I offer you some tea or coffee, or perhaps wine or a beer?'

'No, thanks, I'm fine for now,' she said. She was ushered through the villa, past reception rooms, a room dominated by a baby grand piano, and a wall taken up with a glass-fronted cabinet full of crystal awards and platinum albums. Then there were smaller, cosier rooms, a downstairs bathroom and a dining room. Everything was tastefully decorated in classic styles and neutral colours of creams, light greys and ivory. She caught a glimpse of a maid working in a big airy kitchen before Maria led her through a plant-filled conservatory out to a covered terrace overlooking the lake.

'Luis? Carrie is here,' Maria said, her tone gentle.

Carrie saw a man relaxing in a comfortable armchair facing the lake. He had his back to her. At Maria's words, he rose to his feet and just before he turned in her direction, she saw he was wearing a grey fleece with the word 'Crew' emblazoned across the back. She blinked as he faced her. He was wearing distressed denim jeans and the front of his zip-up fleece bore the legend 'The Beatles'.

Luis was taller than she'd expected, and he must have lost weight with his illness because he was a lot thinner than the man she'd seen on YouTube. He had high, razor-sharp cheekbones that some women would pay a small fortune for, and a wide, noble-looking brow. His hair was cropped close to his head, and was pure white. His eyes were closed, but Carrie felt he could almost see her, the way he tilted his head towards her. He held out his hand and she took it, his grip firm. Then he guided her towards him, his hands lightly touching her shoulders as he bent down and kissed her on both cheeks. She caught his clean, lemony scent.

'You are very welcome, Carrie, and thank you for coming.' Even with a heavy accent, his English was perfect, his voice was deep and musical with a hint of amusement in it. Could this man really have known her mother? Her first impression was that, like Maria, he seemed far too genuine to be making up fairy tales.

Maria indicated an armchair close to Luis'. 'Please, sit down, Carrie. I'll leave you to chat to Luis for a little while. Are you sure I can't get you anything?'

'I'll have some water, please.' Her throat was dry, her tongue stuck to the roof of her mouth with sudden nerves.

'Still or sparkling?'

'Still, please.' She sat down in a big, comfortable chair drawn up beside Luis, also facing the lake. Maria disappeared inside and she was left alone with Luis – the man who was claiming to have had an affair with her mother.

No way.

Chapter Fourteen

September 1980

She doesn't set out to betray her husband, she never thought she'd be unfaithful to him, but when it happens with Luis, it's so removed from the frame of reference of her marriage and so different to what she's experienced so far that it doesn't seem like a betrayal.

'Can you imagine how dull a life without music would be?' she asks Luis. 'Supposing there was no such thing as a song or a melody? Or a musical instrument?'

It's early evening again, a Monday evening, and, once again, they've met in the pocket of time between the housekeeper finishing up and Luis' father coming home, sitting in what has already become their usual spot, a sheltered hollow in the sand dunes, up from the strand. They didn't meet over the weekend because Luis went up the coast with his father – besides, she prefers to stay away from the beach, safe in the knowledge that she won't be spotted by weekend visitors.

'Life without music would be incredibly flat and colourless,' she says. 'Supposing there had been no Beatles, or no Beethoven, no David Bowie or Bach? How boring it would be.'

'Ah, I see where this is going now.'

She doesn't say anything for a moment.

'You are trying to persuade me to play the piano again.'

She watches him cup handfuls of sand that he lets trickle between his fingers.

'Did I say that?'

'No, but it's what you're leading to.' He sounds amused, though, not annoyed.

'And is it working?'

'It's a different way of telling me I owe it to you.'

She moves around and kneels behind him.

'What are you doing?' he asks.

'Shush. Stay quiet.' She opens her bag, takes out a pair of headphones, and she puts them over his ears.

'Sylvie? What are you up to?'

'Don't talk. Don't say anything. Don't even think anything. Just listen.'

'Are you giving me orders again?'

'Absolutely.'

She lifts out a small cassette player and balances it just inside her bag, careful not to get sand on it, then she sticks the plug of the headphones into a socket, and presses the play button. Still kneeling behind him, she puts her arms around him and rests her chin on his shoulder. She'd picked out three songs from her selection of tapes. She figured she'd be lucky to keep his attention for the duration of three songs without him protesting. She knows it's not exactly the kind of music he plays, but she'd given it lots of thought and these were the most suitable songs she'd had with her, and she hopes they will appeal to him.

Luis listens to George Harrison's 'While My Guitar Gently Weeps' without moving a muscle. Next up is 'The Air That I Breathe', during which he clasps her hands with his, followed by Simon and Garfunkel's 'Bridge Over Troubled Water', by which time they are swaying together in time to the music. Eventually, he gives a great, convulsing sigh, removes the headphones and turns his face towards hers.

'Ah, Sylvie. What are you doing to me?'

He pulls her close, his mouth hungry for her, and she slides around onto his lap, arms wound around his neck, her mouth clinging to his as he deepens the kiss until she feels she is dissolving into hot, thick air. Eventually they draw apart, her heart hammering, her fingers trembling as she clutches his T-shirt and steadies herself against his chest.

'Where did you learn to kiss like that?' she asks crossly. 'You're only nineteen.' It's not so much his expertise as the way the raw hunger in his kiss has moved her; she's cross because she's finding it hard to accept that she's never been kissed like this before in her life.

He laughs. He reaches out for her hand, finds it and presses it tightly to his chest. Then he brings her hand to his mouth and kisses it. 'I'll be twenty soon, thanks to you. It's good to surprise you. I was thinking of you over the weekend ... a lot.' His face drops for a minute. 'I miss ... being with a woman.'

'You've had girlfriends?'

'Yes,' he says. 'But that's all over now.'

'Don't be ridiculous. If you kissed like that after a few songs, I can't imagine what you'd be like after playing your music.'

'Don't tease me.' He pulls roughly at the marram grass. 'I don't think I can ever play again after ... what happened. I'll keep seeing my mother there.'

'Just as well Paul and John didn't say that.'

'What do you mean?'

'As in Lennon and McCartney? They both lost their mothers when they were young. Can you imagine what the world could have missed out on if they had said the same as you?'

'Now you're comparing me to the greats. That's not fair.'

'Who said life was fair?'

'You're very hard on me.'

'I can't help thinking that if your mother was so very proud of you playing, she would have wanted you to continue more than anything in the world.'

'Yes, but I don't think I'm brave enough.' A spasm cuts across his face.

She feels for him, and the note of desperation in his voice finds a resonance inside her. She knows what it's like not to feel brave.

'Do you miss the piano?' she asks

'Of course,' he admits. 'When I played – before it all went wrong – I felt privileged. I was in a different place. It was like I held the whole world in the span of my two hands. I just had to put my fingers in the right places and it came, like something outside of me.'

'That's okay,' she says. 'I understand you don't feel brave enough. How could you?'

His face relaxes. 'See? Even you agree that it's too difficult.'

'I didn't say that. It might be too difficult to feel brave, but that's not the point. You don't have to actually *feel* that. All you need to do is pretend.'

'Pretend?' He is clearly perplexed.

'Yes, pretend you're brave.' She sits back and stares out to sea, watching the tide rolling in, and the wheeling gulls like white specks of whirling confetti against the headland. 'What would you do if you were no longer afraid? What would you do if you were bold and adventurous? The trick is to pretend to be that person when you sit down to play. The piano is not going to know that you're scared, once you pick the right notes. Neither will anyone else. After a while, it'll get easier.'

'"Pretend", you say.'

She's trembling herself as she faces him and she hopes it doesn't come out in her voice. A sort of pretence has got her through the worst of times and kept a smile on her lips, but she can't admit that. She strokes the contours of his face and, sounding as confident as possible, she says, 'Yes, absolutely. Brave people are those who go ahead and do things, even if they feel afraid.'

'How do you know all this? How are you so wise for your age?'

'My mum taught me a lot about life and making the best of it. It can be unfair and cruel, and sometimes it can really bring you down, but counting your blessings every day, no matter how small they are, is one way of getting through.'

He sits quietly, absorbing her words. Then he says, 'My father told me this morning that we're going home next weekend.'

It's her turn to absorb what he has said, and her heart gives a painful lurch. The past few days have been a bubble of time suspended from everything else, away from her real-life concerns, her worries and, most of all, her fears. Everything has distilled to the time she's spent with this man.

'Sylvie, if–'

'Yes?' She can't believe how disappointed she is.

'If I wasn't afraid of your answer, if I was brave enough I would ask you to ... no, I can't.'

'Yes, you can. Go on.'

'If I was bold enough I'd ask you to come to bed with me,' he says. 'My father will not be home until seven this evening.'

Something flashes through her, leaving her weak. 'If you played some music for me, I might be tempted.' She's taking her own advice, sounding brave even though she's trembling inside.

'I'd be nervous,' Luis says, fidgeting with his hands.

He'd be nervous? Not half as nervous as she'd be. She catches his hands again and brings them to her mouth, kissing his fingers. 'That's allowed. I've heard you play already, haven't I? You can try it out with just me and see how you get on. There's nothing to be nervous about. Luis ... you can try everything out with me to see what it's like.'

A pause. 'Everything?'

'Yes.'

'I'd be nervous of that too.'

There is another silence. 'We have a week,' she says, 'that's all.

After that it's over and we go back to our own lives.' She smiles. 'Call it a holiday romance if you like.'

* * *

The big house at the end of the track is comfortable, spacious and full of light. It belongs to a friend of a friend of his father, Luis explains, who thought it would be suitable for the professor and his son. Luis finds his way around by trailing his fingers off the walls and doors with a practiced ease. The bedrooms and bathrooms are on the ground floor, but only one bedroom looks fully lived in. Through the half-open door, she sees an assortment of personal possessions and, on the bedside table, a crystal-framed photograph of a beautiful blonde woman in her forties. Luis' father's room. The first floor, with a wraparound balcony and fantastic sea views, is taken up with a modern kitchen and living area. There are long, low couches, shelves with books and cassette tapes and LPs, and a music centre with speakers. There is a piano, close to a window, and she watches the white-capped waves rolling in, in silent, slow motion from this vantage point.

'What is it?' Again, his perception is sensitive and acute. 'You've changed your mind?'

'No,' she assures him. 'It's just different, being here with you.' They are both standing in the living room but neither of them is making a move towards the other.

'How so?'

It's difficult for her to tell him that, along with confidences, kisses and embraces are easier exchanged on a beach, where the essence of life is carefree and buoyant, like the playful breeze, compared to the personal intimacy of a home.

'This is your private space, where you live; even though we've talked about lots of things, I feel like an intruder in a way. But when I see that wonderful piano in the room,' she goes on, focusing on him, 'I want to ask you to get going on it before I do change my mind.'

'I can't have that.'

Luis sits down on the piano stool and at first his hands skitter across the keys, finding chords and limbering up. Then, it is as though he forgets she is there. He launches into music she has never heard, and it ripples around the room, plucking at her heart, snatching at her senses, making her throat swell with a peculiar kind of ache. Everything about her life that has been building up inside her over the past few weeks comes together in a wave of emotion that is suddenly unbearable.

Luis finishes up with a Beatles medley. After he stops, with a final flourishing sweep of his fingers up along the keys, she gets up and, feeling as though she is sleepwalking, goes across to where he is sitting.

'You must never give this up, Luis,' she says gently. 'When you play, it's like giving life to something ... It's far bigger and more important than your fear, and it makes me want to ...'

He turns to face her. 'Want to what?'

'This,' she says, her heart almost jumping out of her chest as she puts her hands on his shoulders and bends to kiss his mouth. It is just a butterfly touch. At first. She kisses him again, and he puts his arms around her and draws her down to him so she is sitting on his lap.

They kiss deeply, hungrily, her arms going around his neck, coming together with a raw fervour that seems to rise up from her toes, up through her hands and her body, so that it overflows from the pores in her head, making her light and dizzy.

It's not enough. She wants more, wondering what it would be like to go to bed with him, or even, she trembles, to satisfy this sensitive, hungry young man. She's afraid of what might happen next – not just afraid, scared to death – and she's glad he can't see it in her face. She tells herself to pretend to be daring. She takes his hand and puts it on the swell of her breast, over her clothing. Surprise flickers across his face, and then it tautens in desire as she takes his other hand and guides it towards the buttons on her blouse.

'Sylvie, are you—?'

'Yes, I'm sure. I want to show you what else you can live for.' She kisses his face, the side of his mouth, the curve of his jaw, his closed, sightless eyes. 'Which room is yours?'

The blinds are still drawn, the light shadowy. There is a double bed, a built-in wardrobe and a chest of drawers, but apart from a pair of jeans folded over a chair, there is little else to indicate that anyone uses the room. He closes the door, leaning against it for a moment, and they are then together in the dim light, pushing each other's clothes aside, tugging at buttons and zips, his hands reaching around to get at the fastening of her bra.

She's not really breaking her marriage vows because it's not really her feeling this depth of desire, she tells herself as his fingers scorch her skin. In the thick silence, Luis' fingertips slide down along the contours of her body, taking away any lingering fears and doubts. As his hands and mouth run across her breasts and hardened nipples, she closes her eyes and quivers under his tender touch. She brings him across to the bed, breathless, tingling with anticipation, every pore in her skin buzzing with need as she lies down and guides him towards her.

He is suddenly unable to hold back, driving himself into her with an urgency that inflames her, shuddering to a long climax that helps her feel vibrant and so, so alive, as well as awed that she has been able to give him this pleasure. In the moment after he comes, he is totally defenceless and it touches her heart. He buries his face in the side of her neck, catching his breath.

'Thank you,' he says eventually, his voice hoarse. 'Sorry it was too quick.'

'There's time for more,' she says.

Luis strokes and kisses her skin, taking his time, touching her in a slow, tentative way that no one else ever has. There is something intensely erotic in the way he is using just touch and taste to get to know her body. She is open to him, and she lets him trace every part of her, which he does with a deep and thorough attention, as though he is forming a picture of her in his mind. She is astounded at her capacity to respond to him, all barriers down, her body almost convulsing with a primal need when his fingertips reach down and stroke the sensitive folds between her legs. She hears someone cry out, and doesn't recognise herself as she writhes under his touch, doesn't recognise herself as she asks him not to stop, the sensations building up until it's almost unendurable, and then her whole body is bubbling over with ripple after ripple of sweet pleasure.

'Thank you,' she whispers.

'I can't believe this is happening,' he says.

'Oh, it is.'

'Sylvie, that was ... I can't describe it. Are you ... okay?'

She stares at the ceiling. She hasn't been doing anything wrong. This is how it is meant to be. She has sensed, like an echo in her heart from some old knowledge, that this is how it could be and should be. 'Yes, it was brilliant.' *Yes and no. I'm okay this very minute, I'm full of happiness this very minute, but I know that other things are not okay and they will have to be faced sometime in the near future. But not just yet.*

'I don't know how to thank you.'

I don't know how to thank you for showing me what it can be really like and making me feel like this. Powerful. For a precious short while, I'm free from the unhappiness that has sucked me into a whirlpool of fearful anxiety.

She turns into him, needing to feel the hot solidity of his young, strong body against hers. 'You can thank me by giving me more,' she says. They would have the rest of this week. The intensity and joy of it all would be enough to last the rest of her life.

Chapter Fifteen

'I owe Maria a thousand francs,' Luis said, inclining his head in Carrie's direction when Maria went inside. A smile lifted the corners of his mouth. 'I bet her you wouldn't come.'

'Did you really? Well, here I am,' Carrie said. What next? A rundown on how well he knew her mother? Or should she cross-examine him to get to the truth of the matter? And then what?

'Maria can be quietly persuasive,' he said. 'I thought you would be far too busy enjoying your life to have the time to give in to a foolish man's request. Especially a man you've never met who claims to have known your mother.'

'That last part is highly debatable,' Carrie pointed out. She needed to get this clear from the start. 'I don't accept you and my mum were ... lovers. Or in a relationship. Absolutely no way.'

He let the silence rest between them. Out on the terrace, there were tubs brimming with pink and white flowers, a splash of deep green from patio planters holding ferns and vibrant shrubs, and, in the near distance, the tinkle of a fountain. Beyond the terrace, the expanse of the lake shimmered, rimmed by the distant mountains. On any other occasion, Carrie would have sat back and soaked it all up.

Luis finally spoke. 'Well, then, Maria's powers of persuasion must be far greater than I realised. You don't believe me but you still came.

I understand you have big doubts, particularly as it seems – and forgive me, I didn't know – your mother was married at the time. Please be assured I had no intentions of causing hurt to you.'

She was opening her mouth to protest when he continued.

'I believe you knew nothing about me, so I imagine you're sitting there with lots of questions and much denial, but can we agree something?'

'That depends on what it is.'

A maid came out from the conservatory with a tall glass of chilled water for Carrie, which she placed on a small table. Carrie smiled and thanked her.

'We'll leave all that to one side for now. I won't upset you with talk of the lovely Sylvie or how special she was to me. I found her a very ... inspirational person, warm, generous of nature and full of life. It must have been very hard to lose her out of your life.'

In spite of her doubts, she liked the way he said her mother's name and spoke about her, as though he was speaking about a priceless gift. She nodded her head, forgetting he couldn't see her, but he continued as though he hadn't been expecting her to reply.

'I'm glad she had a lovely daughter. Maria told me what you were like. She said you had a beautiful smile. So, for now, I'm glad you came, Carrie, even if it was just to argue with me, because I like the sound of your Irish voice and it pleases me to have a visitor from Ireland after the special time I spent there.'

'That's okay by me,' Carrie said. 'That's what I was thinking when I agreed to come. Just a visit, no strings. I've never been to Switzerland, and I'm not going to waste time arguing with you over something I don't accept. Besides ...'

'Besides what?'

'I knew I'd regret it if I didn't come.'

'Why?'

'Because of ... well, your circumstances.'

'Ah. You want to please me because you've a soft heart and Maria told you I was dying. That's very noble of you.'

'I wouldn't say that,' she rushed to explain herself, not wanting to give a wrong impression. 'I'm not that kind of person in general, and my heart is anything but soft, it's as tough—'

'Tough?'

'Yes, as leather.'

'Oh.'

There was a silence. Luis sat quite still and relaxed in his chair, his legs stretched out in front of him as though he could sit like that forever and had all the time in the world to wait for her to talk.

She took a sip of water before continuing. 'I'm here because it's giving me a chance to do something useful with myself.' She was surprised at how honest she was being with him. In a funny way, it was easy to talk to him, knowing he couldn't see her. It was like talking to a stranger on a plane, knowing you'd never see them again; easier somehow to talk to an anonymous person who didn't know enough about you to judge you or find you wanting.

He smiled. 'So I'm your good deed? I'm truly honoured.'

God. He seemed to think she was some kind of merciful angel and she felt uncomfortable being there under false pretences. 'I'm not being totally selfless,' she said. 'I also have my own agenda.'

How could she say she was hoping he might have the answer to her mother's fateful last words, when she refused to believe they had a relationship? It just showed how mixed up she was. Instead she said, 'I needed a break from the mouldy pit my life had become.'

'"Mouldy pit"? What's that, Carrie?' He looked confused.

She tried to explain herself. 'In other words, my life is all messed up, it's a bit of a disaster at the moment ...' She paused, embarrassment crawling through her veins. What right had she to talk like this when if anyone's life was messed up, his was? He was *dying*, for God's sake – 'three months-ish', Maria had said, what could be more disastrous than that? And here she was putting her foot right in it by chattering away about her mouldy life. Luis was most likely in pain, too, and covering it up as best he could to talk to her.

'Just forget what I said.' She spoke hurriedly. 'Everything.'

'You're embarrassed because you think no one's life could be more dismal than mine,' he said gently.

'I shouldn't be complaining.'

'Surprisingly enough, Carrie, my life isn't all that dismal,' he said. 'I've had a joyful life, a full, rich, roller-coaster of a life. A life warmed by love and affection. A life that mattered. I still have that life, right here and now. It might be over sooner than I had hoped for, and it will be sad to leave Maria, but it was wonderful while it lasted. And I know I said I wouldn't speak of her but just this once I will. Only for Sylvie, my life would have been over many years ago. Since then, every day has been a gift.'

'Even though you'd lost your sight?' It had to be said. She couldn't just ignore it. How could his life have been so joyful with such a terrible affliction? Even now, they were sitting in front of some of the most spectacular scenery she'd ever seen, but it was lost on Luis.

'I'll be honest with you, Carrie. I appreciate that you are honest with me. At first I thought I couldn't cope. The blackness was terrible and it swamped my heart as much as my head. I was in huge pain; an angry young man, frustrated, confused, raging against fate. Then I met Sylvie and she taught me to live again and love again, to enjoy the ordinary things, to count my blessings. I owe my life to her. She wasn't all sweetness, she was very cross with me at times. I know you don't accept this as the truth, and I am not going to try and persuade you to change your mind.'

Her mother had loved her father. Sylvie had been a vivacious, effervescent person, spilling over with fun, happiness and joie de vivre. All of this had been lavished on Carrie as well as her husband. Was it possible, in any way, that there had been room in her big heart for more than one man? That she had, indeed, had a fling with this very talented man sitting beside her? Was Luis the private matter she'd wanted to reveal?

'So is being here any improvement on your mouldy, disastrous life?' he asked.

'Absolutely.' She looked out across the lake. 'This place is like heaven. It's so beautiful, like something out of *The Sound of Music*.'

She fell silent. Again, this man with the quiet kind of charm and attention caught her mood.

'That makes you a little sad?'

'As a child I watched it on the TV each Christmas with my mum, before we headed down to Willow Hill for a few days. We'd cuddle up on the sofa with the Christmas tree lights on … I know all the songs.'

'Good. I'll have you singing them to me before you go home.'

'Want to bet?'

'A thousand francs.'

'Right. Seriously, though, it's a long time since I was anywhere as beautiful as this.'

'What do you see?'

She tried to talk about the lake and the mountains and then she faltered. 'God, I'm sorry, I'm banging on about a view.'

'It's not a problem. Maria describes it every morning. I know what it looks like in my heart. I still see everything in there. I was luckier than some. I got to see the sunrise and sunset, my parents and family, the beautiful lake, the mountains. I get to play music that flows into people's hearts and souls. I'm a lucky person.'

'Lucky? How can you say that, when you know you're dying? I mean—' She fell silent. One of the things that still disturbed her sleep was how scared and terrified her parents must have been when they realised they were about to crash. 'Don't you feel scared? Or angry and furious with fate that you're going to leave all this?'

'What good would that do? It won't change anything. A kind of calmness comes over you when you surrender to your fate and leave it in the lap of the gods. I have the opportunity to say goodbye to those I love and put my affairs in order, to insist to Maria that she make the most of her life after I'm gone. If I'd had my way years ago and had exited this earth, I'd never have known all the good years that life had waiting for me. We are all going to die, Carrie,' he said a little wryly, 'but not all of us get to truly live.'

He didn't mention her mother this time. Instead he said, 'Are you going to tell me why your life is a disaster?'

She ignored the ache in her heart and moved to a safer topic. 'Well, my job is a bit of a disaster, I know I'm hanging on by my fingernails. No one seemed to care that I wanted a week off,' she said. 'It made me think they'd hardly notice if I left for good. So I can't be that valuable to them.'

'How do you know? Maybe they thought you really needed a break, a chance to have some rest and relaxation and come back refreshed.'

'I doubt that. I don't get anything much out of my job. I don't feel it matters. I spend my days looking at flow charts and sales figures and customer surveys, and quite a lot of time sorting out staff problems.'

'Where do you work?'

She told him about Jade.

'And you don't think it's good to be working in an industry that brings pleasure to others? Maria loves shopping for clothes, she enjoys retail therapy. She needs it from time to time.'

'I suppose I'm useful in a way, but I can't seem to find my proper niche. I've spent the last few years flitting from job to job, finding them unfulfilling and boring. In a way, I blame myself.'

'Why do you blame yourself?'

'Well, it's obvious.'

'Not to me. You have to tell me.'

'I can't seem to commit all my energy to a job. I just seem to do enough to get by and no more. I'm not interested enough.'

'And why do you spend your life going from one job to the next if you're not interested?'

'It's better than sitting at home doing nothing. It gets me up and out of the house.' *And please don't ask me why I need to get out of the house.*

'Ah, Carrie, you sound like you need some sparkle in your life and I know exactly how to do that.'

'What do you mean?'

'You're here until Thursday, is that right?'

'Yes.'

'Good, that gives me a chance to put some sparkle back into your life and feed your soul. We can do a few things and start by going out on the lake tomorrow afternoon. Okay?'

'Sounds good, but I'm rather a hopeless cause.'

'Hopeless? There's no such thing, there's always hope.'

'I'd rather you didn't waste your valuable time on me. Wouldn't it be better if you saved your energy for making the most of the days you have left?'

'Humour me. Give in to a dying man. Give me a bit of distraction, Carrie, a few days to take me away from what's knocking on my door.'

'You're serious, aren't you?' She couldn't help smiling. 'And pulling your ace card? That's manipulation of the worst kind, Luis.'

It was hard not to remember Mark and the tricks he'd used to get her to Paris. Maybe that was why she felt drawn to this man, in spite of his unlikely convictions about her mother.

'It certainly is manipulation,' he grinned. 'And the best thing of all is I don't give a damn. If it came to that, I'd rather face God a little earlier having used up my last bit of life and energy on you. Call it karma. Sylvie helped me; now, in turn, I'd like to help you. It might earn me some brownie points on the other side. So I'm not being completely unselfish.'

'That's the thing,' Carrie said slowly. 'I don't believe in God or any of that claptrap. As for having a soul, I don't think there's anything out there. Or any afterwards. When you're gone, you're gone. Sorry if I'm being insensitive, especially in your situation, but that's me.'

'If that's what you believe, fine,' Luis said. 'I don't propose to change anything like that in the course of two or three afternoons. But I'd like to send you back to Ireland with a bit more fire in your belly to get you out of your "mouldy pit" as a way of saying thanks for coming to visit me.'

'Are you going to play some music for me?' she asked, distracting him. He was taking on an impossible task. Carrie was quite happy in her mouldy pit, wasn't she?

'Would you like me to?'

'If it's okay.'

'Come with me,' he said, getting to his feet.

'Just how many piano rooms are there in this house?' she asked as he brought her through. In his jeans, with his Beatles fleece loose across his frame, he looked like a born-again hippie. From behind, you'd never think he'd been robbed of his sight he knew his way around so well, using the lightest touch of his fingers to guide him.

'Three,' Maria said, coming towards them. 'He's never too far from one of his precious pianos – are you, Luis?'

'I cannot live without them,' he chuckled. 'Neither can I live without the lovely Maria,' he added.

They went into another room overlooking the terrace outside and the lake beyond, a cosy room with cream furniture and shelves containing books, DVDs, CDs and scattered with ornaments and more picture frames.

'This is where we like to relax,' Maria said. 'We sit here in the evenings, and sometimes Luis will play, other times I read to us, a book or some poetry. And we are getting lots of fan mail in, from people all over the world who are wishing Luis well, so sometimes I read that out as well.'

Carrie wondered what Maria was going to do with her long, lonely evenings when Luis was gone. At least her parents had gone together. It was a consolation to her that neither of them had been left to live with the heartache of missing the other. Luis sat down and struck a chord, picking notes out of the piano, notes that were fluid and resonant, soaring and joyful – and she was gone. The music swelled, catching Carrie by surprise, stealing into all the emotional corners of her heart. Luis played for a while, and when he finished, there was a ringing silence in the room.

'That was … fantastic,' she said. 'Thank you. You composed that yourself?' She knew her question was inane, her words totally inadequate in a response to the spellbinding sound, but she was so stirred up she felt at a total loss.

'I didn't actually compose it,' he said. 'I listened for it and allowed it to come.'

'It can't have been that easy.'

He laughed. 'You're right, Carrie. It wasn't easy. Nothing worthwhile in this life is easy. It took a lot of discipline, and long hours sitting at the piano, and I had to learn to ignore the voice that said I couldn't do it, the voice that said I was kidding myself. I had to quieten all that and allow myself to listen to the music, and then I had to practice over and over.'

'I'm in awe of you,' Carrie said. 'Yet I can't believe someone like you would have any self-doubt.'

'Plenty, but I had a way of telling it to get lost.' He smiled at her as though he was recalling someone or some kind of fond memory.

'You must be very courageous,' she said. 'A lot of people, who are far less challenged than you, would give up and settle for the comfort of mediocrity,' she said. *Like me, for instance.* Unwilling to fully grasp her life by the throat, she stayed away from responsibilities, such as commitment, love, trust and hope. It was safer that way.

'How to be courageous is another trick I learned, many years ago,' he said wistfully.

She knew instinctively he was talking about the time he spent in Ireland and this time Carrie felt humbled. How come Luis, who had found himself so depressed that he had considered ending it all, managed to turn his life around and produce such amazing music and a full, rich life? What had happened all those years ago? Unless she allowed Luis to speak of it, even if that meant talking about her mother, she would never know.

Both Maria and Luis invited her to stay for dinner, but Carrie declined, saying she was tired and would prefer to go back to the hotel. She could see the invitation had been issued out of good manners, but that Luis was tiring and she herself felt a little overawed after the experience of meeting him. After Christophe brought her back to the hotel, she was going to sit at a window with a view of the lake and have dinner and a couple of glasses of wine. Then relax with a long soak in the bath using all the hotel's luxury toiletries. And she was going to put everything else out of her mind.

Famous last words. She curled up in the comfort of the hotel bed and spent most of the night dreaming of Mark.

Chapter Sixteen

When it was all over between them, Carrie tried to console herself by clutching at straws – she hadn't been herself the day they'd met, otherwise she wouldn't have behaved as she did, and Mark would never have been on her radar or in her life. She'd known Fiona's wedding day was going to be difficult, but it was far more bitter-sweet than she'd expected and, even now, it still filtered through her head as a series of jumbled feelings and images. It had taken a huge effort to smile, her gut twisting as she'd watched Fiona glide up the aisle on her father's arm and it had hit her forcibly like a punch in the head that she'd never walk up the aisle like that with her great big bear of a father. And when her breath had hurt for a moment as a wave of loneliness and loss swept over her, she'd ignored it and plastered her smile back firmly in place. When envy had curled in her stomach at the warm, secret smiles shared by Fiona and Sam, she'd ignored it. When she'd wanted to ask them what the magic ingredient was that told you it was love, she'd ignored it.

Into this mix of potent emotion had come the flowing champagne, the country hotel decorated with feel-good sparkly Christmas lights and romantic candles, and the huge Christmas tree in the foyer, reminiscent of the tree in Willow Hill, and running through it all had been the sense of happiness and warm celebration that had risen in waves around the milling guests and which had been totally at odds with the way her life had thudded to a full stop.

It was no wonder she had glugged so much champagne and that her usual defences were down. It was no wonder she had kept seeing him every time she looked around – the tall, skinny groomsman with the messy black hair and sexy eyes, catching him watching her from across the room like a heat-seeking missile, and knowing he was also catching her watching him.

* * *

'Carrie, I don't think you've officially been introduced to Mark yet, have you?' Sam said, when the bridal group broke up after a photograph.

'No, but I've heard all about him,' she said, surprising herself by looking at Mark from under her lashes.

'Good things? Unofficially?' Mark said hopefully, his eyes crinkling in amusement.

'Nah, very bold things,' Sam joked. 'We had to warn her in advance. Take my advice and keep away from him, Carrie. You're far too good for the likes of him.'

'I think Carrie should be the one to decide that,' Mark said.

'Who says I'm interested in revising Sam's opinion?' she said.

'It was worth coming back from Singapore to be thrown a challenge like that,' Mark said, making a flourish out of lifting her hand and kissing it and looking, she thought with a shiver, like a ravishing Spanish pirate in his dark suit and purple cravat.

Later, he looked like a tall, thin flamenco dancer as the bridal party walked out onto the floor in the wake of the bride and groom, his white shirt unbuttoned at the collar and billowing at his narrow waist, his cuffs open and rolled up to show his lean wrists, his tight bum encased in black trousers. They were dancing to Snow Patrol's

'Chasing Cars' and, instead of pairing off with the second bridesmaid, Fiona's friend, whom he'd accompanied back up the aisle, he stood in front of Carrie.

Mark took her hand and whirled her out under the colourful strobe lighting as though he was unfurling a matador's cape, then he pulled her in close to him. After the effort of keeping a rein on her emotions all day, she let down her guard, threw caution to the wind and responded to him in a heady miasma of lust and anticipation that raced through her veins like quicksilver. They didn't talk. They danced together as if they were the only couple there, as if they'd known each other forever, Carrie's eyes never leaving his as they circled each other, strutting their stuff and their bodies, laughing and falling together when it got too intense, as though it was a wonderful game.

'You probably *are* far too good for me, Carrie,' he said eventually, when the band announced a short break. 'That's why I'm taking extra special care of you and not letting you out of my sight for the rest of the evening.' He took her by the hand and led her outside towards the hotel bar, where he bought drinks and they sat in a corner away from the wedding crowd.

'I hope you haven't got a big, strong boyfriend who can't be here today because he's at a martial arts competition somewhere,' he said.

'Not the remotest chance, why?'

'Because I wouldn't fancy my chances with him after the way we danced. He'd be insanely jealous.'

Mark looked like he needed a good feed, but she sensed from the way he moved that he was strong and hardy.

'I'd say you can give as good as you get,' she said. 'And what about you?' she went on. 'Anyone likely to come after me, brandishing long, red talons?'

'Nope to that as well. Glad we got that out of the way first.'

They talked, and Carrie found out that Mark worked in Bizz,

having been headhunted by the Dublin branch of the worldwide internet firm. He'd never had a serious relationship, he said, as he'd spent a lot of time travelling in Asia for work.

'Sounds more romantic than it was,' he admitted. 'I fitted in some amazing sightseeing and got up close to the whales, but mostly it was about hanging around in a lot of boring hotel rooms, where room service was better than eating alone in a restaurant. What about you?'

'I'm part of the mad Sullivan family, and I've just started a new job in Jade, a luxury fashion company, but I lead a very quiet life. The only amazing sightseeing I've done is thanks to the television and I never tried to save the whales. Today is the most excitement I've had in a long time.'

'What's that they say about the quiet ones?' He laughed gently.

'And my parents are dead,' she went on hurriedly, wanting to get it out of the way, 'so I'm kind of on my own, but it's not something I talk about.'

'You don't have to talk, Carrie – whatever makes you happy – but you don't have to be on your own,' he said, tightening his grip on her hand, his light-grey eyes looking at her thoughtfully.

She couldn't help wondering what it would be like to have that gaze skimming across her body, and the bolt of pleasure that shook her sent her spinning adrift from reality.

Later, they danced again when everyone was circling the bride and groom and his hand on her waist felt hot through the material of her dress. Towards the end of the night, Carrie bumped into Sam when she was coming back from the ladies.

'Nice to see you hooking up with Mark,' he said.

'So you're not warning me off?'

'No way, he's one of the good guys. He's also brilliantly clever at his job and quite good at rescuing stray kittens.'

'I hope you don't think I'm his next stray kitten.'

'No way, Carrie. Besides, you don't need rescuing from anything, do you? And don't let on I told you but he's house-trained. He can iron several shirts and whip up a meal without breaking a sweat. He might look like he needs feeding up, but he eats like a horse and he's as solid as they come.'

Later still – and sometimes she still blushed at this memory – she allowed him up to her room, unheard of for her on a first date, if it could be called that. But it was as though they knew they could skip the preliminaries and dispense with flirtatious games to get straight to what mattered the most. They wanted each other.

'I've never done this before,' she said, locking the door after they had tumbled through, the sight of this man in her room sending feverish excitement ripping through her.

He stopped dead. 'Never?'

'I mean,' she laughed shakily, 'first time, first night …'

'Guess what, me neither.' He drew her into his arms and cupped the back of her head. 'Hey, Carrie, at last I can kiss you in peace. I've been dying to kiss you all night.'

They clung together; it was their first real contact, and the nearness of him, the feel of the lean power of his body against hers made her feel dizzy and disorientated. His kisses were deep, searching and satisfying. Every nerve-ending in her back and shoulders prickled as he stood behind her and released the diamante clasp holding up her tumble of shoulder-length, dark, wavy hair. Then he pushed her hair to one side and kissed the back of her neck so gently that she thought she was going to faint. She shivered as his fingers found the zip of her Grecian dress and slid it down into a cloud of chiffon at her feet. She stepped out of it and away from him. Still wearing her lacy underwear and silver stilettos, she fluffed her hair into shape as she turned to face him, watching desire flicker across his face as his eyes slowly absorbed her.

She shivered. She tingled. She laughed nervously as he dragged off his shirt so quickly he popped some of the buttons. She couldn't remember the last time she'd wanted a man so much.

She couldn't remember the last time she'd wanted a man.

She was outside of herself, she was certainly far outside her normal rules of behaviour as he backed her across to the bed until they both fell onto it, entwining their legs, kissing deeply, getting to know the scent and feel and taste of each other, skin sliding off skin as her wispy underwear was peeled away.

'Now, Carrie?' He drew back and looked at her face.

'Yes, now,' she gasped, hooking her leg around his hips, wanting everything about this man and her breath snagged at the feel of him filling her up. She arched her hips and strained against him, desperate for the long, sweet throb of release. After she came, he did too, and he rested his head on her shoulder, and she thought she could listen to the sound of his breathing all night.

Then they took it more slowly, teasing each other, laughing a lot; she surprised herself by how carefree she sounded. She loved the way he moved down the bed, trailing his tongue along the valley between her breasts. He kissed her tummy, resting his head on the tiny swell, looking up at her with a question in his light-grey eyes before she gave a tiny nod and he moved down further again, drawing a long, shuddering sigh from her. Afterwards, she slid her hands across the breadth of his chest, down towards the narrow sweep of his hips, following her hands with her mouth, feeling free and deliciously loosened, and so replete with fun and excitement and a magic kind of headiness because of this man.

They slept through breakfast the next morning and organised a late checkout.

Six weeks later, just in time for Valentine's day, he moved out of his rented apartment and into Faith Crescent, shoring up all the corners of it with his presence, his books and impressive vinyl collection and decks, his jokes and friendship, and, most of all, his love.

When he had settled in, and she felt it was safe, she opened her laptop one night, logged on to her email, and passed the laptop across to him.

'I don't want to read this myself,' she said, 'or look at the photos; once was enough, and I don't want to talk about it either, but I want you to read it and see them.'

It was the last email she'd got from her parents, along with the last photos taken of them in South America. Mark was very quiet when she took back her laptop and powered it off. He opened a bottle of good wine and played a selection of his most treasured music, Depeche Mode and Spandau Ballet, swinging her around the small front room as they danced to some of them, and he was extra tender when he made love to her that night.

When he finally persuaded her to come to Paris, just over six months after he'd moved in, he kissed her on top of the Eiffel Tower on a glorious sunshiny afternoon, and asked her to marry him.

'You're far too good for me, Carrie Cassidy,' he said. 'You're precious and important to me, and you bring out the best in me. I never felt like this about any other woman. I want to spend the rest of my life taking care of you, loving you, minding you, watching you sleep at night and wake up in the mornings, and I love hearing you in the shower and the squeaky clean way you look when you come out … and the neat way you bite your toast … never mind the way you touch me …'

'Hey … stop it …' She felt tears in her eyes and she dashed them away and flapped a hand at him as he was still on one knee. Touched with his honesty, and caught up in the romance and excitement of the moment, she said yes. They spent the rest of their trip talking about their wedding. They would have a small, intimate wedding in Paris the following summer and throw a party for Mark's family and hers, when they came home.

'Does that suit you?' he asked her a couple of days after their engagement, as they sat sipping champagne on a terrace overlooking the city at sunset. In the hazy evening, the terrace still held the heat of the day, Carrie relaxing into the warmth of it settling around her shoulders.

'It won't be a big extravaganza,' Mark said. 'Just you and me and our commitment to each other.'

'Absolutely. A small wedding, just us, the important people, with Fiona and Sam as witnesses.' It was all she wanted in the circumstances. After all, she had no father to walk her proudly up the aisle, no parents for photographs or for sitting at the top table. There would be a gap in her wedding album, if she were to have a traditional wedding.

'And our honeymoon?' He caught her fingers in his, looked at her warmly.

'Dunno,' she smiled. 'We could do Rome, if you can persuade me. I haven't been there yet.'

'I was thinking farther afield.'

'Like where?'

'Would you like … Carrie, would you like to go to South America?'

As she began to protest, he tightened his grip on her fingers. 'Carrie, don't say no immediately, just hear me out.'

She found it hard to sit still, to remain patient while he had his say.

'I just thought it might be a special trip for you, for both of us. To visit the last few places where your parents were happy and carefree. Judging from the photographs they sent you, they are among the most beautiful places in the world. It might help …' He paused then, obviously silenced by the darkening expression in her face.

'Help what?' she asked, staring at him, jutting out her chin, feeling prickly all over in her defensiveness.

'Just help you to … something …' his said. 'You see, Carrie, you've never really talked to me about your parents. You've never let me into that part of your heart. Surely you can trust me with your feelings by now? Sometimes I wonder if you're still, well, hurting about it.'

A pain cut across her stomach and she didn't answer his question. 'You think I'd be happier if I saw a few pretty butterflies fluttering about the Inca trail or dancing over the waterfall, because I might think they're somehow watching over me?' she said, giving a half-laugh. 'That my parents are hovering overhead, looking out for me in some weird and wonderful way? I don't believe in any of that bullshit, Mark. They're gone. Dead. Finished. It's been over four years. That's enough closure in itself.'

'Forget it, sorry, wrong thing,' he said calmly, refilling her glass. 'Rome, then, or perhaps Spain, maybe the beautiful Seville? I'll let you choose.'

Chapter Seventeen

As soon as Christophe brought Carrie to the villa the following afternoon, they headed down to the lake.

There was a cruiser tied up on a jetty down by the side of the house and Christophe took the wheel, having ensured Luis was sitting comfortably. Carrie sat beside him. Today, he was wearing a pair of dark glasses, faded jeans and a navy zip-up jacket with 'The Who' emblazoned across the front and 'Crew' across the back. Maria came too, wearing oversized sunglasses and a straw hat tied with a scarf under her chin.

Carrie didn't know what to expect. Luis had been very matter of fact about it, as though a lake trip wasn't all that special, so she tried to keep her amazement to herself. It was one thing to have seen the lake from her hotel room or Luis' terrace, but being out on it, and feeling the pull and swell of the water around the cruiser was a different experience. *Picture postcard land*, Carrie thought, watching the dazzle of sunlight dancing on the water, the town with its medley of quaint rooftops and spires and towers, and all around, the backdrop of towering mountains, sheering down to vertical cliffs, or sloping to green meadows.

'You're very quiet,' Luis said.

She wanted to say she was too busy soaking up the view for chit-chat, but how could she put it to him like that, reminding him of what he was missing? He seemed to be happy enough, sitting contented and relaxed, with his face tilted to the sun.

'Is this boring enough for you?' he asked, his voice teasing. 'Would you prefer to be out here or sitting safely in your hotel room?'

They were cruising along parallel to land now, where lush green forests hugged the slopes and swept down to the lake in a wonderful flourish.

'Okay, I get the point,' Carrie said. 'It's even more beautiful to be out here, it's amazing. And up closer, the mountains are breath-taking …'

'That's our next trip. We're going up to the top,' Luis said. 'Tomorrow afternoon.'

'Sure we are,' Carrie laughed, not believing him for a minute 'It's one of my favourite hobbies, climbing mountains.'

'Isn't that one of the songs out of *The Sound of Music*? About climbing mountains?'

'Yeah, so?'

'You'll enjoy it. But first, can I ask you to do something?'

'Like what?'

'Close your eyes.'

'Close my eyes?'

'Yes. Close them until I tell you to open them again.'

'How will you know when I have them closed?' Carrie asked.

'I won't. I'm trusting you to humour me.'

He trusted her. She closed her eyes. It was amazing how difficult it was, to simply sit with her eyes closed. At first she felt strange and self-conscious, wondering what Maria must be thinking. But after a while, she relaxed back in her seat and let her hands rest in her lap. Gradually she began to realise that she could enjoy the lake through her other senses. The deck swayed under her feet and the taste of the breeze was on her lips, the thin warmth of the sun licking across her face. Tendrils of her hair were lifted and teased by the eddy of the breeze, as though it was playing with her. She heard the smack of the cruiser cleaving into the waves, and the noise of the spattering spray. Everything was heightened with the loss of her sight. She noticed the blood running through her veins all the way down to her fingertips, and the breath coming in and out of her body. She knew, in a moment of clarity, what it felt like to be fully alive to this moment.

She didn't know how long she sat with her eyes closed until Luis told her to open them. 'Well?' he asked.

She blinked in the sunlight, the panorama all around her so richly colourful that it was almost an overload.

'Wow. That's all I can say. Thank you.'

Later, they sat on the plant-filled terrace facing the lake. Maria insisted that Carrie have a glass of wine, and then she brought out a dark blue rug for Luis and asked Carrie if she would also like one.

'Yes, please, it looks so comfy that I'm jealous of Luis,' she said, making him smile. Sitting back in the leather recliner, she swaddled it around her, enjoying the simple pleasure of feeling tucked up as she gazed out at the lake and listened to the fountain gurgling away.

'Tell me about you, Carrie,' Luis invited. 'I want to hear your Irish voice. You were happy, growing up?'

'Very. I couldn't have had a better childhood. We lived in Dublin, I went to school and college there, but I spent a lot of my childhood summers running free in the fields around Willow Hill; we went down at Christmas as well. We were very close, Mum, Dad and me, and I was very much loved.'

'You don't know how glad I am to hear that,' he said.

'Why?'

'It's one of the reasons I wanted to talk to you. You see, Sylvie – sorry Carrie, I know I said I wouldn't mention her.'

She tucked the blue rug closer around her and hugged herself with her arms. 'You might as well say whatever it is you were going to say.'

'I'm glad you felt loved and that Sylvie's life was happy. It gives me great reassurance and it's just what I was hoping to hear from you when I asked you to visit. Because at the time I met her she wasn't happy.'

'That doesn't sound like my mum.'

'There was something deeply troubling her. She was adamant no one could know about us, I understand that now, of course, as she was already married, but it was more than that …'

'Go on.' Carrie burrowed further under the rug.

'Towards the end of our time together, she confided in me. She said I had saved her life just as much as she had saved mine. She had needed rescuing from a difficult situation as much as I had. She told me she had me to thank for giving her back some meaning to her life.'

'That doesn't make any sense to me.'

'Well, it wouldn't, if you only knew her to be a happy person. She told me her life had taken a dark turn and fallen apart. She was fearful and very unhappy about something that had happened before we met. She said she'd been running away from circumstances that had become intolerable, and she couldn't continue with it any longer.'

'You're joking.'

'I wish I was. She was at a crossroads of sorts, she said, but being with me had helped her to make a big decision about her future. I wanted her to come back to Lucerne with me, but she refused. She also refused to stay in touch with me. Later, when I was home and went over everything that had happened between us, I deeply regretted letting her go so easily. I worried about her, but I had no way of knowing how her life had turned out, or if she had made the right decision. Then, as time went by, I met Maria and my life grew very busy. In recent weeks, as I looked back and had time to think, thoughts of Sylvie weighed heavily on my mind. That's why I wanted to see you and I'm so glad you came, Carrie. You don't know how immensely relieved I am to hear that Sylvie went on to enjoy such a happy and contented life.'

Could this be part of the 'old history' her mum had talked about? An intolerable situation? Something fearful? Surely not. 'None of this adds up for me.' For a moment, Carrie felt her breath fluttering in her throat. What Luis was saying was surreal, just as surreal as it was to be sitting here like this.

'Please forget whatever I said if it upsets you in any way. I promise I won't talk about Sylvie again. It's a great comfort to me to know she was eventually happy.'

'What you have said sounds off the wall to me. All I know is that I had a great childhood, secure and loving, thanks to my parents. End of.'

'It's good to hear that, Carrie. Right now, it's all that counts.'

Snuggled in her rug, Carrie absorbed the panorama beyond the terrace. She gazed across at the graceful dip and sway of the sailboats cruising across the sparkling lake, she heard the faint chug of the steamer in the distance, and she recalled how it had felt earlier as she sat on a deck, her senses alive to the moment. She breathed a little deeper and presently she was calm again.

'I think all the love spoiled me for what was to come,' she found herself admitting.

'Too much love never spoils anyone.'

'Either way, everything changed.' She could have left it there; she sensed Luis wasn't going to push her, but something about the afternoon made her want to talk.

'When it happened – the accident – life had been so perfect before it that I wasn't able to cope and everything crumbled around me. It was devastating, I still miss them. To the outside world I'm fine, but

I know I haven't come to terms with it, or had any sort of closure, not really.' The honesty in her voice surprised her. The words were coming from a place inside her she rarely visited.

'And why do you want to do that? Why do you want closure?'

'That's how you cope, isn't it?'

'But Carrie, don't you think it's such a cold, final word? I don't want Maria to close her heart to me after I've passed.'

She smiled, because hearing it said like this, the idea seemed totally outrageous. 'Yes, I get you. That's what I've been trying to do. And I never thought I'd be here, sitting beside you on this lovely terrace, looking out at that fab view, telling you all this. I haven't talked to anyone at length about my parents.'

'Ever?'

'Not really. I had bad days at the beginning, in those early weeks, of course, and my cousins and relations were all tip-toeing around me. But then I blanked it out and just kept going.'

'But these were your wonderful parents. You lost people you loved very much. You're allowed to be sad and talk.'

'I didn't want to inflict my self-indulgent, self-absorbed tears and sadness on anyone else. Worse things happen to nicer people than me. Losing a parent is in the natural order of things, compared to losing a child. I didn't think I had the right to become a snivelling wreck. I was twenty-five when they died, an adult. It's not as if I was just fifteen. My parents were in their fifties, they'd had a good life. It wasn't a tragedy in the sense of the word when compared to some of the awful things that happen to people, especially children and young people, and parents of young children whose lives are cut very short. You only have to read the newspaper or look at the news, every day there are terrible accidents and disasters happening to innocent people, and families as well as lives are being torn apart.'

She'd discovered that there had been children and babies on the flight. When she'd braced herself enough to skim through an online article, she read that a family of five had been wiped out. Accompanying the article, their innocent, smiling, family photograph, complete with a gap-toothed grin from the youngest, broke her heart all over again.

'Yes, there are,' Luis agreed. 'But in what way does that diminish the death of your parents?'

She was silent. After a while he went on. 'Carrie, my dear, losing a loved one can't be processed like that. All neat and tidy and boxed away. You go with the flow of your feelings, whatever they say.'

'Yes, but people expect you to get on with things,' she said. 'After a while they stop asking you how you are, except for maybe one or two close friends. If they haven't experienced bereavement themselves, they don't know how you feel, deep down, or how painful it can be. It still comes over me like a wave now and again, so for everyone's sake it's best to put it to one side and get on with things.'

'Ah, Carrie, you've been far too hard on yourself. Did you give yourself time to grieve? To cry? To rage against fate? To hold photos close to your chest and bawl your eyes out? To pick up their clothes and rub them against your face, and pass your fingertips over their special things?'

His words cut her to the quick. 'I didn't do any of that,' she whispered. 'I couldn't face it. I stayed down in Cork, hoping I'd die myself, hating it when I still woke up each morning and had to face all the minutes and the hours of each day. My aunt and uncle went through our family home and got it ready for letting out. I haven't been in the house since, even though it's been five years.'

'You should give yourself permission to wallow in it for a while – be angry, be cross, be tearful. I think you're stuck, something like the way I was years ago.'

'I'm not stuck at all,' she disagreed. 'It's the opposite. I've more than moved on, I've been a busy bee, moving from job to job, not staying too long in the one place. Besides, I didn't feel it was right for me to wallow in it.'

'Why not?

'You see, Luis,' she said, dragging the words out of their hiding place, 'I was partly to blame. If I hadn't nagged them to spread their wings because I was going around the world myself, they wouldn't have been on that flight.'

He shook his head. 'Don't tell me you've been carrying around that burden ever since? Did you personally book the flight tickets? And then bring down the plane?'

'No.'

'They booked the tickets of their own free will. The crash was due to mechanical failure together with human error. There is an account of it on the internet. Maria read it out to me. Carrie Cassidy was in no way to blame. You did not climb on board and take over the controls, and neither did you attack the instrument panel with a hammer. As far as I know.'

He made her laugh, with the picture he put into her head. 'I couldn't help feeling guilty,' she said.

'That, too, is perfectly normal. Didn't you try to talk to someone about all this?'

'Not really, no.'

'So you put on some bullet-proof armour to face the world and got busy skipping around from job to job.'

'More or less.'

'Living life on the surface.'

'Sort of.'

'Drifting along, letting it take you where it pleased.'

She didn't answer that.

'Are you happy?' he asked.

'Hey, this is getting all very serious. I'm not sure this is what I came out here for.'

Luis chuckled. 'You don't need to answer that. I forgot. You've already told me you came out here because your life was messed up, and in a dirty pit.'

'A "mouldy pit",' she automatically corrected him.

'In that case, we will definitely go up into the mountains tomorrow. And they will lift you out of this pit.'

'The mountains.' She laughed. 'Sure, Luis.'

'You don't believe me,' he said, flashing her a smile. 'You will see, tomorrow. We will go to Rigi.'

Chapter Eighteen

Adam had never been one hundred per cent, absolutely certain that it was all completely over, that there were no threads left to unravel. He knew one pulled thread was all it would take to unpick the carefully constructed fabric of his life.

What, exactly, was she doing in Switzerland? More to the point, Lucerne? Something cold ran down his spine as the information pinged into his brain, stirring his conscience. He logged off Twitter and put down his mobile. He stared out the window at the city skyline from the choice vantage point of his penthouse suite. Was it starting, the one thing he'd feared, old ghosts of the past coming back to haunt him?

It was far too much of a coincidence. Wasn't it? He didn't believe in coincidences. He tried to think it through, as rationally as possible. She hadn't mentioned any friends or travelling companions and the photographs she posted were just scenic so from what he could gather, she was travelling alone. It wasn't as if she was part of a hen weekend, although Lucerne wasn't the kind of town that attracted a lot of Irish hen parties anyway – and it wasn't a weekend. It was unlikely to be a sudden urge to visit the city, beautiful as it was. There were far more exciting European cities that would appeal to a thirty-year-old. He should know. He knew all there was and more about the levels of excitement available as part of the nightlife of Europe's top flesh pots, high and low. Was it possible there was any kind of connection between Carrie Cassidy and Luis Meyer 'attending to some personal matters'? Or, maybe there was something she was about to find out.

Later, the knowledge slithered around the back of his head, spoiling his night at the opera in the corporate box office.

His companion touched him on the arm, sensing his withdrawal.

'Are you okay?' Her voice was hesitant, as if afraid of disturbing him. 'You seem a little distant.'

'It's the opera. I'd forgotten how tragic the story was.' He gave her a little rueful smile, as if embarrassed that she'd caught such a successful financier being moved by a scene in the opera.

'Of course.' She smiled sympathetically and tightened her grip on his arm.

She was beautiful and glamorous, one of Ireland's former top models, and she probably thought that sex might be on the agenda later, but she'd be sadly disappointed. He wasn't going to run the risk of introducing her to his particular tastes. He looked down at the stage where Romeo and Juliet were exchanging vows of love. Problem was, he didn't know how he'd find out if Carrie was talking to Luis Meyer. He'd no connections in the clean-cut city of Lucerne. He'd checked out the big villa by the lake years ago, but had discounted it. From what he could see, it was impregnable. And the Meyers lived an impeccable lifestyle far above the orbit of mere ordinary mortals, yet in the glare of a certain public spotlight that precluded any whiff of scandal. Besides, Luis Meyer knew nothing about what had really happened in Willow Hill.

He'd read the original newspaper article translated on the internet. The man was dying, and spending the last of his time quietly at home. Given the height of the Meyers' elevated status, and their current plea for absolute privacy, it was inconceivable that Carrie had been invited over to visit them.

During the interval, he gulped down his gin and tonic and ordered another, congratulating himself as he made easy small talk with his companion. After a while, he convinced himself that he was just imagining the worst, jumping to conclusions because of his guilty conscience. Most likely, Carrie was over in Lucerne at a retail conference or on a junket for that job of hers in Jules, no, Jade. He had to curb his impatience and silence that little slithery voice at the back of his head. He had to blank out the vision of Beth's eyes staring into his, never mind Sylvie's blue eyes, heavy with secret knowledge, meeting his across a crowded room. Thanks to his careful planning, he expected to luxuriate in a comfortable niche for the rest of his life. There was no need to imagine someone might throw a curve ball into it – certainly not Sylvie's daughter.

He stared unseeingly down at the stage, where the final scene of the opera was playing out. Was she anything like her gutsy, spirited mother? Was there the slightest chance history might repeat itself? Back then, his life had been under control, until Sylvie Cassidy had turned it upside down. Nothing like that would happen again.

Chapter Nineteen

January 1980

'Engaged? You're not. Beth, I don't believe you.' Sylvie felt a thud in her chest as Beth extended her left hand and allowed her diamond ring to twinkle under the overhead lights. Instead of feeling excited for Beth, Sylvie couldn't shake off the gut feeling that this was all wrong and all happening too fast.

They were having lunch in a restaurant on Trinity Street. It was the first week in January and outside the day was darkened by the lowering black skies. Sheets of rain spattered against the steamed-up windows of the restaurant and overflowed into gullies on the street. Sylvie's feet were damp and cold after her gallop through the streaming wet pavements from the bus stop.

She was still on holidays as schools had not reopened after the Christmas break. She'd been a little disappointed when Beth hadn't come down to Willow Hill to join in the festivities at any stage over the holiday, preferring to stay in her bedsit in Dublin. Beth had explained that she'd very little time off work, and she'd be visiting Adam and his parents on St Stephen's Day. Then Beth had asked to see her as soon as she was back from Willow Hill, telling her she had something important to show her.

As soon as Sylvie sat down, tucking her sopping umbrella under the table and sliding off her damp scarf, they ordered chicken and chips and a pot of tea. Then Beth made a show of lifting her hands and peeling off her gloves to reveal her ring.

'Why shouldn't I be engaged?' Beth said. 'I never in a million years thought I'd be this happy.' Her face was a circle of innocent joy as it beamed across the table at Sylvie.

Sylvie made a supreme effort to swallow the catch in her throat. 'That's great, Beth. I'm just a little surprised, that's all. Adam didn't waste any time. How long are you dating now?'

'Five months. Once he knew I was the girl for him, he didn't see the point in waiting. I can't believe I'm going to be Mrs Adam Gilmore. It's too much to take in and all my dreams come true.'

Sylvie was unable to bite her tongue. 'Marrying Adam or getting married?'

'Adam, of course,' Beth said. 'Look, Sylvie, I know I'm not pretty like you. I don't have your dazzling confidence or way of laughing with the world …'

Sylvie shook her head. 'For God's sake stop talking like that and putting yourself down. Doesn't Adam … well, does he help you to feel good? Make you laugh?'

'He makes me feel the world is a magical place,' Beth said dreamily. 'All I ever wanted was an ordinary kind of a life; a man to love and have his babies, a house with a front and back garden. I'm not asking for the earth. I'll have all that and more with Adam. Aren't you happy for me?'

'Oh, I am. If you're happy then I'm happy, Beth. I'm just a little surprised at the speed of it all. I thought—'

'What did you think?'

'Life has been tough for you, I know that. Whenever we talked about your future in Willow Hill, I imagined you enjoying some freedom for a couple of years, going out with the girls in the job, having dates, a few boyfriends and plenty of laughs before you settled down.' Sylvie stopped and laughed. 'Listen to me – I sound as if I'm still in the classroom. Seriously, Beth, I know your dream is for marriage and children, but after all the hard years you put in, I'd like to have seen you finding your feet and having some carefree years before you waltzed up the aisle.'

'I've had a tough time, yes, but that's why Adam wants to take care of me. He knows all about it.'

'Does he?'

Beth coloured. 'Well, most of it. He knows about Mum dying, but I told him my dad went to work on the oil rigs before I was born and there had been an accident.'

'Was there?'

'No way. He walked out on Mum before I was born. They were never even married. But how could I tell him that? Although I think he kind of guessed the truth. He was very nice and understanding about it, really.'

Oh God, Sylvie wanted to say, *if you're going to marry him and trust him with your life and have his babies, you should be able to confide in him.* Their food arrived and Sylvie waited until the waitress had left them alone before she poured some tea and continued. 'I'm only asking questions because I love you, Beth McCann, and I want you to be very sure you're doing the right thing. Somehow, I didn't think Adam was the marrying kind.'

Beth froze, the salt cellar in her hand. 'Why, what kind did you think he was?'

Sylvie didn't know what to say. She'd only met Adam three or four times, as he and Beth kept to themselves a lot, but when she had met him, the slightly arrogant and suggestive look in his eyes had made her feel uncomfortable. How could she say this to Beth? Beth, with bright eyes lighting up as though the sun, moon and stars had been handed to her? Still, maybe Sylvie had been overreacting, imagining something that wasn't there. She searched her mind for something to say that might give Beth pause for thought and help her to fully consider what she was about to do. She leaned forward across the table. 'Beth, I just didn't think Adam was ready to settle down, to love and honour one woman for the rest of his life. There was an article about him in the newspaper last year—' She faltered, picking up a chip and dunking it in her mayonnaise, anything to cover her uneasiness, as she hated talking to Beth like this.

'What article?'

'He was included in a handful of up-and-coming bright Irish stars of the 1980s. Adam was interviewed and I got the impression his career came first, it was the only thing he was interested in, and settling down was the last thing on his mind.'

'Well, of course his career is important,' Beth said, her eyes alight, having never thought she'd have a husband with such a glittering future. 'Adam has said it's going to support the rest of our lives.'

Sylvie tried a different approach. 'I didn't think he was the kind who was ready to settle down just yet,' she said, treading very carefully. 'You know what they say about sexy, virile men?' She gave a half-laugh in an effort to lighten it. 'They need time to sow their wild oats and have some fun playing the field before they commit themselves to living faithfully ever after.'

Beth looked at her blankly. 'Do you think Adam would have a problem being faithful to me? That he's too sexy and virile?'

'I didn't say that. I'd have some concerns because, from what I've read, a lot of career-focused men of his age who work hard like to let off steam by playing hard. Before they settle down to marriage.'

'Adam's not like that. He's a perfect gentleman.'

'Then I was wrong, wasn't I?' Sylvie said, feeling helpless. 'I must arrange a night out for the four of us. We'll celebrate your engagement in style and have a proper drink, not just stewed tea. Hey, we could go down to Willow Hill for a weekend and have a decent knees-up, I'm sure you'd love to show him where you grew up.'

Beth's face clouded a little. She stirred her tea, not meeting Sylvie's eyes, her blonde hair falling forward like a curtain. 'I'm not sure about that. I feel I've moved on from my childhood – it's all behind me now. Anyhow, we'll be cutting back on socialising because we're saving for the wedding.'

'I'm sure you've plenty of time to save for that.' *And in case you've already forgotten, John and I are your best friends.*

'We're hoping to get married in March.'

'March? You can't mean *this* March?'

'Yes, *this* March.' Beth pushed her hair back over her shoulders. 'Don't look so surprised, Sylvie, Adam can't wait to marry me. *Me*! Can you believe it? Sometimes I can't. It'll be a small wedding, sooner rather than later.' She lowered her voice. 'To let you in on a secret—'

Sylvie couldn't help her eyes flying to Beth's stomach. 'You're not pregnant?'

Beth laughed as she sat back in her chair. 'What makes you think that? Adam doesn't *have* to marry me. I told you, he's a real old-fashioned gentleman. He wants us to wait until we're married,' Beth said in a proud voice. 'He's not just after one thing.'

'Isn't he?' Too late, Sylvie knew she shouldn't have said that, but remembering the sexual vibes she sensed emanating from Adam like a silent undercurrent, while Beth seemed to think he was an old-fashioned gentleman, the words had escaped her lips with a life of their own.

Beth gave her a funny look. 'I used to be jealous of you and John but, from what you're saying, I wonder if you're jealous of me now.' She tore off strips of her chicken and pushed them around her plate.

Sylvie took a deep breath and counted to five. Instinct told her that Adam mightn't be the old-fashioned gentleman he was cracked up to be, but Beth had been dating him for five months now and seemed to be happy. Then again, perhaps the undercurrents she sensed were caused by his struggle to contain himself until his wedding night. 'I never knew you were jealous of me and John,' she said.

'Once upon a time I had a big crush on John, and so had every other girl in St Imelda's Vocational School. You must have known, Sylvie – but he only ever had eyes for you. I never dreamed I'd be getting married before you, and I'm hoping you'll be my bridesmaid.'

'I'd be thrilled and honoured to be your bridesmaid,' Sylvie said, catching her hand across the table. 'We'll go wedding dress shopping together.'

Beth's face glowed. 'I'd love that. I don't have anyone else to go shopping with.'

'What about the other girls in the bank? They must be delighted for you and Adam.'

Beth played with the napkin. 'Not really. They've passed a few remarks but Adam says I'm not to listen to them, they're just green with envy.'

'What kind of remarks?'

'They were wondering how I managed to snag him … I've overheard bits of conversation – have I got what it takes, you know … sleeping with the manager …' Beth's cheeks were stained with an angry red.

'He hasn't gone out with any of them, has he?'

'No, he hasn't. That's why they're all being so bitchy. Anyway, it doesn't matter because I'll be putting all that behind me when we get married.'

'How come?'

'I'm leaving the bank. Resigning.' Beth announced this as though it was something to be proud of. She looked at Sylvie as though daring her to disagree. It was a look that made Sylvie think of a truculent teenager – which Beth had never had the opportunity to be.

Sylvie couldn't pretend she was happy about this. 'Beth, please don't give up your job just yet. I know how much it means to you, I'll never forget how excited and happy you were when you passed the entrance exam. Would you not wait until you start a family?'

'I can't very well stay in the bank after we're married,' she said, laughing. 'Come on, can you imagine what it would be like? It's not appropriate for the up-and-coming manager to have his wife slaving away in the typing pool. It could put a strain on our marriage. I'd be watched like a hawk; it could be embarrassing and might even compromise Adam's career. Anyway, the best thing is, I won't even need to work. We're moving into a new house as soon as we're back from our honeymoon—'

'That fast?'

'Adam knows a few builders and he'll automatically get a preferential loan, so that will cut some red tape. A new home will keep me busy for a while. And with the dole queues the way they are, it's not fair of me to take up a job I don't need when someone else could do with it.'

'Says who?'

'I'm in full agreement with Adam.'

Beth sounded so convinced and her gaze was so steady that Sylvie began to question if she might just be a tiny bit jealous of her quiet friend after all. Maybe she was so used to having Beth look up to her that she felt a tiny bit disgruntled and surplus to requirements now that she'd been pushed to one side in favour of the brilliant Adam who had turned Beth's life around so sensationally. Maybe she was even a little resentful that Beth had somehow managed to attract such a confident, self-assured man, an up-and-coming name to watch, who might be ambition personified but was gentleman enough to hold off until he whisked her up the aisle, and who could afford to grant her a life of ease in a brand-new house.

And maybe she was just imagining those risqué vibes he was giving off.

Chapter Twenty

Christophe was a little tense when he called for Carrie at noon the following day.

'How's Luis today?' she asked, sliding into the back of the Mercedes.

'He's great, so great that we're all going to Rigi, just like the tourists.'

'You're not happy with that?'

'I'm happy once Luis is happy, but I think he is a little – ah – ambitious?'

'You think he should be behaving himself by resting at home and not climbing mountains?'

'Who knows? He wants to go and Maria has said it will be good, but David is coming with us. One of his nurses.'

'I haven't met David.'

'He visits twice a day to check Luis' medicine for his pain.'

'Right.'

Whatever preconceptions Carrie had of the assorted group of them climbing up a mountain, she needn't have worried. David was a slightly younger version of Christophe, and both of them stuck closely to Luis, aware of his every movement, alert to whatever he needed, without appearing to invade his personal space.

But it was Maria who was Luis' anchor. They seemed to move as one, as fluidly as though they were used to being together, Maria imperceptibly guiding him, his hand light on her arm as he followed where she led.

Once again, Carrie feasted all of her senses as they took the cruiser across the glittering lake to a small town on the other side, at the base of the mountain. From there, they took a train up to the summit, 'the first cogwheel train in Europe', Luis told Carrie. She sat by the window entranced by the unfolding view as the train climbed up from the lake at a steep angle, chugging up through alpine farms sparkling in the spring sunshine, and meadows seeming to slant precariously across the horizon, the sound of cowbells tinkling in the air and dotted with quaint alpine huts reminiscent of her childhood Heidi storybooks.

'We could have driven, and taken a cable car,' Luis said. 'And there are many walking trails around the mountain, some more difficult than others, but I thought you'd prefer this.'

'You were right,' she said, 'I do. It's magical.'

'Wait until you get to the top.'

He was right again. They got off the train and Luis decided to sit out the final part of the trip with Maria and David on a bench overlooking the spectacular view, where the ground fell away beneath them and the mountain tops unrolled all around seemed within touching distance. Christophe escorted Carrie on foot up a farther track that led to a more elevated viewing platform. It gave her an uninterrupted, spellbinding view of the snow-capped mountains, the deep valleys, with the lake and Lucerne, resembling miniature toy-town versions, far beneath.

The air was crystal clear and slightly chilly. She drew in slow gulps of it, breathing it in while she soaked up the view, thinking there was something majestic in the slumbering, silent mountain summits, something beautiful and powerful and ancient, that made light of the petty concerns of everyday life. There was something deeply soulful about it all, if you believed in that. Then again, if you even recognised it, didn't it imply you had some sort of soul? Maybe she wasn't quite as washed up at thirty as she'd thought. She watched paragliders drifting on the wind thermals, suspended in the air, and envied their guts.

Christophe pointed out the various summits – the Matterhorn, the Eiger, the Jungfrau. She shook her head, bemused.

'I've only ever heard of these in books or films,' she said.

'Take your time, have a good look around. Would you like me to take some photos of you?'

'Yes, great.' She took her phone out of her bag and gave it to him. Christophe took some photos of her against the stunning backdrop. When she was back home she could look at them and remind herself of where she'd been and how it had felt. After a while they went back down to the others, who had moved into a coffee shop.

'You liked it?' Luis asked her when he sat down beside him.

'It's wonderful. So wonderful I can't begin to describe it.'

'Good. I'll bring you paragliding tomorrow.'

'Sure thing,' she said.

'I mean it, Carrie. For your last day you have to do something special. You won't be on your own, you can go in tandem. It will be perfectly safe.'

She'd thought he was joking, until she heard him talking about it to Maria later, as they relaxed on the terrace by the lake.

'You don't really mean this, do you?' she asked.

'I want to go up myself, for the last time, Carrie. The feeling is just wonderful. In the air I can fly. I'd love it if you had the experience also.'

'No way. It was bad enough flying over here, I was terrified, but …' she paused.

'You were terrified?'

'I have a great fear of flying ...'

'I can understand that, after your parents, yet you managed to get over it to come. You were very brave.'

'I wasn't, not really, I had help,' she admitted in a soft voice.

'Even if you had help, you were still brave. Who is he?'

'Who do you mean?'

'The person who helped you. I know by your voice this person is someone special and I hope there is a little romance in your life.'

'*Was*. It's all over,' she said flatly.

'Oh dear, I have put my feet in it.'

'It's okay, how were you to know? But it's over and I don't want to talk about it.'

Luis accepted what she said, without probing further, mindful of her firm voice. But all the way back to her hotel – and later, as she showered and did her hair – it was as though the floodgates had opened and in spite of her amazing day on the mountain, all she could think about was Mark.

* * *

It had been all very well to agree to marry him in the romance of the moment. But as time went by and the New Year arrived, and their wedding day was just months away, Carrie found herself full of uncertainty. What was she doing? How could restless Carrie Cassidy promise to love someone for as long as she, or he, lived? She felt hot and cold. She woke at four in the morning with a kind of dread stealing over her. She picked silly little rows that developed into big rows and brooding silences, until one Friday evening at the end of January, when Mark came home from the office looking a little agitated, he confronted her and asked her to spit it out.

'Spit what out?' she asked, her heart squeezing.

'Come on, Carrie,' he said, sliding off his tie and rolling it around his fingers. 'You've been going around for the past two weeks like I'm dirt on the end of your shoe and you can't stand the sight of me. What's up?'

'I think this is all a mistake, us getting married,' she said, her voice choked, after two weeks spent soul-searching desperately, trying to get to the bottom of why she felt a net closing around her as her wedding day drew near. She knew she had begun to snap at him, because she felt irritable and ill at ease instead of feeling ecstatic and full of the joys and tingling all the way down to her toes, much as her mother had described true love to her once upon a time.

'"All a mistake"?' He looked bewildered. 'Could you explain that to me please?'

She twisted her engagement ring around and around, the one he'd bought in a quaint little jewellery shop in Paris. 'I think I said I'd marry you because I was carried away in the moment ...'

His face paled. 'Go on.' At the open neck of his shirt, she saw his throat contract.

'It's all happened so fast with us. It's been such a rush, a whirlwind. I barely know you a year. How can I promise to love you forever?'

'I knew the minute I saw you that you were the woman I wanted to marry. I came back from Singapore expecting to pick up where I'd left off, free and easy and enjoying the clubbing scene; instead I saw you at the altar and wham, I was gone. I love you, all of you, even if you do hog the duvet or look like a ten-year-old without your makeup or eat Rice Krispies out of the box. I want to be with you forever, that's all you need to know.' A muscle moved in his jaw ... the jaw she used to love running the tips of her fingers along. He looked suddenly vulnerable and she hated herself for putting that look there.

'How do I know it's for real? Or that it will last?' she said, voicing the questions that were causing her to lose sleep at night. How could Carrie Cassidy be responsible for the happiness of one person she'd known just over a year? And surely there should be no doubts whatsoever.

'Ah, Jesus, don't you trust me?'

'It's not that. I don't know what to think. The night we met … at the wedding … you swept me off my feet, caught me at a raw moment. It wasn't me, I never behaved like that before, I was …' She struggled to make sense. 'Like I was someone else. A sexy, flirty Carrie Cassidy. Acting a part. That was never me.'

'Wasn't it?' He looked at her sadly. 'I could have sworn you were with me all the way when we made love.'

'I was more swept away with the moment. Swept off the edge I was clinging to, and sent freefalling into thin air. Sometimes I think I'm still freefalling into a void. It's like I've been caught up in something outside myself ever since I met you. I feel more untethered than ever now and I'm scared of where I'm going to fall. As for marriage and commitment …' she paused, '… I don't think I can do it. I don't think I can take that risk.'

She didn't tell him about her parents' marriage, and how devoted they'd been to each other, that it had been as perfect and steadfast as any marriage could be. Like a rock. It was the kind of marriage she wanted for herself, but she didn't think Carrie Cassidy had it in her to be anyone's rock. She couldn't quite put her finger on what was bothering her. But the fact that something bothered her was enough to question things, wasn't it?

The silence between them was thick with tension.

'Okay,' he said, his voice a little warmer. 'Forget about weddings and engagements for now. Forget about any kind of commitment. Blank it all out of your mind, and we'll see how we get on.'

Blank it all out of her mind – she was good at that. She'd blanked a lot out of her mind since the phone call from Sean Sullivan telling her about her parents' accident.

For her thirtieth birthday, three weeks later, he brought her down past Waterford city, through twisty narrow roads towards a picturesque seaside village, to a luxury hotel built into the cliff face, where all they could see from their bedroom window was the breadth of the rippling ocean. Mark opened the patio door and she stepped out onto the glass balcony. She was entranced by the sight of it.

'I didn't even know this place existed. It's amazing. Look at the light, look at those colours.'

He stood behind her and pulled her back gently so her head rested against his shoulder.

'See, Carrie, how wide and deep that ocean is? That's how full I am with feelings for you. Can't you take me on trust?'

She twisted around to face him. 'It's myself I don't trust – not you, Mark,' she said. 'I'm the proverbial rolling stone, always flitting hither and thither. I haven't even held down a job for longer than a year. That seems to be my time limit. I'm a wanderer. Unreliable. You deserve more than to be saddled with someone like me.'

'Saddled?' He looked at her ruefully. 'I thought we were equals in this.'

She shook her head wearily. 'Anyhow, I thought we were going to forget all about us for the weekend.'

'Sure,' he backed away slightly. 'We're forgetting about weddings and commitment, but that doesn't mean I can't show you how much you mean to me.'

Before dinner they went for a walk along a cliff trail, high up behind the hotel, where the sky seemed to go on forever and the landscape was beautifully stark before the last of winter slowly released its grip. Mark talked of his plans for his career and his hopes to set up his own business in two or three years' time. He talked to her of Singapore, and the experience he'd gained. Over dinner, which was superb, and served in an equally superb dining room, where walls of glass faced the ocean, Carrie watched this lovely man with the intelligent face and kind eyes talk about his future, and she grew quieter and quieter.

'I'm talking too much,' Mark said, catching her hand in his.

'No, go on, I like hearing all this,' she said.

It was helping to make her realise that she was right not to marry him. Mark deserved far, far better than Carrie Cassidy with all her baggage, and her flighty behaviour, her insidious doubts and fears. Things that could, over time, nibble away at the fabric of a marriage. How could she seriously expect this lovely guy to take her and all her insecurities on board? It wasn't fair on him.

'What about you? When are you going to make the break from Jade?'

He knew she was just going through the motions, going in and out to work each day. 'It's a job, isn't it?' she said.

'I'd prefer to see you working somewhere that fills you with enthusiasm.'

He made slow, tender love to her that night, and she soaked it all up, leaning into him, luxuriating in every stroke of his hand on her body, staring into his eyes as he lifted her hips and entered her, trying to wrap up the special moment as she wrapped her legs around him, and save it forever in a corner of her heart.

She remained silent as they drove back to Dublin the following morning. Mark's face grew more taut the closer they got to the city.

'I guess it didn't work,' he said, when they reached Faith Crescent and he lifted their bags in out of the car.

'You were great, Mark, it was a lovely weekend …'

'But?' His eyes were shadowed as they flicked to her face.

'I still think getting married would be a mistake. I'm just not the committed type. I can't take the risk of promising to love you for as long as we live. And it's all happened too fast. We're better off making the break now than when we're a couple of years married.'

He shook his head. 'I don't understand why you have no faith in our love.'

She laughed, tears in her eyes. 'Going by my track record, I have no faith in anything I do.'

'I'm beginning to believe you at last,' he said coldly. 'If this weekend didn't convince you that we have something special, then nothing will.'

He slept in the spare room that night, and the following day he never came home from work. He moved out that weekend while she stood by silently, watching him fill his car with his clothes, his books, his music, his favourite mug; all the pieces of his life that he'd shared with her. She watched him drive up Faith Crescent and disappear around the corner. She decided it should be renamed the 'crescent of no faith whatsoever', and made a supreme effort to blank the past few months with him out of her mind.

In Carrie's back garden, clumps of daffodils were bravely pushing bright green stalks through the ground, their tips swollen with yellow buds; the first signs of spring and renewed hope after the long winter, something to gladden the heart. But never had the house or her heart seemed so cold and empty than after he'd gone.

Chapter Twenty-one

'So are you up for it, Carrie?' Luis asked. 'The paragliding?'

He'd phoned through to her hotel room just after breakfast. She hadn't slept well, memories of Mark interrupting her dreams once more. She'd sat by the dining-room window, picking at her breakfast, thinking how crazy it was that she'd come to Lucerne to get away from her dull existence, and yet everything she'd tried to box off seemed to be cracking open in glorious Technicolor in front of Luis' calm, intuitive presence. And what's more, she wasn't any closer to the truth about Luis and her mum. True to his word, and mindful of her feelings, he hadn't mentioned her at all after Tuesday afternoon.

'It's booked, but can be cancelled,' Luis continued. 'I think it would be a good experience for you. If you are nervous, I can give you the magic words to get over that.'

She hesitated, annoyed with herself. Okay, the circumstances were unusual to say the least, but Luis and Maria had done their best to make her feel welcome and show her a good time. And now this very talented man, who had lost his sight and was dying of cancer, wanted to give her an experience she'd remember, and she was hesitating.

'You won't be on your own,' he said. 'You'll be strapped to an experienced pilot. How long we can stay up will depend on the thermals, we could do a mini-flight of fifteen or twenty minutes. I could tell them you want a gentle flight. That's all my nurse is allowing for me anyway,' he chuckled.

It was her last day. She was flying home that night. Another airport ordeal she hadn't had the chance to psyche herself up for. Was she always going to be such a dull, boring wuss?

'You're on,' she said.

'I'm on?'

'I mean, yes, yes, yes, I'll go.'

'Good, Carrie. I'm pleased to hear that. Make sure you wear your boots, a warm jacket and gloves. If you have no gloves, Maria can lend you some. We'll collect you at your hotel in half an hour and drive straight from there.'

She ended the call with a rush of panic – all the boundaries that she controlled so tightly were falling away.

'So what's the magic formula?' she asked Luis, as the Mercedes sped around the lake through breathtaking scenery towards the launch site. Maria was sitting in the front chatting to Christophe while he drove. She gathered that David was going to meet them at the site.

'Simple, Carrie. You pretend you are brave.'

'I'm an expert at pretence. I'm so good at hiding my feelings from people at times.'

'I don't mean it like that,' Luis said. 'I mean when you're scared, or have self-doubt, you pretend to be brave enough to grab life, make the most of each day and the life you have. Being brave enough to open your heart, and not to hide your feelings, even from yourself or those you love.'

Easy-peasy, she decided, staring out the window and watching the way the sunshine glimmered off the lake.

The next couple of hours sped by in a mist of anxiety for Carrie. David joined them as they ascended the final slopes of the mountain by cable car, while Christophe went off in the Mercedes to have it ready at the landing area. She would have cried off but she knew she couldn't let Luis down at this stage, he seemed determined that she would enjoy the experience, and was full of enthusiasm.

As they met their respective pilots close to the launch site, Carrie tried to breathe slowly and concentrate on the list of instructions she was being given before she was helped into her helmet and harness; her heart almost tripped out of her ribcage as she was zipped up and buckled in. She was told she just had to sit back and relax in her harness, and enjoy the sensation of freedom. 'It's the closest you'll ever get to flying like a bird,' her pilot said. 'Let me do all the work.'

Luis went first. Carrie watched as he took a few running steps across the sloping meadow, helped and propelled from behind by his pilot, until – and it happened so smoothly she could hardly believe it – they were floating out across the air. Standing behind her, her pilot checked everything one more time, playing out the ropes attached to the giant parachute. Then she, too, was running down the field, the pilot running close behind her, nudging her along, and, before she knew it, they were soaring out across the space between the tranquil sky and the verdant tumble of valleys far below.

'Hey!'

'It is good?' her pilot asked.

'It's brilliant,' she said, choked up at the wonder of flying through the air above the mountains and valleys. The wind snatched at her clothes and her breath, but her anxiety melted away and her heart soared as her pilot brought her over the ridge of a deep-green forested valley and back up over the silent lake. Up here, in the gentle haze, it was incredibly peaceful, almost spiritual, and the world seemed a beautiful and benign place. She closed her eyes for a moment, gently drifting, feeling part of it all, absorbing the tranquillity as though she was imprinting it on her bones.

* * *

When they came down from Rigi, they went for lunch in a pretty restaurant and, at Luis' insistence, Carrie went back to the villa for a post-lunch digestif. They sat in their usual spot on the terrace facing the lake, which was sparking with silvery filaments under the dazzling sun. Once again, Maria brought out the blue rugs for extra comfort in the shade. Carrie leaned back against the cushions, with the rug tucked around her legs. She sipped her cherry schnapps, knowing it was her last hour or so to be sitting here like this. Luis would be going inside for a rest shortly, and she was going for a final stroll around the quaint part of town, and hoping to pick up some souvenirs to bring back to Fiona and baby Lucy.

'I broke up with my fiancé about two months ago.'

'I'm sorry to hear that,' Luis said.

The painful words slipped out, freed by the fact that it was her last afternoon, and she knew she would never be here again. Besides, she wanted to hear what Luis had to say.

After a while he spoke. 'May I guess – was Carrie afraid to love?'

Afraid to love? Her heart almost cracked when she pictured Mark and remembered their last weekend and the sight of his car turning the corner at the top of Faith Crescent.

'On the contrary,' she said quietly. 'I loved him so much that I thought he deserved better than me.'

'Carrie! Shame on you for talking about yourself like that.'

'I thought we both had a lucky escape when I called it all off,' she admitted. 'Going by my frivolous record of skipping from job to job and drifting on the surface, I didn't think I could take the risk of seeing if I'd last the course – marriage, commitment, whatever. I think I was just getting married to see if it would give me some kind of anchor. Only as the wedding date drew near, I realised Mark made me feel more untethered, more wobbly. All the time I was with him, from the day we first met, it was like I was outside of myself. I was spinning, freefalling. Thoughts of getting married to him were giving me a meltdown. I felt I was losing my grip on things. I was beginning to feel anxious a lot of the time.'

He was quiet for so long she thought he was shocked with her words. Then his next words surprised her. 'Did you feel vulnerable?'

'Yes, I suppose that's a good way to describe it.'

'That was good, Carrie, that meant you were coming out of the safe little comfort zone you've been hiding behind and coming back to real life, to living, to loving and all the heights and depths it can bring you to.'

'No, thanks. Whatever it was, it scared me.' She stopped for a minute, surprised she'd said that.

'Why?'

'I don't know. I'm still trying to figure it out, scared of having my heart broken again, I guess.'

'Did Mark love you?'

See, Carrie, how wide and deep that ocean is? That's how full I am with feelings for you.

'Yes.'

'Why did it scare you?'

She stayed silent.

'Maybe I should have asked if Carrie was afraid *of* love?'

'I didn't want to take a risk.'

'Why not?'

'Same thing. I was afraid. It feels safer in my dull little life. That way nothing much can go wrong. My house is my safe place, solid and red-bricked, tucked into a cul de sac.'

'Did you tell Mark how you felt?'

'Sort of – he was very hurt.' The taut paleness of his face still haunted her.

'Was he the person who helped you to fly again?'

'Yes. Then he wanted us to go to South America on our

honeymoon, to see some of the beautiful places my parents visited before they died.'

'Had you talked to him about your parents?'

'A bit.'

Truth was, she hadn't. That first night at Fiona's wedding, she'd told him what had happened to her parents as unemotionally as possible, to get it out of the way. After that, they'd talked to each other about hopes and dreams and lots of things in between, but she'd never talked to him in a deep, heart-searching way about her parents. He'd asked how she really felt, several times, telling her he was there to listen whenever she wanted to talk, but she'd always made light of it, telling him she was fine, not wanting to make too much of a fuss, or open the floodgates.

'Besides, it's five years ago now.'

'Carrie, the passage of years means nothing when it comes to losing people you love,' Luis said. 'Time doesn't heal, but love does.'

She bit her lip and tucked her rug around her a little tighter. She stared out at the lake.

'I don't believe you ever get over the loss of someone you love,' Luis said. 'You learn to incorporate that loss into your life, you learn to accept that life is changed irrevocably, but they'll always be part of your life. If you loved them, how could they not be? Mark was trying to rescue you, he thinks you haven't faced up to what has happened.'

'I don't need to face anything or to be rescued. That's what I'm trying to say. I'm fine.'

'Flitting from job to job and then calling off your engagement? I can see you are fine and all is well. You are living a great, meaningful life, full of richness and purpose.'

'You're teasing me.'

'If that's the way you want to pass your days, then you don't even know you're alive.'

Alive? *That's how I felt in Mark's arms*, Carrie thought, a shiver running through her as she recalled the way every pore in her body had hummed with energy whenever they'd made love. But in a way, it had been scary. It hadn't felt like the Carrie Cassidy who had spent the past few years making sure she kept her thoughts and emotions safe and in control.

'You have choices, Carrie,' he said. 'You can live a half-life in the shadow of your parents, or go out there and honour their memory and live it on your own terms.'

'I felt alive this week,' she said. 'I've done things I've never done before. Especially today. Thanks for urging me to fly off the cliff, it was wonderful.'

'It was wonderful for me too,' he said, smiling at her. 'I asked you here because I wanted to meet the daughter of the woman who gave me back my life, and have some kind of reassurance that she'd been happy. Thanks for coming to visit and I hope I put some sparkle into your life, the way Sylvie did with mine. I didn't want to say too much about her in the circumstances, but whatever you believe or don't believe, please know that she was very special.'

Carrie made a noise that neither agreed nor disagreed with Luis.

'Apart from telling me she was at a crossroads and had a big decision to make,' he continued, 'she'd also had some sadness in her own life. Someone close to her had died, and she was terribly angry with me when I wanted to do away with my life. So I'm very relieved to know that she had a contented life.'

'I don't know who could have died around that time, did she tell you?'

'No, she told me it was someone she loved who was close to her.'

'Strange. That doesn't add up for me either. Nobody in my family died then.'

'I'm not sure how recent it was,' Luis said. 'When she talked about it, she said she knew what it was like to have her heart broken into tiny pieces.'

Nothing added up. A crossroads? A decision? Sylvie being fearful of an intolerable situation? Sylvie, heartbroken?

Carrie knew she'd have to do some digging of her own to find out what had happened in September 1980, as soon as she was back in Dublin.

'And now,' Luis said, 'I will have to go inside before Maria gets very cross and shouts and stamps her foot at me.'

Carrie couldn't help smiling at this. She pushed her rug aside and got to her feet. 'I don't know how I'm going to say goodbye to you,' she said, suddenly stricken.

'Then don't say goodbye now. Pop in on your way to the airport this evening.'

This time, when she was leaving, she kissed him on the cheek. Christophe drove her into the town, and all the way Luis' words rang in her ears: 'Time doesn't heal, but love does.'

* * *

Later, when Carrie called in to say goodbye, Luis was still resting.

'I'm sorry, Carrie,' Maria said. 'He's fast asleep and, according to his nurse, I can't disturb him. You won't get to say goodbye, but perhaps it's better like this?'

'He's dying, isn't he?' Carrie said with a pang.

'Yes,' Maria said. 'It'll be weeks rather than months.'

They were standing in the hallway and kept their voices low. The late-evening sun slanted across the walls and sent columns of light across the marbled floor. The doors were open all the way through, and she could see the silver glitter of the lake through the picture window at the end of the hallway. The surface seemed to be dancing under the rays of the sun, causing it to spark here and there like the glint of diamonds. It looked alive and very beautiful – joyful, even – and she found it hard to picture Luis sleeping in his bed, unable to fully appreciate the beautiful evening, and knowing full well he wouldn't be seeing many more.

'I don't know how you can be so calm,' she said to Maria. 'I'd feel like roaring and shouting if I were you.'

'Believe me, Carrie, I have felt all that and more. In the beginning, I was full of rage and disbelief. I didn't believe it could be happening to him. I felt sure the treatment would work. I couldn't believe that he wouldn't be cured. It was inconceivable. You hope, you always hope, a mistake has been made or that the doctors can do something. Then little by little, the bad news added up and didn't go away. I have to be strong on the outside for Luis, but in my heart I have cried an ocean of tears, and railed against the fates and begged the universe to heal him. I think even now' – she smiled a sad smile – 'that I still carry some hope that tomorrow might bring a breakthrough or a healing. I will go on hoping until the very end.'

Carrie stepped forward and hugged Maria's thin frame. Her fragrance was light and floral, understated, like the elegant woman herself. However, Maria felt suddenly brittle in her arms and Carrie wondered how much of an effort she was making to hold it all together.

Carrie stepped away a little, her hand on Maria's arm. 'I'm glad I came.'

'I am too, and so is Luis. You are exactly the kind of daughter he would have wished for, had we been fortunate enough to have children.'

Carrie felt uncomfortable. 'Really? I thought he might have been disappointed in me. I thought he might have been expecting someone strong and courageous, the kind who saves other people's lives.' *The kind of person who's not afraid to engage with life.*

Maria covered Carrie's hand with hers and squeezed it gently. 'I didn't hear all your conversations with Luis, but I don't understand how you can talk about yourself like that, Carrie,' Maria said. 'You're a beautiful, warm-hearted woman. You gave of your precious time to Luis, a stranger you'd never met. You answered his request. What could be more generous than that?'

'I suppose …' Carrie felt tears prick her eyes. She dashed them back in the face of Maria's stoicism and squared her shoulders. 'I can't say my motives for coming here were entirely unselfish.'

Maria smiled. 'In the past few weeks, Luis has been living here very quietly, not wanting any visitors. It's a long time since I've seen him as happy as he's been with you this week.'

Glancing at the clock on the wall, Carrie knew it was time to go. Time to leave Luis and Maria in the hushed quiet of their beautiful home and face a noisy, bustling airport and a journey home. Time to pick up the threads of her own life – or try to make some kind of life, more to the point.

'You'll stay in touch with me?' she asked Maria. 'Let me know …'

Maria smiled, visibly pulling herself together. 'Of course. And thank you again, Carrie.'

Carrie felt her heart contracting as she stepped away from Maria and went outside into the sunny evening, where Christophe waited. They didn't talk much on the journey to the airport, and Carrie was glad of that because she felt close to tears all the way, feeling them gather thickly at the back of her throat. In a funny way, she didn't want to go home, she would have preferred to stay on for a little longer, wrapped up in the mood of the past few days, an ambience that had softened all her spiky edges a little.

When they reached the airport, Christophe looked after her with the kind of old-fashioned courtesy that she found touching and which she thought should never have gone out of fashion. She needed his solicitous attention also, because she was disorientated in the airport, which was teeming with people, with the prospect of getting on the plane causing shards of panic to spear across her stomach. Christophe must have sensed her anxiety because he stayed with her all the way until she reached the security barrier.

'You'll be all right?' he asked.

It was on the tip of her tongue to say she was scared of flying, until she thought of how scared Luis and Maria must be feeling at the prospect of what lay ahead, a fear they hid behind a stoic courage. 'I'm grand,' she said, tightening her grip on her tote bag, willing herself to believe it.

'Safe journey,' Christophe said. He put his hands on her shoulders and, bending down, kissed her lightly on both cheeks.

'Thanks for looking after me,' she said, her words futile to express the emotion building up inside her.

In the departure lounge, she was removed from the busy minutiae of it all, her mind full of images of her visit to Lucerne. When her flight was called, a moment of panic almost caused her to run in the opposite direction, but her life was back in Faith Crescent and Jade, and she needed to go home and uncover the mystery of her mother's relationship with Luis, as well as come to terms with the lingering ache of her breakup with Mark. She joined the queue for the boarding gate, thinking of Luis facing the ultimate test with a quiet dignity, and Mark's warm encouragement when he brought her to Paris, lacing his fingers within hers, and telling her calmly to take slow, deep breaths.

She fastened her seatbelt, glad that her fingers shook a little less this time. As well as unearthing the truth of what happened to her mother in 1980, something else she would like to do was make some kind of peace with Mark, but that would take a miracle, wouldn't it?

Chapter Twenty-two

'A great meaningful life, full of richness and purpose,' Luis had said. Oh, yeah. Carrie's gaze drifted around the pale-grey walls of the office, where the ergonomic workstations, the ugly, metal filing cabinets, even the photocopier and printer seemed to blend into the dreary monotony of the walls, and she wished it was half past five. Was this it? Since she'd arrived home from Switzerland, and April had slid into May, she'd gone in and out to work in Jade, forcing herself out of bed in the mornings, knowing she was going through the physical motions on autopilot. She answered emails, went to meetings, smiled mechanically at Shelley and Elena, ducked out of the office at lunch for some fresh air, walking around in a daze until it was time to go back. Her heart and her head were miles away, in an airy, light-filled house overlooking a lake, recalling Maria's gentle smile and the shadows under her beautiful eyes that told of sleepless nights, but mostly she thought about the days she'd spent with Luis. They whirled around at the forefront of her mind, sharp and clear, dizzying in their intrinsic honesty and bittersweet in their urgency, showing up her routine life as dull and boring.

On Thursday afternoon, the office walls began to close in around Carrie. Three whole hours stretched ahead, minute after minute, like an endless grey fug. The rest of her life stretched ahead like an endless grey fug. Her heart thumped loudly in her chest and sweat ran down her back. She rose to her feet so abruptly that she knocked against the desk, sending her keyboard flying. Shelley looked up immediately.

'Are you okay?' she asked.

Carrie swallowed hard and fought down a sensation of panic. She nodded her head and went out to the ladies, drawing in gulps of air – even that was artificially freshened. The sanitised scent caused her to gag. Was this it, her life? Right now, the weight of dull routine in a job she hated was pressing down more and more on her.

A job she hated. How could she waste another moment trapped in such a soul-destroying daily grind? Still, she needed something to get her out of bed each morning and make her face the world. Yet how dare she feel like that, or need something to get her out of bed each morning when Luis hadn't got that luxury? She stared at her face in the mirror and blinked, as though seeing it properly for the first time in a long time. Why was she wasting so much time, drifting on the surface of everything? But walking out of yet another job surely reinforced her lack of staying power, didn't it? Shouldn't she try harder to make it work?

The arguments batted to and fro in her head as she went back to her desk and made an attempt to fill in her time productively until half past five. Shelley kept throwing odd glances in her direction, which unsettled her further. When she finally reached the sanctuary of Faith Crescent that evening and closed the door on the outside world, she was almost weeping with relief.

Until the bells of the nearby church began to chime at six o'clock, and she thought of the way church bells would chime for Luis, in the not too distant future, and her head was filled with the cold finality of what they would signal.

The following morning, after a sleepless night, Carrie summoned all her bravery and handed in her notice.

Steve's reaction was more or less as she'd expected. 'I don't think you were quite the right fit for Jade,' he said, with the smug air of a man who had been proved correct about something he'd suspected all along. 'It's probably just as well for both our sakes that we part company at this time. Actually, Carrie, you have pre-empted a performance-related conversation I wanted to start with you. I'll arrange with HR to give you a reference, of course, don't want to scupper your chances of getting another job,' he said, smiling at her as though he was doing her a wonderful favour.

Shelley's reaction shocked her. 'You don't know how much I envy you,' she said, when the news flew all around the office that afternoon.

'You are joking?'

'I wish I had your guts.'

Carrie laughed shortly. 'You must be confusing me with someone else. I don't have any guts.'

'I know you couldn't stand working here,' Shelley said. 'There were times when I couldn't stand you working here either.'

Carrie thought she'd misheard. 'Sorry?'

'Don't pretend you don't know. I knew by the way you looked at me, during our meetings, secretly laughing at me as though you thought I was being ridiculous for fawning all over Steve. You really don't care about anything at all, do you? That's what I envy, your cavalier attitude, that ability you have to shrug your shoulders, as though nothing about Jade matters at all.'

'Well, it doesn't, in the great scheme of things.'

'I agree. You don't seriously think I'm concerned about our cutting-edge philosophy, do you? But some of us have to act as if it matters. We have to toe the party line, lick up to the boss, go the extra customer-focused mile just to make sure we get to keep our jobs.' She smiled faintly. 'Because we have bills to pay and futures to build, and we need the money and some kind of temporary security, and if we've found it almost impossible to get a permanent job after leaving college, well, we need to do our very best to hang on in there, even if we're tired of 360-degree feedback and repeating by heart the brand values. Only I've no intentions of sleeping with Steve—'

'Christ. Has he asked you to?'

'Not in so many words,' Shelley gulped. 'He's far too clever for that. He's full of innuendos. He drops hints about needing to see me on the top of my game, that he likes to see me on the ball, and asks if I'm truly passionate about unleashing all my talents in front of him. It's all in the way he says it, and I'm struggling to stay one jump ahead.'

'That's sexual harassment, Shelley. That shouldn't go unchallenged.'

'And do you think I'd be able to prove anything – even in this day and age?'

There was silence.

Shelley went on. 'So, Carrie, I'd love to have enough guts to walk out the door and say to hell with the consequences, only I can't afford to. I need the money too much.'

'No money is worth that kind of misery.'

'Oh, it is, if you've finally managed to take out a mortgage and get a foothold on the property ladder. It might be the holy grail, but it traps you, you know? For the guts of thirty years.'

'I'm really … I don't know what to say,' Carrie said, feeling suitably chastened at the way she'd privately slagged Shelley.

'Don't say you're sorry, I couldn't bear that. There'll be a flood of applicants for your job, and the successful one will spend a weekend celebrating their good fortune and enjoy a wonderful honeymoon period until the boring reality sinks in. Who knows, if she's younger and prettier than me, it might take the heat off me with Steve. That's who you should be sorry for.'

'I apologise unreservedly if I upset you,' Carrie said contritely.

'I'll keep you in mind if I hear of any jobs or openings you might be interested in.'

'Thanks.' Shelley had already straightened her shoulders and was once again absorbed in her computer screen as though their conversation had never happened.

But the conversation echoed in Carrie's head as she walked home from the office, a sudden empathy for Shelley surprising her. One more week – the notice she'd had to give – and she'd be free of it all. Relief washed over her in waves. The May evening air seemed extra sweet after the oppression of the office, and slanting sunshine highlighted the fresh new leaves on the trees that lined her route home, uplifting her heart.

Leaving her job in Jade didn't mean she was about to lob around Faith Crescent in her PJs and slippers. She had other, more important, things to do. Things like making a kind of peace with Mark. But first on her agenda was finding out what Sylvie had been up to in 1980. The relationship that Luis had had with Sylvie was puzzling, bewildering, almost incomprehensible to her. Luis didn't seem the type to be given to fantasy, but she couldn't rationalise anything he'd said against the reality of the devoted parents and loving mother she'd known. The truth was buried somewhere between Waldron Avenue and Willow Hill, and she would find it. The obvious place to start was Waldron Avenue, which, up until now, had been a no-go area in her heart.

But not, of course, half the no-go area that Mark was.

'Pretend to be brave,' Luis had said.

That night, Carrie dropped in to Fiona and, ignoring her cousin's dropped jaw, asked for the keys to Waldron Avenue.

Chapter Twenty-three

Fiona had offered to accompany her, but Carrie said she'd be fine. She didn't want Fiona to witness the reality that she might need to hold photos close to her chest and bawl her eyes out, as Luis had mentioned. She might need to pass her fingertips over her parents' special things. And she might find something that would explain what had happened in 1980 – she most definitely wanted to be on her own.

Her throat almost closed over, such was the thick surge of emotion that swamped her as she walked up the garden path. It took her three goes to open the hall door. Five years, five days, five minutes. She was there, in that hall, looking at her parents' suitcases – brand new, pristine and expensive, as befitted the trip of a lifetime – and laughing over the meticulous details written in her mother's neat hand on their luggage tags.

The sound of her carefree, absolutely know-it-all, twenty-five-year-old voice. 'You don't need to write your whole life story on a luggage tag ... so uncool on top of having immaculate-looking cases ... you'd swear you had never gone away before ... course that's right, you haven't. In this day and age, mainland Europe is practically the back garden ...'

Her dad's teasing voice. 'Hey, less of your mockery. At least we're making up for lost time, now that you've finally decided to give us some space …'

'Oh, yeah, blame me, it's all *my* fault. I kept you tied to mainland Europe all these years …'

This afternoon, early-summer sunshine poured through the fanlight over the door and slanted off the walls, much as it always had. In one sense, everything seemed the same, but there was an empty space in the hall where the shiny new luggage had been, and a thick silence where her parents had teased and laughed. The table was still there, holding the same lamp and a couple of flyers. There was a child's bike propped against the wall and a small pair of bright-red wellingtons lined up on an old mat inside the door.

The Quinns were in Galway for the weekend and had given Carrie's visit their blessing. Carrie wondered if Fiona had warned them that it would be her first time to walk through the door since her parents had died. She stood in the hall for long moments, trying to steady herself against the disorientation that came at her in waves. There was a different scent and a different feeling to the house, yet the doors and the walls and the stairs were in the same place, and it was easy to imagine that her father would saunter out of the living room at any moment, the newspaper or a book in his hand, or that her mother would come up out of the kitchen.

And yet they were old spirits, who had visited her subconscious and flitted through her dark dreams over and over so that here, today, the impact of their absence wasn't quite as agonising as it might have been. Carrie walked down the hall and pushed open the door to the kitchen, bracing herself against a surge of memories. It was the same and yet not so – the same configuration of kitchen units, same table and chairs and magazine rack and bookcase and view to the garden, but indefinably altered with the gloss of another family and the pieces of their day-to-day lives overlaying everything. Different photographs on the shelves, a selection of a child's crayon drawings attached by magnets to the fridge. The memories came in a flood, all right, a kaleidoscope of images swamping her senses. She took a deep breath and walked around the kitchen, and the love and warmth of those memories seemed to resonate from the walls. She went across to the window, and then, out in the garden, she saw the apple blossom tree.

It was bursting with colour, the branches weighed down with thick, fat blossoms. It had always been their lucky tree, announcing the arrival of spring. Her mum never tired of extolling the wonders of nature, saying the tree heralded new life and fresh beginnings after the dying of the old year. Her dad had never tired of telling her that he had planted it the year she was born in honour of her birth into the world. And here it was, still blooming with life, vigour and beauty, years after her parents were gone.

Gone. Dead. Departed. Passed away.

It hit her then, standing in the kitchen, that the warm memories were just that – recollections of what had happened in the past. No matter how much she wished for it, those moments would never, ever, come again; her parents would never be here again, looking out this window, sitting by the table, reaching idly for a newspaper or a magazine, sipping coffee or laughing as they poured a glass of wine. No matter how long she lived, she would never again see her father's mischievous wink or the twinkle in his eye, or hear her mother's soft laughter. Her father would never again tell her that the apple blossom tree had been planted the year she was born.

Suddenly she was crying. The tears came in torrents so that she was gasping for breath, and she bent over, sobbing her heart out, clutching her stomach, the pain almost too much. It was a long time before she recovered enough to look for some kitchen roll, so that she could dry her eyes and blow her nose. It was a long time before she recovered enough to go upstairs into the room where Evelyn and Sean had stored her parents' belongings.

Once more, Carrie braced herself as she unlocked the door and let herself in. The bed had been taken out and plastic Ikea storage crates were neatly arranged around the room. Behind them, her parents' good paintings and mirrors lined the walls. As she looked around and tentatively opened some of the crates, the first thing that Carrie realised was the debt of gratitude she owed Evelyn and Sean. They had had to deal at first hand with the trauma of losing family in a very tragic way, and then clear up all the red tape left behind while coping with their loss along with Carrie's dejection. *And* get the house ready for letting out in the face of Carrie's blasé detachment. They'd gone to a lot of trouble to painstakingly label each and every crate with a list of contents, and within them, carefully pack away the items for safekeeping. She could see at a glance where the Waterford crystal was kept, the glasses and flower vases, the silverware, the china dinner sets, her father's all-important sound system, the most cherished of their books and CDs. Other crates held less expensive but more precious items: Carrie's school sports trophies, mementoes she had had in her bedroom, and then all the family photographs, some of them in frames, some arranged in albums, and others in folders, all of them dating from the time Carrie had been a baby.

She knew her mother had kept a selection of older photographs in a rather battered album, and that was the one she wanted to find. It was down at the bottom of the crate and Carrie had to pull out an old address book to get to it, and her heart clenched.

There was a brown A4 envelope caught inside the book that used to sit on the shelf under the hall table. Her scalp pricked. She sensed what it was, even before she examined it.

She sees her mum coming up to the hall, where Carrie has been teasing her dad over the shininess of their cases:

'Darling, have you seen the envelope with the flight tickets?' Her mum's calm voice, talking in loving tones to the husband she had apparently betrayed years earlier.

Her dad winks at Carrie. 'I wonder could it possibly be this one here, on the hall table, the brown one labelled 'Flight tickets' in a blue felt pen?'

'Is it? Oh, you!' Her mum's laughter as her dad slides the envelope out from under his newspaper and hands it to her.

'I can't even find the spares I printed out, just in case …'

'Knowing you, you have probably tucked them away too well.'

And here it was, years later, a slim brown envelope labelled in blue felt-tip pen in her mother's neat handwriting: 'Spare copies'.

Carrie let the envelope drop to the floor as though it was on fire. She replaced the lid of the crate and put the photo albums into her tote bag. Feeling sick and shivering with nerves, she picked up the envelope and tucked that in as well.

Afterwards, she could hardly remember locking the door of the room or putting on the alarm code before she left the house. She must have been at serious risk on the roads, because she scarcely remembered driving home to the sanctuary of Faith Crescent. She was trembling as she closed her front door and leaned back against it, as weak as if she'd climbed to the summit of a mountain, fighting for breath, her tote bag almost burning the side of her body where it touched against it.

* * *

Later that evening, she went around the house, shutting all the blinds and pulling the curtain across the French doors, and then lit a fire in the front room, more for cheer than anything else. All she had to do was stay here, cocooned safely within the walls of Faith Crescent, and do nothing at all. Not even think. She took a bottle of white wine out of the fridge, turned on the telly, kicked off her boots and curled up on the sofa for the night.

The wine helped. Two glasses in, she began to feel a relaxation of sorts sliding through her veins, numbing the edge of the nameless anxiety that had dogged her all afternoon. There was a family quiz show on, which was light and undemanding and, more importantly, noisy with silly, canned laughter.

By her third glass of wine, she began to remember the cosy Saturday nights in she'd shared with Mark, when they'd done nothing but order a takeaway and open a bottle of wine. And then go to bed. Was he sharing a cosy Saturday night in with anyone else right now? Or was he out on the pull, prowling around the town? If he was, she had no one to blame but herself. She remembered the way his face had dropped when she'd told him, in a voice full of false bravado, that she was thinking of heading off to Switzerland. Like she hopped on a plane every day of the week. Like she was almost thumbing her nose at his thoughtful and carefully executed – his *lovingly* executed – mission to get her to Paris.

He deserved a proper explanation.

Without thinking too much about it, she picked up her mobile and brought up her text messages. There had been a time when his name would have been top of her list, now she had to scroll down to find him. His last text jumped out at her.

On the way. Beef or chicken? X

He'd been picking up a Chinese on his way home from work. She saw him coming through the door, carrying a brown-paper bag of food, tipping cartons out onto plates she'd already warmed in the oven, pouring curry sauce into a jug, popping a chip in his mouth, dunking a chip in the sauce before feeding it to her. It was three nights before they'd had their last major row.

Can we have a chat when you get a chance?

She sent the message before she could get cold feet.

Then she knew what to do to take her mind off Mark. She padded out to the hall in her stocking feet to where her tote bag sat drunkenly in a corner near her bookcase, like some kind of slumbering alien.

She brought it into the front room and was about to chuck the envelope with the copies of the flight tickets onto the coals when she decided it would be more of a ceremony to feed the tickets to the fire, one by one. She slid out three sheets of paper, printed with her parents' various flight details, her eyes sliding over the sight of their names together, and the flight information.

She felt a pain in her chest as she held the first sheet over the coals until it caught fire, the flame running up along the side of the paper, and then she dropped it, watching it crumple in on itself and dissolve into the red heart of the fire. She did the same with the next sheet, listing details of the penultimate flight, the doomed one. She watched in a kind of fascinated horror as it perished in the fire. Afterwards, she took a long gulp of wine. Then she picked up the final sheet of paper, for the homebound flights they'd never used.

There was something odd here. Something that didn't add up. She remembered her mum ticking off the itinerary on the fingers of one hand, giving Carrie a quick rundown of the homeward journey.

'Brazil, Paris, London, Dublin.'

'Why can't you fly from Paris directly to Dublin?'

'The timings are awkward.'

'I can't believe you'll actually land in London and only see the inside of the airport. It's a missed opportunity. You haven't been there since your honeymoon.'

'Sure we'll have plenty more travelling days ahead of us. This is only the start.'

But according to the copies of their tickets, John and Sylvie Cassidy were spending two days in London, and were not flying home to Dublin straightaway. Her parents had been due to land in

London midday on a Monday and fly back to Dublin on Wednesday evening. Carrie stared at the dates, convinced that she was so tired and emotional and wine-fuddled that she was reading them incorrectly. The canned laughter on the television reached a crescendo and she lifted the remote and muted the sound, plunging the front room into silence, except for the crackle of the fire. Carrie couldn't bring herself to feed the final flight ticket to the flames.

Instead, she poured the last of the wine into her glass and sat huddled by the fire, picking up the old photograph album. She was glad of the soporific effects of the wine as she opened it. But before she flicked through the album, three photographs fell out from a loose pocket at its front.

The first was a group birthday photograph taken at the kitchen table in Willow Hill with Carrie's beloved grandmother and a very young Sean and Andrew, a pleasant-faced, buxom woman wearing an apron and a shy-looking girl standing beside a teenage Sylvie. There was another photo of her parents as teenagers, in amongst a group of friends on a football pitch, her mum's hair tossed in the breeze. Finally, there was a strip of four small black-and-white photographs, the kind taken in a photo booth, and used at one stage for a passport or driver's licence. They were of her mother and the shy-looking girl in the birthday photo. This time, they were a few years older. The two of them were squashed together in the booth, arm in arm, heads pressed together as they laughed into the camera. In the last photo on the strip, they were holding their left hands up in front of their faces, showing off their engagement rings.

Carrie turned the strip around. The words written on the back in pencil had faded over time, but she could just make them out: 'Sylvie and Beth, February 1980.'

Beth. She'd heard that name before, but it had been years ago and so fleetingly that it hadn't really registered with her. She must have been a very good friend of her mother's, once upon a time …

Chapter Twenty-four

Adam had never been one hundred per cent, absolutely sure that he was safe from an unexpected phone call from the police, but as time had gone by, and one year had rolled into the next, Willow Hill had become a memory and he convinced himself that he was in the clear. There would be no fresh evidence coming to light. Not now. Besides, everything had gone cold, especially after Sylvie Cassidy had met her unfortunate end.

Not that he had anything to feel guilty about, he told himself as he took a bottle of blue label Johnnie Walker out of a cabinet and poured a generous measure. It was six o'clock, more than time for a relaxing drink. There was nothing to implicate him whatsoever. Now he was busy securing his retirement with a series of painstakingly planned manoeuvres that would result in sufficient funds to see him living out the rest of his years in comfort, as far away from Dublin as possible. He looked around his spacious office – two more years here, maybe three, was all he needed to consolidate everything.

He should have already retired by now, after all; he'd got off to a very promising start by making a small fortune on the back of the Asian crisis in the late 1990s. Unfortunately, he'd seen his wealth badly dented when funds he'd ploughed into prime real estate had collapsed in the wake of the Irish recession. He might have had to offload some developmental properties for a fraction of what he'd paid for them, but he'd managed to stay afloat and had narrowly avoided liquidation. Many empires had crumbled, never to rise again, but not his.

Spending a few months on Wall Street at the time so many others had gone to the wall had been the best thing he could have done. He'd reinvented himself, brushed himself down, invested carefully in distressed assets and, thanks to ruthless cost management, was well poised to take advantage of the emerging resurgence in the Irish property market.

And he'd been clever enough to keep his private equity group disentangled from his investment portfolio. He was still there, at the helm, waiting for the right moment to sell and bag a hefty sum to take with him into his golden years. He reached out and with a flick of his wrist, he spun the globe at the side of his desk. He just had to decide where he was going to go. Somewhere, preferably, where laws were lax, morals were loose, and a modest amount of money could get you whatever sexual thrills and excitement you desired.

No one was going to scupper his carefully crafted plans, least of all an uppity thirty-year-old who hadn't a clue how hard he'd worked to get where he was. She was home from Lucerne by now, but he was none the wiser about what she'd been doing there.

He would continue to keep an eye on her, as he had done over the past five years, like her mother before her. Just in case. See if she went to Willow Hill. Christmas visits were one thing, but coming on top of a trip to Lucerne, it might be too much of a coincidence. Then he would know he might have a problem on his hands.

Women! Interfering bitches, most of them. Only good for one thing. He pressed a few buttons on a remote and selected a movie from a menu on a wall-mounted television screen. He took a few sips of whiskey, relaxing into the butter-soft leather chair. After a while, he convinced himself that it was ridiculous, really, to imagine there might be a problem. It was all ancient history.

But with the benefit of hindsight, if he was back there again, he'd never have married the prim and prudish Beth McCann …

Chapter Twenty-five

March 1980

Beth walked out of the University Church on St Stephen's Green on a mild March afternoon, telling herself that Beth McCann was gone and in her place was Mrs Adam Gilmore. Already she felt different. She wasn't an illegitimate daughter any more – or a housekeeper's daughter. Funny how Adam had transformed her into someone different, someone new, in the space of a few minutes with the exchange of vows in front of an altar and a signature on a register of marriages.

It was a small wedding and Adam's parents were polite, but clearly less than overjoyed to see their son marrying her for better or worse. The wedding photographs were taken in St Stephen's Green. Beth posed for the camera with Sylvie and John, as well as Sylvie's parents, who made up for the lack of guests on Beth's side by being larger than life, warm and effusive.

At first, Adam hadn't been too keen on Sylvie being bridesmaid.

'Isn't there anyone else you could ask?'

'Adam! Sylvie's my best friend. Of course I have to have her as my bridesmaid.'

'Have her if you must, but it might be best not to see too much of them after we're married.'

In one sense Beth was relieved. She'd been afraid that Adam might be attracted to Sylvie with her contagious laughter and bubbly confidence. Compared to the effervescent Sylvie, Beth had always felt dull and boring, but now all that was behind her.

After the photographs were taken, the wedding party moved on to a reception in the Shelbourne Hotel, which Adam had insisted on paying for. She danced with him in a daze, still pinching herself. Beth could almost hear Molly McCann's voice bubbling over with excitement and pride as she told her she was so lucky to be marrying a lovely man like Adam, who would take good care of her for the rest of her life.

They stayed in the Shelbourne for their wedding night, Beth's body tinging with heat, anticipation and nerves as they left the reception. She felt unbearably shy when she slipped between the sheets in her new silky nightdress, bought with some trepidation, and heard Adam cleaning his teeth in the adjoining bathroom.

Up to now they'd kissed, and he'd swept his hand across the curves of her breasts, but they'd never gone very far, Adam explaining that he was afraid of getting carried away and doing something he might regret before their marriage. She couldn't wait to love him fully. In her single bed in the bedsit, she'd allowed her hands to roam across her body, imagining they were his. There had been no way of imagining what real intercourse would be like, of course. Now every pore of her skin was tight with anticipation, and she felt an ache building up between her legs.

She heard the last of the water gurgle down the sink as he finished cleaning his teeth. He snapped off the bathroom light and walked into the bedroom, wearing blue pyjamas with sharp creases that told her he'd just taken them out of the cellophane packaging. He lifted the coverlet and the mattress dipped as he slipped into bed beside her. She froze for an instant.

'Beth?'

'Yes?' She smiled up at him; she hoped it was an inviting, womanly smile with no sign of her nerves. Her cleavage strained against the top of her nightdress and behind that her chest felt suffocated.

'You must be tired after everything today,' he said. 'I'm not going to expect anything of you tonight. Let's just to sleep, okay?'

A crashing disappointment. He wasn't going to expect anything? She wanted to show him just how much she loved him. She wanted to surprise him with all the pent-up passion she had been storing these past few months. And, anyway, what about her? Or was she not supposed to have any desires?

'Are you sure?'

'We have the rest of our lives, haven't we?' He clicked off the lamp and lay down on his back. 'It was a great day, wasn't it? I think everyone enjoyed themselves. You looked beautiful, Beth.' He turned away from her, careful not to dislodge the bedclothes.

'Thanks.'

Her tears were close to the surface and her body ached all over as she lay in the dark and told herself that she must be more exhausted than she realised. So he was right, in a way. The past few weeks had been hectic and they were both tired tonight. No point in messing up their first time. It was a long time before she went to sleep. She'd never shared a bed with anyone before, and it felt strange and unfamiliar. Funnily enough, she sensed that he too was lying sleepless in the bed; it was much later when she heard him snoring.

The day after the wedding, they went to Spain on their honeymoon. Beth had never flown before. She tried not to look too excited as she followed Adam down the cabin and found their seats because she hadn't actually admitted this to Adam, especially when she knew he'd been abroad several times. She realised belatedly that he must have noticed her shiny new passport, but he didn't pass any comment.

She tried not to look too wide-eyed when they arrived in Torremolinos and the heat and scents of the Spanish resort wrapped around her, foreign and enticing. It was all very strange for someone who'd only lived in Cork and Dublin, but Adam knew what to do, how to behave, what to expect at their hotel. She just had to let him take charge and look as though she'd been on foreign holidays hundreds of times before. Her case was full of holiday clothes, and sexy night clothes and underwear. It was going to be brilliant.

But it was the third night of their honeymoon before he made love to her.

Not that it deserved to be called that.

He'd had too much to drink. He'd started on beer and then moved on to spirits, knocking them back too swiftly for her peace of mind. By the time they went up to their hotel room, he was unsteady on his feet. As before, he waited out on the balcony while she got ready for bed but, this time, when he joined her in bed, he reached out for her.

At last. He had just been nervous. Maybe he'd needed the benefit of a few drinks to relax him. She turned into his arms, expectation and desire rising up inside her. He kissed her and felt her breasts through the thin material of her nightie. She tried to manoeuvre herself into a sitting position, to take off her nightie but, to her surprise, he turned her around to that she was lying on her stomach. He pushed up her nightie and drew down her pants.

'Adam?' she said, feeling horribly vulnerable, her voice muffled against her pillow. He said nothing as he lifted her hips so that she was on her knees. She turned her head and looked back over her shoulder. He was kneeling behind her, bare-chested, his pyjama bottoms down around his knees, his hand jerking something big and red and purple that sprang from a nest of dark hairs. Blood thrummed in her head when she realised what it was.

Oh God.

'Don't talk. I prefer it if you don't talk,' he said in a thick voice.

She stayed quiet, the sheets clenched in her grip, wondering if she was doing the right thing. It was her first time, so she didn't know what to expect, but her romantic, soft-focus imaginings of them making love had looked nothing like this. She didn't know Adam would have wanted it like this, especially for the first time. She didn't know how clumsy it could be as he prodded his thing against the cleft of her buttocks. She squirmed around, trying to look at him, to connect with him, but he kept pushing her face down into the pillow. It took him several attempts to enter her; his fingers seemed to be everywhere, in all the wrong places, pinching and bruising her skin, and when he forced himself inside her and began to move roughly, she thought she was going to be torn in two.

He pulled out after a couple of minutes and went into the bathroom. Eventually, she heard the flush of the toilet, the running of a tap, and she tensed when he came back to bed.

She heard his whisper, echoing sibilantly in the darkened room, 'Thanks Beth, thanks for letting me do that.'

She closed her eyes and pretended to be asleep. The soreness pulsing in her body was almost as painful as the ache in her heart.

The following morning, she didn't know what to say or how to act. How to pull the edges of herself together, she felt so raw and frayed, all her romantic expectations in smithereens. They were going on an excursion to see some caves and visit a jewellery factory. Adam seemed to behave much as normal, she wasn't sure if he was avoiding her eyes or if it was her, feeing edgy around him. Miserable and confused, she went along with him, passing the bread politely, pouring his tea. After breakfast, they waited with some other tourists outside the hotel in the dazzling sun for the tour bus. The daylight seemed bright and clean, and somehow safe after the trauma of the night before in the darkened bedroom. She reminded herself that they were husband and wife. Sex was part of the package.

Beth couldn't help looking at other couples, wondering if what had happened between her and Adam was a normal part of married life. What was wrong with her, that she didn't care for it? Was she frigid? She'd heard the term bandied about and now wished she'd joined in the secret talks and giggles that had taken place behind the bike shed in school. She might have learned something. She wished she'd had more information besides a third-hand copy of a book on the facts of life that her mother had handed to her when she was ten. She wished she'd had the cop on to get her hands on a few books on the subject of married sex, or to have studied some of the racy magazines she heard the girls in the typing pool talking about at tea break. They'd talked as though everybody knew everything there was to know about sex. She'd smiled and gone along with them.

It would get better. She had every trust in Adam. He fussed around her during the trip, and like the perfect gentleman, he held out his hand to help her down the steep steps of the coach every time they dismounted. Still, she felt cold inside every time he gripped her.

* * *

Three nights later it happened again. They'd spent the evening in a bar overlooking the beach. She sipped a cocktail and looked out at the night time falling across the beach and the twinkly lights of the resort coming on. Someone was playing a Spanish guitar and she was beginning to relax into the pleasant, exotic kind of night, far away from Dublin, when she noticed he was drinking quite fast. Knots of tension formed in her stomach as they strolled back to their hotel room. As before, his hand glided across her breasts before he turned her around, away from him. This time she tried to stop him.

'Adam ... please,' she begged. 'What about ...' What could she say? I don't like it? To the man who had made all her dreams come true by marrying her? The man who had bought them a house, and made sure it would be ready by the time they returned from honeymoon. Who'd said he didn't believe in sex before marriage, that he didn't want her to think he was that sort. The awful thought struck her that she might not have married him had she known what it would entail or how vulnerable it made her feel.

He was stronger than she realised and caught her two wrists in his hand and held them over her head, pinning her to the bed.

'Shut up,' he said, in a low voice. 'I like it this way. And I prefer it if you don't talk.' His other hand was heavy in the small of her back as he roughly nudged her legs apart with his knee and she tensed, bracing herself for what was to come.

Chapter Twenty-six

Sunday dawned wet and miserable, a veil of rain lingering into the afternoon so that, for once, Faith Crescent seemed dull and oppressive; even the church bells ringing at regular intervals sounded mournful in the murkiness of the day. Carrie put on some music very loudly and scrubbed her cooker until it gleamed, then she emptied whatever was left in the fridge, washed it out and mopped the floor.

In the late afternoon, the rain lifted, a streak of blue sky pushed through the clouds and then the sun came out, flooding her home with summery light, sparkling off the wet grass in the back garden. Feeling grubby after her exertions, she went upstairs to shower and change her clothes. As she came downstairs, the doorbell chimed and, without thinking, she opened the door.

Naturally, it was Mark. *Who else could it be?* she mocked herself. She couldn't stop her heart from leaping at the big, vital sight of him.

This time he was facing her, his hands shoved into his jacket pocket, his expression neutral. Her grip tightened on the doorjamb. She took a quick gulp of the late-afternoon air pouring in through the open door, it was fresh and cold and rain-scented. Over his shoulder, at the top of the cul de sac, traffic passed by, the sunlight glinting off chrome and glass. From nearby came the sound of children's voices and a football being thunked against a wall.

'You seem to be the only person knocking on my door these days,' she said. 'Don't tell me – you left something behind.' She was glad he hadn't found her in her PJs, that she'd put on her best jeans and a white shirt after she'd showered. She'd even put on makeup and sprayed some expensive perfume as part of her attempt to be more positive about her life.

'Not this time,' he said, his detached expression changing to one of surprise as his eyes skimmed over her face.

'You're looking for some post?' she asked cheekily, crossing her arms as a defence against the way he was looking at her.

'Huh?'

If she was trying to protect herself from the puzzled vibes he was now giving off, it didn't work. They ricocheted around her like an invisible hail of arrows.

'I'm not here for post, Carrie,' he said. 'Have you forgotten?' He shot her a look that put her on edge.

'Forgotten what?' A short pause. 'Oh, flip.'

Her text. Last night. She'd forgotten it completely in all the emotion and confusion surrounding her parents' flight tickets and the photographs. Her heart tripped with a mixture of embarrassment and discomfort, but she'd no choice but to ask him in. Whatever bravery she'd summoned the previous night, there was no sign of it this evening as he marched into the kitchen. He stood and looked at her, his face pale and leaner than ever, his grey eyes sombre.

'What's up?' he asked. 'You wanted a *chat*?' He emphasised the word 'chat' and the way she was feeling right now – off-balance, vulnerable and unsure – he might as well have been asking her if she wanted to be fed to the lions.

'Yes, well, it seemed a good idea last night …' The words died in her throat. Totally wrong thing to say. She hadn't been expecting him to drop by like this. When she sent the text, she'd thought he might eventually text her back and agree to meet at a future date, on neutral ground somewhere, like a hotel bar or a café, where there would be other, welcome distractions.

'Why, what happened last night?'

She supposed it was better than him asking her outright how many bottles of wine she'd knocked back. She shrugged, trying to muster some courage. 'It was the way I headed off to Switzerland. I realised I didn't give you a proper explanation.'

'I think you did. Very comprehensively.'

'I just wanted you to know that I wouldn't have been able to go only for you.'

'Me? What did I do?' He leaned back against the counter and folded his arms, but instead of looking relaxed, he was as taut as a wire.

'It was the way you managed to talk me into going to Paris, it was very good of you, very thoughtful, and I really appreciate it.'

He stayed silent.

'It helped me to get on the plane to Zurich and back again without panicking too much.'

He still didn't say anything.

She blundered on, searching for words. 'So in case you got the impression I was being cocky about flying again, I didn't mean to sound like that.'

Silence stretched. Eventually, he said, 'And you brought me here to tell me this?'

'I wasn't expecting you to call, I figured we'd meet in a bar or something … You see, I thought it was important for us to talk.'

'Why?'

'Because …' She tried to think clearly. 'The way I spoke the last time you were here was probably a little dismissive. It was wrong of me.'

'Dismissive? Carrie, I don't think you have a clue what you're talking about. Much less what you brought me here for.'

Why was he doing this? Putting her on the spot. Drunken tweets were one thing, as least they could be deleted, but drunken texts. And to Mark. She felt hot and cold. Never again. She was flustered under his direct gaze. She saw him looking at her from across the aisle of a church at the start of it all, when the bouquet-scented air had been full of swirling possibilities. She thought of the way they were now and wanted to cry.

'I just want to set a few things straight,' she said. 'I realised that I was probably a bit dismissive with you the last time you dropped by, and I'm sorry if I caused you any hurt.'

'What brought this on?'

He was looking at her as though he didn't particularly like her, and she had to force out the words over a lump in her throat. 'A few things came clear to me around the time I was in Switzerland. I had time to think and last night—'

'How long were you in Switzerland?'

'Four days.'

'And you went to see …?'

She didn't like the glint in his eyes. 'I told you already. A man who was an old friend of my mother.'

'So on the basis of your holiday or whatever, you decided you were sorry for being dismissive of me on that occasion?'

'It was more than a holiday. It was a very special few days. It made me look at life in a different way. We did things—'

'What kind of things?'

'We went up into the Alps, it was like *The Sound of Music*, it was beautiful. We went sailing on the lake, Lake Lucerne, and he even brought me paragliding—'

'Paragliding? I don't believe you.'

'Yes, it was great.' She couldn't help but smile at the memory. 'It made me take a fresh look at my life. You'll be glad to hear I've even left Jade.'

'Oh, yeah?'

'Yes, I handed in my notice and finished up on Friday.' She thought he might have approved of the way she was starting to turn her life around. Instead, he looked as though he was going to explode.

'Are you telling me that some old friend of your mother managed to do in four days what I wasn't able to do in six, seven, eight months?'

'It wasn't like that.'

He laughed. 'Hold on a minute. You went out to the airport and got on a plane, all by yourself?'

She nodded.

'You spent a few days doing the kind of things you haven't done in five years – that you wouldn't do with me.'

Something felt hollow inside her.

'You actually went *paragliding*.'

He was angry. She had never seen Mark this white-faced before.

'You went up into the mountains. You were out on the lake.'

'You're making it sound …' She shook her head.

'Go on.'

'Like I shouldn't have.'

'On the contrary, I think it's nothing short of a big fucking fantastic miracle that you turned your life around in just a few short days – to the extent that you even left a job that did nothing for your heart and soul. I think it's fantastic that Carrie Cassidy has finally woken up and smelled the coffee. What I can't understand – what's pissing me off big time – is how someone else managed to get through to you in a way I never could, someone you've known only for a few days. And you're standing here now –' his voice rose, thick with pain '– telling me you're sorry if you sounded dismissive the time I came to pick up my car stuff?'

'Mark, I—'

'I'm not finished,' he fumed. 'And you had the nerve to haul me over here to tell me that? Carrie ...' He shook his head. 'Is this for real?'

She was trembling. 'Why? What did I do?'

'You sure know how to kick a man when he's down.'

'I didn't mean—'

'Have you any idea how totally dismissive you were with me, the last few weeks we were together? All the times I tried to talk to you, to lift you out of yourself. All the times I cared for you and loved you ...'

His voice cracked. She thought she was going to break in two at the sound of it.

'I couldn't give a shit if you looked crooked at me the last time ... whenever ...' He threw up his hands. He looked at her as though he couldn't believe what he had heard. 'Because you'd already dissed me in the most horrible way imaginable. You'd already stamped all over me. How dare you drag me over here to tell me that a virtual stranger encouraged you to look at your life anew, in a way I couldn't. What has he got that I hadn't? And how *dare* you think it's okay to apologise for treating me to a once-off, cheeky grin, when you've already done your best to make me feel like a whole big heap of stinking hot crap.'

Pain sliced through her once more, robbing her of breath.

He started for the hall and she grabbed his arm but he brushed her off. 'Don't touch me. I can't get my head around this, asshole that I am.'

'Look, Mark, you have it all wrong ...'

He stared at her without saying anything. His face was sad now, and it cut her to the quick. Then, he was gone. She slammed the hall door to shut out the daylight streaming in and the sight of him driving out of the cul de sac. But she heard him all right: the rev of his engine, the clash of gears as he manoeuvred the car out of a parking spot, then the squeal of him accelerating away.

Chapter Twenty-seven

'Are you going to tell me what happened?' Fiona asked.

'Why?' Carrie didn't falter, but kept up her pace as they walked briskly along the pathway cutting through the overhanging trees.

'You have bags under your eyes the size of football fields and your face is as pale as skimmed milk – and kind of greyish.'

'That all?'

Sparks of sunlight darted through the overhead branches, dancing off fresh new leaves, and silhouetting their lacy patterns on the track in front of them as they walked along. The May afternoon was warm and Carrie pulled down the zip of her grey tracksuit, and shrugging it off, she tied the sleeves around her waist over her T-shirt.

'Did you find anything upsetting in Waldron Avenue?'

'No, I already told you I'm fine about that,' Carrie said, brushing aside her niggle of concern with the flight ticket. It probably meant nothing at all.

'I don't want to pry but you look kind of shattered,' Fiona said.

'I left my job last Friday and I'd a huge row with Mark on Sunday evening. How does that sound?'

'What?' Fiona stopped. Carrie halted alongside her. Two runners clad in Lycra sprinted around them both without slowing for even a nanosecond.

'Jesus, Carrie, I can't keep up with you lately. Talk about major life events in the space of a few days. You left your job *and* you saw Mark? What really happened in Switzerland?' Fiona tipped her bottle of water against her mouth and took a long slug. Then she held the bottle between her knees as she pulled off her scrunchie, combed her hair back with her fingers and tied it up again.

'Come on,' Carrie urged, 'we have to get around this park in half an hour. Otherwise we can forget about the mini-marathon.'

As they walked smartly, following the path that brought them around the perimeter of the football field, Carrie gave Fiona a quick rundown of her resignation and her row with Mark.

'You actually *asked* Mark to drop in?'

'I sent him a text. On Saturday night, after a glass of wine. Two glasses of wine. Maybe three.'

'You didn't.'

'I never thought he'd arrive at my door so fast – and in person. It all went south after that. You didn't hear about it?' she asked, bracing herself in case Mark had been talking.

'Not from Mark, if that's what you mean. Sam might have met him for a drink but I haven't seen him in a month or so. I can't believe you've actually left Jade, though. What brought that on?'

'I didn't fit in, Fiona. I couldn't play the company game any longer, so I resigned before I got the push.'

'What are you going to do now?'

Carrie moved aside to avoid a young child careening towards her on her pink bike. 'I'm going down to Willow Hill. I've already been on to your mum. It's all arranged.'

'Oh, great. Free access to the spa and lots of spoiling for a few days, just what the doctor ordered, as in Dr Me. A few days down there will help. You'll come back a new woman and, who knows, we might even complete the mini-marathon in under two hours,' she said, as a trio of runners raced past them at speed.

It wasn't why she was going down, but there was no need to try and explain the inexplicable to Fiona.

* * *

On the outside, the natural stone façade of Willow Hill looked much as it had for fifty years, during the time Carrie's grandparents had raised their family there, her mother had grown up and Carrie had spent her childhood holidays running between the homes of her grandparents and her aunts. The big, square Georgian house sat on a couple of acres of land on a high incline overlooking the sweeping pastures of County Cork, surrounded by landscaped gardens to the front and a well-tended kitchen garden to the south-facing rear.

Carrie swung in off the main road, tyres crunching on the gravel as she followed the driveway around to the car park at the side of the house. She stepped out of the car, all her senses assaulted. The clean tang of the summery air was infused with the scent of freshly cut grass. Late-afternoon sunshine bathed the countryside in a soft golden haze, and a chorus of birds chirped from the nearby orchard. Her spirits immediately felt lighter. The journey from Dublin had taken just over three hours thanks to the motorway, which was a huge improvement on the journeys she'd made as a child.

As Carrie stepped into the spacious hallway, her mind flooded with memories; a huge, sparkling, pine-scented Christmas tree, an aromatic turf fire, a drift of cold December air sweeping through the open hall door as her dad ferried through cases and bags bulging with presents, Carrie skipping around him, her mother's soft laughter and words of admiration for the decorated tree. Her smiling grandparents, coming to meet them. All gone now, they'd passed through this life and left it. *I miss you guys.* Carrie blinked, feeling suddenly alone and teary, wanting, ridiculously, the warm feeling of Mark holding her hand in his in the empty hall.

The black and white floor tiles were still there, and there was a polished wicker basket of logs arranged in the big marble fireplace. The mantelpiece now held scented candles and crystal awards, and the walls were decorated with framed qualifications and Spa of the Year awards. The reception desk held a vase of fresh flowers as well as pamphlets and leaflets listing the treatments available.

Evelyn Sullivan came out of the office behind the reception desk, where she'd been doing some paperwork. 'Well, look at you,' she said, coming around from behind the reception and throwing her arms open in welcome. 'It's lovely to see you here, Carrie.'

'I hope I'm not barging in …'

Evelyn put her hands on Carrie's shoulders and held her at arm's length. 'Don't start. Sean and I are delighted you're here. We've a bedroom ready for you, you're to do nothing but relax for the next few days, and this is the perfect place. You don't have to talk to us if you don't feel like it, you can spend your day lazing in the spa in your dressing gown and slippers. By the time you go home, you'll be a new woman. Just make sure you Twitter plenty. Or is it twit or tweet?'

'Are you not on Twitter yet?' Carrie grinned. 'You're missing out on a valuable opportunity to spread the word.'

'There, see? I knew you'd help us out! As for those eejits in Jade who let you walk away,' her voice dropped to a confidential tone, 'they're barking mad to have let you slip through their fingers. If you ever want a job and don't mind relocating … I'd be delighted to hand over some of the reins here. And Clare feels the same. She and Andrew are away in Portugal for a week, they'll be sorry to have missed you.'

Carrie smiled. 'I'm not expecting you to offer me a job. You've already done more than enough for me.'

'We're not doing you a favour, we could do with your marketing brains and some fresh ideas,' Evelyn said. 'And you'd be worked to the bone. I'm going to bring you around to show off some new facilities, and make sure the gang here know to allow you access to all areas, some of them won't have met you before, and, lastly, I'm going to book you in for a stress-busting massage tomorrow. How does that sound?' She looked at Carrie with warm concern in her eyes, and Carrie could have collapsed into her arms.

Her grandfather's construction supplies firm, begun in the outbuildings behind the main house, had long since relocated to a modern, purpose-built premises a couple of miles away. After both her grandparents had passed away, just over ten years ago, the inside of Willow Hill had been transformed into a luxury spa, keeping as many of the original features as possible. A glass passageway through a pretty landscaped area linked the back of the house to the outbuildings, which had been rebuilt to house a tranquillity pool, thermal suites and an outdoor vitality pool.

The large, south-facing Willow Hill kitchen still retained its homely atmosphere but had been remodelled and upgraded to cater for the healthy lunches and snacks the spa's clients needed. The living room and old playroom, where first Sylvie and then Carrie had played, had been converted into a farmhouse dining room, with views over the rolling pastures to the north and the distant sea to the south. The ground floor also held a relaxation area and luxury changing rooms, as well as a reception and a small office. Upstairs, the first-floor rooms were now top-of-the-range treatment rooms.

As soon as Evelyn had finished showing Carrie around and booked her in for twelve o'clock the following day, Carrie drove to Evelyn and Sean's spacious bungalow. It was set on an acre of land beside Willow Hill, a line of beech hedging marking the boundary between the properties. Up in the guest room, where Evelyn had left out towels and magazines, Carrie showered and changed, and had a relaxing evening meal with her uncle and aunt, and a glass of Sean's best Malbec, before falling into a lavender-scented bed for an early night. She wasn't going to think of anything – not her job, nor Mark, or even her mum and Luis, or what might have happened in 1980. Not tonight, at any rate. Within minutes, she was sound asleep.

She slept for hours and by the time she woke the following morning, both Evelyn and Sean had long left for their respective jobs. Carrie helped herself to fruit and yogurt and strolled to the spa through the connecting pathway. Her aunt welcomed her warmly, ushered her into the changing rooms and told her that Clodagh would be looking after her massage.

Carrie donned a big fluffy towelling robe, tying it around her waist, and almost fell asleep during the expert massage. Sometime in the afternoon, as she listened to music on her mobile, relaxing on a heated recliner and gazing out past the rear gardens and the undulating terrain down to the far-off sea, she began to realise that the tension she didn't even know she'd been holding was slowly but surely evaporating from every bone in her body.

She was glad of the distance, both physical and mental, between the shock of Mark's angry face the previous Sunday and now. Something about their last row was floating intangibly right there in front of her. It was more than his anger and the whiteness of his face. She went back over it again, replaying it in her head, trying not to get swept up in the emotion, and, after a while, it came to her. He had sounded resentful, almost jealous that someone else had managed to get through to Carrie in a way he hadn't. She would have to find some way to explain what had happened with Luis. She owed him that much at least.

She'd emailed Maria before she'd left for Cork and Maria had replied to say Luis was holding his own.

'Some days are better than others,' Maria wrote. 'He tires easily. But we are both very grateful that you came to visit. Luis is smiling at the thoughts of you going back to Willow Hill, close to where it all began.'

Luis had told her that they met in a sheltered spot in the sand dunes in the evenings. He knew it was quite sheltered from the sound of the waves and their voices. She knew where he meant. As children and teenagers, she and her cousins had swarmed down the track through farmland and woodland leading from Willow Hill to the sea. The same track had been there in her mother's time. Now it was closed up as a golf course had been built across it during the boom years, but there was nothing to stop her driving around to the cove and looking at it with fresh eyes, seeing where it had all happened.

'A belt of the sea air will do you good,' Evelyn said when she mentioned her plans that evening. 'It'll put some colour in your cheeks. I'll book you in for a facial in the late afternoon, so.'

'You're too good,' Carrie said. 'I owe you and Sean so much.'

It was on the tip of her tongue to say she'd called into Waldron Avenue, and really appreciated what they'd done for her, but she let it go for now. It would have meant explaining why she'd been there and she wasn't ready for that just yet. Evelyn was gazing at her with a faraway look in her eyes, the look that told her she was thinking of Sylvie and John.

'Wait until you get the bill,' her aunt said, laughing, pulling herself together. 'I hope you'll have your credit card handy or else you'll be cleaning the bins in the spa and helping in the kitchen.'

* * *

As she walked briskly along the beach, Carrie realised that there was no way of knowing which house Luis had stayed in all those years ago. There were several bungalows and cottages set back from the strand into the lee of the bluff, and others cheek by jowl in adjoining fields, but far more than there would have been in Luis' day. A few looked like they dated from the 1940s, others from the 1960s or

1970s, but these were all outnumbered by several modern holiday homes that had been built during the boom years.

The vista of the sea from the small, sheltered cove would have been much the same in Luis' day. Not that he had seen any of it. He'd told her that Sylvie had described it all to him, so he could paint a picture in his head. Carrie took out her mobile and took some photos. At least she could send something to Maria, who could describe the views to him afresh. As she looked out, it all seemed calm and placid but, as children, they'd been warned about the dangerous currents lurking underneath the surface, and the way the beach shelved steeply away a few hundred feet out.

After her walk, she sat for a while in the sand dunes, listening to the hiss of the sea, feeling the breeze running through her hair, trying to imagine what might have happened in her mother's life to make her fall into Luis' arms. Now that she was here, in and out of a Willow Hill filled with memories of her mother's laughing, happy face, it seemed more incomprehensible than ever.

Her route back from the cove took her past the graveyard where her parents were buried. She'd ignored it on the way down, but now she slowed her car to a crawl as she approached the wrought-iron entrance gate, wondering if she had the guts to go in. Some people claimed to get solace from visiting their loved ones' graves, that it was a kind of pilgrimage and healing. She didn't know if any of that would work for her as she'd never set foot in the cemetery since the day of the funeral. It was something else she could try, in an effort to face up to what had happened, she decided, pulling into the parking area by the side of the road.

The calmness of it all under the soft glow of mild spring sunshine surprised her, along with the warble of the birds, so joyful, considering the tears and heartbreak this small parcel of land had witnessed down through the years. Some of the graves were bedecked with flowers and mementoes, photographs of loved ones, a few decorated with teddies and colourful windmills. They were the ones that clutched at her heart. At least her parents had had a rich and full life. She saw their grave two or three rows ahead, the names etched in gold on a black marble headstone, and she faltered, unable to go any closer to the spot where they had been put into the ground.

Five years, five days, five minutes.

What difference did the length of time make? They would never come back, but she was here still, a legacy of their love. She felt suddenly alive in this moment, the sun gentle on her face, the twitter of the birds floating across the air, and she had an urgent need to grab the life she had by the throat and wring the very best from it. She drew in deep gulps of air and turned to leave. Threading through the pathway between the graves, her attention was caught by one particular headstone and what was inscribed on it: 'Molly McCann, aged fifty one, 30th January 1976.

Her beloved daughter Anna, aged twelve, March 1962.'

How sad. What a tragedy for Molly and her family. But there was more. Resting on the grave, balanced against the base of the headstone, was a separate marble plaque in the shape of a heart. The inscription and date jumped out at her: 'In loving memory of a beloved daughter Beth Gilmore, lost at sea, September 1980.'

Carrie froze at the sight of the name and the date. Something icy trickled down her spine. Beth. A name that was on the back of her mother's old photographs. A friend of hers. Molly's daughter? And the date – was this what she'd been looking for? Someone close to Sylvie had died, Luis told her, and she was angry with him for wanting to end his own life.

This had to be the answer she'd been looking for. Her devastated mother had fallen into Luis' arms seeking comfort after her good friend had died. 'Lost at sea' – what exactly did that mean? Whatever had happened to Beth had surely been a tragedy.

Chapter Twenty-eight

April–July 1980

When they returned to Dublin and began to live in the house of her dreams, Beth felt she was acting some kind of part. On the surface, Adam was kind and pleasant, taking care of all the bills and expenses. He went out to work each morning in a freshly ironed shirt and a good suit. In the evenings, they had dinner together, Beth secretly relieved with her skill in the kitchen. They watched television or read, and sometimes Adam brought work home from the bank, staying on at the kitchen table to deal with it. He was also studying for his accountancy exams and he went to college two nights a week. At the weekends, he brought her shopping for groceries, out for occasional meals and sometimes to the movies. To the outside world, they looked like a newly married couple in love. What was happening in their bedroom stayed there, behind closed doors. Sometimes when she looked at Adam, she wondered if she was dreaming it all. But the bruises on her body told her she wasn't.

She thought of Sylvie's words: 'I didn't think Adam was the marrying kind,' and wondered what she had really meant by that.

'Why don't we have Sylvie and John over some night,' she suggested when they were a month married. She'd just cleared away the dinner plates and Adam was relaxing with a cup of tea before he opened his books.

He didn't turn around to look at her, but she could see the rigid set of his shoulders. 'Sylvie and John? Why?'

'Why not? They are our friends and they'll be getting married soon themselves.'

'*Your* friends, you mean ...' he said in a faintly dismissive tone of voice. He let that sink in for a minute and then he went on in his persuasive tone of voice. 'Beth, we're making a whole new life for ourselves as far removed from the life you had in Cork as you can imagine. We need to be rubbing shoulders with the right kind of people, people who can help us advance, and not hanging on to people from our childhood.'

'They're not just people,' Beth insisted, 'they're our *friends*. They came to our wedding. I've known Sylvie since ... oh gosh, I was six years old.'

'Precisely,' he said, rising to his feet and taking her into his arms. 'We'll have new friends, friends we have a lot more in common with than people you grew up with. I told you I never really took to Sylvie,' he said. 'I find her very irritating. Nor did I like the way she looked at me.'

Once again, Beth was torn, not knowing whether to feel a tiny bit relieved that he hadn't fallen under Sylvie's vivacious spell, or a little sad that her husband and best friend didn't seem to get along.

'As a matter of fact,' Adam continued, 'I wasn't going to spring this on you just yet, but I'm hoping to invite some bank people to dinner.'

'Like out of the branch?' she asked. She'd met them for lunch one day, her friends from the typing pool, but it had been very awkward. Now that she was *married* to the junior manager, the strain had been evident. He'd been right to suggest that she leave her job – after the lunch, she knew for certain that she couldn't have continued to work in the same bank as Adam.

'No,' he said. 'Friends of my father who will be useful to me in the future. And, by the way, I won't be able to make Sylvie and John's wedding. I have bank exams on that day and you know how important they are. You can always go to the wedding yourself if it means that much to you.'

Even though it did mean a lot, she knew she wouldn't go. She knew by his face not to. And, after all, Adam was on his way to the top, a vice-presidency, a seat on the board. She owed him everything for marrying her and securing her future. She would never have to worry about money again. Mind you, Adam was holding on to the purse strings. He took care of everything. She didn't have to worry her pretty little head, as he said, checking the bills that came in through the letterbox.

She didn't know what was going to happen, though, when her savings were gone. She'd been using them to buy a few necessities for herself, but they wouldn't last forever and before they were depleted, she would have to find a way to talk to Adam about some kind of an allowance or pocket money for herself. It's not something that had seemed important before they'd married.

She'd raised the subject of getting a part-time job somewhere, but he hadn't been keen.

'Beth … you don't really need to go out to work. I'm earning more than enough to support us. Besides, it doesn't really suit me or the position I'm going to be in to have you out at work. My mother never worked outside the home, her job was to take care of her husband and me. And if you look at the lengthening dole queues, it wouldn't be right if you took a job you didn't really need and deprived someone else of the work.'

Beth wished she could have talked to her mother. Though her mother would probably have said what everyone else seemed to think – Beth was very lucky to be married to Adam. She tried to talk to Sylvie and, without telling him, she had her friend over for lunch one day when she was back from her honeymoon. To her surprise, Beth felt envious when she heard all about Sylvie's big country wedding down in Willow Hill and her short honeymoon in London.

'I'm really sorry we weren't able to go,' Beth said. 'Adam had exams that day, and I needed to be here for him. He gets very nervous.'

Sylvie's eyes were expressionless. 'Yes, it was a pity, I'd love to have had both of you there.'

'Even Adam?'

'Yes, of course, even Adam. He's your husband now, he would have been very welcome.'

'So you like him after all? I didn't think you were all that gone on him,' Beth said, wondering if she dared admit that Adam thought Sylvie had been flirting with him. She didn't believe him for one moment. Not when Sylvie had John. Adam had just mistaken her friend's effervescence for something else.

Sylvie smiled. 'I thought he whisked you up the aisle in a bit of a rush, but look at your fabulous home, he seems to be taking care of you all right.'

'It's rather nice, isn't it?' Beth glanced around her kitchen with the brand-new fitted cupboards, acres of worktop and gleaming appliances. How could she admit that it didn't feel like her home? That it was like feeling her way around an elaborate stage set.

'You don't know how lucky you are,' Sylvie said. 'You have everything you could need and this house is like a palace. We have to gut and renovate everything in Waldron Avenue. We'll be a while waiting for a carpet for the stairs, and we're still sitting on two armchairs. But we're happy. You must be really happy, Beth. Imagine how proud your mother would have been. Molly would have given her eye teeth for a kitchen like this. She must have sprinkled some magic dust on you from above.'

Beth couldn't bear to think about her mother. 'Don't laugh, but sometimes I miss going out to work,' she admitted.

'Yes, I thought you were a bit hasty to give up your job,' Sylvie said. 'I suppose you're bound to miss the office, but I can see how busy you must be running this big house, and the good thing is you won't have to worry about childcare when your family comes along or make the hard decision between working or staying at home. You know you can afford to stay at home. That's if you are planning on a family?'

Beth felt her face going bright red at the reference to sex. She felt suddenly choked. How could she admit to Sylvie that things were far from right in the bedroom? Unspoken questions teemed through her head. *What made you think Adam wasn't the right one for me? Was there anything apart from a newspaper article that made you think he wasn't the marrying kind or good enough for me? How can I tell you that my dreams are falling down around me already and I don't know how to put it right?* 'We are, of course,' she said smoothly. 'It just hasn't happened yet.'

'Well, you know what to do,' Sylvie smiled.

'What do you mean?' Surely no one knew what was going on between her and Adam? Was it written on her face?

'Keep trying,' Sylvie laughed. 'Make the most of it. I'm on the pill. We don't want to start a family until we're more financially secure and have the house in order. I can't believe the freedom it gives, compared to our mother's generation. We can do it as often as we like without fear of pregnancy.'

'That's great.' Beth was overcome with another unexpected stab of jealousy. Sylvie spoke with all the confidence of a woman in love, a woman having regular, satisfying sex. With John. Beth was horrified to think she might be still carrying a torch for him in her heart when she was now married to Adam.

'And you'll be wonderful.' Sylvie was still talking. 'Warm and motherly, just like your own mum.'

It hadn't happened, Beth knew, because what went for love-making in their marriage wasn't happening properly. She'd tried different approaches, making it her mission to break down the barriers between them. A reserved man, Adam had never been one for casual touching and kissing and she'd kept her distance from him ever since the disaster of their honeymoon sex and everything else that had followed. Maybe that had been the wrong thing to do. She had then tried losing her inhibitions, being more tactile with him, coming over to him at the dinner table and hugging him, kissing the side of his neck. A couple of times, he'd hugged her back, but she'd sensed it was empty of warmth.

Goaded by her jealousy over Sylvie's happy sex life, the next time she was in the city centre she plucked up the courage to buy a couple of books on health and sexuality in a large bookstore, convinced a spotlight was shining on her when she picked them up and hurried with them to the cash desk as though she was holding red-hot coals. She bundled them into the end of her shopping bag, in a fever of anxiety, until she reached home and looked around for a suitable hiding place.

The hot press. She wrapped them in a spare pillow case and slid them in between the piles of carefully arranged bedding and towels. The following afternoon, when she knew Adam would be late home because of a college lecture, she took them into the spare bedroom and with a thumping heart, began to read.

* * *

'Adam, I think … in the bedroom …' Her voice dwindled to a whisper and faltered.

Adam put down his fork and stared at her with an irritable frown. 'Go on …'

She should have waited until they were away from the table. He hated his meal being interrupted before he was finished. She had made a big, creamy pavlova for dessert and he was still tucking into his. Bad timing. It's just that the words had been on the tip of her tongue all week and now they had gushed out of their own accord.

'I was just thinking …'

'Yes?'

'We might … it could be … different.'

'What could be different?'

'Us. You and me. I'd like to see your face when we …' She swallowed.

His face darkened with anger. She thought he was going to explode.

'See, Adam, I don't know if I make you happy … and if we want to have children …' Her voice trailed away at the chill in his eyes.

'But you do make me happy, Beth,' he said, looking at her closely. 'What on earth made you think you didn't?'

She was nonplussed. 'I do?'

'Yes, of course. Do I make you happy?' he asked, his eyes watching her thoughtfully.

'Oh, yes, yes, Adam.'

'But you thought it could be different. Why was that? Who were you talking to?' He shot out this comment so fast that she didn't have time to control her reaction, and her face went brick red.

His expression darkened. 'You were talking to someone. About us.'

'No, I wasn't, honestly. I just read it in an article. In a woman's magazine. That was it. It was an article about … about becoming pregnant.'

'Show me.'

'Well, em, I don't have it now, I guess I threw it away in the rubbish.'

'An article.'

'Yes.'

'In a woman's magazine.'

'Yes.' She held his gaze, but her voice was a whisper.

He pushed away his plate so that it slid across the table and rose to his feet. He went over to her and, grasping her by the arm, lifted her to her feet.

'Something different, you said.' His face was stiff with rage.

'Yes, Adam, but—'

'How's this for something different?'

He twirled her around and pushed her face down across the table, so that her hair trailed into the remains of the Pavlova. His hand locked around the back of her neck, securing her there.

'*Nooo*, Adam …'

'Shut up.'

'Please, noooo …'

He ignored her protest, as her flailing hands reached behind her and tried to push him away. But she was too stunned to protest when his free hand shoved her skirt up to her waist and yanked down her panties, too shocked to cry out when he hit her forcefully – twice, three times, four times … she lost count – too frightened to say anything when she felt his feet kick at her ankles to spread her legs apart, but she heard a whimper tear out of her throat at the sound of him opening his zip.

Afterwards, he told her how sorry he was, he didn't know what had possessed him, he loved her, he really loved her. It would never happen again.

Chapter Twenty-nine

'They never found the body,' Sean Sullivan said.

Carrie shivered. Evening sunshine flooded through the dining room. Beyond the long picture window, the sandstone patio was colourful with tubs of primroses and spring flowers. A row of delicate silver birch trees bounded the easterly aspect of the rear garden, green fuzz licked by the low sunshine. It was hard to be sitting here, tasting slow-roasted lamb and sipping merlot, while her thoughts were with a young woman whose life had been cut so short.

'It must have been very sad for everyone,' she said.

Sean lifted the wine to refill Carrie's glass, but she put her hand up.

'Pour away, Sean, Carrie needs a drink listening to all that sad talk,' Evelyn said, helping herself to some cauliflower cheese. 'What started all this chat off anyway?'

'I did, when I asked Sean about Beth's memorial plaque,' Carrie said. 'Mum never talked about her, but I vaguely remember her name and I've seen her in photos with my mother.'

Sean explained. 'Beth practically lived in Willow Hill. She and Sylvie were good friends. Beth's mother Molly was housekeeper here until she died, then Beth stepped into her shoes until she went to Dublin. But after that we hardly saw her, if at all. She surprised the lot of us by marrying very quickly and very well.'

'How did the tragedy happen?' Carrie asked.

'I'm not sure,' Sean said. 'Andrew and I, we were in Canada that autumn. Sylvie was here in Willow Hill looking after Mum, who'd had an operation.'

Carrie's heart squeezed. It fitted with what Luis had said.

'We only heard about Beth second hand,' Sean continued. 'She was a good swimmer, but she must have ventured out too far, where the beach shelves quite sharply. There's a dangerous current beyond the headland as well. It's all too easy to be swept away. When we came home at Christmas, I remember being warned not to ask Sylvie about it because she was very upset.'

'She must have been in bits,' Carrie mused.

'Beth's husband is someone else who was very cut up,' Evelyn said. 'They'd only been six months married.'

'God. Did you know him? Was he from around here?'

'No, she met him in Dublin. I never even knew Beth, I only got to know Sean the following year,' Evelyn said. 'And I didn't meet Beth's husband until years later, when he came to the funeral.'

Going by the delicate tone in her voice, Carrie didn't need to ask whose funeral she meant.

'For all his wealth and good looks, Adam never married again,' Evelyn continued. 'According to interviews in the newspaper, even recent ones, he never got over it. You met him, Carrie.'

'I did?'

Immediately Evelyn's hand covered hers. 'You won't remember, of course, kiddo. He came up to me after the funeral and asked to be introduced to you, so he could express his condolences. He told me how close he and Beth had been to your parents once upon a time. Sylvie had been Beth's bridesmaid. They'd gone out as a foursome, but it had never been the same after Beth went missing. He found it too upsetting to socialise with Sylvie and John. He was a lovely, really charming man. It was all such a terrible shame.'

'It was very sad,' Sean shook his head. 'For such a shy girl, Beth had a brilliant future ahead of her, something she could only have dreamed of. I mean, look where she'd be now.'

'Why, where would she be now?'

'Married to Adam Gilmore, you know, one of Ireland's biggest noises in financial services and private equity,' Evelyn said. 'He has golden fingers in a few golden pies. Unlike a lot of them, his company survived the recession. Gilcorp – you must have heard of it.'

'The name rings a bell, I think I've seen him on the telly, all right. So he's the guy who married Beth?'

'He is. His group looks after tax and accountancy as well, including your parents' estate.'

'Really?' Carrie felt a stab of annoyance that she knew so little about her parents' affairs.

'He offered to help us out, around the time of the funeral. We were only too glad, weren't we, Sean?'

'Absolutely.'

'There was a lot of red tape. He worked with your parents' solicitors and even came to Waldron Avenue to help us go through the paperwork, and make sure we had everything accounted for.'

'That's what you call going the extra mile,' Sean said. 'It's a pity more of the financial wizards in this country, or should I say what passes for them, don't follow his example.'

It was the opening Carrie had been waiting for. 'Is there much stuff here belonging to Mum and Dad?'

'You don't have to worry about any of that,' Evelyn said.

'I might like to … just have a look,' she said.

'We've all the important paperwork here, certificates, annual tax returns, solicitor's letters, and everything about Waldron Avenue,' Sean said. 'You're welcome to look any time, Carrie, it's all in a big lever-arch file in a cabinet in the study.'

'I might take a look before I go back to Dublin.'

She was thirty years of age. It was about time she faced up to certain things. She hadn't even seen her parents' death certificates.

'And there are more family photographs, belonging to your grandmother, ones with your mum as a child that we cleared out of the presses in Willow Hill before the spa went in. They're all stored together.'

'Good.'

'Anyway, enough of this sad talk, let's talk about the present,' Evelyn said. 'Another thing we'd like you to do is set up the spa on Twitter. See? We're really slave drivers behind it all,' she joked.

Carrie smiled. 'I'll do that first thing in the morning and it'll be a pleasure, you've so much to offer. I can't believe you managed without it for so long.'

* * *

Carrie went straight over to the spa after breakfast the following morning and took some photographs on her mobile. She went into Evelyn's office and logged on to the PC, where she set up a Twitter account for the business. She tweeted about it herself and asked all her followers to retweet and give them a follow.

@carriecassidy: You can't afford to miss #luxury #indulgence #totalbliss @WillowHillSpa

One of her followers came back almost immediately.

@happyduck: sounds great, enjoy.

Whoever @happyduck was, she was always quick to respond, following Carrie's tweets with supportive comments.

That evening, when Sean and Evelyn had gone to the theatre in

Kinsale, she decided to brave the cabinet in the study. The first things she found were folders full of old photographs. They dated back to the time her mother had been a baby. Carrie had looked at them as a curious child, but had forgotten about them. Now she gazed at them, feeling a soft ribbon of love untangle inside her. And something else. The fashions of the 1950s were not to be laughed at. She looked at Granny Sullivan and Molly, in the kitchen, in the sitting room, at Christmas or on the children's First Holy Communion days, and there was something gracious, womanly and glamorous in their clothes and their hairstyles.

If she were still working at Jade, she'd tell them to take a reference from the 1950s for their new branding. It was something that she could suggest for the spa, though, embellishing what they had with a touch of luxury, retro-glamour.

There were copies of photographs that Carrie had also seen in Waldron Avenue, her mother's birthday parties, surrounded by half a dozen friends, including Beth. She stared at Beth's face, her heart snagging at the fate that befell the young woman. Beside Sylvie, whose sparkle and energy jumped out of the picture, Beth looked plain and composed, timid even, in the slight dip of her head, her hair falling like a curtain around her face. Another folder contained photographs Carrie hadn't seen before – several photos of Sylvie, John and Beth down at the cove and in Willow Hill, which looked like they'd been taken with a polaroid instant camera, and then there were photos of Beth's wedding day.

Carrie recognised St Stephen's Green in the background, and the photos included her parents and grandparents along with Beth and a very handsome man. Beth was wearing a simple white dress with a lace bolero and a Juliet cap on her long blonde hair. She carried a small flower bouquet. She looked a little overawed, standing beside her new husband. There was also one of Beth and her mother, arm in arm.

Carrie had never seen any of these photographs in Waldron Avenue. For some reason, her mother hadn't kept copies of the wedding of her good friend. Too upset after her death, Carrie guessed. Which supported the idea that she'd fallen into Luis' arms purely out of shock. She replaced the wedding photographs and saw an envelope labelled 'Inquest Report'. Something else that Sean and Evelyn must have decided to spare her from. For some reason, it had been put away with the old photographs instead of the lever arch file. She was on the point of opening it but stopped. Not this evening. Looking at the photographs had drained her.

Carrie couldn't settle to sleep that night, her mind was racing. Her mother had also told Luis she was at a crossroads of sorts and needed to make a decision. Had that anything to do with her betrayal of her husband? Had she ever admitted it to John or had she made the decision to put it all behind her and start again? At least one of her questions had been answered. Her mother had been so devastated by her friend's death that she'd been temporarily unbalanced enough to sleep with Luis. According to Sean, Beth had practically lived in Willow Hill. They must have been like sisters, Sylvie and Beth.

Chapter Thirty

August 1980

'Adam's a very lucky man,' Teresa Graham said.

'Hear, hear,' Tom, her husband, agreed.

'A lovely home and a beautiful wife, *and* she can cook like an angel. What more could any man want?'

Tom proposed a toast. 'To Adam and Beth, may you have a long and happy life,'

'To Adam and Beth.'

There was the sound of glasses clinking as the visiting couples sitting around the polished mahogany dining table toasted the hosts. From across the table, Adam half-smiled and tilted his head slightly in Beth's direction in a gesture of appreciation. Beth was sitting beside Margaret MacBride, who was here with her husband Eoin. Both Eoin and Tom held senior positions in the same bank as Adam's father. He, too, was here tonight, along with Adam's mother. Beth knew she was being carefully scrutinised as to her suitability to support Adam in his rise to the top as both a hostess and his wife.

And, for once, in front of her critical in-laws, Beth had done something right. She hadn't spoken out of turn, she'd been perfectly mannerly and charming to all her visitors. She'd agreed with

everything Adam had said and hadn't voiced a different opinion
– though, in truth, she didn't have a different opinion. She wasn't
informed enough. She found it was best to stay quiet in case she
said something stupid. They all read the *Financial Times.* They were
talking about the recession and the government, and politicians she
hardly knew; however, she wasn't stupid enough not to grasp from
their chat that they had property developers and senior politicians
in the palm of their hands, through bankrolling their various pet
projects.

No one could fault her beautifully arranged table décor, and
the food she had cooked was superb. She'd had a full week with
nothing to occupy her mind except the planning and preparation
for this dinner party. A full week during which she'd needed lots of
distraction.

Adam had barely spoken to her since the evening he'd beaten
and raped her across the kitchen table – and it *was* rape. She hadn't
consented. She'd cried for him to stop. She'd been sore for days after
that episode. But because they were married, he'd broken no law.
The evening after it happened, he'd acted as though it had never
taken place. He'd been his usual self as he told her of his plans for
the dinner party. He'd opened his wallet and peeled off some notes,
telling her to get her hair done and buy some new clothes to wear.

'You're beautiful, Beth,' he'd said. 'I want you to do yourself
justice. I want to show you off.' His eyes had looked lost for a
moment, and she wondered what he was really thinking behind his
composed façade.

She'd put his money away, unused.

'Can you help me, Margaret,' she said, turning to the woman
sitting beside her at the table, 'I'd like to find out more about the
best place to buy my linens.'

* * *

The following week, he came home early. She was in the spare bedroom, sitting on the bed, reading a chapter on female sexual response in her book when she heard his key in the lock. Her heart fluttered into her throat. She slammed the book shut and shoved it hard under the bed, sending it flying. Then she smoothed the coverlet and came out onto the landing, her footsteps as light as possible so he wouldn't guess where she'd been. She began to walk down the stairs, her legs like jelly.

'Adam? You're home early …'

'What were you up to?' he asked her, standing in the hall, watching her come down the stairs. It was as though he sensed her anxiety, not surprising considering it was pouring out of her in waves.

'Nothing.' Fear jumping in her chest. 'Why?'

'You look a bit flushed.'

'I've been dusting. The bedrooms,' she said. She didn't look like she'd been dusting. There was no sign of a cloth or spray in her hands.

He looked at her blankly for a moment. He was beautifully dressed in a navy suit and white shirt. He had a navy-and-yellow striped tie. Then he said, 'You can leave that for now. I've a surprise for you.'

She reached the bottom of the stairs. He was smiling. In that moment, he reminded her of the Adam she'd fallen in love with. She was painfully conscious of the gap that existed between that naive, innocent Beth McCann and the disillusioned Mrs Adam Gilmore.

'Out front,' he said, jingling a set of car keys.

Out front, slung across a lot of the space in their driveway, was a brand new car, a long navy silhouette gleaming in the sun.

'Nice, isn't it?'

'It's lovely, Adam. Is this yours?'

'It's ours, Beth. I'll arrange to have you insured on it.'

'Me?' She felt faint. She didn't even have a licence. The prospect of driving this magnificent car was thrilling and daunting. If her mother could see her now …

'But not just yet,' Adam said. 'You'll need lots of practice, and you'll have to pass your test first.'

She wondered how that was going to happen, or how she was supposed to get some practice. 'Maybe I could go for driving lessons, with a registered instructor.'

He smiled. 'That's if I find someone I can trust enough to allow my wife in the car with them.'

John Cassidy had taught Sylvie to drive, as soon as he'd bought a second-hand Renault. She'd passed her test first time. She knew John would probably be kind enough to give Beth a few lessons, but she also knew she daren't suggest it.

'It would have to be someone I approve of,' he went on. 'You're very precious to me, Beth. Don't ever forget that.' She knew by the intense way he looked at her that he meant every word.

Adam jingled his car keys. 'We'll go for a spin, show it off to the world.'

They looked good, taking the road out towards the coast, the picturesque route from the village of Blackrock out to Dalkey, where Dublin Bay shimmered in the evening haze, like a silvery sheet unrolling off to the horizon. It brought her back, for a long nostalgic moment, to the view of the far-off sea from the kitchen window in Willow Hill.

Her heart squeezed. Another life. Already long ago. Thinking of Willow Hill was like looking through a telescope at an old, nostalgic Christmas card that depicted a warm, secure scene. A bygone scene. She blinked and inhaled the cloying scent of new leather coming from inside the car. She thought about John and Sylvie and their Renault. It rattled a lot and bits had fallen off and Sylvie had made her laugh when she recounted some of the times it had broken down on them. She'd even had to take off her tights one day when they were up in the Dublin Mountains and John used them as an emergency fan belt to get them to the nearest garage. They hoped they'd get another year out of it.

She hardly saw Sylvie any more, they moved in different circles, but her friend made sure to keep in touch.

They'd give their eye teeth for a car like this. Beth could see the enviable picture she and Adam made, the powerful car smoothly taking the inclines, the thrum of the engine, and the couple sitting in it; they could be in an advertisement for the perfect life on the television. Almost. She wondered how Sylvie would feel, sitting in a car like this with John. On top of the world, surely. She wondered what it was like, to be the kind of wife who looked forward to sex with her husband, to be making love as often as you could. She wondered what it was like to go to bed with someone like John. She looked at Adam's hand gripping the steering wheel, and found it hard to imagine those hands on her body in a slow caress.

* * *

The book – *Everywoman: A Gynaecological Guide for Life* – came hurtling through the air so that it landed on the ironing board, right on top of Adam's blue shirt.

She froze.

'What's all this about?'

She faced him. His eyes were very blue. Not blue like the sea, blue like chips of glass.

'It's just …' She straightened her shoulders. 'Look, Adam, it's mostly about women's health, our bodies, what happens when we get pregnant. That sort of stuff. I need something like this … to give me information for when I get pregnant. She gave a forced laugh that came out like a squeak. 'Otherwise, I'd be clueless.'

Silence. She waited for the explosion. She heard the clock over the window ticking off the seconds. It had been a wedding present from a cousin of Adam's. 'Wishing you every happiness for the future', the card had said. It had had a silver picture of wedding bells on it. She had kept all their wedding cards with their lovely messages for a bright, new future. They were tied up with white ribbon from her flower bouquet and kept in a box in the wardrobe.

Then, calmly, 'Is this the "magazine" you were telling me about?' She nodded.

He picked it up again, flicked through the pages, pausing now and again to glance at various diagrams. 'You should have told me. Why did you keep it a secret?' His voice was neutral.

It was like there were two Adams: the husband who was bright and ambitious enough for both of them, who never complained about the office but simply worked hard to pay all the bills and keep up a good home, the husband who said he loved her; and then there was the dark Adam, as she began to think of him. The Adam she didn't recognise, who wanted vastly different things from the intimacy in their marriage than she did.

'I didn't think you'd be interested.'

'I'm interested in everything about my wife. Everything. Take care of that shirt, will you? It's one of my best.'

He turned on his heel and marched out of the kitchen, taking the book with him. She stood immobile for long moments listening to the ticking of the clock before she picked up the iron and swished it across the collar of his shirt.

* * *

She watched the level of brandy in the bottle being reduced inch by inch, as he refilled his glass time and time again. It was the expensive brandy Tom and Teresa Graham had brought to the dinner party, just last week.

Later, she lay in bed, dreading the inevitable, knowing she had nowhere to go. The money in her post office account was dwindling. She was now hiding it away from Adam. And who would listen to her, let alone believe her? She was the luckiest girl in the world. Too bad if she didn't like the way her husband preferred sex.

She felt him pushing up her nightdress and she waited for him to stab himself into her, hoping he'd get it over with quickly. She was confused when she felt his hand going around her neck and his knee in the small of her back, locking her into place. She heard a rush of something coming through the air before her buttocks seared with pain as his belt connected with them.

'*Nooo*, Adam, please ...'

She struggled to get away, but he was too strong for her. Through a mist of pain and outrage, she heard him talking. She had been bold and needed to be punished. He would kill her with his bare hands if she dared to tell anyone. Did she understand what he was saying? She bit down hard on the soft inside of her lip. She tasted blood. She thought of the view from the kitchen window in Willow Hill. Especially around now, in the summer. How beautiful the blue-grey sea looked in the distance beyond the yellow rim of gorse-frilled fields. She could be there, now, in her mind, instead of here. She didn't have to be here at all.

Even when he pushed inside her and told her he loved her, and thanked her for letting him do that, and he was sorry if he hurt her, but she had really given him a shock, gloating over books like that behind his back, and the pictures in them, she imagined herself walking in the garden at Willow Hill and knew she had the power to be anywhere, or anyone ...

* * *

It only registered with her two days later. How had Adam managed to find her book? It had been thrown under the bed in the spare room, and she'd left it there for a day or so, feeling it was safe enough from his eyes. How come he'd stumbled across it? What had he been doing in the room that had caused him to look under the bed? Adam left all the housework up to her. The question ran around and around in her head.

She picked a morning when he said he'd be extra busy in the office. There were meetings on and talk of promotion, he said, and he was determined to do his best. He thanked Beth for his crisp, clean shirt. He lifted her chin and told her she was a great wife and that he loved her.

She waited half an hour after he had left and then went into the spare room. It was simply furnished with a single bed, a built-in wardrobe and a chest of drawers. The single bed was pushed against the wall and Beth got down on the floor and looked underneath. Nothing. Just a few blobs of dust on the surface of the carpet. She was about to get up when she noticed that in one of the corners, the edge of carpet seemed to have come slightly away from its anchoring grips. It took her a while to pull out the bed, she had to inch it out bit by bit, but eventually she had it dragged out enough to check the carpet. Climbing across the bed, she stood in the space where it had been. In the corner by the window, the carpet *was* loose. She lifted it and pulled it all back by about three feet, the autumn-shaded carpet together with the felt backing, revealing the floorboards. And something else.

Magazines. Carefully lined up under the carpet. About four of them.

She wasn't quick enough to avert her eyes. She saw immediately what they were about. She thought it was funny that marital rape wasn't against the law, but what she saw in the magazines probably was. There were also loose photographs inside one of the magazines.

Photos of young women and men, together, some of them barely over the age of consent. At first, she couldn't make out what exactly she was looking at, with the hot mist in front of her eyes. Then she hurriedly replaced them, a scalding embarrassment washing over her.

She made it to the bathroom just in time. After she was sick, she looked around that room as well. Something prickled at the back of her skull when she thought of the time he spent in the bathroom after his attempts at sex. Eventually she found two of them, rolled up, on top of the cistern and slightly wedged in behind it, way out of her sight and out of her reach. She wouldn't have found them, except her instinct made her bring in the step ladder from the garage to check the only place she couldn't reach.

She wasn't his wife, not in a true sense. She wasn't enough. She would never, ever be enough. No matter how much love she had in her heart, it would never be enough. The house closed in on her. The beautiful house of her dreams.

Chapter Thirty-one

'I think the spa bookings are up already thanks to your campaign,' Evelyn said, when Carrie came through the door on Thursday afternoon.

Carrie smiled. 'Campaign? Hang on, it's only in its infancy. It'll take a while to build up a good following and spread the word.'

'What would you like today? Can I book you in for anything? We've a couple of spare slots. Facial? Massage?'

'Thanks, but I'm just going for a swim,' Carrie said, 'then I'm going to laze on a lounger for a while. Keep your appointments for the paying customer. I can put it out on Twitter that you have spare slots, but they're going fast and it's first come, first served.'

'Gosh, looks like you'll be keeping us on our toes.'

'Absolutely. You'll need extra staff by the time I'm in full flow.'

'Oh, wow.' Evelyn waved a brochure in front of her face as though she was in danger of passing out.

Carrie went through to the dressing rooms. Taking a towel with her, and wearing her swimsuit under her robe and a pair of spa slippers, she walked through the glass-enclosed passageway out to the pool area, where the dim lighting made water seem like black silk, illuminated by small coloured lights around the perimeter of the pool.

She took off her robe, drew a deep breath, closed her eyes and slipped into the water. For a while she just floated, sliding through the water, emptying her mind, her movements languid, being aware of nothing but the caress of the warm water against her skin and her weightless limbs. She swam over to the Jacuzzi area, letting the water bubble up around her, gently massaging her damp skin, keeping her buoyed. Then it was back to the main body of the pool, and more floating on the darkened surface while she thought of nothing at all.

After that, Carrie took off her wet swimsuit and snuggled into her towelling robe, and in the relaxation area she stretched out on a warmed lounger with a view of the wild-flower garden, and beyond that the countryside, sloping down as far as the rim of the sea in the distance. From here, it resembled a benign strip of pale blue painted between lush green fields and the paler sky on the horizon.

How had it happened? How had the sea taken Beth? Was that why they'd been warned as children to be vigilant?

She needed to take it easy this morning, because for the first time since she'd arrived in Willow Hill, she felt limp and exhausted. She hadn't slept well, her dreams interrupted by images of the girl with the timid face, who'd been innocent of the cruel fate awaiting her. Carrie had tossed and turned, the photographs she'd seen of Beth and her mother coming between her and sleep. She tried not to think too much of her mother running into another man's arms, such was her desolation at losing her friend. It had been very short-lived and her mother had obviously made a supreme effort to put it all behind her when she returned home to Waldron Avenue, to the extent that she never even spoke of her friend or the terrible tragedy. Her parents had always seemed settled and happy, their marriage so solid and impregnable that she'd taken it for granted. They'd been four years married before Carrie had been born, so she'd no way of knowing what life had been like for them in those early years.

Then at one time during the night, disorientated from her

dreams, she'd lain in that semi-conscious zone between waking and sleeping, and thought she was still at home in Faith Crescent, in bed with Mark. She'd rolled over, half-expecting to come up against the reassuring heat of his body lying next to hers. Instead there was cold, empty space. Bed was the worst place to entertain memories of Mark, because they inevitably led to what it had been like with him. Warm, delicious and sensual.

And now, even though she was lying on a heated lounger, something icy cold flared through her body at the way she'd ended things between them, leaving a bitter taste in her mouth. She'd stamped all over him, despite the way he'd loved and cared for her.

* * *

Later, she found herself drawn back to the graveyard, bringing on impulse some fresh spring flowers. She placed them on Molly McCann's grave, right in front of Beth's plaque. Then drawing together every atom of courage she possessed, she took faltering footsteps across to her parents' grave. Her eyes slid across the inscription on the headstone, unable to look at it too closely. She was so tense she thought she was about to snap in two; she looked down at the pebbles covering the surface of the grave, still unable to comprehend that the parents she had loved with all her heart were buried several feet deep underneath.

She thought of her dad, years ago, drawing a smaller circle inside the big circle.

'And this is you, Carrie,' he'd said. 'You're part of us, and always with us.'

At no time since they'd perished had she felt them around or imagined they were with her. There was just a cold, silent emptiness in the space where they'd loved and laughed and held her close. She wondered what they would have said to her, if they'd had one more opportunity to talk. Or if they'd known, on that fateful flight, that they'd just minutes left, what would have been their parting words? They'd surely have repeated that they loved her – but was there anything else they'd have wanted her to know, to help her wring the best out of a life that had become dull and so very, very sour?

Be happy.

The words rose up inside herself; she didn't imagine for one moment that they'd been whispered by a ghostly spirit hovering overhead. The words had come from the part of her that knew the vital essence of her parents, which was as intrinsically familiar to her as her own life blood.

Be happy.

Two simple words, but they resonated inside her and she felt a tension melt away, like an invisible straitjacket falling off.

Chapter Thirty-two

August 1980

He loved Beth. He really did. It was just that, sometimes, she overstepped the mark.

He wasn't going to follow in his father's footsteps. At least, that's what he'd thought. He'd grown up to the sounds of his father's fists, sometimes his belt, connecting with his mother's flesh in the late-hour quiet of their bedroom. As a young child, he'd opened the door one night, not knowing what he was hearing. In his confusion, he didn't know what to make of the mounds of pale flesh and disarrayed clothing on the bed. His father, standing by the bed, belt in his hand, had let out a roar. Then, the bundle of disorder shifted and turned around and his mother's face had appeared above it all, scaring him. She had told him to go back to bed, her dull voice so at odds with the electric charge in the room that it chilled him. After that he did his best to shut his ears to the noise and to blank from his mind the sight of her face and the flat sound of her voice.

He also knew what it felt like to be thrashed, at the hands of both his father and the stern, disciplined teachers – what had passed for committed teachers – in the upmarket boarding school he'd attended in his teens, following in his father's footsteps. The worst time had been when he'd been caught with the magazines. One of the Danish students in his class had smuggled them in after the Christmas break, but he'd been the one caught with them in his possession. He'd been proud of the fact that he hadn't squealed on his classmate. Nor had he flinched, not once, when he'd been lashed with the leather in front of the class. Lashed again by his father when he'd been suspended from school.

He'd almost been expelled and, to this day, he wasn't sure of the exact nature of the exchange that had taken place between the abbot and his father, the upshot being they'd allowed him to return to Hargrove Hall and complete his final two years.

The magazines had kept on coming, as a reward for keeping his mouth shut, and he became very clever at hiding them. Especially when the magazines started to be accompanied by some very explicit photographs that would have meant instant arrest, never mind expulsion. He went to sleep most nights with the images in his head.

College and his early career brought a new freedom. He dated a few women, and enjoyed going to the movies and out for meals, but when it came to the end of the night, he didn't know what to do for the best with his hands, with his mouth, let alone his body. Little by little, he learned to gloss over his lack of both experience and confidence with a bold, knowing, larger than life attitude to everything. He knew it left most women feeling that they were the ones at fault if Adam Gilmore didn't find them attractive enough to make a serious pass at them. But college trips and holidays abroad were full of new thrills and excitements.

Then four years into his job with the Mutual Banking Corporation, when he was approaching twenty-five years of age, his father started to drop hints about him settling down.

'A wife in the background would give Adam a certain maturity and an air of responsibility.'

'A wife in the background would give Adam a stable home base.'

'A wife in the background would be good for Adam's career in terms of the corporate aspect, which would become more and more important as he ascended the ladder to a seat on the board.'

Just like his father had his mother supporting him every step of the way.

He wondered if his father knew about the collection of magazines and photographs that had been discreetly added to on his holidays abroad and which were slowly but surely supplanting his need to form a proper physical relationship with a woman, with all the messy, bodily women's stuff he only knew one way to handle. It made him feel uncomfortable. He hated feeling uncomfortable. Worse, he hated feeling vulnerable. He hid that part of himself away under a layer of carefully cultivated assurance.

When he first laid eyes on Beth McCann, he knew he had found the kind of quiet, docile woman who would be perfect for marrying and who would fit into his life quite easily. He only had to look at her, and her face flushed. He smiled, and she gave him a tentative smile in return. She looked at him with her soft eyes as though he was God and Elvis Presley rolled into one. Not that he wanted to be compared to Elvis.

Too bad if Beth didn't impress his parents at first because of her lack of education. Too bad if she couldn't boast of any important connections, because she was more or less alone in the world. When he'd first brought her home to the period red-bricked house in Rathgar, his mother's eyes had scoured Beth from head to toe, clearly disdainful of her chain-store skirt and top. His father's blue eyes examined her curiously from under thick brows, clearly trying to figure out what spell she had cast on his son. That they didn't consider her good enough to clean the underside of his shoes, never mind support him in his stellar rise to the top, was clear in the way they spoke to her as though she was of no consequence whatsoever, but they were coldly civil because she was a guest in their home.

But Beth was exactly the type of wife he wanted. He had his own reason for selecting the shy, submissive girl, who wouldn't cause a fuss. Her situation suited him down to the ground. Besides, he knew she would win his parents around in time with her housekeeping and cookery skills and, most importantly, the way she worshipped their son and heir. When he walked back up the aisle on his wedding day, he was glad he had lived up to his father's expectations, and relieved to be married in the eyes of the world, with the seal of conventionalism it stamped across his life.

But after that, everything fell apart. After a while Beth started to look at him as though he was the devil incarnate – and he couldn't have that now, could he?

Chapter Thirty-three

On Saturday morning Carrie left Willow Hill, promising it wouldn't be too long before she returned.

'I'll be down again soon,' she said to Evelyn as they had a cup of coffee in the spa dining room before she left. 'In the meantime, I'll work on building up your Twitter profile. Text me anytime you have special offers or a few spare slots and I'll put the word out.'

'Thanks, Carrie, and don't forget, if you're looking for a change of scene for longer than just a few days, you're welcome to stay here.'

'You're too generous.'

'Generous?' Evelyn laughed. 'I'd put you to work, seriously, in the spa. Clare and I won't be going on forever.'

Carrie hesitated, breaking up her blueberry muffin into bite-size pieces.

'Of course I know Dublin has its attractions.' Evelyn gave her a meaningful glance. Do you think …? You and Mark …?'

Carrie sighed. 'I don't know. The more I think of what happened, the more I realise I was very unfair to him. It's probably far too late now to be mending any fences.'

'Would you like to? Mend fences?'

'Yes, but I don't think he'll listen to me.'

Evelyn shook her head. 'You can only try. Give it a shot. I firmly believe that what's for you won't pass you by.'

'That's something Mum used to say,' Carrie smiled.

'Hey – I think that's the first time you've actually brought your mother up in conversation all by yourself.'

'I did, didn't I? And not before time,' Carrie said. 'I called into the house a couple of weeks ago to have a look, Fiona organised it for me, and I can't thank you and Sean enough for what you did. You've been brilliant.' She felt a lump in her throat.

'It was the least we could do,' Evelyn said.

'So I think it's about time I got more involved if there's any business stuff to do or problems with the house. I have to learn to stand on my own feet and can't be always leaving it up to you pair.'

'That's fine, Carrie, it's mostly just annual returns and the very occasional problem with the upkeep of the house, but, yes, you should know what's involved as it's your inheritance and we won't be around forever anyhow.'

Carrie shook her head. 'That kind of talk is not allowed. However, I'm finally acting my age and taking some of the paperwork home with me to try and get my head around it, for starters.'

'Atta girl.'

It was a sunny morning when she drove to the outskirts of Cork city and took the motorway back home, her small case in the boot of her car along with a carrier bag containing the lever arch file and folders of photographs. She'd already hooked up her mobile and set it to the playlist Mark had selected for her before they went to Paris. As she let the music wash over her, she told herself that at least she now knew why her mother had a brief affair with Luis. He just happened to have been in the right place at the right time when she went into a sort of meltdown after her good friend had perished in the sea. How sad it must have been for all of them.

Standing in the cemetery, nothing had seemed more important

than getting the best out of life. She knew that meant having the courage to mend some fences with Mark and, even if he never wanted to have anything to do with her again, letting him know how grateful she was to have had him in her life. But remembering how he'd stormed out of Faith Crescent, it was difficult – if not impossible – to know how she might get around to that conversation.

She sped up the motorway, the countryside unrolling like a lush, green carpet. Was it best to ask Mark to come to Faith Crescent or to meet him somewhere neutral for coffee? He'd more than likely refuse, that's if he even bothered to take her call or reply to a text in the first place. She could send him an email, but judging by the mood he'd been in the previous Sunday, he'd probably delete it without even opening it.

On the other hand, she could take up the invitation she'd got to a thirtieth birthday party that evening, and risk coming face to face with him. The fiancé of one of Sam's friends was having a big bash in The Purple Room in the Q Hotel on the quays. Everyone was invited, including Sam and Fiona, and there was a good chance that Mark would be there.

It would take some guts, though. Traffic thickened as she approached Dublin and she argued with herself as she slowed down – which would she prefer to be doing that evening? Sitting at home in her PJs in front of the telly, feeling sorry for herself, or going out and taking a chance on talking to Mark? The worst had already happened when he'd flung himself out through the door of Faith Crescent. After that experience, she could deal with the possibility of him blanking her, or refusing to talk, or acting as if she wasn't there. She imagined what she might do if he stonewalled her and, in spite of that, something fizzed inside her at the prospect of simply seeing him again. No matter how much he might ignore her, she would find a way to get through to him and make him listen to her so that they could at least be on speaking terms again.

Chapter Thirty-four

August 1980

Beth began to realise that Adam had married her under false pretences – Beth will be easy to fool, Beth will be so grateful to marry me, Beth will never question my authority or what I want to do to her, in bed and out of it. Beth, all alone in the world, no one else to look out for her. No one else close enough to sense the gaps in her marriage. Or sense the unhappiness in her.

She asked herself if she could change him. There must be something lacking in her, something she was missing, that made him feel angry with her and made him want to hurt her. Surely if she loved him enough for both of them, something good would come of it? All her pent-up love and longing would help to fix their marriage, wouldn't it?

Filled with a new-found purpose, she waited for him in bed one night, wearing just her underwear. Fighting down her nerves, she hoped he'd find the lacy bra and pants attractive. But he just looked vaguely annoyed, and his eyes flicking over her had the same effect that a bucket of cold water would have had.

'Cover yourself, Beth, you'll catch a cold.'

In bed, he turned his back on her. She might as well have been a stuffed doll.

The following night, he beat her again.

* * *

Sylvie's friendship was the only thing that kept Beth sane.

During the school holidays, Sylvie began to pop in with cream cakes or chocolates once a week, and kept Beth up to date with snippets from Willow Hill. She brought fun and laughter to the kitchen, and she reminded Beth that another life existed beyond the walls of this house. Most importantly, she stayed friends with Beth even though Beth refused her invitation to a meal, or out to drinks with her and John. Sylvie must have known that Adam didn't want her around; after all, the four of them never socialised, and even though Beth fobbed off her invitations, thankfully Sylvie kept up the threads of a friendship with her.

She wondered if Sylvie sensed that all was not well in her marriage, not that her friend knew anything about what was going on behind closed doors. Adam was very careful not to hit her where the bruises could be seen. More than once, she was tempted to confide in Sylvie – all she had to do was lift her jumper, or show her the bruises on her thighs – but stubborn pride held her back. Sylvie had tried to stop her from rushing into marriage, she had tried to suggest that Beth needed more experience of life and of men in general, but foolishly Beth had thought she'd got one up on her friend and that Sylvie was jealous. How stupid could she have been? Even now she was being stupid, unable to handle Adam.

'You know I don't have anything in common with them,' Adam had said, when, once again, Beth told him – very casually, so as not to pester him – that Sylvie had invited them for drinks. 'Don't tell me you're still in touch with her? I find Sylvie very annoying, the way she continually laughs at nothing and flutters her eyelashes.'

Beth had wanted to say that Sylvie had a great sense of humour and a lighthearted attitude towards life, but she'd known that wouldn't go down well. It had been quite obvious that Adam was trying to put a wedge between her and Sylvie. He wanted Beth all to himself. He didn't even want her to go out to work, where she'd be mixing with other people. He wanted her tied to the house and totally dependent on him.

'And as for John …' Adam had left that hanging for a moment as his eyes flicked over her face. There was a tense pause. He couldn't know, could he? That Beth had regarded John with something bordering on blind adoration throughout her teenage years. God help her if Adam ever suspected that. 'I know they're your old friends,' Adam had said, 'but we've moved on and left all that behind. We've far more exciting times ahead, Beth.'

It was impossible not to agree, partly because she didn't know if any remnants of her teenage crush would show in her face if they were out with John and Sylvie. She couldn't risk Adam seeing that.

* * *

'I'm going back to Willow Hill for a few weeks next month,' Sylvie said.

Beth made herself look pleased as they sat at her kitchen table and she poured the tea, even though something dark closed in on her. 'On top of your long holidays?'

'They'll have to do without me in the classroom for a few weeks. Mum's having a hip operation and will need my help. Sean and Andrew will be in Canada, they'll be over there until Christmas on work experience, and then they're taking over most of the business from Dad as he's semi-retiring.'

'And what about John? You're leaving him on his own?'

'He'll survive,' Sylvie said, helping herself to some milk. 'Mind you, he could be eating a lot of scrambled egg, it's about all he can cook. We're hoping to have central heating put in to Waldron Avenue, so he'll be looking after that as well. Things are starting to take shape in the house. We're now the proud owners of a second-hand divan, courtesy of John's Aunt Bridget. It's our new sofa and it's very versatile. We can open it out into a bed and we're like Darby and Joan lying with our feet up.'

'Sounds very cosy.'

Sylvie cut a generous slice of cake for both of them. 'Oh, it can be, especially if I take out Aunt Bridget's huge brown quilt that came with it and throw it over us. Mind you, she'd probably have a stroke if she knew what we were doing underneath the quilt in our sitting room. Or,' she laughed, 'sometimes on top of it.'

Beth swallowed. Best not to think of Sylvie and John rolling around their second-hand divan bed, laughing and joking amid the folds of Aunt Bridget's quilt. Best not to think of her own heart, once brimming with love and hope for the future, and her body, aching to lavish the very best of her love, now horribly bruised and damaged.

'Although we'll never catch up with you, Beth.'

'Sorry, you've lost me. What do you mean?' Beth forced a smile.

'You do realise you're living in the lap of luxury,' Sylvie teased. 'And you can't talk about holidays, it seems to me you have a permanent holiday.' She laughed. It was such a carefree laugh echoing across the kitchen that Beth winced. She couldn't remember the last time the kitchen had rung with such laughter.

Of course that was how it seemed to Sylvie. Lucky Beth, nothing to do all day but suit herself, living the dream life in a beautiful palace. Only it was really a gilded cage.

'There's nothing to stop you from visiting Willow Hill when I go down, if you can tear yourself away from here,' Sylvie said. 'Mum would love to see you, she'll be bored silly, laid up at home. You could pop down for a week.'

'I'll think about it,' Beth said, knowing it would never happen because Adam would never let his wife go off like that. She was trapped, like a bird in a cage. With a husband who didn't really love her. She broke up the slice of cake on her plate into small pieces and found herself saying, 'I'll see what Adam says.' It was like she wanted to put something out there in front of Sylvie. A hint. A suggestion. That somehow she was under his thumb.

Sylvie frowned. 'Surely, it's up to you? Adam would hardly stop you, would he?' She laughed as though the idea was sheer nonsense. 'This is Willow Hill, your second home.'

'He likes me to be here when he comes in from work.'

'Ready and waiting for him?' Sylvie teased.

Beth didn't answer. She popped some cake in her mouth, but it tasted like dust.

'He can hardly object to a visit to your old home,' Sylvie said lightly. She tilted her head and looked at Beth as though she was seeing something different about her. Something puzzling. 'Or would he? Beth, is everything all right?'

Beth pulled herself together. 'Yes, everything's fine. I'll have a look in my diary and see how I'm fixed,' she said, feeling suddenly nauseous.

'Let me know next week and I'll make plans … it would be great to have you …'

It would be lovely to be there, feeling safe in the bosom of the Willow Hill kitchen. If only she could turn back time, if she could be back there, swishing the mop across the stone-flagged floor, with the scent of apple tarts cooking in the oven and the sea a thick blue line in the distance.

* * *

'Who was here?'

'What?'

'You heard me, Beth, who was here today?'

Adam had just finished his dinner. He'd come home from work a little distracted, and she'd fluttered around him serving the food, knowing better than to make small talk. He'd read the paper as he ate his meal, his brow furrowed. Now, he lined up his knife and fork to one side of his plate, and folded the newspaper. He sat back in his chair as though he had all the time in the world. His eyes were blue as they stared at her, not blue like the sea, but blue like shards of glass.

Her heart began a slow thump. 'Why should anyone have been here today?'

'Indeed.' He smiled. 'Why should anyone have been here today?'

She rose to her feet, her legs like jelly. 'Adam … I don't know why you're going on like this.' She began to clear the table as though nothing was wrong, picking up condiments and cutlery, praying her hands wouldn't tremble too much. She pretended she could be clearing the table in Willow Hill, after the lads had tucked into a huge meal. It could be another summer evening, scented with the freshly cut meadow, and they are talking about the match in the sports field up in Kinsale.

'I'm going on like this, dearest Beth, because of what I found in the bin.'

The bin. She saw herself, after Sylvie had left, going out to the bin in the garage and shoving into the dark recesses whatever was left of the shop-bought Madeira cake Sylvie had brought, to hide any evidence of her visit. He couldn't have checked the bin … could he?

'I don't know what you're talking about,' she said, deciding to bluff it out. The cutlery rattled in her fingers. She picked up two plates, placing the knives and forks on top.

She was halfway across to the sink when he said, 'I don't like my wife keeping secrets from me.'

In spite of her resolve never to challenge him, she whirled around. '*I'm* keeping secrets from *you*?'

She froze on the spot, her hands clenched round the plates. What had possessed her? The room grew silent, a silence so thick it surrounded her in waves, almost suffocating her. He continued to stare at her as if trying to makeup his mind about something. She stared back at him. Without her realising it, the plates began to slip from her grasp until they crashed to the floor, the cutlery falling with them, clinking against the tiles. She stared down at the mess.

'Now look what you've done, you silly girl.'

She saw him rising to his feet as if in slow motion. There was a mist in front of her eyes as he closed the gap between them. He reached for her hair, grasping it at the crown, pulling it back so that her head was jerked backwards and her neck exposed. He hit the side of his hand off her throat, winding her. Tears pricked the back of her eyes. He put his mouth close to her ears. 'What are you? Nothing but a silly girl.' Still grasping her by the hair, he propelled her across the room, slamming the side of her head into the kitchen press. 'A silly, stupid girl.'

'Please, Adam.'

'I could kill you.' He could have been talking about the weather, he sounded so casual.

'You can't. You'd be arrested.'

'Not if I made it look like an accident.'

'You can't do that either.'

'Oh no? I think I could, quite easily. Then I'd be a widower, earning due sympathy and respect for my status in life.'

'And what about your dinner parties? Isn't that what our marriage is all about? You need a wife to support your career?' she said, risking his wrath.

'Not if I was too broken-hearted to ever marry again,' he said. 'I can buy anything I need in that sense. Anything at all. Why do you think I'm keeping a secret from you?'

'I never said that.'

'You implied it.'

'I didn't mean it to sound like that.'

'You didn't? So tell me, are there any secrets between us?'

'No. None at all.'

'We're perfectly happy, aren't we?'

'Yes.'

'I was only joking, of course. I'm not going to kill you.' He let go of her suddenly so that she slumped against the press. She rubbed the side of her head where it smarted.

'Sorry if I hurt you, I didn't mean to, I just get so afraid—'

'Afraid of what?'

'That you won't love me anymore.'

'I will love you, always.'

'Show me.' His voice had changed.

'How?' What did he expect her to do?

'I love you, Beth. I want to keep you safe with me forever. I don't want anything or anyone to come between us.'

'It won't.'

'Then show me how much you love me.'

She couldn't look at him, sensing the change in his tone of voice, the sudden charge in the atmosphere, something about him putting her on red-hot, sickening alert. She knew he was fiddling with the buttons in his trousers and wondered if he'd expect her to bend over the table or the back of a chair. She was starting to back away when he grasped her by the hair again and pushed her down to her knees in front of him, down on top of the broken plates, cutting into her knees, right in front of his thick, angry-looking erection. And then she knew.

* * *

In the days that followed, she sensed him watching her closely. At home, he scarcely let her out of his sight. When he was in work, he called her at home two or three times a day, just to see if she was 'okay'. She wasn't okay. She would never be okay again. She was beginning to feel nauseous all of the time. And it wasn't because she was pregnant. She was afraid. But her fear wasn't just a feeling, it was a physical thing; heavy, like lead, and it spread through her whole body, and gripped her stomach and her guts. She spoke as little as possible to him, mentally drawing away from him, as if she was closing down to him, switching off, becoming invisible.

Chapter Thirty-five

On Saturday night Carrie dressed in her favourite Karen Millen champagne lace dress and nude shoes, and went to the Q Hotel. She saw Fiona and Sam in the bar and walked over to join them.

'Where did you come from?' Fiona asked, rising to her feet and giving her a hug.

'Home, and Willow Hill before that. Why?'

'No, I mean the new you.'

'The *new* me?'

'You look fab tonight. Gorgeous.'

'That's thanks to all the spoiling I got in Willow Hill,' Carrie said.

'It's more than that. You look …' Fiona put her head to one side and studied her, 'kind of brighter, more relaxed. Dare I say, happier?'

Carrie grinned. 'Yeah, I think I'm starting to feel a bit more in charge of me, if that makes sense.'

'Wow, watch out world,' Sam joked. 'Cocktails, ladies?'

'Sure why not,' Carrie said.

'I couldn't believe it when you texted me,' Fiona said, when her husband had gone to the bar. 'You know Mark might be here?'

'I know, and I promise to behave myself,' Carrie said. 'Actually I—'

'Yes? Want to kiss and makeup?' Fiona gave her an impish glance.

'I wouldn't mind bumping into him. More to talk to him. Tell him a few things, like …' She hesitated.

'Like?'

'Well, some kind of apology from me is definitely needed, after all the hurt I caused.'

'I know it was all a mess, but don't expect too much, Carrie.' Fiona looked worried. 'I'm not sure that The Purple Room on a Saturday night is the right place for a heart to heart.'

'I think it's better in a crowd, I just need to get used to being around him. And there's safety in numbers.'

'There'll be a crowd all right.'

She felt unaccountably nervy when they took the lift up to the penthouse after their cocktails. The venue was spectacular. One side of the room was made up of floor-to-ceiling windows facing the Liffey, giving fabulous views of the quays. Outside, the river was at full tide, the dark, rippling water surging towards the open sea, as though it danced to an invisible tune, sparkling with the wavy reflection of multicoloured lights coming from streets and buildings and the bridges over the river. Purple leather sofas were scattered around, people were standing and chatting in groups, and there was music pumping out of the speakers. Pencil-slim laser lighting played across the room from floor to ceiling, intermittently changing colours and design, adding to the energy of the occasion and the sense that something exciting could happen.

'If this is Dublin on a Saturday night, I didn't know what I was missing,' Carrie said, feeling she'd stepped onto a different planet.

For half an hour or so, she moved through the crowd with Fiona, catching up with old acquaintances, including people she'd met at Fiona and Sam's wedding and their milestone birthday parties. Then some sixth sense told her that Mark had arrived. A sixth sense caused by the hard clench of her gut at the worried glance Fiona suddenly threw in her direction.

Her grip tightened on her glass and the wave of noise in the room suddenly receded. She blinked. Mark, coming through the door. A tall, thin, rakish Mark, with someone by his side. Someone blonde and pretty in a figure-hugging white dress and silver sandals. Hanging on to his arm, and to his every word by the look of it. She was giggling at something Mark had said, her vibrant face tilted towards his. In turn, his was tipped towards hers as together, they swept into the party, looking like they were sharing a funny and very private joke. Pain seared through Carrie's heart. She'd mentally prepared herself to be blanked and ignored, but not for Mark to be with another woman. She had to remind herself to breathe, and thought how ridiculous she'd been not to anticipate something like this. Mark O'Neill was attractive and sexy and honest-to-goodness kind. He was bound to be in great demand. Pity if it made her feel crushed, but she'd already rejected this man and crushed his love for her under her spiky stilettos.

Fiona stood in front of her, deliberately blocking her view, her face anxious. 'Jeez, Carrie, I'm sorry about this, I'd no idea Mark was going to bring someone.'

It took every ounce of Carrie's self-possession to shrug and to refrain from looking over Fiona's shoulder. 'Don't worry,' she said, her voice thin, her body as brittle as an eggshell. 'Why shouldn't he bring someone? He's a free agent. And it's not going to be handbags at dawn,' she laughed. 'We're finished, me and Mark. I'm fine about it.'

She forced her biggest smile, even though her face cracked with the effort. But she must have convinced Fiona, because her cousin stood back and Carrie had a clear view to where Mark and his stylish date had joined a group, and were busy chatting and laughing. Mark's hand was resting lightly on the woman's shoulder as though to announce to all and sundry that she was with him. She knew how that felt, a sense of belonging, a sense of unity, and she was insanely jealous. He was wearing jeans and a navy shirt with the sleeves rolled up to his elbows. Then the party crowd shifted and re-grouped and she lost sight of him.

Fiona invited her to chat with some people she knew, and Carrie took refuge in their conversation and laughter, letting it wash over her, trying to look as though she was part of the crowd instead of feeling painfully separate from all of it, watching the other couple through occasional gaps.

He saw her, then. He turned, raising his head a little as though alerted by something. He caught her staring at him, and she thought he saw him flinch, then he deliberately looked away. She'd prepared for that, she wasn't going to let it faze her. She kept him under scrutiny, trying not to look as though she was watching him, and when his girlfriend whispered something in his ear, took her bag and went to the ladies, Carrie saw her chance.

She excused herself from the group she was with and weaved through the throng until she reached his side, dizzy with the effort it had taken to behave normally; dizzy, too, with the effort it took to stand within three feet of him and stay upright.

'Hi, Mark.'

'Carrie.' He moved slightly away from the group he'd been chatting with. His eyes were cold as though her interruption was a nuisance. She'd prepared for that too, in her head.

'I'm glad to see you. I was hoping we could have a few words.'

'What about?'

'Could we go somewhere a little ... less crowded?'

'You know how to pick your moments,' he said. 'I'm here with Sienna, or had it escaped your notice?' He lifted an eyebrow in a way that told her he'd been quite aware of her scrutiny.

Sienna. She had a beautiful name, naturally. She couldn't help torturing herself by wondering how it would sound on his lips, in bed.

'Sorry, I didn't mean to goof. I just wanted to say ... that last time … and everything that went wrong, I only realised later how totally unfair I was to you.'

'Unfair?' His eyebrows rose. 'I think that's an understatement.'

'That's why I want to apologise. I know I really messed up. With us.'

'Carrie.' He shook his head. 'Forget it. Just leave well enough alone. I don't need this right now.'

'I knew it would be hard to get you to listen.'

His face tightened, his mouth set in a grim line. He glanced around the function room and took her by the elbow, guiding her closer to the window and out of earshot of the crowd. 'Get me to listen?' His voice was clipped. 'That's rich. Have you any idea how long I waited for you to talk to me, really talk?'

'I know.' She shook her head. 'I wasn't in the right place. I was scared of … letting myself go.' She felt tears prick the back of her eyes. Not now. Please. She swallowed hard. Too late, because they'd pooled into her eyes and he'd spotted them.

'Tears, Carrie? That's a new one. I don't think you cried, once, all the time we were together. Don't tell me you're turning on the tears now.'

'For God's sake, I'm not doing it on purpose,' she said. 'I just want you to be happy.'

'*What?* You've a damn funny way of showing it.'

'Well, sorry if I'm not doing this right, I'm pretty good at cocking things up, I'm well aware of that, but that's all I want. You to be happy. Okay? I'm sorry I put you through hoops of fire. Sorry for stamping all over you. And thanks for everything you did for me. I didn't appreciate it at the time.'

Out of the corner of her eye, she saw Sienna coming back into the room, crossing the floor ultra-carefully on her spindly high heels, her big, soft, brown eyes searching for Mark.

'Right, I'm gone,' she said, her voice choked. 'Sorry for the interruption, as well as everything else I messed up.'

She jammed her clutch under her arm, lifted her chin, and walked out of the room, heedless of where she was going, just intent on recovering her composure and getting the hell away from Mark. The corridor was cool after the heat of the party, and an open door gave access to a decked area with rattan tables and chairs. She stepped out onto the glass and chrome balcony overlooking the river and walked across it to catch her breath.

Out there, the dark, blowy night was relatively peaceful compared to the frenetic party noise. The air was cool and chilly and carried a damp, briny scent, and she shivered in her sleeveless dress. Far down below, the river rippled along between the quay walls, the reflection of city lights refracted in the moving current, and across on the other bank, windows of apartment blocks were lit up intermittently. From behind her, laughter, conversation and party music swirled out; the DJ was now playing a sensual kind of love song, and she thought of Mark and Sienna together, while a breathy voice pulsed around them. Would they dance like she and Mark had, the first time they met? Slow and sensual. Wild and passionate. Touching hands and fingertips, a heady anticipation spinning between them?

She leaned against the balcony, took a few deep breaths of the cold air and blinked back her tears. She'd be fine. She'd be great. Right now she might feel raw and vulnerable, but Carrie Cassidy would come out of all this a stronger person. She owed it to her parents. She also owed it, in a way, to Luis. Most of all she owed it to herself.

She turned to go back inside and froze. She wasn't alone. Mark was walking out towards her. For the second time that night, she found herself struggling to control her breathing. She stayed silent until he joined her by the balcony, resting his arms on it as he leaned forward and looked out to the river.

'Dammit, Carrie,' he said. 'You sure can pick a time and a place.'

His voice was marginally softer, as were his eyes when he glanced at her before looking away again, as though he didn't want to see her face. Or was it just the shadows of the night? She wasn't sure.

'I'm sorry.'

'There you go again. I've heard more apologies tonight than I did in the entire time we were together.'

'Shouldn't you be inside, with Sienna?'

'She understands I need five minutes out.'

Five minutes. She focused on that rather than the shared understanding part, which cut her to the quick. 'I don't want five minutes. I can't butt in on your night any further.'

'Sienna knows we have history. I told her I needed to draw a line under it.'

'I see.' *Great. Not.*

'But before that, I thought the least I deserved was a proper explanation for your … surprising comments. So I'm ready to listen to what you have to say and hear you out.'

'I told you I just wanted you to be happy. How much of an explanation does that need?'

She wished he wasn't standing so near. So near she caught the scent of him, could have reached out and touched him, could have leaned into him the way she used to and felt his arm curving around her shoulders in response.

'That's not the part I wanted explained.'

'No?'

'I understood that part all right.' He turned and looked at her with curiosity before looking back out across the river. 'The part I didn't understand was …' he hesitated, 'you being scared of letting yourself go.'

The answer to this question wasn't in her prepared script. She stayed silent.

'There's a minute gone already,' he said.

'That wasn't … what I wanted to talk about. Look, I just came here tonight on the off-chance I might see you and apol—'

He put up his hand. 'Don't say that word again, Carrie. Come on, spit it out, what was it about me you were scared of? You see, I want to make sure I don't screw it up again with someone.'

She laughed. 'I wasn't scared of *you*, Mark, anything but.'

'You must have been if you couldn't let go.'

'It was me,' she said in a small voice. 'I was scared of … life, I suppose.'

Something honest in her voice must have reached him. 'In what way?' His tone was a little kinder.

She took a breath. 'I don't think …' She shook her head. 'This isn't the right place.'

In response, he moved a little closer so that their forearms were touching as they stood together on the balcony, staring out into the night. She shivered. If Sienna or anyone else, even Fiona, walked out, they would look like they were having a romantic interlude under the stars.

Some hope.

'This is as good a place and time as you're going to get. And you now have three minutes left. So come on, if you really want me to be happy, prove it. Tell me in what way you were scared of life. I thought you were only scared of flying. Although maybe … ' he actually laughed, 'you're too afraid to tell me.'

Ah, feck it. She might never talk to him like this again after tonight. 'Okay. Stop me after three minutes and go back to Sienna.' She paused, gathering her thoughts. 'If you must know, I thought I was afraid of getting hurt, of putting my heart on the line and having it bruised.'

'Well, weren't you? You couldn't take that risk with me.'

'It was more than that. I was afraid to let go, I was scared of getting too involved and reluctant to commit to anything major at all, because my greatest fear was that I didn't think I deserved to be truly happy. With you. I felt I didn't deserve such happiness.'

'Happiness. With me,' he repeated.

'Yes, because deep down, I was caught up in some kind of … I guess … survivor's guilt. So I just, I dunno, skimmed the surface of life.'

He interrupted. 'Survivor's guilt?'

'Yeah. See, it goes back to my parents. I was the one who influenced their decision to go away. Deep down, I felt at fault over what happened, so with them gone, I didn't think it was right for me to be happy and contented, and that coloured everything I did. I know now it was wrong of me to think like that, that I didn't actually cause the accident, and I should have dealt with this before now, maybe talked to someone, even you, properly, about it.'

'Yes.'

'I even felt to blame over the way their love for each other had perished in that accident.'

'Carrie!'

'Now I know that their love is still very much alive, as it lives on in me,' she said softly. She lifted her chin, swallowed hard. 'All this … it stopped me from living my life … like, I didn't think I deserved you, so I pushed you away. I didn't think I deserved a fulfilling career, so I skated on the surface, not fully engaging with anything. I felt I didn't deserve much. I was too scared to move out of my comfort zone and take a few risks, and try to be happy. But I was wrong. I let myself slide into a half-hearted kind of life, and my parents wouldn't have wanted that.'

'Are you saying that you and me was half-hearted?' he asked. 'You've another minute, by the way.'

'No, Mark. Most of the time you and me were full on. That's what scared me as well.' She gave a little gulp. 'It was like the ground under me was gone. The safe, solid place I was stuck at in my head.

It was easier to crawl back to my tight little comfort zone of safety than risk letting go and maybe getting happy.'

'And what brought all this on? Your visit to Switzerland?'

'That and other things … I kind of had a road to Damascus moment.'

'Like what?'

'Something happened in Switzerland …' She paused, realising with a pang that she would have loved to introduce him to Luis, they'd get on like a house on fire, but that would never happen. 'Then I was down at Willow Hill this week and it kind of hit me that if I wanted to honour the memory of my parents, I should be making the most of life and squeezing it by the balls, rather than skiving off, half-arsed at everything. It hit me too that, more than anything, they would just have wanted me to be happy.'

He threw her a sideways glance. 'All parents ever hope for is that their kids are happy. That's hardly rocket science. What made you think otherwise?'

'I lost sight of it for a while. I told you – I was all screwed up. You were right in something else …' She hesitated.

'Come on, spit it out.'

'I never let myself grieve for my parents, not properly. You're supposed to go through five stages, you know, but I shut it all away and papered over it with my casual attitude to everything.'

'I wish – Jesus Christ, Carrie, I wish we could have talked like this sooner. And don't you dare say you're sorry.'

'I won't.' She turned and smiled at him in the shadowy light. He was looking at her with such a soft expression in his eyes that her heart caught in her throat.

'Thanks, anyway, for being so honest,' he said. 'I know how hard it must have been for you.'

'I just wanted to mend a few badly broken fences.'

'Badly broken?' He lifted an eyebrow. 'You mean mauled, mangled and smashed into smithereens.'

They stood for a moment in silence. The enormity of the hurt she'd caused him sat heavy in her chest. She didn't think she'd ever be free of the weight of it.

'Be happy, Mark, won't you? I wish you all the best. Seriously. And light a fire under them all in Bizz.'

'And you, what are you going to do now you've left Jade?'

'I'm taking a month or two out to get my head back where it should be, and then I'll decide. I've been told there's a job for me in the Willow Hill Spa if I want it.'

'Nice one.'

'It would mean relocating to Cork, though.'

'Big decision.'

Another silence. If they could have started all over again. If this could be a new beginning. Their first date. The promise of more to come. But he'd moved on now. Besides, it had been a silly idea, she'd hurt him far too much and damaged their relationship too much. Still, it was wonderful to be just chatting like this, even if it was making her head swim.

'You'd better go back in to Sienna.'

'Yeah. My five minutes are long up. Take care, won't you?'

'Same to you.'

'See you around.'

He leaned towards her. She stayed very still while he kissed her on the forehead. She closed her eyes. When she opened them, he was gone.

Relocating to Cork was suddenly looking very attractive; at least she'd be away from witnessing any romance budding between Mark and Sienna. She might never have to lay eyes on Mark O'Neill again.

Chapter Thirty-six

September 1980

'So I don't know when I'll see you again,' Sylvie said, sitting in Beth's gleaming kitchen on Wednesday afternoon. 'It'll be at least five or six weeks.'

Six weeks. Beth found it hard to get the words out over the lump in her throat. 'Is it this weekend you're off?'

'Yes, Mum's coming out of hospital next Monday, so I'm going down on Friday to make sure everything is ready for her. I know you said you'll be too busy to come down …' There was a hint of concern in Sylvie's face.

Willow Hill. Beth had a huge longing for the warm security it stood for, but she hadn't dared ask Adam if she could go, not even for a couple of nights. 'I have some dinner dates coming up,' she lied, 'and Adam wants to bring me over to London.'

'Great.' Sylvie didn't look too convinced. 'If you change your mind, you're more than welcome anytime, you know that. Even if you and Adam wanted to come down, together, some weekend.'

There was no chance of that happening. From the hallway came the strident peal of the phone, cutting through the afternoon. 'Excuse me a minute,' Beth said, bile rising in her throat.

'And how's my wife today?' Adam asked.

What would he have done had she not answered? How often would he have called before he came dashing home to see what she was up to?

'I'm fine,' she said. She heard noises in the background, someone else talking on a phone, a peal of laughter, and she envied the girls going about their day in the bank, grumbling about the weather or that it was two whole days until pay day, the sheer normality of it all seeming like a slice of heaven to her.

'*Dallas* is on the television tonight,' he said. 'You like that, don't you?'

'Right. Okay.' She couldn't summon any enthusiasm. And then what, she wanted to ask – another rape? Another beating? She was still all colours of the rainbow after the last one.

'What are you doing this afternoon?'

Was his pleasant voice tinged with intimidation, or was she imagining it? By habit, she bit down on her knuckle, then she hastily removed the offending knuckle from her mouth. He hated her doing that. 'I'm going to vacuum the floors.'

'Good. I hope to have another dinner party soon; you'd like that, wouldn't you? Tom and Teresa were very impressed with you. They like you. And they're very influential people, with connections into Leinster House. I'd better go now. See you tonight.'

She put down the phone and walked back to the kitchen, a kind of slow suffocation sliding through her veins. 'That was Adam, calling to see how I am.' Even her voice sounded thick and distorted.

'Really? You must be very happy, Beth,' Sylvie said.

'Me?' She looked at Sylvie blankly.

'Yes, all this,' Sylvie waved her hand around to encompass the kitchen, 'and a husband so madly in love with you that he calls you from his busy job to see how you are. Your mother would have been absolutely thrilled for you.'

'Do you think so?'

'All Molly ever wanted was for you to be happy and contented.'

'Happy.' The word dropped like a stone into her heart.

'She loved you to bits. She'd like to think Adam was taking good care of her precious daughter. She'd like to think Adam loved you as much as she did, and more.'

Beth had the feeling that Sylvie was deliberately avoiding her eyes as she picked at cake crumbs with the top of her finger.

'Adam calls me every day.'

'He must be very devoted.'

'Sometimes twice a day.'

'Is he really that devoted? No wonder he doesn't want you to come down to Willow Hill.'

Beth gulped. 'I never said that.'

'Not in so many words, no. Beth …' Sylvie looked up and gave her a worried glance. 'Is everything … Look, Beth, are you okay?'

Beth felt as though everything was unravelling inside her and she made a huge effort to pull the edges of herself together before they fell apart completely. 'I'm great. Why are you asking me such a silly question?'

'Is it silly to be concerned about a good friend?'

'There's no need to be concerned.' Beth made one last attempt at bravado. 'I'm living in a palace with a man who is very devoted, aren't I? Every woman's dream come true.'

'Sorry if I said the wrong thing, or spoke out of turn. I thought you looked a bit … well, off-colour or exhausted … or something.' Sylvie looked at her watch. 'Is that the time? I'd better go.'

Beth saw her lifeline slipping away from her as Sylvie stood up, picked up her bag, and checked for her car keys. Her friend looked lovely in a pair of blue jeans and a flower-print shirt, her dark hair freshly trimmed. How come she irritated Adam?

Six weeks.

She followed her out into the hallway, where Sylvie took down her jacket that had been hanging at the end of the stairs. *I'll surely be dead in six weeks' time if I don't get away from Adam.* There were only a few paces to the hall door ... *and there is only one person who can help me ...* In a minute Sylvie would step through the door, go home, head off to lovely Willow Hill for six interminable weeks, and her lifeline would be severed.

Her mother only wanted her to be happy. Not rich or well connected or living in a gilded prison.

Sylvie walked to the door and turned around with a big bright smile, ready to hug her goodbye, only realising then that Beth wasn't following her.

'Beth?'

She stood by the staircase, opening and closing her mouth. No words came. She gasped, she choked, she tried to suck in air but the slow suffocation had crawled all through her body and now her lungs seemed frozen solid.

'Beth, are you okay?' Sylvie's face was wreathed with concern, her eyes affectionate, her voice gentle and friendly, and everything about her overlaid with her reassuring blend of warmth and love. Everything about her exuded the calm security that Beth had envied for years.

'Beth? What's the matter?' Instead of going out through the door, and disappearing down to Willow Hill for six weeks, Sylvie retraced her steps down the hall.

At the last minute, the lifeline hadn't, after all, been severed. Beth gulped air into her chest and then she pitched forward into Sylvie's arms.

Chapter Thirty-seven

Monday evening in Dublin was showery. In Carrie's back garden, her small patch of grass and surrounding foliage glowed bright green against the soggy patio stones. Beads of rain rimmed the edges of her bird feeder, plopping off one by one, and over the back wall, angled against the grey sky, the slate roof of the church gleamed wetly. Earlier, she'd heard the bells chiming out, cutting through the quiet of her house.

She'd been going through her bookcase. Old favourites and those she wanted to read again were put to one pile. Other books were put in another pile for the charity shop. She'd also come across books belonging to Mark caught up in the untidy shelves, which she'd put to one side. It hadn't exactly been an invigorating afternoon, but it had been absorbing and, most important of all, it had kept her busy. But unfortunately not busy enough to replay in her head from time to time the moment Mark had walked into the party with Sienna. She was glad when Evelyn called her, pleased to talk to her aunt after her solitary day at home.

'Carrie, I'm not sure how to put this, but …' Evelyn began.

'Fire away,' Carrie said cheerfully, holding her mobile as she relaxed onto the sofa. She tucked her feet under her and watched rivulets of rain sliding down the window pane.

'It's sort of about Waldron Avenue, and Gilcorp,' Evelyn said. 'Funny – we were just talking to you about it, so this is very timely.'

Her stomach tightened. Relax, Carrie. She could do this.

'Is there a problem?'

'No, there's nothing wrong, but Adam Gilmore has contacted Sean and suggested it might be a good idea for you two to meet.'

Carrie sat up straight. 'Meet? You're joking. Waldron Avenue is only chickenfeed to the likes of him.'

'It's not about the estate. Decisions will have to be made later this year, about the investments in general, and Adam knows that Sean was authorised by you to manage the estate and deal with Gilcorp; he understands you didn't feel up to it. Apart from that, Adam thought it would be an appropriate time to meet you and have a chat. Just informally.'

'I don't know what to say. I can't understand why he'd be bothered meeting me. I'm sure he's far more important things to do with his time.'

'His accountancy staff look after the routine admin, but because of his connection with your parents, Adam has always had a special interest in making sure the affairs are managed as beneficially as possible, or so he says,' Evelyn said. 'It's not so much to talk about the estate, he explained to Sean, it's more he'd like the opportunity to meet Sylvie's daughter, on account of that connection. For old times' sake.'

'He actually said that?'

'Yes, more or less.'

'It's all a bit … surprising,' Carrie said.

Adam Gilmore, Beth's husband, wanting to meet her. He would have been there, in Willow Hill in 1980, at the time of Beth's disappearance, wouldn't he? Maybe he knew something that could help Carrie sort out what had happened.

'Sean and I are surprised too. Adam has been interviewed lots of times over the years,' Evelyn said, 'but the one subject he has always refused to discuss is his late wife. He has said it's a dark spot in his life he never wants to revisit. That he never got over it. That he keeps expecting her to walk through the door. You don't have to meet him, of course, Carrie, it's just a suggestion. He said he'll respect your wishes if you want to pass on this.'

'Maybe it's time I began to stand on my own two feet,' Carrie said. 'You and Sean have been fantastic and I still need you there at my back. Very much so. But it might be no harm to meet this guy and see what he has to say.'

See what he has to say about Beth and Sylvie.

'Only if you feel happy with it,' Evelyn said.

'I'll have a look through the paperwork I brought from Willow Hill first, so I'm not totally clueless if he does start asking questions.'

'There's no rush on the business end, a couple of term accounts will be up for review, but not until later this year. Sean can run through anything you're not sure of, in plenty of time. So I'll tell Adam to contact you directly himself?'

'Thanks. Email would be best.'

After the call, Carrie went back out into the hall and continued to sort through the books, lining up her favourites and those she wanted to read again in order of importance. She went into the kitchen and fetched two paper carrier bags, putting the books for the charity shop in those. She left them by the hall door, ready to drop into the shop in the morning. Something swirled through her, something positive. She was taking charge of her life. After years of living on the sidelines, she was going to get her life back, slowly but surely. The real, messy, sometimes complicated, far from perfect, genuine life of Carrie Cassidy, where she had good days and bad days, where she even stepped out of her comfort zone from time to time, no matter if they were baby steps to begin with and she fell flat on her face. It would be infinitely better than living a half-hearted, excuse of a life.

'Carrie is grabbing her life by the balls,' she murmured.

Mark would have had something to say about her stealing his positive-thinking talk. In spite of her sore heart when she thought of him, it made her smile a little. She couldn't allow herself to dwell too much on Mark and Sienna. She would need a good cry all right – several good cries – and to indulge in a few weepy moments now and again, but grabbing life by the balls meant not torturing herself thinking about what might have been or imagine what he was up to in his free time. She'd said her piece on Saturday night. They'd both drawn a line under it. She'd made her excuses to Fiona and left the party early with her dignity intact.

Fiona had texted her later that night and called on Sunday, hoping she was okay. Carrie had said she was fine, she'd had a good chat with Mark, but didn't want to talk about him now.

Carrie picked up his books, three of them altogether. If they'd been paperback novels, she would have put them in the charity shop pile, but they were reference books and an autobiography, books he'd dipped into now and again.

She saw them lazing together on the sofa in Faith Crescent on a particular Friday night, both of them reading, propped up at opposite ends so their legs intertwined together in the middle. 'Did you know that Steve Jobs once returned Coke bottles for the five-cent deposits so that he could buy some food?' he said.

'Uh.'

'You're not listening.'

'Shh. I'm reading.'

'Did you know that Steve Jobs once dated Joan Baez?'

'Um.'

'Did you know that Carrie Cassidy has lovely long toes, and there's a soft spot underneath her feet that is very ticklish? Like this?' Quick as a flash he pulled off her pink spotted socks and tickled her feet.

'Oh, you!'

She blinked hard at the memory and drifted around the house, searching for a large envelope; finding an unused jiffy bag, she put the books into that. Using a felt marker, she addressed it to Mark at his work address.

'What will I do if there's any post for you?' she'd asked, hugging herself against the stab in her chest as he'd shifted the contents of his life from her house to his car. It had been easier than: Where are you going? Will you be bunking in with someone? *Have* you somewhere to stay in the ridiculously overpriced, short-in-supply rental jungle that Dublin has recently become?

His reply had been tight and terse. 'My work address will do fine.'

There had been little or no post. He'd obviously been on to his bank and whatever else the minute he'd left Faith Crescent. On Tuesday morning, she slid the package across the post office counter and watched it being weighed and stamped before being swallowed up by a grey sack. She tried not to think of the look on his face when the envelope landed on his desk in Bizz, but that was almost impossible.

She spent Wednesday going through her kitchen cupboards, and clearing out her freezer, a catharsis in itself, considering the amount of convenient, out-of-date foodstuffs she had to consign to the bin. She logged onto Twitter and updated her status.

@carriecassidy Cleared out kitchen cupboards to make room for new treats. Bring it on #spendingspree

A reply, shortly afterwards.

@luckyduck well for some ;)

At least she could count on one very faithful follower.

* * *

On Wednesday evening, her mobile rang. She stared at Mark's name coming up on her screen before accepting the call.

'Carrie … um …'

'Yes?' Why, oh why did her traitorous heart gallop at the sound of his voice? Even after Saturday? When would she ever learn?

Mark's voice was composed and matter of fact. He could have been ordering a takeaway. 'I'm calling to say thanks for sending the books. You didn't have to do that.'

'No bother,' she said.

'I could have picked them up and saved you the postage,' he said.

'At least I saved you the bother of calling here again.'

'That wouldn't have been a problem.'

Oh, yeah? What about Sienna? And what about Carrie having to look at him one more time, and endure the paralysing feeling of him standing close to her in her narrow hall, when she needed to forget all about him, and excise every single memory of him from her heart.

'If I find anything else I'll let you know,' she said brashly. 'As long as Sienna understands why you're calling here.'

'It shouldn't concern Sienna in the least,' he said.

'Because she knows we're history?' Carrie prodded. Was she already so far down Mark's priority list that she was off Sienna's radar?

There was silence.

'Carrie, do you think Sienna and I are … um … together?'

'Well, aren't you?'

'Do you … I …' he spluttered. 'Do you seriously think I'd hook up with someone else already? After us? What planet are you on?'

The anger in his voice was unexpected, and she didn't know

whether to laugh from nerves or cry from overwhelming emotion. 'Mark, hey,' she said, swallowing hard, 'You said it yourself last Saturday night. You were with Sienna. What was I supposed to think?'

'Jesus. I was at the party with her, for fuck's sake. Nothing more. Sienna's an old friend from college, she's just moved back home from London after her marriage broke up. I brought her along with me to cheer her up. It was her first night out since she came home and she didn't know anyone there, so I didn't want to leave her all alone or standing like a twit for too long.'

Something heavy rolled away from her, leaving her head all swimmy. 'It's not my fault I got the wrong impression.'

'I suppose not, but still ... for you to think I'd already be getting it on with someone else ... Christ.'

'Mark, you probably have half the women in Dublin climbing over each other to get into your jocks. So, yes, I didn't think you'd be able to resist temptation for too long.'

'Two things, Carrie,' he said, his voice hard. 'One, I'm not aware of any women throwing sex at me; maybe they are, but I'm not in that frame of mind so it's not registering. Two, if you think I could forget about you all that easily, you need ... duh ...' He sighed in such a way that she could picture him running his hand through his hair distractedly.

'What do I need?'

Silence.

'Ah, jeez, you said you were getting your head together, it can only be a good thing. Let me know if any more of my stuff turns up and I'll collect it.'

For the rest of the evening, chiming through her head, like the bells of the church, was the fact that there was no Mark and Sienna – they weren't an item. The information had the effect of a long drink of cold, refreshing water. She had to tell herself forcibly that it didn't mean anything. It didn't mean Mark couldn't hook up with anyone else because he still had feelings for Carrie. Carrie was bad news as far as he was concerned. It meant, she figured, that he couldn't forget about her, or hook up with anyone else, because she had burned him so badly.

When Adam Gilmore sent her a very informal email later that night, she was glad to take her mind off Mark and she agreed to meet him in the Gilcorp offices on North Wall Quay on Friday afternoon. As she pressed Send, running through her head was the image of the handsome man in the wedding photos, and the way Beth had looked a little overawed standing beside him. Alongside that, she couldn't help seeing Beth's memorial plaque in the graveyard at Willow Hill. Since, according to Evelyn, he didn't like to talk about his wife, she wondered what kind of 'old times' sake' Adam had in mind.

Chapter Thirty-eight

September 1980

'No one must know …'

'They won't.'

'You have to promise me, Sylvie.'

'I promise, on my heart and soul … I might need to tell John, though, but that's all.'

'Oh God, I'd hate him to know.'

'More than you'd hate to stay living with Adam? After what he's been doing to you?'

Beth stayed silent.

Sylvie hugged her yet again. Beth caught the scent of her floral perfume as she clung to her friend. Never had anyone seemed so reassuring. 'Beth, darling, you don't deserve this. You did nothing wrong. You were far too good for him. We could need John's help. It would be good to have him onside. Adam will come looking for you and I'll bet Waldron Avenue will be on his list.'

'Then it's best if John knows nothing. Otherwise his face might give him away.'

'Maybe you're right. John would want to give Adam a most unpleasant injury. A few of them, mind. I'll say nothing for now but let me think about it. Then again, from what you've said, I can hardly imagine Adam admitting to John that his wife has run away and he doesn't know where to find her.'

Beth shivered. 'That's what I'm doing, aren't I? Running away. What kind of a coward am I?'

'Don't dare put yourself down. I think you're being very courageous.'

'I don't feel very courageous.'

'Of course you don't. You're terrified. That's why it's taking great courage to do what you're doing.'

'I never thought of it like that.'

'Well, it's true. Courage is doing the thing you're most scared of. So even if you feel sick inside and you're trembling from head to toe, all the better. You can tell yourself you're being very brave indeed.'

'I still don't want people to know, even in Willow Hill. I don't want anyone seeing me as a victim or feeling sorry for me.'

'Who's there to tell?' Sylvie grinned. 'Sean and Andrew are away, Dad will be working all the hours possible, and Mum will be laid up.'

'Good. I don't mean "good" that your mum is laid up—'

'Relax. It's all good, Beth, it'll be an adventure.'

'Willow Hill could be next on Adam's list. That's if he even remembers the name. He was never interested in talking about Cork or my childhood, which suited me. I'm glad now I never brought him down.'

'I can't imagine him knocking on the door asking for you. He might come down and prowl around, but he'd be spotted immediately and we'd run him off.'

Beth couldn't help but smile.

'And he can sniff all he likes around the vicinity, but he won't find you,' Sylvie went on. 'You'll be miles away by road. No one knows about that track except us. The summer house might need cleaning and airing, though.'

'No bother. It'll keep me busy and give me somewhere to hide out until I decide what to do with the rest of my life …'

'You're not hiding, you're just taking some time out.'

'Time out. I like that.'

She wasn't hiding away like a scared little mouse. She was taking her life into her own hands and having some time out until she decided what to do about Adam and their marriage.

'Can you hold out until Friday?' Sylvie asked.

'Just about. I've a few things I need to sort out before I leave anyway.' Like empty the few savings that were left in her post office account. And check all her papers and belongings to make sure there was no reference anywhere to Willow Hill.

'Good. If anything happens between now and then, just walk out the door and ask someone – anyone – to call me.'

* * *

Like someone throwing out a buoy to a swimmer in distress, Sylvie had given Beth a way out. She would collect her on Friday afternoon and bring her down to Cork. Not to Willow Hill, of course, but to the summer house, a small chalet owned by the Sullivans, tucked into a quiet spur of land close to the sea. It had been used occasionally by the family over the years, and Beth was going to stay there for a while. Nobody would be anywhere near it, certainly not in the next few weeks. It was six miles from Willow Hill by road, but it was less than two miles away on foot, through the patchwork of fields and woods leading down the incline from the back of Willow Hill to the sea. It was a route known and used only by the Sullivans. Sylvie would pop down to Beth some evenings after her father came home from work. If by chance any of the locals happened to ask if it was occupied, she would just say that a college friend of hers was using it for a couple of weeks to write up her thesis in peace and quiet.

Beth had dithered over leaving a note for Adam. Anything she said was going to antagonise him. That she had even had the temerity to go anywhere without him was going to antagonise him. Hah! That she had even dared to leave was going to send him into a furious rage. She couldn't bear to imagine what he'd be like when his phone call wasn't answered on Friday afternoon, or how angry he'd be to come home to an empty house. Never mind how furious he'd be if he found her.

So she packed the bare minimum and left a note to say she had gone to Manchester in England to take care of her elderly aunt, who was dying. She didn't know if he'd believe one word of it, but he could use it to save his own face and explain her absence in the short term. Although Adam would be well able to use his charm to cover up the fact that his wife was missing.

As to the long term, she hadn't a clue what it held. When she closed the hall door on the house of her dreams, she knew Adam could never find her. Because if he did, he would kill her.

Chapter Thirty-nine

On Friday afternoon, Carrie stood outside a six-storey steel and glass building and watched the reflection of a blue sky dotted with clouds mirrored across the expanse of glass. Gilcorp was based in this impressive-looking building. She walked up a short flight of granite steps and pushed through a revolving door into a huge lobby. Two identically dressed receptionists, with perfectly polished hair and perfectly glossed red lipstick and matching headsets, sat behind a black marble table. They would have been equally at home on the stage of the 3 Arena strutting around as sexy backing singers for a rock star. Carrie felt herself being scrutinised and found wanting. She began to smooth back her hair and then she deliberately mussed it up again.

'I have a 4 pm appointment with Adam,' she said, enjoying the way they snapped to attention at the mention of his name. She leaned against the reception desk and raised an eyebrow, adding nonchalantly, although she knew it was completely superfluous, 'Adam Gilmore?'

One of them checked her name off a computer screen and the other spoke briskly into her headset. A high-tech tablet slid across the counter and she signed her name with a stylo in the space indicated by a long red talon. She was given a visitor's pass, with strict instructions to return it before she left the building, in the kind of automatic voice that had issued the same instructions many times before.

And this was only one of Adam Gilmore's gigs, she told herself, refusing to be fazed by it.

'Michael will show you up,' one of the receptionists said.

Only then did she notice the security guy in a corner of the lobby beside the bank of lifts. She stepped into a glass bubble that gave her a bird's eye view of the reception area as it slid silently up to the top floor. You wouldn't want to have a head for heights, or wearing no panties, she thought giddily. She stepped out onto a small, square corridor on the sixth floor. Michael ushered her through a double fire door and out to a narrow, thickly carpeted corridor. There was another fire door to the left and a heavy, opaque glass door facing her. Outside the opaque glass door, Michael entered a code into a keypad. There were a couple of clicks that reminded her of a safe being opened, and he led her into a big, wide room.

The first thing she noticed was the fantastic view of the docklands area through the floor-to-ceiling windows, which took up two sides of the room. The other walls held some paintings, a huge flat-screen television and a row of black lacquered cabinets. Then she saw the man standing up from an enormous, glass-topped desk.

She'd seen him on the television and in the newspapers, and as a young man in photos with Beth, but nothing had prepared her for the impact of meeting him in real life. The young man was long gone, his body filled out so that it was heavy and square, and as well as the razor-sharp suit that sat perfectly on his broad shoulders, and the arrogant lift of his head, Adam Gilmore oozed an aura of power and affluence that surrounded him like an impenetrable shield.

'Thank you, Michael,' he said, dismissing the security man. 'Carrie, you're very welcome to my office.' He came around from behind his desk and clasped her hand in his. 'It's good to meet you at last.' He was even more polished from head to toe than his reception staff; so smooth and finished he was like a perfect mannequin of sorts, she decided. Carrie could have sworn he'd had Botox and eyelash tints. And his teeth must have cost a fortune. She looked at his ridiculously sized symbolic desk, with a row of small, flat-screen monitors embedded in the surface, and couldn't help wondering what kind of car he drove.

The door closed behind Michael with a series of soft clicks. Carrie was suddenly conscious that she was alone with this man at the top of a high-storey office block, with no one within shouting distance. Who else knew she was here? Had she actually told Evelyn and Sean that she'd be meeting Adam this afternoon? She dismissed her creeping anxiety and told herself to get a grip. Michael and the receptionists knew she was here.

Adam indicated a meeting table to one side of the room. There was a tray already arranged with china cups and refreshments. 'I thought it would be more relaxed if we sat over here,' he said. 'Tea? Coffee? Or there's water if you prefer.'

'Water, please,' Carrie said.

He walked across to the table, carrying himself as though he was royalty. She sat opposite him, finding it an effort to pull out the heavy chair, but he made no move to help her. He handed her a crystal tumbler, diamonds twinkling in his ice-white shirt cuffs, and asked her if she preferred sparkling or still.

'Still, please.'

Adam poured some water for himself too, as well as a cup of coffee. 'Carrie, it's lovely to talk to you at last,' he said. 'I met you before, although you probably don't remember.'

'Yes, I believe you came to the funeral.' She managed to get the word out without choking on it.

His expression immediately altered to convey respectful sympathy. She had the unaccountable feeling that he'd a full repertoire of facial expressions ready to be donned as appropriate. 'Yes, it was a very sad affair,' he said. 'I didn't know your parents were over in that part of the world. I was working in Wall Street at the time. I was very shocked. I can't imagine how devastated you must have felt.'

'It wasn't easy,' she said. Understatement of the decade.

He went on. 'Such a shame. I think it was the first time they'd taken themselves off around the world like that.'

He looked at her enquiringly, as though he expected her to confirm or deny this, but her gut rebelled. The last thing she wanted was a man she didn't know raking over the embers of her parents' death, albeit an old friend of theirs. Then she remembered that he was no stranger to tragedy himself.

In loving memory of Beth Gilmore, lost at sea.

She found it hard to place the reality of this strong, controlled man alongside the image she had of a timid, unassuming Beth. Still, it had been years ago. The Adam Gilmore of today, with all his success and power, was the result of a lifetime's worth of hard work and dedication. No doubt Beth would have acquired some of that poise, had she lived long enough.

'I apologise,' Adam asked, taking her silence for some kind of distress. 'It must be still difficult for you.'

'It is.'

He smiled. 'Sometimes it helps to talk things over with a stranger.'

'Actually,' she said, his white-teethed smile putting her on edge, 'I'm the kind of person who prefers to talk things over with friends.'

'Good for you, Carrie. You remind me of your mother a little.'

'I do?'

'Yes, you seem to have the same kind of spirit. Sylvie was unique in that. Young people today are far more confident than they were in my day. Back then, you were supposed to stay in your corner, be seen and not heard, but Sylvie was the exception.'

Carrie stayed silent, sipping her water. She didn't agree. She knew her parents had never had that kind of repressed upbringing, and she couldn't imagine Adam, with his blazing self-assurance, suffering any kind of oppression. Though maybe the unfortunate Beth had been a little inhibited.

'And like a lot of your generation,' he went on, 'you've probably travelled the globe by now.'

'Not particularly,' she said.

He raised an eyebrow. 'Maybe you don't see it as travelling the globe – your generation would take it for granted – but I bet you've probably been away three or four times already this year,' he said.

She shook her head. 'I lead a very quiet life,' she said, wondering why he was giving her so much of his valuable time. The guy probably charged a fortune for you to shake his hand, never mind the eye-watering amount you'd part with for the benefit of his expert knowledge. Unless he had been a much better friend of her parents than she realised. But why hadn't they mentioned him at some stage? She didn't recall ever seeing him in Waldron Avenue. He waited, watching her thoughtfully, allowing a silence between them, and she had the uncomfortable feeling he was expecting her to say something. What, though? She was hardly going to admit she'd been to Lucerne to meet her mother's supposed old lover, not that he'd know anything about that.

'It's good to talk to John and Sylvie's daughter, after all these years,' he said. 'We were great friends once, but we drifted apart after my wife died tragically. It was never the same after that. There were so many memories of the four of us, together, that it was too painful for me to keep up the close friendship. I'm afraid I threw myself into my work and allowed my friendships to slide.'

'I was very sorry to hear about your wife. I think my mother felt the same,' she said.

'She did?'

The intensity of his shrewd blue eyes surprised her. 'Well …'

Carrie hesitated, thinking of the absence of photographs of the four of them, and the absence of wedding photographs in Waldron Avenue. 'She never talked to me about you and your ... wife.'

'Didn't she?' he said. He looked at her a little quizzically. 'Forgive me, Carrie, but in that case, how do you know how your mother felt?'

'I guess she didn't talk about it for the exact same reason as you don't talk about it,' Carrie said. 'She found it too painful.'

He looked at her questioningly as though he was expecting her to elaborate.

'My mother was a very positive, outgoing person,' Carrie went on. 'She didn't dwell on her problems but looked on the bright side of everything. It obviously made her feel sad to think of Beth if she never spoke of her.'

'So you didn't know how close she was to Beth?'

She was here under false pretences, Carrie decided. If Adam thought they were about to indulge in a good heart to heart about Sylvie and Beth and their close friendship, he was wrong. She wasn't going to try and second guess him, it was best to be as honest with him as she could. 'The way it is, er, Adam,' she said, 'I didn't know anything at all about Beth until ... oh, last week, when I came across the photographs of her and Sylvie.'

She felt a chill run around the spacious room. It crept up the back of her neck. Then she realised Adam's whole demeanour had altered. He leaned forward, resting his elbows on the table, and his blue eyes were cold as he said, 'What photographs?'

'Photographs of your wedding. I saw them when I was down in Willow Hill.'

'My wedding.' He gave a slight laugh. 'Of course, Sylvie was our bridesmaid. Forgive me for being curious, Carrie, I might put the fear of God into my executives, but behind it all I'm just a sixty-year-old man reminiscing about a part of the past no one knows enough to talk about. Funny to think you were looking at photographs of our wedding. It's good to chat to someone with the same connections as darling Beth.'

'I don't know much about connections myself,' Carrie said. 'It was only when I saw the photographs that I realised how close they were, and soon after that, I came across Beth's memorial plaque.'

'Her *what*?'

His face closed over, but not before she saw the spark of surprise. He didn't appear to know about his wife's plaque. For a man who was supposed to have loved her so much, surely he would have been at least aware of it? If not responsible for it?

'Her memorial plaque,' she said. When he still looked blank she went on, 'In the graveyard close to Willow Hill. That's how I knew she'd died.'

He visibly swallowed. 'Of course,' he said. 'It was rough … losing Beth like that. I've hardly been back down there.' Adam took a sip of water. He looked at Carrie, his blue eyes as unblinking as a snake's. 'So you didn't know anything at all about Beth and her tragic accident until then? I must admit I find it surprising in a way that Sylvie never once spoke about it, given the depth of their friendship.'

Why did she feel she was being put through a wringer? It was like being at a job interview where they came at you from different angles. It wasn't so much a chat for old times' sake as a grilling, as though Adam had a hidden agenda for calling her here.

'I believe my mother didn't even talk to her family about it, at the time,' she said.

'I see.' He pursed his mouth. She looked at his fleshy lips, trying to figure out if he'd had dermal fillers.

'In fact,' she said, 'I appreciate you've experienced a tragedy and don't like talking about it, but I was hoping you'd fill in some of my blanks, Adam.'

'Like what?'

'You must have been down in Willow Hill at the time of the accident.'

His eyes blinked. He seemed to be holding himself very still. 'What makes you say that?'

She shrugged, trying to dissipate the sudden tension. 'Well, obviously, after Beth went missing, weren't you …?'

'Yes, obviously, I was then.'

'I've no one to talk to either about this, and I'm trying to get a picture of what exactly happened.'

'But you just said it yourself, Carrie,' he said evenly. 'It was a tragic accident. No one knows what happened.'

'I was thinking more of my mother, how she managed to cope.' *Or not cope …*

He met her eyes and his were as smooth as glass. 'The truth is, Carrie, I don't know. I was distraught, as you can imagine. I don't know what was going on around me at the time.'

'But you must have been talking to her?'

'I must have, yes,' he agreed. 'But it's all such a blur, I can't remember.'

Instinct told her he was lying. Instinct told her that the perfectly controlled Adam recalled every minute, but for some reason chose not to talk about it.

'All I remember,' he went on, 'was Sylvie sitting in the big reception room in Willow Hill and your father with his arm around her.'

Her father? Carrie was momentarily immobilised. Her father would have been there to support her mother. Sylvie wouldn't have been left to cope on her own in the aftermath of Beth's accident. So where did Luis fit in?

'Are you okay, Carrie? You look like you could do with some more water.'

She lifted the glass, letting the cool liquid slide down her dry throat.

Adam sat up straight. 'Forgive me, Carrie, it's been too easy to talk to you. I indulged in too many painful memories that must have been equally upsetting for you, having lost your parents. I appreciate your time is just as valuable as mine. You're probably due back in the office …'

'Well, you needn't worry about that,' she blurted out, still unsettled. 'I'm not due back anywhere as it happens, I'm between jobs right now.'

'What?'

Something slithered through Carrie's gut at the surprise in Adam's eyes. It made her want to breathe fresh air. 'I've left my job, that's something else I need to sort out, and in fact I do have an appointment at five, across the city.'

'Can we talk again?'

'I'm sure you're a very busy man. Why should you have time for me?'

'Sylvie was such a good friend to Beth that I'll always have time for her daughter,' he said. 'I trust you're happy with the investment end of things? Your portfolio is in good hands.'

'I don't doubt that,' she said.

'It's no harm for you to give thought to your long-term financial future. I could arrange for you to talk to one of my best advisors.'

'I'll think about it,' she said, pushing back her chair and standing up, feeling the urge to get far away.

He also rose to his feet. He extended his hand and good manners obliged her to shake it, although for some reason she didn't want to have to touch him. 'Thank you for coming in, Carrie, and sorry if I upset you in any way with the trip down memory lane.'

'It's fine,' she said.

He went across to his desk, pressed a switch and unlocked the door. He escorted her down the corridor to the lift, and although she guessed he was just under six feet, he seemed taller, thanks to the way he carried himself, and his strong, muscular build. No wonder Beth looked overawed standing beside him on her wedding day. She'd probably been as nervous as hell about sex with her new husband, as, strictly speaking, it was frowned upon before marriage in those days, and from the look on Beth's face, she hadn't been the kind to break any rules.

When the lift door opened, Michael was waiting inside.

'Michael will see you out,' Adam said.

Her final thank you was lost as the doors slid closed. She returned her pass to the receptionists and signed out on the flat screen. Then she left the building and walked towards the quays. She had a sudden urge for a long, cleansing shower. She didn't understand why she'd a funny taste in her mouth, or a prickling feeling between her shoulder blades, as though she was being watched. She quickened her pace until she turned onto the quays, grateful to draw in deep gulps of the air blowing up off the Liffey.

Chapter Forty

Adam stood by the window and looked down several storeys to the street below, where the figure in the red jacket crossed the road and headed towards the river. From his high vantage point, people resembled toy miniatures as they scurried about. No sound came through the triple-glazed windows, not even the barest hum from the tiny cars below, the call of the gulls that drifted in the air currents outside or the noise of the aircraft climbing into the sky on their curving ascent out of the airport.

She knew something. He didn't know what it was, but it was likely she didn't know either, otherwise she'd scarcely have agreed to meet him by herself. Otherwise she'd scarcely be talking about filling in some of her blanks. Blanks in what? And she'd said nothing at all about her trip to Lucerne, even though he'd given her a suitable opening and gone on to use the silent technique. Most people hated that. If you had the patience to wait long enough, they said something to fill the silence, usually supplying you with the information you were looking for. For some reason, she hadn't wanted to talk to him about Lucerne – which could mean she was hiding something.

And yet she'd talked about Willow Hill quite freely. Even startling him with talk of a memorial plaque. He'd struggled to cover his surprise and the weird feeling of something walking over his grave. When had that happened? The only time he'd been in that godforsaken graveyard was for the funeral of Carrie's parents. He hadn't seen any memorial plaque to his wife. That cow Sylvie must have arranged it at some stage.

But he'd almost shot himself in the foot when he'd been unable to contain his surprise about Carrie having left her job. He didn't normally make such a basic error. It proved he didn't know everything there was to know about her after all. If he hadn't known something as basic as that, what else did he not know?

There was something else nagging him. He thought back to what had been said, but couldn't put his finger on it. Maybe it was just that Carrie had reminded him of her mother. And one thing that still played on his mind over and over was the deliberate way Sylvie had looked at him across a stuffy Coroner's Court, her eyes cool and calculating, yet deep with secrets. It was a look that had got under his skin, that had made him itch to slap it off her face, a look that had stalked his nightmares until he'd seen her coffin being lowered into the ground.

He sat by the window as, on the floors below him, workers streamed out of the building departing for the weekend, and the onset of twilight dropped a light veil across the city. His phone gave a low buzz. It was Michael, informing him that the receptionists had left and the building was being secured.

'Fine, Michael, enjoy your weekend.'

'Do you need anything before I leave?'

'No, thanks.'

The penthouse was on a separate circuit to everything else, including the alarm system. Because as well as having his very plush and accommodating office, the rest of the floor was taken up with Adam's private apartment. All he had to do was step outside into the corridor and go through the security door into his private domain. It even had a separate lift that went straight down to the basement garage where he housed his car. If he wished, he could spend the whole weekend undisturbed in his fortress.

Undisturbed by everything except thoughts of flighty Carrie Cassidy filling in some blanks and meddling around with the details of Beth's accident. He didn't like his conscience being ruffled or the sense of foreboding that was creeping around the back of his neck.

Chapter Forty-one

Saturday was one of those unexpected summer days where the sky was an endless blue vault and everything seemed fresh and new. Even the church in the grounds behind Carrie's house looked beautiful, the sunshine gleaming off the spire and sparking off the granite walls, winking against the stained-glass windows. It seemed a solid and comforting anchor after the nasty taste her meeting on Friday afternoon had left in her mouth. Not that she believed, of course, that there was some entity or other looking out for her or looking after her.

The soft warmth of the afternoon enticed Carrie out into the back garden, where she brought out a bottle of beer and the file and folders from Willow Hill. She sat at her patio table, going through photographs, staring at Adam and Beth on their wedding day, along with her parents. Adam looked very attractive, smooth, the promise of his future success stamped all over that confident, expectant smile. What was it about him that had unsettled her? He had to have been a very astute businessman to be where he was today, still hanging on to some kind of empire after the great recession. She went through the file for Waldron Avenue and all the paperwork and annual returns seemed to be in perfect order. She saw where she had put her signature on various documents, as advised by Sean Sullivan.

Then, at the back of the file, behind the final tab, she came to the ultra-sensitive stuff, all arranged in plastic pockets.

Bless Evelyn Sullivan. Carrie knew it had been all her careful attention to detail, ready for the day Carrie would have the mental energy to go through it. She skipped past a copy of her parents' death certificates, their marriage certificate and, lastly, their respective birth certificates. It was madness to think the important details of their whole lives were contained between three A4 plastic pockets a few millimetres in thickness.

Yet they weren't, were they? She was here, wasn't she? The result of their love for each other.

Thank you, she thought. She closed her eyes for a moment, remembering how alive she'd felt sitting on a boat on Lake Lucerne. Then she picked up the file again and the next document she came to was labelled in Evelyn's handwriting: 'Accident report'. It was in a foreign language. Even though she didn't take it out of the plastic folder, the date jumped out at her. Eighteen months ago. Not long before Fiona's wedding.

Then she remembered Sean Sullivan telling her about it, but she didn't have to concern herself with it. Besides, he knew she was off to Brighton with Fiona and a gang of her friends for the hen weekend that Friday morning. Flights and accommodation had been booked and a weekend of pre-wedding antics planned. Carrie had only half-listened, blocking most of it from her head, hiding her panic and sick fear, under the laughter and jollity of getting ready for the weekend.

Hang on. She paused, frowning. If this was her parents' accident report, carefully filed away by Evelyn Sullivan, what was the inquest document she'd passed over earlier? She went back to the folder with the photographs, sifting through the prints until she found the brown envelope labelled 'Inquest report'. As she pulled it out, her heart tripped a little.

It was an old report, typed on a manual typewriter, the print a little faded over time, the corners of the pages yellowing slightly. Carrie was hardly aware of her surroundings as she opened it out and began to read. To her surprise, the report wasn't about her parents. It was dated 1988 and it was about Beth. And as Carrie read it, skimming over some details, reading other paragraphs twice or three times, words jumped out at her and her whole world tilted.

According to the report, Beth had taken her own life in September 1980. Sylvie Cassidy had found a note. *A note?*

It seemed that Beth had been staying in a summer house down by the cove beyond Willow Hill for a couple of weeks preceding the incident, but her husband thought she'd been in England.

Luis Meyer and his father had returned to Switzerland two days *before* Beth went missing.

Shell-shocked, Carrie sat frozen, unable to take it in, trying to grapple with the facts and sort them out in her head. Beth had been married for six months. She'd been staying in the summer house, but she'd told her husband she'd gone to England. Sylvie couldn't have fallen into Luis' arms because she was broken-hearted over Beth. There was a yellowing newspaper clipping in the envelope, carrying a much sparser account of the inquest, merely reporting that Beth Gilmore was now legally declared missing, presumed dead.

It was impossible to make sense of anything. Had Beth gone down to the summer house of her own accord or had she had some help? Her mother had been in Willow Hill at the same time. Why had Beth left Adam, and the glittering future she could have had?

Something else whirled into Carrie's head. If Beth had been in the summer house, a few hundred yards away from Luis … could it have been Beth who was with Luis all along? Pretending, for some reason, to be Sylvie? There was no way she'd ever find out the truth though, was there? And timid Beth didn't seem the type to indulge in an affair, especially if she was married to Adam.

She rummaged through the pile of photographs until she found the photograph of Beth and her mother, arm in arm on Beth's wedding day, their faces smiling out to her. Goosebumps rose on the back of her neck as she examined the photo closely. There might be some way of uncovering the truth, if Luis remembered. She picked up her mobile and checked the time.

Switzerland was an hour ahead, so it was just late afternoon over there.

Since she'd come home, she'd kept in regular contact with Maria through email and an occasional text. Now she called Maria's mobile, hoping she wasn't going to disturb Luis, who according to Maria's latest email, was in good spirits but weaker by the day. She pictured the phone ringing out across the elegant reception room in Lake Lucerne, windows open to the shimmering lake.

Just as she was composing a message for voicemail, her call was answered.

'Carrie? How are you?' Maria's voice, low and calm.

'I'm good, Maria, how are you and Luis?'

'He's resting right now, he's on stronger medication so he's sleeping a lot.'

'And are you resting as well?' Carrie asked her. 'I hope you're minding yourself.'

Maria laughed softly. 'Not very much, no. But that doesn't matter right now.' *I'll have plenty of time to mind myself … afterwards.* The words hung between them, unsaid.

'What's the weather like over there right now?' Carrie asked.

'It's a beautiful evening,' Maria said. 'The sunshine on the lake is very pretty, like millions of diamonds twinkling. I have already described it to Luis. But you didn't call to ask about the weather?'

'I don't want to be a nuisance,' Carrie said, 'but I have a question for Luis, if you don't mind asking him when he's more awake.'

'Of course, Carrie. What is it?'

'It's about the time he was in Ireland. It might sound silly, but I have a reason for it. Although I'm probably expecting too much of Luis; after all, it was years ago,' she said, hesitating. This was stupid after all.

'You can but ask, and we shall see.'

'He might have no idea at all, but please ask him if by any chance he can remember … what my— Sylvie's hair was like. If it was long or short.'

If Maria thought the question was off the wall, she hid it well, replying to Carrie in her usual calm voice, 'I'll ask him, certainly.'

'Thanks. You don't mind?'

'Why should I mind, Carrie? Luis is always pleased to talk of you and he will be glad you called and happy to help. I'll talk to him when he's awake.'

* * *

Maria called back later when Carrie was in the kitchen, mixing the ingredients for an omelette, instead of whipping something out of the microwave, even though she didn't feel very hungry.

'Hi, Carrie, Luis says hello and he hopes you are keeping well. He'll talk to you himself. I'm going to put you on speaker, okay?'

After a minute, Luis spoke, his voice a little hoarse. 'Carrie! How are you?'

'Hello, Luis, I'm fine, how are you? Sorry for disturbing you.'

'It's a pleasure. You're welcome to disturb me anytime.'

Although I don't have much time left, she almost heard him say.

'You are asking about Sylvie?' he said. 'You want to know more about your mother and me? You have accepted things?'

'Yes, but my question might sound silly to you and I don't want to bother you with silly things.' What she really meant, but couldn't say, was, *I'm sure you have far more important things to concern yourself with than the minor incidentals of an affair over thirty years ago.*

'No matter. I'm always happy to talk to you about the lovely Sylvie.'

'Even if Maria is listening?' she said, hardly able to believe she was teasing him.

'Especially if Maria is listening,' he said, his voice tinged with laughter. 'You see, I need to keep her on her toes. So what if she gets insanely jealous?'

She heard Maria laughing in the background.

'So, Carrie, you are asking about your mother's hair?'

'It's an unusual question, I know—'

'Don't fret, I recall it quite easily. Sylvie had long hair, right down past her shoulders.'

'You're sure?' She could have bitten her tongue, but he was ill, and it had been a long time ago.

'I'm very sure,' Luis said, his voice warm. 'I couldn't see it, of course, but I remember running my fingers through it several times. And I probably shouldn't be telling you this but, to hell with it' – he laughed softly – 'I remember, ah, the way it fell against my chest when we— never mind. I'm perfectly sure. I remember every moment of the time we spent together.'

'I'm very jealous, Carrie,' Maria said. 'I never had long hair to seduce Luis with.'

Carrie was only half-listening. A funny kind of shock was running icily through her veins and even though she was leaning against the kitchen counter, staring out into the garden, she thought she was about to sink to the floor. In Beth's wedding photograph, Sylvie Cassidy had short, dark hair cut in a page-boy style. No way would it have grown very long in the space of six months.

But Beth had long hair – long, blonde, straight hair that flowed down past her shoulders. Beth, who had been lost at sea, two days after Luis had gone back to Switzerland.

Chapter Forty-two

September 1980

She knows she is playing with fire, but she can't help herself. In the interlude she spends with him each evening, she makes Luis play the piano for a short while before they fall into bed together.

'My father keeps asking me how I am,' Luis says, stroking her hair.

'Good. He doesn't know about me, I hope.'

'He knows something has changed because I'm different with him.'

'How?' She shimmies around in the bed so she's facing him. She loops her leg so that it rests between his, enjoying the intimacy.

'I'm talking to him now, instead of ignoring him and sulking. It is not as difficult between us.'

'Good, but he must never know about me,' she says, squeezing his shoulder to emphasise the importance of this.

'Don't worry, he won't. I tell him I like the sea air and he seems satisfied with that. He has bought more tapes, of music and books, and I'm listening to them. I've told him I have started to play again but I'm not ready to play in front of him yet. He's happy with that and he wants me to learn Braille when we go home ...' Luis falters.

'You're not sure about that,' she says.

'I don't want to be someone who has to learn Braille.'

'Why not?'

'Because it means ...'

'Yes?'

'It means I'm starting to accept ... that I'll never be able to see again.'

'And is that a bad thing? The acceptance?' She lies so that her head is on his chest and she can hear the rumble of his voice reverberating inside him. Her hand is resting on his hip, splayed across it. In a minute, she will tease him with her fingers, marvelling that she is doing this.

'Why should I give in?' Luis asks. 'I'm still fighting it – in my head. I'm still angry and I don't want this.'

'Of course you don't. But is there anything at all you can do to change what has happened?'

'Not one thing, and it makes me feel helpless.'

'You can't change what has happened, Luis. Sometimes life throws terrible things at us we don't expect. The only thing you can change is your future.'

She tucks those words away for herself.

'What future could I have?'

'Better than you think. You can spend the rest of your life feeling helpless, and angry and stuck in your fate, or you can make the best of what you have.'

'You make it sound too simple.'

'I didn't say it was easy. It's tough. You'll just have to pretend again, that you feel brave, because learning Braille could open a whole new world for you, Luis. You're nineteen. What could you be doing when you're twenty-nine? Thirty-nine? You can hide away and spend those years wasting life and your talents. Or you can decide to ignore all the fear and do something that scares you and brings you alive again.'

He is silent for a moment. 'Putting it like that makes me think. It's good with you, I trust you, I can talk to you, but after this ...'

'After this, after me? You could give hope to lots of people with your music.'

'You have all the right words, Sylvie. Words that make me think I can do things. Words that can even' – he laughs – 'make me think I can fly. I wish I could remember them when I am back home.'

'You won't remember everything I say, but you might remember that I made you feel strong, full of hope, full of love.'

'Love?'

'Yes, Luis, I love you I will always love you and you will always be special to me. I don't think you will ever realise how much ... you see ...'

'Go on.'

'You have rescued me as much as I have rescued you.'

'Have I?'

'I didn't tell you the full truth about me.'

'Tell me now.'

It was impossible to tell him everything. 'I'd just like you to know that my life – when I met you – was full of worries. I was living in an intolerable situation. I didn't know what to do, what way to turn.'

'I knew something was making you unhappy.'

'It was more than just being unhappy,' she admits. 'I was anxious and afraid.'

'Afraid of being found with me?'

'That too, but mostly it was something that happened before we met. I was happy once, life was great, and then things turned very dark and frightening. When I came to Cork, I was at a crossroads, with a big decision to make. But thanks to being with you, I now know exactly what I have to do.'

He pulls her face to his and begins to kiss her. She is drawn into his deep kiss and her hand flutters across his hip to find he is ready for her again. She feels the tremor running through his body at the light touch of her fingers and it makes her feel like a powerful woman. With a sigh of pleasure, she slides across on top of his body; straddling his hips and drawing him deep inside her, she lets him fill the ache at the core of her. They rock to and fro, and she straightens up and arches her back a little, feeling free and desirable, beautiful and brave. He reaches around to cup her buttocks, his fingers splayed as he holds her tightly, and for an infinitesimal moment she flinches, but he can't see the marks of the scars Adam has inflicted, and the memory doesn't hurt her any more, lost as she is in the moment with this man.

Then wanting to give him as much pleasure as possible, she leans forward to kiss him, her hair brushing against his chest. He cups one breast, stroking the hardened nipple with his thumb, sending a curl of pleasure rippling right through her. She gives herself up to the wonderful sensations and desires she thought she'd never enjoy.

'Sylvie ...' Her name on his voice is but a soft breath.

She closes her eyes against the lie.

Sylvie.

* * *

How could she have done it? Pretended to be someone else? Her friend's name had slipped out unintentionally that first, frantic afternoon.

Beth knew she shouldn't be venturing out of the summer house, but she couldn't resist the short walk to a secluded spot in the sand dunes in the quiet evening time, just for some bracing sea air. On Saturdays and Sundays, she stayed put in the summer house, in case there were any weekend visitors around. As she'd sat in the sheltered dunes, in the calm evenings, she'd escaped the worst of her worries and unhappiness by pretending she was someone else. She wasn't Mrs Adam Gilmore, with her marriage in ruins, or Beth McCann, shy and diffident, easy to manipulate. She was someone like Sylvie – sometimes she imagined she *was* Sylvie – confident and full of life, happy and joyful. Fearless. All those qualities she'd envied in her friend and wanted for herself. If she pretended hard enough, she might begin to believe she was as confident and fearless as Sylvie.

And then there was Luis, and that fateful evening ... He couldn't know her real name, just in case. 'No one must know I'm here,' she'd said to Sylvie.

Since she'd walked out, there had been a deafening silence from Adam. He hadn't called to Waldron Avenue after all, or made any attempt to contact either John or Sylvie. There had been no sign of him in the small village in Cork or skulking around Willow Hill. Sylvie would have heard immediately if anyone had been asking after her or Beth or looking for directions to Willow Hill. She wondered if he'd gone looking for her in Manchester, half-believing her note and never guessing that Beth had had the temerity to actually leave him. Surely it was only a matter of time before he began to search in Cork.

She'd told Adam very little about Willow Hill, or the modest council house she'd shared with her mother on the edge of the village outside Kinsale. She'd never brought him to visit her birthplace. It was lowly by his standards and, to her shame, it wasn't somewhere she'd wanted to show off. She'd turned her back on her past life, thinking it hadn't been good enough, that *she* hadn't been good enough.

In a dark way, she'd felt it served her right when her marriage turned so sour. It had been some kind of karma. Who did she think she was? Why had she denied her background? Her hard-working mother, who'd kept cheerful and positive in spite of the terrible knocks life gave her? She still missed her so much. Then her beautiful sister, Anna. Beth had been six when Anna had died of tuberculosis, and it was something she'd never forgotten.

Surely she had been as deceitful as Adam, hiding away her humble beginnings much in the way he'd concealed his true nature? In a sense, she'd felt she deserved Adam's beatings, his cruel attempts at having sex, as far from making love as you could imagine. Then she thought of what Molly McCann would have said about her the real nature of her daughter's marriage, and the answer had been clear as a bell.

If Molly McCann were alive today she would tell her daughter she was far too good for the likes of Adam Gilmore.

If Molly McCann were alive today and knew of Adam's cruelty, she would personally go after him and strangle him with her bare hands.

No life of privilege and security was worth the wretched way he treated her. Beth was right to have left him, and right to have grabbed moments of happiness with Luis.

* * *

She's glad Luis can't see her face on their last afternoon together. It's Friday, and he'll be travelling home to Switzerland with his father on Sunday.

'What will I do without you?' Luis asks, as they lie in bed, his arm curled around her. The light of the afternoon sun presses through the curtains and bathes the room in a warm glow. She has the sensation of time inexorably slipping past, of the futility of trying to hold on to this moment. All she can do is imprint it indelibly on her mind, and hope it will shore her up in the months ahead.

'You won't be without me,' she says, pressing her body as close to his as she can, skin to skin. 'I want you to forget about my name, but I'll always be in a corner of your heart like a loving thorn, reminding you never to give up. When you sit down at the piano, in front of hundreds of people, I'll be the one poking you in the back telling you that you can do it. When you get tired of the long hours of practice, I'll be the little nagging voice in your ear, reminding you of all the comfort your gift is bringing to people. I'm not saying it'll be easy, but you owe it to me. Right?'

'I hear you.'

'Good. If you feel down at times, just ask yourself if you'd prefer your life to be over, where nothing and no one can touch you, not even a slice of sunshine or a spatter of rain or a woman's love. Isn't it better to be alive enough to sit at a piano and feel the music coming out of your fingers?' She lifts his hand and kisses his fingers one by one.

'I'll never love again.'

'Of course you will.' She lifts her head and looks at his profile, his high forehead, strong nose and full mouth, his thick blond, wavy hair. 'You're not allowed to say "I'll never". If you hear yourself say that again, picture me being very cross with you. You're only nineteen, your life has barely begun.'

'Can't you come with me? Back to Switzerland? You said you were at a crossroads, why not leave everything behind and come with me?'

For a long, glittering moment she considers this. 'No, Luis. This week with you was always just going to be a moment out of time before we go back to our separate lives.'

She senses the sharp edge of his unhappiness as keenly as her own and she presses even closer to him, reminding him she is still there. 'Luis,' she says, 'no feeling sorry for ourselves. Let's enjoy the time we have left. Let's always remember how good it was between us. Remember you have given me as much as I have given you. Nothing can ever spoil what we have shared.'

She presses her face close to his until, at last, he turns and kisses her. He wraps his arms around her, folding her into him so that she feels sheltered and safe, warm and secure in his love. This, now, she will always remember. He moves on top of her and she savours every movement, full to the brim with the hot feel of him inside her, and after a while, every particle of her dissolves in a white hot blur of sweet fulfilment. She lies still, soaking up the sound of his breathing, drinking it into her senses, knowing she will need every ounce of this memory to sustain her in the days ahead.

Then feeling outside of herself, and slightly in shock that this is indeed the end, she lifts her arm away from him, wriggles her body away from the heat of his, already feeling a chill at the gap between them. 'Luis ... it's time.'

Chapter Forty-three

The letter for Mark arrived on Monday morning.

From the kitchen, Carrie heard the rattle of the letterbox and her gut automatically tightened. Since talking to Luis on Saturday evening, she'd stayed close to home. A sense of nameless anxiety clouded everything, immobilising her so much that she'd barely made it to the local shops for some milk. Her sleep had been interrupted by disturbing dreams she couldn't fully recollect on waking, dreams mixed up with visions of her mother and Beth, and Adam chasing after her, brandishing a pen. And everything Adam had said on Friday afternoon became coloured in a different, more sinister light.

Something had happened in Willow Hill all those years ago, and she couldn't figure out exactly what just yet. Why had Beth pretended to be Sylvie when she met Luis? Why had she left Adam, after just six months of marriage, and the fantastic future ahead of them? How come Beth's life had ended so tragically? She'd probably never know the truth.

Carrie was still in her PJs, feeling jumpy and nervy, when the post arrived. She went up to the hall, telling herself to relax, she was safe here. It wasn't as if Adam Gilmore was about to magic himself through the letterbox like a dark genie stealing out of a bottle. Picking up the post she saw it was for Mark, stamped 'Private and Confidential'.

Wonderful. Just what she needed. After a breakfast of toast and coffee, she sent him a text.

Letter arrived 4 U, looks important.

It was early afternoon before he replied and her eyes widened as she read it, because he seemed to be calling a truce.

Tks. Will call to collect later this week.

Later that afternoon, she called Evelyn.

'Hi, Carrie, how did you get on with Adam?' Evelyn asked.

'I don't know,' Carrie said, gripping the phone, quite unable to put on her old mask of glossing things over and pretending they were great. 'I was at a loss to know what to say to him. Mum and Dad never spoke of Beth, or the accident. But that's not what's bothering me. Yesterday evening I came across a copy of Beth's inquest report in with the photographs. Have you ever read it?'

'The inquest report? Can't say I have.'

'Do you remember it at all? Did Mum talk about it?'

'I remember there being an inquest all right, a few years after Beth went missing,' Evelyn said slowly. 'I was expecting Conor at the time and when I saw Sylvie afterwards, in the Willow Hill kitchen, she looked so wretched that I knew better than to ask about it. But I never saw the official report. Someone must have got a copy of it and put it with the photographs, whether it was Sylvie or your grandmother, I don't know.'

Carrie took a deep breath. 'Then you probably don't know that, according to the report, Beth took her own life. She'd been staying in the summer house by the cove. She left a note and Mum found it.'

'Good God. No. *No*. How terribly sad. Sean and I thought there was something a bit odd all right about the circumstances of Beth's death, but it was never spoken about.'

'That makes it even more sad.'

'I know. It was different in those days, Carrie. Things were hushed up, not like nowadays where everything is out in the open. I just know all the Sullivans were devastated that Beth was gone, so we didn't really talk about it very much.'

'As well as that, it seems she'd left Adam.'

'What? Did he tell you that?'

'No way. That was in the report as well. Beth had been staying in the summer house for a couple of weeks before the accident.'

'That was kept very quiet too.'

'A few things were well and truly hushed up. There was a newspaper clipping in with the report but it only had a couple of lines in it and made it out to be an accident.'

'What a terrible tragedy. No wonder Sylvie was so broken-hearted.'

'No wonder Adam doesn't want to talk about it in the media,' Carrie went on, piecing things together. 'His wife running out on him in the most final and awful way possible, after just six months of marriage.' No wonder he'd reacted the way he did last Friday when she talked about the circumstances of Beth's death.

'Well, you can't blame the man,' Evelyn said. 'Even though he'd plenty of women chasing after him, Adam never married again on account of Beth. That's how cut up he was.'

'Even years later? I'd say he was enjoying himself too much to be tied to one woman.'

'Carrie … grief does different things to different people.'

Carrie fell silent. 'You're right, if anyone knows that it should be me. Whatever about Beth, it just seems weird that Mum and Dad never mentioned Adam's name to me. Especially if he was supposed to have been such a good friend and given that he was in the newspapers and even on the television.'

'We did speak about him to Sylvie and John once or twice, when he started to make a big name for himself,' Evelyn said. 'But it was all very casual and your parents were very non-committal. I got the impression they didn't want to talk about him because of Beth. I'm sure Sylvie was heartsick imagining the kind of life Beth could have enjoyed.'

'Heartsick is right. Mum never kept any photographs in Waldron Avenue of the four of them, not even the wedding photos. What does that say? Then he turns up at their funeral?'

'He probably regretted letting the friendship between them lapse.'

Carrie made a noise that sounded like agreement even though she didn't agree.

Afterwards, she replayed her Friday-afternoon meeting with Adam again. All that talk about friendship drifting apart because it was too painful was a load of rubbish. Beth must have had help to get to the summer house. Sylvie, her close friend, had to have known she was staying there. And Adam must have known that Sylvie knew. Why, now, did he feel the need to talk to Carrie about this dark spot in his past?

She tried to piece it all together. Luis Meyer was now terminally ill and the press release ensured that information was in the public domain. But if Adam had suspected that Luis might have been involved with Beth, he would have acted long before now, surely? He wasn't the type of man to tolerate being deserted by his wife, let alone being betrayed. Why turn his attention to Carrie? Why now? In what way could he possibly think she posed a threat to him?

Carrie recalled the long silence after he'd remarked that she'd probably been away three or four times already this year. She'd replied that she led a very quiet life, instead of saying that she'd just been as far as Switzerland – as though she had something to hide. But there was no way Adam could have known Carrie had been visiting Luis. Her imagination was running away with her.

Once again, the biggest fear that had stalked her since Sunday made her feel nauseous; maybe Adam had found out about Beth and Luis back in 1980 – maybe he had already acted. The body had never been found, Sean Sullivan had said. Anything could have happened to Beth ...

Chapter Forty-four

September 1980

'I've been seeing someone,' Beth said.

Puzzlement swept across Sylvie's face like a cloud. 'Seeing someone? Who? *How?*'

'He's been staying in the big house at the other end of the headland.'

'Who's "he"? What do you mean you've been *seeing* him? Beth?' Sylvie's tea cup rattled in the saucer as she put it down.

'It's all over now, he's gone home … to Switzerland. Luis. I met him when I went … out to the sand dunes one evening, and we got talking and things …' Beth's voice softened. 'Things happened … that made me realise I was right to leave Adam.'

'Of course you were right to leave Adam.' Sylvie's face was wreathed with concern. 'But Beth, I hope you didn't take any chances. We agreed it was best for you to stay close to the summer house.'

Beth twirled the small milk jug around and around. 'I've been very careful. I wasn't spotted, if that's what you mean, nobody was around whenever I went out for some fresh air. Anyway, it's over now, he's gone home.'

'I won't even ask the details …'

'You don't need to know the details, but …' Beth hesitated, wondering how Sylvie would take this, 'the thing is, I told him my name was Sylvie. When we got chatting first, I pretended I was you, it was a sort of safety mechanism. And I kept it up.'

Sylvie grinned. 'I won't fall out with you over it, so long as John doesn't think I've betrayed him.'

'I never thought of that, sorry.'

'You did sleep with him?'

'I did – and I've no regrets.'

'Good. Whatever happened, I can see by your face it was good for you.'

'It was very special.' Beth gazed out through the front window of the summer house, to the sand dunes outside. The sound of waves crashing along the strand carried through the window. The tide was on the turn.

'Are you hoping to keep in touch with this Luis?'

'God, no, it's over. It was just a holiday thing. Luis has gone back to his life. We won't be in contact again.'

'The most important thing is, what are you going to do now?' Sylvie asked. 'Mum's making a great recovery and I'll be going home in two weeks' time. I won't be here to look out for you.'

'I'm not going back to Adam.'

'Of course not. No way.'

'In a way I hope he finds me …' Beth gathered the tea cups and saucers along with the spoons, remembering the way plates and cutlery had slipped through her fingers and crashed to the floor under Adam's cold gaze. No way could she go back.

'You're joking?'

'I'm not joking. I need your help, one more time. There's something I've been thinking about doing … just hear me out.'

The warmth of Sylvie's smile was like a candle in the dark. 'Sure, Beth. Anything.'

Chapter Forty-five

When the doorbell chimed in Faith Crescent on Tuesday afternoon, Carrie hurried downstairs, her heart tripping. Mark? She wasn't expecting him until later in the week. Flustered at the thoughts of seeing him face to face again, she hurriedly checked her reflection in the hall mirror. Two spots of colour came and went in her cheeks.

Carrie and Mark will not have cross words. She flung open the door.

Adam Gilmore stood there.

Carrie's utter shock must have registered on her face because he took an automatic step back as though she had thrown him a physical punch.

Then he smiled. 'You weren't expecting me.'

'I was expecting my boyfriend,' she said. He'd be less of a threat, she thought, if he thought there was a boyfriend about to appear on the scene. She pictured Mark standing behind her, solid and strong at her back, and decided she wasn't going to let this man see that she was nervous of him in any way. She tried to rein in her imagination and not think of his hands going around Beth's neck.

He lifted an eyebrow. 'Oh, a new boyfriend?'

'What makes you think that?' she said, amazed her head felt so clear.

'It's common knowledge that you've had a recent breakup,' he said smoothly.

'I didn't know it was that widely known in your exalted circles.'

'Ah, Dublin's but a village, everybody knows everybody's business.'

'Well, certain people appear to know some business anyhow, but not all,' she said, thinking of the way he'd been unaware she'd left Jade.

'Carrie, to me that sounds like a challenge.'

She felt as though an invisible gauntlet had been thrown down. Without her realising it, he was standing in her hall. Adam Gilmore wasn't the kind of man who'd be willing to talk on a doorstep. She couldn't bring herself to close the hall door because she didn't want to be stuck in the narrow space of the hallway with him. Neither did she want to bring him any further into her home. Her eyes darted on instinct to her bookcase, where she had placed the folder with the photographs and inquest report. She tried to breathe evenly, appalled to realise that he was only a few feet away from the report that had been quietly put away and never discussed. Belatedly she realised he'd intercepted her gaze. Feck it, anyway.

'I was passing,' he said.

As you do, she thought. *I'm sure you pass by Faith Crescent every day.*

'I notice your house alarm is a bit askew.'

'Thanks. I'm trying to figure out how you know where I live,' she said, hugging herself defensively, realising too late – and rather stupidly – that her address would be on the files in Gilcorp, even though correspondence was sent to Sean Sullivan.

'And have you?'

'I'm sure my address is all over your files.'

'Is that a problem?' he asked.

'I hope not.'

'Good. I'm sorry to interrupt but I called to see if I could have a look at your photographs.'

'Photographs?'

'Yes, you said you had photographs of my wedding day. I've moved around so much since then that my copies have been misplaced. It would be good to have a look at them again.'

'Sorry I can't help you, I saw them when I was down in Willow Hill.' She looked him straight in the eye as she mentioned Willow Hill, wondering if it would provoke a reaction, then asking herself in the next breath if she was stupid to think about antagonising him. Despite her worst fears, she'd no proof that he'd had any hand in Beth's death.

He smiled. 'Why does everything start and end with Willow Hill?' She noticed it was only his mouth that moved. His eyes remained a particularly icy shade of blue. She wondered if those eyes had ever chilled Beth. How had someone so meek and mild managed to land someone like Adam? Had she been totally bowled over by him? What could have happened that she'd plucked up the guts to leave him? Nothing good, for sure.

'Are you sure you wouldn't find it too sad to look at them,' she said, 'given the way Beth died?' She was skating on thin ice, but what the hell. This man put her on edge for some reason and she didn't like him. Neither did she like the scent of his aftershave stealing around her hall.

'"The way Beth died,"' he repeated her last words, his snake eyes back again.

'Yes, it was a most unfortunate accident.'

'What else could it have been?' He was very still.

'Whatever kind of an accident it was, it was very sad for Beth,' she said.

Unscrupulous. *That* was the word she'd been looking for. He might be wearing a beautiful suit, with expensive cufflinks gleaming at his wrists, but to her mind, there was something devious about

Adam Gilmore. Then again, he wouldn't have got where he was today without being extremely clever.

'It was, yes, and for everyone else,' he said. 'That includes me and your mother. I hope you weren't upset on Friday. You see …'

She waited. She wasn't going to fall into the trap of saying something to fill the silence.

'You remind me so much of Sylvie,' he said. His eyes were veiled as they glanced at her. 'And I feel Sylvie must have been talking with Beth, down in Willow Hill, before she … died. I might have a brilliant lifestyle, Carrie, and want for nothing financially, but sometimes I drive myself mad wondering how Beth was, or what frame of mind she must have been in to be so careless with herself. How terrified she must have been, fighting the tide. She should have known better than to go out of her depth. As her only daughter, I thought Sylvie might have shared some confidences with you.'

Carrie shook her head. 'I can't help you at all. As I explained on Friday, I knew nothing about any of this, even about Beth, until recently.'

He looked at her very shrewdly. What had she said wrong? *Recently?*

'When I was down in Willow Hill, as I told you last Friday,' she added, mentally kicking herself for sounding on the defensive.

'Well, of course, what else could you mean?' He smiled, and it sent a chill right through her. 'Here's my card, it has my private direct line,' he went on, taking a slim wallet out of his jacket pocket and plucking out a business card. He held it out to her between perfectly manicured fingers that brushed hers as she took it from him, and she just about managed not to flinch. 'If you think of anything I might like to know, no matter how small it is, or if you come across any more photographs, please contact me.'

From his tone of voice, it was more of an order than an invitation for coffee. As soon as he had left, she sagged weakly against the hall door, hardly able to move, hardly able to breathe, wondering what his hidden agenda was and what had really happened to Beth. Even though she'd left a note, surely someone who'd made such valiant attempts to save Luis wouldn't have thrown her own life away?

Luis had said Sylvie was at a crossroads. She had a decision to make. Her life had taken a dark turn and she was anxious and unhappy. It hadn't been the happily married Sylvie he'd been talking about of course, but Beth.

Chapter Forty-six

September 1980

'Did you really think I wouldn't find you?'

'Adam …'

Under the strength of his shoulder, the lock gave way and he advanced into the summer house. Even though she'd half hoped for this, she tasted the wave of smothering dread that seeped into all the corners of the room. Beth struggled to stay calm, her breath fluttering in her throat. Her first thought was for Luis. By now he was back home in Lake Lucerne. There was no way Adam could connect him to her.

He smiled, his eyes cold. 'I knew you were a silly, stupid woman, but if you thought you could hide away forever, you're even stupider than I thought.' His face darkened.

'How did— How did you find me?' Had he followed Sylvie? Down from the back garden at Willow Hill? Dear God, she hoped not. Sylvie should have been well home by now.

'Do you think I'm stupid? Believing that ridiculous note about your so-called aunt in England? There's only one place you'd be capable of running to. I've spent the last three weekends driving around this godforsaken part of the world, until I finally drove past

Willow Hill. Most convenient that it was signposted. I remembered the name. Then I got talking to a man in a pub on the outskirts of the town whom I'd seen hanging around the gardens. He was only too happy to chat to me, once he knew I wasn't a con man down from Dublin.' Adam sneered. 'He talked all about the Willow Hill property as long as there was a whiskey in front of him and I'll bet he's forgotten our conversation already.' His tone was boasting, as though he was pleased with his cleverness. 'I didn't even have to mention your pretty little name. I heard all about the house and the outhouses and then the little summer house. Did you really take me for a fool? How dare you betray me!'

Her blood ran cold. 'B–Betray you?'

He shoved his face into hers. 'What do you call running away from me and our marriage, you bitch! How long have you been hiding out here? Who helped you? That cow Sylvie?'

'Sylvie doesn't even know I'm here,' she babbled. 'Do you think I'd want to tell her about our sham of a marriage? And I'm not hiding away.' She straightened her shoulders. 'I'm taking some time out while I decide what to do.'

He poked the soft spot in her shoulder with his index finger. '*You* deciding what to do? Bollocks. Being my wife, that's what you should be doing.'

She trembled. She had nothing to lose now. He was going to try and beat her to a pulp, and she knew what she had to do. She thought of how powerful she had felt in Luis' arms. She breathed in the memory of him to sustain her.

She faced her husband, staring at him in a way she never had the guts to before. 'Your wife? Really, Adam? You see, I'm not sure it's a wife you need after all.'

'What's that supposed to mean?'

'I don't think you love me – not like a husband should love his wife. You never have. You used me.'

'I've given you everything someone like you could wish for, a wedding ring on your finger, a beautiful home, a husband who is on his way to the top of his profession.'

'And I'm supposed to be grateful for that?'

'Of course, you thick bitch. Although you're too stupid to appreciate everything I've handed to you on a plate. I'll forgive you this once. The car's up on the road outside. Collect your things and we'll get going.'

'I'm not going anywhere.'

'You're coming home with me. Now.'

'No, Adam.'

He stared at her, surprised at her mutiny. There was silence except for the roar of the waves crashing on the strand outside.

'There's no point in arguing. Get in the car.'

'I said no. I'd rather die than go back.'

'What? The hell you will,' he blustered. He raised his arm and hit her across the face. 'Get into that car, you fucking bitch.'

She stood her ground. 'No. Didn't you hear me? I said I'd rather die than go back home to that life I had with you. You're evil. I can't stand it anymore. I've been hiding out here trying to pluck up the courage to end it all. That's what I've decided to do.'

'*End* it all? Are you mad?' His face was white.

'I've nowhere to turn and nowhere to go,' she cried. 'I promised myself that if you did find me, there was only one thing I could do. I mean it, Adam. I'd rather die than go back to that life with you.'

'You little shit. I'll see you dead first.'

The blows seemed to rain down from every direction, landing on her face, her head, her arms, and her back. The room shifted around her, as if reverberating in outrage, the cosy room that had never before witnessed such cruelty. It blurred in front of her vision, and she realised she was crying.

Then she blanked it all out. She wasn't here at all – she was with Luis, lying in his bedroom filled with muted sunshine. He was holding her safely and protectively. They were pressed together skin to skin, hip to hip, entwining their legs, their breaths mingling, lying in a cocoon of heat and warmth and perfect trust. She dissolved into that image as she fell to the floor.

Chapter Forty-seven

Even now, living in the comfort and security of his penthouse apartment, Adam had never been one hundred per cent, absolutely sure that he was rid of her ghost. Occasionally he awoke during the night, seeing her face in front of him, the sheer terror in her staring eyes as well as her disgust of him churning the anger inside him. Occasionally, he had the feeling she was there somewhere, still alive, laughing at him. Taunting him.

Then in the cold light of dawn, everything seemed okay, and his night terrors just that. Ridiculous. He could look back dispassionately on everything that had happened all those years ago and remind himself that Beth McCann – correction, Beth Gilmore – was long gone. Despite his unnerving journey back up from Cork that fateful day in September 1980, he was sitting at his desk, perfectly composed, when the call came through early on a Wednesday afternoon.

* * *

The police were downstairs and wished to talk to him. Somewhere private. He'd better prepare himself, they said, because it seemed there had been a terrible tragedy. His wife's shoes and cardigan had been washed up on the strand by the cove south of Willow Hill. And she'd left a note.

'A *note*? What kind of a note?' he said, his astonishment genuine. 'Dear God. This can't be real. Not Beth, my dearest, darling Beth. Not *my* Beth. She's spending time in England, looking after her sick aunt.'

The police were silent in the face of his outburst. Then the younger one said, apologetically, 'Unfortunately, what you've just said seems to back up what we fear.'

Adam couldn't remember either of their names. 'We don't have the note, it's down in Cork,' the young policeman continued. 'We can tell you what's in it.'

'Yes, I think you'd better,' Adam said, bracing himself.

The younger policeman consulted his notebook. 'Beth wrote that she was deeply sorry for any upset she'd caused,' he said, reading from his notes. 'She hadn't gone to England at all, there had been no sick aunt. She'd been hiding out in the summer house for the past three weeks trying to pluck up the courage to end it all. If they found this letter, and she was missing, then they'd know what she'd done.'

'What?' Adam couldn't hide his shock. Beth must have meant every word she'd said to him that night. She must have planned this. Good God. He was afraid to listen to the policeman, thoroughly alarmed.

The policeman continued. 'She said she knew the cove was a good place, with the strong rip tide. She didn't see the point in living anymore, as she feared she couldn't have children and she didn't want to tie Adam down to a childless marriage. Neither did she think she was good enough a wife for Adam, and she wanted him to be free of her. This was the only way out.' With that, he closed his notebook.

Adam let out his breath. Thankfully, there was no mention of what had really driven Beth into the sea. He knew he was ultimately responsible after the way he'd mistreated her. God forbid anyone found out.

There were questions, of course. Respectfully asked, in view of his distress.

'When was the last time you saw your wife?' the older man asked.

He swallowed nervously. 'Before she went to England to look after her aunt. That's where I thought she'd been for the last three weeks.'

'How had she seemed then?'

'She was sorry to be leaving me alone in Dublin, but it would just be for a month.'

'Did you talk to her when she was in England?'

'No, Beth told me her aunt didn't have a house phone.' *Liar.* He almost heard her ghost whisper in his ear.

'What had your marriage been like?' the older policeman asked. 'Any problems? Did Beth seem unhappy?'

'There were no problems at all, we were very happy. You could talk to some of my friends, they'd corroborate this.'

'Corroborate?' The older policeman threw him a shrewd glance. 'You're not in a witness box, Mr Gilmore.'

Yet, her ghost whispered.

'We held regular dinner parties for my colleagues and friends in the bank, and Beth had always excelled herself,' he said. 'She really enjoyed them. I can't believe this is happening …' He put his head in his hands.

After a short silence the older policeman said, 'We have to ask – where were you on Monday night, Mr Gilmore?'

'What made you think anything happened on Monday night?'

'A few things point in that direction,' the young policeman said. 'A local fisherman thought he heard a cry, late that night. The remains of food in the house pointed to someone being there very recently.'

Adam shook his head slowly.

'Not that you are in any way suspected of anything in relation to your wife, but we just need to eliminate you from all our enquiries.'

'I was at home, getting papers organised for an accountancy course I'm due to begin in October. I could show you what I was working on.'

Accountancy course? It that what he called those disgusting magazines?

Adam thought the magazines had been disturbed, but given his agitation, he told himself he was imagining it. Beth would never have been clever enough to find their hiding place.

'You're needed down in Willow Hill ... there are details to be accounted for. After that you'll have to make an official statement to the police.'

'Oh, God, that makes it seem so real. This is a nightmare. I can't take it in.'

'We're afraid it is real. Very much so. Do you need transport to Cork? You're hardly in a fit state to drive.'

'My father will drive me down – my father, the vice president of the Mutual Banking Corporation.'

'Of course.' The older policeman gave a deferential nod.

He was disgusted that it filled him with relief.

* * *

'This is a nice mess,' his father said, with thinly veiled fury. 'It'll have to be cleared up quickly. We can't afford a scandal. It couldn't happen at a worse time, you know we've an important merger on our hands. Didn't you realise your wife was unstable when you married her?'

He didn't talk to his father the whole way down to Cork. Willow Hill and the nearby village, where Beth had spent so much of her time, was plunged into mourning. According to the police, her good friend Sylvie had made a statement. Under his blind panic he was feverish to know what she'd said. The local police brought him to the summer house in which he'd threatened Beth. He acted as though he'd never set foot in it. He examined the signs of her living there as though he couldn't quite believe it; provisions such as powdered milk, tinned food, cereals; dishes draining on the counter, books on a shelf and her tape recorder. In the bedroom, he identified her clothing and toiletries. Her handbag was there, containing her appointment diary. Scattered throughout the diary, in her distinctive, childish handwriting, were brief notes of the food she'd prepared for dinners they'd hosted, to avoid, he guessed, serving the same menu twice. He also identified her handwriting on the note, which had been found behind her tape recorder, feeling all the time he was in the grip of a nightmare and she was going to jump out from behind a door and denounce him for the immoral coward he was.

Outside, he gasped in the blowy air and saw the lifeboats out in the cove and beyond, fishermen searching for her body. He heard them talk about strong currents and high tides and if they didn't find her soon they might never find her. Then he met Sylvie and John in the living room in Willow Hill.

Sylvie was sitting in an armchair by the window, her face blotchy from crying, her eyes red-rimmed. John sat protectively on the arm of the chair. She had already given a full statement to the police, as had Seamus, the handyman who'd found her clothing.

'Adam! I can't believe this has happened,' she said, making no move towards him to comfort him. 'Poor Beth. What happened? What could have possessed her?'

'I don't … How did …?' He didn't know how to phrase it. He sat down opposite them. 'When did you find out?'

'Seamus was out this morning, down by the beach, and he came back to tell me he'd seen clothing that looked like it had been washed up by the tide and that the door of the summer house was wide open. I drove around to check it out and I saw Beth's stuff … around the place' – she gulped – 'then I found the note.' She broke into fresh sobs. John rubbed her shoulders. 'I called the police immediately.

Oh, God, and she seemed so happy.'

'She did?' he had to ask. He watched her face closely.

Sylvie's red-rimmed eyes were blank as she looked at him. 'The last time I spoke to her, just before I came down here to look after my mother, she seemed so happy. So much in love. You even took the time to call her from the office when I was there, to see how she was. If that's not love, I don't know what love is. She was even talking about another dinner party ... she must have been very broken-hearted, deep down inside, when there was no sign of any babies. I wish she had spoken to me.'

'All this time I thought she was in England. I was expecting her home at the end of next week. Did you think she was in England?'

'No.' Sylvie shrugged. 'I thought she was still in Dublin. She didn't say anything to me, the last time we spoke.'

'I don't know how she managed to hide out there by the beach all by herself, or how she even thought about it,' he said. 'Have you any idea how she could have done that?'

'She was often down in the summer house. She'd have known it would be quiet down at the cove with the school holidays over. And she had a key ...'

'Still?'

Sylvie gave him a level glance. 'Beth had a key to the summer house as well as a key to Willow Hill. We never asked for them back when she moved to Dublin. My mother wanted Beth to look on Willow Hill as her second home; we're practically family and she's spent most of her life here.'

John Cassidy stood up. He was tall and broad with it, a formidable figure silhouetted against the window. Then his father, white-faced with barely concealed irritation, stood in the doorway. No trace of anything yet. They were organising some volunteers to search the coastline on foot.

The search was called off after five days.

Chapter Forty-eight

It took a while for Carrie to calm down after Adam's unexpected visit. Needing to do something, she took everything out of her wardrobe, sorting out clothes, picking out the shirts and suits she'd worn in Jade and deciding not to use them again, wherever she worked. She put them to one side for the charity shop. She found she enjoyed going through her clothes, seeing where separates she'd bought could be mixed and matched, and carefully hanging up the dresses she bought in Jade as she would certainly use them again.

Later, as she sat curled up on the sofa, her mobile pinged with a text message.

> Carrie and Mark will not have a row when he calls to collect his letter tomorrow evening.

His text gave her a warm glow after the sour aftertaste of Adam Gilmore's unexpected visit. She took her courage in both hands and replied.

> Carrie is relaxed and she will not row with Mark.

A few minutes later, he texted her again.

Mark and Carrie might even talk when he calls to collect his letter.

Her heart thumped. What did he mean 'talk'? Exchanging pleasantries without anyone getting angry or did he mean something more meaningful? She took a deep breath and, feeling a little giddy, she texted back.

Carrie is happy to talk to Mark.

After a short while he replied.

Mark is happy that Carrie is happy to talk to him.

The warm glow she felt spread out and tingled like anticipation in her tummy. She read and re-read his text as though she was grasping at straws, anything to focus on something good and positive to do with Mark, instead of the coldness of Adam Gilmore's eyes. She went to bed, feeling as though Mark had enveloped her in a hug, or kissed her gently on the forehead, just like he'd kissed her at the party. So what if she was making far more of his texts than he intended? It made her feel good for a while.

Wednesday afternoon was bright and summery, so rather than spend it tucked up in Faith Crescent, becoming more and more jittery by the minute, she put on her tracksuit and yellow Skechers and took the DART out to Killiney beach, where she spent a couple of hours striding up and down, inhaling the fresh sea air, her senses filling up with the calming rhythm of the sea, the view of the Wicklow mountains in the far distance and the elegant Sorrento Terrace to the north. There was something cathartic in letting go of everything and just relaxing into the moment. It was one of the things she'd taken home from her visit to Luis.

Afterwards, she walked up Killiney Hill, where the views of the city, the sea and the mountains were even more spectacular. It wasn't quite Rigi, but the city looked peaceful and placid and from this vantage point, Adam and the veiled kind of threat she sensed coming from him receded until she could look at it all objectively. Her imagination was on fire, that was all. Whatever had gone wrong in Willow Hill, it was over thirty years ago, so it was history. She wasn't used to dealing with the Adam Gilmores of this world, an insanely successful man with a ruthless streak lurking beneath his thin veneer of bonhomie, and that was why she found him a little intimidating. She would talk to Sean later in the week and ask him if she could move all the accounts to the firm that handled his business. So, for now, she just had one thing to concern herself with – seeing Mark later that evening.

Sitting on the DART on the way home, invigorated after her hours out of the house, she checked her mobile and logged on to Twitter.

@carriecassidy: hellooo! What are you up to today? I'm #feelingbored Any trips planned? @happyduck

She replied.

@happyduck No trips planned but #feelinggood

After she sent her tweet, she gazed idly out the windows at the panorama of Dublin Bay to her right. Sitting there, lulled into a relaxed state with the movement of the train, a thought flashed into her head that had the same effect as being doused in a bucket of cold water.

How did @happyduck know Carrie wasn't in the office today? The tweet had been sent earlier that afternoon and it had sounded like @happyduck knew Carrie wasn't working. Carrie had never logged on to Twitter during working hours. Nor had she ever mentioned work specifically, preferring to keep her job in Jade off the inquisitive airwaves of social media. Most of her tweeting was done at night, responding to other tweets and commenting on TV, books, movies and general stuff about her social life. She took out her mobile again and scrolled through her recent tweets. She'd never tweeted about leaving Jade, and had said very little about working there. She checked @happyduck's profile and it was innocent enough; a fluffy duck avatar, lover of shoes and shopping, movies, food and wine, with two hundred followers and several hundred tweets. When she looked out the window again, they were passing by other people's back gardens and then the DART was slowing down as it pulled into Tara Street. Carrie put her mobile into her bag and stood up, joining the queue shuffling off the train, trying to shake off her uneasiness. It was entirely possible that @happyduck had tweeted her during the daytime before with similar tweets, and she just hadn't noticed. She hurried down the steps as though someone was after her, came out of the train station and turned down George's Quay, trying not to feel a prickle across her shoulder blades at the thought of Adam Gilmore sitting by the window of his steel and glass office further down the river, watching all going on around him.

Adam Gilmore, who had been taken by surprise to hear she'd left her job. That's what had niggled her after their meeting. It hadn't just been the normal kind of surprise that someone would walk out of a job in today's climate. It had been a disconcerting surprise, as though he had been thrown off balance at the news – and thrown off balance because he felt he should have already known. How, though?

Adam Gilmore, saying she'd probably been away three or four times this year … and the long silence when she hadn't volunteered any information. Like, for example, that she'd been in Lucerne – which she'd tweeted about. By the time she turned into the cul de sac at Faith Crescent, she was sweaty and uncomfortable, and in need of a long, refreshing shower. She would put on her good jeans and a

Zara top, and fix her hair and makeup, and try to calm down before Mark arrived.

Mark is happy that Carrie is happy to talk to him.

That was all she had to think about. Nothing else. She quickened her pace, jogging slightly as she hurried around the crescent towards her house and almost jumped out of her skin when a man got out of a parked car just as she drew alongside it.

'Hey …' she said, feeling shaken.

'Carrie? Are you okay?'

It wasn't Adam Gilmore, coming after her. It was Mark. Tall, lean, Mark, getting to his feet on the pavement beside her, shutting the car door before activating the alarm, here already, to collect his letter. Her brain stopped in its tracks, paused, switched gears. No time to shower and change, never mind do her hair and makeup. But never had the sight of him been so welcome. She stood there, suddenly vulnerable as though her outer layer of skin had been stripped off, laughing giddily, unable to stop tears running down her cheeks.

'What's up?' he asked.

'Sorry,' she gulped. 'Don't mind me. You weren't expecting this. It's not exactly Carrie being happy to talk to Mark.'

'I got here a bit early. I was sitting in the car and just about to text you,' he asked. 'What's the matter?'

'I don't know.' She dashed away tears. 'It's nothing,' she said, flapping her hands in agitation. 'Just me being stupid. At being caught like this. Look at me.' She tugged at her grey tracksuit top. 'I thought I'd have time to shower and change and look respectable before you arrived. I was rushing so I didn't even see your car.' She laughed, or rather she tried to laugh, but it came out like a strangled gasp. 'Oh God, I'm making a right mess of this.'

He put out a hand as if to steady her, his eyes full of warm concern. 'Slow down, Carrie. Why don't I come inside, you have your shower, and we can talk then.'

Chapter Forty-nine

Carrie stood under the shower spray, slathering herself with coconut-scented shower crème, closing her eyes, tipping her head back and letting the warm sudsy water sluice all over her body until she was rinsed squeaky clean. Having Mark downstairs gave her a feeling of something solid against her back, and she laughed at this. Not so long ago, she'd sent him away because he made her feel as though she was stepping off the edge of space into an abyss. Now she felt nothing but relief that he was here.

She was beginning to realise that nothing in life could stand still. Being alive meant it would always be fluid and fluctuating, full of unanswered questions, quirky possibilities and no guarantees whatsoever.

Afterwards, wrapped in a terry robe, she opened the steamed-up window to the calm, early evening, where silvery sunlight reflected off the church spire. Silhouetted against the pale blue sky, it looked beautiful and serene, solid and invincible, like the mountains in Switzerland. She put on her jeans and top, dried her hair, slicked on some mascara and a trace of lip gloss, and lastly a spritz of scent and she was ready to go downstairs where Mark was waiting.

He was sitting on the sofa in her kitchen, going through emails on his phone, his legs stretched out in front of him, angled at the knees. She'd forgotten the way the kitchen sofa was too compact to contain his tall frame. He looked up and smiled automatically at her as she came through the door and her breath stalled at the look in his light-grey eyes. It was nothing more than his normal friendly smile, she cautioned herself.

'Did you get your post?' she asked.

'I did, thanks,' he said, pointing at the holdall he used for ferrying around his laptop that was propped against the bottom of the sofa.

'It looked urgent.'

'It was. Very.'

She wondered, if it was all that urgent, why he hadn't ensured it was sent to his correct address, wherever that was. He showed no sign of getting up and walking out the door and leaving her in a cold but peaceful silence. Peace? There was no peace in his absence, just a raw ache that attached itself to all the contours of her heart like a layer of cling film. There was no peace either in imagining what might happen in the next few minutes. Her nerve endings jangled. The wrong word could lead to more angry words, and she didn't want to hear Mark's anger or see him storming out of her house again.

'Are you feeling better?' he asked.

'Much.'

'How have you been?'

'Fine.' She stood behind the counter, unsure what to do. Offer him a drink? Beer? Coffee? They were miles away, surely, from that level of relaxed amiability.

'Carrie, I'm not going to bite,' he said. 'I thought it would be good to have a civil conversation without either of us tearing strips off each other – though I think it has been mostly me tearing strips off you lately. I was glad you talked to me at the party last week, I know it must have been hard for you.'

'It was. Sort of.' She gave him a half smile.

'Especially after you saw me arriving with Sienna.'

Was that a teasing glint in his eye? She lifted a shoulder as though to say Sienna being there had made no difference, ignoring the way she'd been wracked with envy.

'Seriously, I was glad you thought you could trust me, but I was surprised by some of the things you said.'

'Like what?' She felt a wall going up inside her.

'Things I didn't have time to ask you about properly, that need more explanation. Like the part ...' He paused. His gaze locked with hers. 'That part where you said you didn't think you deserved such happiness. Were you that happy with me? So good you felt you didn't deserve it?'

Oh, hell, it was a lot harder to talk here, in her kitchen, than at a party with enough distractions going on to dilute the intensity of it all. She had the sense that she was climbing a mountain.

'I didn't realise it at the time,' she said truthfully. 'I was mixed up and confused. You cracked open my safe, risk-free little world. I thought I was scared of falling off the deep end, afraid of commitment, of falling short, of not being good enough – and I was, in a way, but bigger than all of those was the fear of being happy. It scared me. I didn't think I was entitled to feel so ... wonderful.'

He was on his feet by now, but something in her eyes must have stopped him from coming too close to her. He remained on the other side of the counter, leaning carelessly against it.

'Carrie, I ...' He paused, grinning disarmingly. 'I'd love to play a game of "What If".'

She shook her head, 'A *game*, Mark?'

'It's something we do in work from time to time,' he said.

'In *work*? Sounds more like fun to me.' She forced the joke out through her dry mouth.

'Yeah, sometimes it's fun. That's the whole point. The more you're relaxed, the better the ideas. We ask ourselves lots of questions to get the creative juices flowing, look at things from different angles and attempt to link them no matter how mad or outlandish they are.'

'What if.'

He placed his hands down flat on the counter and leaned forward a little. 'You see, it's been going around in my head ... After we split, I was so angry, so furious with you, I was too mad to think straight. But now ...'

'Go on.'

'I've been asking myself a few things, like, what if Carrie had talked to Mark properly, from the beginning?'

She stared at him but remained silent.

'But what if Mark had been a little more sensitive,' he went on, 'so that he had seen things from Carrie's point of view, instead of his own? It might have helped Carrie to trust him.'

'You did try,' she said, her voice husky.

'What if Mark had tried harder? Taken it slower, and not rushed Carrie into important, life-changing decisions like an engagement? What if he had listened more? And talked less?'

She shook her head, incapable of speech.

'What if Mark hadn't been so knocked for six when he first saw Carrie that his head went out the window and only one part of his anatomy was speaking to him ... Or he hadn't thought he could plonk a big, magic sticking plaster over everything, over all of Carrie's sad history, and expect Carrie to be healed?'

She put up her hand. She struggled to find her voice. 'Mark – stop, please. You tried. I just wasn't ready.'

'Maybe I should have known and respected that ... and had more patience.'

'Should.' She smiled. 'The most useless word there is. I'm surprised to hear it coming from you, the master of go-do-it, positive thinking.'

'Sometimes I charge in with my big size tens where angels wouldn't tiptoe. I make mistakes too, you know.'

Silence dropped between them. All of Carrie's nerves felt stretched to the point of snapping. Outside the window, a flock of birds took flight from her garden and soared together into the air. Inside, all she could hear was the hum of the fridge and her heartbeat.

'I'll leave you on that note, Carrie.' His eyes were warm. Everything about this man was warm and reassuring and she felt a stab of panic that he was leaving her alone in the cold silence of the house, with a million anxieties teeming around in her head. He gave her a rueful grin before he walked across to the sofa to retrieve his holdall. 'Although,' he said over his shoulder, 'you might want to strike everything I said. Given the way we imploded, it's probably far too outlandish and ambitious.' He looped an arm through his holdall and walked to the door.

Panic swelled inside her. He'd be through the hall door in a minute, leaving her alone with the memories of Beth and the slithery Adam Gilmore. And alone with regrets about Mark and their imploded relationship crashing over her in waves.

'What if,' she began, her voice cracking. He paused in the doorway, looking back at her as he waited for her to speak.

She gripped the counter, needing to support herself against it. 'What if Mark and Carrie could start all over again?' she said. 'A new beginning?'

He stood perfectly still. 'Are you— Do you mean it?'

As her eyes held his, she could only manage a nod of her head.

He turned to face her, but didn't come any closer. 'Carrie, I hope you're not playing with me. We both made a mess of things first time around. Let's not rush into anything,' he said. 'Take your time, have a good think about it and make sure it's what you want. *I* need to know you're perfectly sure.' He hesitated, looking a little awkward. 'Thing is, Carrie,' he said softly, 'I don't think I could take any more bruising or battering.'

'I understand that,' she said weakly.

'We can talk about this again. Maybe go for coffee or something. If any other post comes and it looks important, let me know and I'll call over.' He walked towards the front door.

Some kind of panic slid through her veins. 'Mark – wait.'

He turned. 'Yes?'

'There's something—' She didn't know where to start. 'Don't leave just yet. I need to talk to someone ... it's not us, but it's something else, weird things. I dunno ...' For the second time that evening, she felt raw and vulnerable and tears sprang into her eyes. She began to shake.

Mark slid his holdall to the floor. 'What's wrong?'

'I don't know,' she said. 'I could be imagining it all, but I feel kind of uneasy about something.'

Chapter Fifty

He interrupted her incoherent jumble of words about Adam Gilmore, her mother, Beth and Luis three times, and asked her to slow down. He told her to tell him everything, no matter how insignificant it seemed. He said if he was in work, he would jot it all down on a big white board and try to connect some dots. Here in Faith Crescent, he would have to make do with sitting at the kitchen table in front of his laptop and a blank refill pad. And lots of coffee.

'So take a deep breath, clear your thoughts and start at the beginning. Again,' he said, rolling up his sleeves, powering up his laptop, and tearing off a fresh page.

Sitting across the table from him, Carrie did as she was told and went back to the first time she'd met Maria. 'I didn't believe for one moment that Mum had betrayed my father.'

'Yet you decided to go ahead and visit Luis?'

She gave a self-deprecating smile. 'Maria seemed so genuine. I wanted to find out more, prove him wrong, and I needed to get away from the … mouldy pit my life had become after us.'

He glanced at her. '"Mouldy pit"? That's one way of putting it.'

'I was all over the place, and I wanted to breathe different air for a while, so I can't take credit for being unselfish. Luis still wanted to see me even though I didn't accept that he'd known my mum, and given the circumstances, I thought it was about time I did something decent for someone else.'

'Even though it meant getting on a plane?' He said it delicately as though it still rankled a little.

'Thing is …' she hesitated.

'Yes?' He looked directly at her.

She took a deep breath. 'On the way over, I was so upset after our row that getting on a plane was kind of okay. I even brought your playlist. On the way back, I pretended you were with me, holding my hand every step of the way.'

Something in his face softened. Encouraged, she told him everything that had happened since she met Maria in the foyer at Jade, right up to this afternoon. Mark interrupted now and then to clarify and ask a question or two, his fingers flying across the keys.

'Have you talked to Evelyn and Sean about all this?'

'Not yet. I'm still trying to sort it out myself. Sean and Evelyn think Adam Gilmore is above board. It's more a gut feeling I have, that something is wrong.'

'Why? What are you thinking?' He pushed back his chair and stretched his arms over his head. It was a gesture so familiar to her, he had done this hundreds of times after their evening meal together, that her heart ached.

'The worst. I'm adding two and two together and making twelve. Then again, my head has been all over the place …'

'Hey, don't look so woebegone. Let's look at the facts,' Mark said calmly. 'This guy's wife seems to have run off and left him, why we don't know. She was hiding out in the summer house during which time she appears to have had an affair with Luis. Okay? And then she was lost at sea two days after Luis went home. What does that add up to? Either she was very guilty after the affair and took her own life because she couldn't live with it, or—' He stopped, because Carrie was shaking her head slowly.

'No way. She saved Luis' life and talked to him about how precious life was. She'd already lost people she loved, her mother and sister, and was very cross with him for trying to throw his life away.'

'Okaaaay …' Mark chewed his pencil.

'So even though there was a note, which my mother found, I find it impossible to believe that Beth could have done that. She could have written the note under duress.'

'Whose duress?'

'Supposing Adam found her? Down in the summer house? I can't imagine how he'd react if he found out his wife was having an affair and that she'd betrayed him. He'd want to kill her,' Carrie said.

'You don't know that for sure. We know Beth ran away from her marriage but we don't know why.'

'What if Adam found Beth somehow, and was so enraged he killed her, and made it look like an accident?'

'That's very serious, Carrie. I'm sure Adam was investigated at the time. The husband is always the first in the firing line if any foul play is suspected.'

'Even people like him? With a very influential father? God knows how many brown envelopes changed hands back then.'

Mark stared at his scribbled notes and scanned his Word document. 'Getting back to the start of it all, I still can't join the dots between you going to Lucerne to see Luis, and Adam Gilmore himself suddenly deciding to meet you for a chat. It could be entirely coincidental.'

'I think he might have been keeping tabs on me, but, again, I don't know if I'm imagining it.'

'How, though?'

Carrie bit her lip. 'That's what I'm finding creepy. I think he's been following me on Twitter.'

Mark flung down his pencil. 'Twitter? Jesus, Carrie.'

'I copped it this afternoon,' she said, explaining what had

happened. 'That's why I almost jumped out of my skin when you got out of the car. I just felt freaked.'

Mark frowned and shook his head. 'Bloody social media.'

'Am I mad thinking a man in his position would resort to that?'

'It's a handy way of keeping an eye on someone. Especially if they're documenting what they have for breakfast and putting up photograph of their dinners.'

'Here, I wasn't that bad.'

'Guys like him could afford high-tech surveillance, or a private investigator, but that would mean involving other people. And if he has something to hide, the less other people know, the better.'

It was a couple of hours before Carrie had finished recounting everything she could think of. She'd done most of the talking, and the fact that Mark had listened and taken her concerns seriously had soothed her. Despite her heightened awareness of him, it had been easy to talk, and cathartic to unload her worries. Now a different kind of tension was setting in, alerting all her senses. For the first time since their breakup, they'd spent the guts of two hours together. And without a cross word. All this time she'd been subconsciously soaking up the sight of him at her kitchen table, his dark hair flopping across his forehead, those light-grey eyes fixed on her attentively as she spoke, his shirt open at the neck, the slight stubble dusting his firm jaw, the feathering of dark hair on his bare arms emerging from his scrunched-up sleeves. The whole gorgeous package of Mark O'Neill.

They both spoke together.

'I think—' he began.

'I'd no idea it—' she said.

They laughed, and as they met each other's eyes, Carrie's stomach contracted.

'You first,' said Mark.

'I didn't know it was this late,' she said. 'You must be starving.'

She was sorry she'd spoken. He'd agree and say it was time he went home, wherever that was.

'I hadn't noticed the time,' he said. 'I've just twigged something here.'

'What's that?'

'Seamus, the handyman in Willow Hill, around the time Beth was seeing Luis. Is he still alive?'

'Seamus? I'd forgotten about him. Where's he mentioned?'

'In the inquest report.'

Carrie fished the inquest report out of the papers on the table and scanned it again. 'That escaped me, I was so shocked by everything else. If he's still alive he'd be well into his eighties,' she said slowly. 'I vaguely remember him, oh about fifteen years ago. I got the impression he was a bit simple though, and a little too fond of his whiskey, and that my grandparents took him on to give him something to do and to try and keep him on the straight and narrow.'

'If he's still alive he might be worth talking to.'

Carrie hesitated. 'I'd nearly be afraid to talk to him, God knows what else might come crawling out of the woodwork.'

'If you're that afraid, I'll come with you.'

'Mark,' she said, 'why are you doing this for me?'

Echoing through her mind were the angry words he'd hurled at her not so long ago and pulsing through her heart was the way she'd bruised and battered his.

'If you'd seen your face when I jumped out of the car ... it got to me,' he said. 'You looked scared and vulnerable and I rarely got to see Carrie Cassidy looking like that. I want to help, as a friend, especially if this guy is spooking you. I don't like that.'

A friend. Still, a huge improvement. It would take a lot to convince him that she meant every word she'd said about giving them a second chance.

'There are things we can do in the background in Bizz as well, if someone's being stalked on social media. It might mean involving the cops. Think about it.'

'I will,' Carrie said. Her heart sank a little as she watched him shuffling his notes together and powering down his laptop.

'I'd better go,' he said.

'Oh. Right.'

He seemed distant, a little preoccupied, almost uneasy. She cast her mind back to see if she'd said something wrong. He stood up and shoved his laptop, notes and refill pad into his backpack.

'I'll call you tomorrow,' he said. 'Find out about Seamus. If he's still alive, we'll go to see him this weekend. And, in the meantime, promise me one thing. Don't open your hall door. To anyone at all.'

'You hardly think …'

'I don't know what to think, Carrie. But don't let Adam Gilmore in if he's upsetting you that much. And go easy on Twitter.'

'I could always put up a few fake tweets.'

Mark shook his head. 'No way. They'll only sound concocted and Adam Gilmore will know you've rumbled him.'

She felt dizzy as he walked briskly up the hall, opened the door and stepped outside. Then a final quick wave and he was gone. She tried to dismiss the feeling that he couldn't wait to be gone. He was bringing her to Cork, wasn't he?

* * *

The following day, it took one phone call to Evelyn Sullivan to find out that Seamus was still alive.

'Well, now, I'm not quite sure to what degree he's alive and well,' Evelyn said, 'given his fondness for whiskey. Funny to think he outlived them all, considering the damage he must have inflicted on his liver. He's in a nursing home outside Cork.'

'I might pay him a visit,' Carrie said.

'I'm not sure he'd recognise you,' Evelyn cautioned. 'Sean popped in to see him after Christmas and his mind was wandering a lot. Are you sure this is a good idea, Carrie? You sounded upset the last time we spoke.'

'I'm fine. I'm just making peace with the past in a way. Seamus was part of Willow Hill, he would have been there in my mother's time.'

'He was, sort of, if you count in his night-time poaching as well as his hit-and-miss gardening attempts. Sean said he was lucky your grandfather took him on, they were second or third cousins or something. I'll text you the nursing home details, but you mightn't get any sense out of him. And if you're down this direction, feel free to pop in. That job offer is still open, if you're interested. Clare and I want to have someone sorted in the role over the next few months.'

'Thanks a million, and thanks for everything.'

She was still undecided about the job in Willow Hill spa. She was in a vacuum of sorts, a beat of time between the safe world of risk-averse Carrie, and the Carrie who wanted to venture out and grab life by the guts. Sometimes the thoughts of it made her head spin, but in a good way – a way that meant she was alive and feeling the rich possibilities of that life beginning to trickle through her again. She just needed to get that creep Adam Gilmore off her back. Which she would, as soon as possible.

And more importantly, her heart swelled; she would see where she was going with Mark.

Chapter Fifty-one

Much to his annoyance, as he barked out orders down in the Gilcorp boardroom or took a conference call in the meeting room, Adam found himself distracted by the knowledge that he'd never been absolutely sure he was in the clear, even after the inquest to settle Beth's affairs. It had been held eight years after her disappearance and it had been Sylvie who'd made him feel uneasy, Sylvie who had rattled his conscience and given him some sleepless nights.

* * *

As Sylvie gave her evidence all those years ago, there was no sign of the young woman who'd been crying her heart out in Willow Hill. More mature now, with a sophistication and polish that was attractive, she answered the coroner's questions in a low, clear voice. It was a very small gathering. Because of the sensitive nature of the case, his father had paid handsomely to ensure that only those who strictly had to be in attendance were there. There were no reporters, and details were kept from the press, as would the inquest report.

After Sylvie said her piece, her steady gaze met his across the courtroom. He felt a sudden chill go down to his toes and wondered what, if anything, she knew about Beth's true state of mind and the abysmal nature of their marriage. He would have to keep an eye on her. It should be easy enough because thanks to the nature of his career, he had lots of friends now, in all sorts of high places. Still, he was being very careful not to blot his copybook. In Ireland, at any rate. He had started to go abroad three, four times a year, using his annual leave to recharge his batteries in the most agreeable way.

His statement was read out, the one he'd given to the police at the time Beth went missing. It was embarrassing to hear that she'd claimed to be visiting her aunt in England during the time she'd apparently been staying in the summer house.

He had a bad moment when Seamus, the gardener-cum-handyman, was called to the stand, but he looked as nervous as a mouse, twisting his cap in his shaking hands. He stared at Adam as though he was terrified of him, and then he'd kept his eyes trained on Sylvie as he spoke. He confirmed he'd gone down to the beach for sand for the Willow Hill garden when he'd found clothes at the tide line and seen the door of the summer house wide open. It looked like someone had been living there. He'd run all the way to Miss Sylvie and later he'd found out the clothes had belonged to Beth.

The Garda superintendent at the time, who had since retired, gave a full account of the search, including the evidence to the effect that Beth had most likely been living in the summer house prior to the incident. A statement was read out from a Professor Meyer, of Lucerne, Switzerland. He'd been in Ireland on a research project, and had been renting a house further up the headland, at the same time as Beth was purported to be staying in the summer house. The professor and his teenage son had returned to Lake Lucerne two days before Beth went missing, but during their visit they'd kept to themselves and at no time had they been aware of her presence.

Professor Meyer. He'd filed that name away for future reference. No harm to check it out himself.

Sea conditions and tides prevailing at the time were examined.

The note Beth had left was acknowledged, but not read out in court, although it was confirmed that both he and Sylvie testified that it was in Beth's handwriting. On the balance of probabilities, the coroner made a legal declaration that Beth Gilmore was missing, presumed dead. He extended his sympathies to both her family and close friends.

Afterwards, as they shuffled out through the exit, he thought he heard the words 'fucking bastard' murmured close to his ear. But when he looked behind him there was no one within earshot except big John Cassidy, who was staring away into the distance.

'We must keep in touch,' he said to Sylvie, outside on the pavement. 'You're my only link to Beth now,' he went on, his voice smooth. 'I don't want to lose contact with you.'

'Oh, I'm sure we'll be seeing you around,' Sylvie said, equally smoothly. 'I've no doubt whatsoever about that. I have some photographs we must share with you sometime, nice ones, of Beth, some of them taken on her wedding day.'

Photographs? He stared intently at her for several seconds, holding her gaze, wondering if there was an implied threat of any kind in her words, but her eyes were clear and guileless. Then John came along and curved his arm around her; he was the first to look away.

The following year his father had been very disappointed when he'd turned his back on a plumb job with the Mutual Banking Corporation to establish himself as a financier, setting up his own private equity company. Mutual Banking was about to be sucked into one of the multinationals and Adam had his own grand ambitions. A year later, he'd spent a weekend in Lucerne and tracked down Professor Meyer, and the grey-haired eminent scientist and his piano-playing prodigy son were so far out of Beth's league that it was laughable to imagine they might have run across each other in Cork.

But sometimes in the silent hours of the night an unsettling voice inside him whispered that they'd never found a body. Sometimes he thought of the look Sylvie Cassidy had given him. As though she knew more than she was letting on. Other times, he told himself he'd just been imagining it. She and her husband seemed to live a very quiet life. Escaping to the sun once a year, to a vulgar resort overrun with tourists, could scarcely constitute a very exciting existence. They didn't do anything at all to draw his attention to them.

Funnily enough, the one time he'd had a lengthy spell abroad, when he'd gone to Wall Street for six months, they'd obviously decided to expand their horizons and travel to South America. He'd heard on CNN about an Irish couple being amongst other Europeans who'd perished in the plane crash in the Andes, and had been shocked to discover it was the Cassidys. Two months later, when he was back in Dublin, he'd read in the newspaper that their remains were finally being repatriated. He'd allowed himself to feel a small relief at the funeral, as he watched what was left of her body being interred into the hard ground. If Sylvie Cassidy had been carrying any secrets, they had died with her.

Hadn't they?

* * *

He'd probably not have got away with it nowadays, not with mobile phone technology and near-instant communication, and big brother watching you, between the ability to track mobile phone signals and car movements. Besides, legislation had changed completely in favour of women. But some legislation hadn't changed, which was why he had to get his sexual kicks abroad, blending anonymously into the shadows of busy tourist spots, although he was always extremely careful not to use a phone that could be traced back to him.

What was he afraid of? He'd been clever enough to offer his help in sorting out the Cassidy affairs, suddenly paranoid in case there was anything amongst their paperwork to incriminate him, like another note Beth might have left with her friend, or a diary, whatever photographs Sylvie had alluded to after the inquest. He'd thought some of his special ones might have been disturbed around the time Beth walked out on him. Even if Sylvie's daughter just happened to stumble across something, surely a ghost couldn't give evidence against him. Then he told himself in the next breath that if Sylvie had known anything at all that could blacken his name and lead to a prison conviction – like accusations of marital rape, or gross indecency, domestic violence or attempted murder – she would scarcely have kept silent all those years.

Unless she'd had very good reason.

He almost heard Beth's soft voice in the darkest hour of the night. Like what, though? And now Sylvie's daughter was digging around and behaving strangely in front of him and giving him real cause for concern. From his comfortable leather chair, he stared down at the river of humanity swarming the city-centre streets far below. Friday evening brought lots of people into the docklands area, for meals, drinks, coffee, the theatre. Up in his penthouse, he lived in an impregnable fortress, a bubble suspended far up and away from the great mass of ordinary people. Much as he liked to remain above it all, there were times, very occasionally, when he had to step outside his citadel and call in a favour. This appeared to be one of those times. Going across to his safe that was concealed behind a Jack Yeats painting, he took out a mobile he rarely used in Ireland, and he made a call.

Chapter Fifty-two

Saturday-morning traffic was light and the roads were dry, the countryside glinting under early June sunshine. Mark drove, his hands light on the steering wheel, Carrie absorbing his profile against the view of fields and distant mountains flowing by the window. She sat back, letting everything about this man drip-feed through her senses like warm, soothing nectar. They spent most of the journey in silence, music playing softly as they sped down the M8 through the Golden Vale, over the Blackwater River, reaching the outskirts of Cork in just under two hours, and they stopped for lunch in a hotel on the edge of the city.

The dining room was busy but they got a table by the window, where landscaped gardens were visible behind voile curtains shading the floor-to-ceiling windows and children laughed and shouted in a fenced-off play area.

'How are you feeling?' Mark asked.

'Jittery,' she said. Jittery with Mark sitting opposite her, his long fingers unrolling his napkin, his eyes searching her face. So close, yet so far away. He was wearing black jeans and a white shirt, reminding her again of the moment they'd met, the moment the Spanish-looking guy standing by the altar had snagged her heart.

'Jittery, but …'

He raised a dark eyebrow.

'Glad I'm not on my own.'

To her surprise, he reached across the dining table and interlinked his fingers with hers. '"Glad" sounds good. Jittery? There's no need. I'm with you in this.'

She couldn't stop herself from stroking her thumb across the palm of his hand, revelling at this small sense of togetherness. 'I just want all this to be settled,' she said. 'I doubt if Seamus will have much to say anyway. Whatever happens, I'm going to move the finances to another accountancy firm, and cut all ties with Adam Gilmore.'

'Sounds like a plan.'

It would be the start of getting her life back on track. She wanted to begin again with Mark, and show him, somehow, that she had changed from the Carrie Cassidy who'd been afraid to take any chances in life or love, but she knew he would take some convincing.

* * *

The nursing home on the outskirts of Kinsale was a low-rise, modern building with neat, landscaped grounds. Carrie had already called ahead to see if Seamus was up to having visitors, explaining that she was related to the Sullivans of Willow Hill, where he'd worked for years. She'd been told that she was very welcome to see him, but that he was frequently confused.

'He has very few visitors,' the care assistant said as she brought them down clean, polished yet airless corridors to his room. 'Sad, really, he's such a quiet, gentle person. His room-mate has gone home for the weekend, so you can chat undisturbed.' She ushered them into a small, neat bedroom overlooking the side gardens of the home. One bed was unoccupied, the bed sheets perfectly arranged over the blue coverlet and, in the other bed, a wizened old man was propped up against the pillows. The sheets on his bed were also perfectly aligned, as though he hadn't the energy to disturb them. He stared at them uncomprehendingly with his vacant eyes. Carrie was already regretting her trip down. It seemed so unfair to be disturbing this frail, elderly man with her wild-goose chase.

'Seamus?' the care assistant said in a deliberately loud, friendly tone. 'There are some lovely visitors here to see you, it must be your lucky day.' She turned to Carrie. 'I'll leave you to it. Press the bell if you need to call me, otherwise I'll see you before you leave.'

Carrie moved further into the room and over to the bed, which was close to the window. Mark brought over some chairs and they sat down side by side. 'Hello, Seamus,' she said, unable to equate the frail person in the bed with the handyman she'd remembered taking care of Willow Hill. Seamus turned his head slightly in her direction and his faded, blue eyes wandered around the general area where she sat.

After a while he spoke. 'Sylvie?'

Carrie couldn't prevent herself from grabbing Mark's hand.

'Sylvie,' Seamus said, a little stronger. 'There you are.'

Carrie nodded, unwilling to confuse the old man. To her consternation, his eyes filled with tears.

'I wish I was gone,' he said. 'I want to be with Molly. It's been too long.'

'You loved Molly?' Carrie said gently.

'Aye.' He stared into the distance, seeing something in his mind's eye.

'That's nice, to have someone to love.'

'She was the only girl I ever loved, and she went away. She took the boat to England.' He sat in silence, his face crumpled as though some of the life had gone out of it. 'Then she came back with the wee child and I still loved her.'

'When she came back to Willow Hill?' Carrie said carefully. She was afraid of asking too much.

'I got her a job with Mrs Sullivan after Anna, didn't I? I did that for her. It broke her heart, losing Anna like that, and it broke my heart too … to see Molly so full of sorrow. Hers was a hard cross to bear.' Fresh tears glistened in his faded eyes.

It was wrong of her to be here, Carrie decided. She was just upsetting Seamus. He thought she was Sylvie and his mind was back there again. 'He's talking about Anna,' she murmured to Mark. 'Beth's older sister.'

'Molly was too sad.' Seamus lifted a feeble hand and tried to wipe away a tear.

'Yes, it was very sad,' Carrie murmured, not knowing how to console him, privately kicking herself for resurrecting old and painful memories.

'I'm glad she was gone before Beth,' he said.

Carrie tightened her grip on Mark's hand.

'Poor Beth. To go like that … It would have broken Molly completely. Strange too. Beth could swim like a fish … you and her both. Remember? The swimming down in the cove?'

Seamus sat up a little straighter and Carrie wondered how he was balancing his head on his pitiably thin neck. 'But I stayed quiet about the ghost,' he said, his eyes widening as they fixed on hers. 'Like you said, I didn't want them locking me away in St Conor's.'

She remembered St Conor's as an old hospital on the Cork road. Long closed and fallen into disrepair, it had been an oppressive, forbidding building, with a sinister history. She could easily imagine it being used as a threat once upon a time.

'What ghost, Seamus?' Carrie asked gently.

'Remember, Sylvie? I told you I seen her ghost in the woods that night. I swore on my own mother's grave not to tell in case people thought I was for the fairies and the banshees. I still haven't told anyone, like you said. After Molly and Beth and Anna, you were the next person I loved. We all loved you, Sylvie.'

Carrie felt humbled. 'It's safe to talk to me, Seamus. Just tell me again, what ghost did you see in the woods?'

'It was Beth. All white and pale. The ghost of Beth floating through the woods, up towards Willow Hill.'

Carrie didn't even realise she had fallen against Mark until she felt the solid weight of him at her back.

Chapter Fifty-three

September 1980

This time, it was different. This time as Adam's blows rained down upon her, she was dissolving into Luis, gathering strength from the memory of their love, summoning a powerful courage that poured through her veins like liquid steel.

Even when she managed to escape from his blows, drag herself to her feet, throw back the door and run out into the night, she was melting into Luis. And when Adam came thundering after her, his breath heavy behind her in the cold night air, she didn't notice herself shrugging off his arm and increasing her pace. She was lying in a bed of heat, warmth and peace.

The sea was an ocean of pitch-black ink, roaring in the dark, broken only by the rolling waves showing foamy-white tips as they crashed upon the strand. She ran into the shallows, the water so cold that it almost robbed her of breath. She managed, somehow, to drag off her shoes and cardigan before she ran headlong through icy, black waves, her ragged breathing loud in her ears along with the roar of the ocean. She heard splashes and realised they were coming from her tired limbs. She gave a cry for help, and then another.

If Adam attempted to follow her, she knew exactly how to get rid of him. Watching the sea, knowing it from childhood, she'd imagined this moment in her head over and over during the past week. But above the roar of the tide, there was no sound of anyone crashing through the waves behind her. No sound of Adam coming behind her to finish what he had started back in the summer house. Certainly no sound of him coming to rescue her.

Then she was lifted off her feet, and she found herself treading water, waiting for the rip tide to pull her out, far beyond his reach. She knew exactly what to do. Since the first summers that she and Sylvie had learned to swim, it had been ingrained in their minds – stay calm and don't fight it, you'll only waste your energy. If you can't manage to swim parallel to the shore, let the tide bring you out, then afterwards, when it dies down, you can come back in again. She felt the pull and suck of the tide and she relaxed, going with it, looking up at the vastness of the heavens, the glimmer of age-old stars, whose steadfastness filled her with a solid certainty.

He wouldn't catch her now.

When the tide waned, she struck out parallel to the shore, treading water and coming back in to watch for pin pricks of light from the headland. It seemed a long time, but eventually she saw what she was waiting for – the gleam of tiny twin headlights coming from the road up beyond the beach, edging slowly along the headland before they disappeared.

How long had he waited to see if his wife had perished? It seemed like hours since she'd run into the water, but she knew it was probably only fifteen minutes at most. No doubt he was scarpering back to Dublin right now, in his big shiny car, cursing the narrowness of the country lanes until he got to the dual carriageway.

Even though she was starting to feel exhausted, and so cold she couldn't feel her bones, she was free. She splashed her leaden arms and legs, made one more supreme effort, and hoped the tide would be gentle with her as she coasted into shore and dragged her sodden, ice-cold body from the water.

Shivering and shaking, the track up to Willow Hill took twice as long, even though her eyes gradually adjusted to the dark. The wood was full of strange noises that startled her. The spare back-door key was in its usual spot under a planter, ready for all the Sullivan family for the numerous times they forgot theirs. She crept silently through the house as best she could in her sodden clothes, mindful of Mrs Sullivan sleeping temporarily in a downstairs bedroom, then she was tip-toeing upstairs and down the landing until she reached Sylvie's bedroom.

Chapter Fifty-four

After they left the nursing home, they agreed to give Willow Hill a miss, swinging into a service station for coffee before they hit the motorway and home.

'I need the ladies,' Carrie said, picking up her bag with trembling fingers and fishing around inside for some tissues.

Mark brought her across the forecourt to the washrooms, pushing her through the door and closing it after her, telling her he'd wait outside. She moved around like a rag doll in the dim, cheaply scented interior, all her limbs so floppy that they took a few seconds to obey her brain. When they went into the busy service station, she blinked in the noise and bustle of it all, shuddering at the feeling of claustrophobia brought on by the densely packed shelves and glaring spotlights. Mark looked at her face and bought coffees without even asking her, fixing them on a cardboard tray, adding sugar sachets and wooden stirring sticks, buying chocolate and shoving it into his pockets before steering her back out to the car with his free hand.

They sat in a corner of the car park, Carrie's teeth chattering on the rim of her cardboard cup, the first gulp of hot coffee scalding her mouth so that she gasped. Mark placed his cup in a holder, and, lifting hers carefully from the grip of her clenched hands, he blew on the liquid as you would for a child, adding some sugar and blowing on it again before handing it back to her. He took the chocolate out of his pocket, opened the foil and broke off some squares, feeding them to her, pushing them gently through her trembling lips in between her sips of coffee. The soft, sweet chocolate soothed her a little, as well as the touch of his thumb on her lips.

'Do you believe in ghosts?' she eventually asked.

'No, definitely not.'

'So Seamus couldn't have seen Beth's ghost.'

'No.'

'Do you think Seamus saw something or was it just his imagination?'

Mark sighed. 'I don't know, Carrie. His mind is wandering. He thought you were Sylvie.'

'Lots of people think I have a strong resemblance to my mother. I'm not surprised I reminded Seamus of her.' She fell silent again and sipped some coffee. 'I wonder if Seamus saw Beth going up to Willow Hill through the woods, maybe she got fed up hiding out in the summer house. Only why did Seamus think she was a ghost?'

'Because he saw her before she died, but in his confused or drink-fuddled state … who knows? Beth could have taken a chance on going to Willow Hill.'

'And if Adam had been hanging around, looking for his deserting wife, could he also have spotted her?' Carrie went on. 'He could have followed Seamus or my mother and been led to Beth. So supposing the note Beth left had been a red herring, written under duress, but in reality …'

'You still think Adam Gilmore killed his wife and managed to cover it up?'

Carrie shivered. 'Who knows? Why did my mother ask Seamus to keep quiet about the ghost?'

'Because she was fond of the oul' fella and didn't want to see him laughed at for spreading stories.'

He fed her some more chocolate and there was something so comforting in the gesture that Carrie almost wept. Outside the perimeter of the car park, traffic roared past, but she felt they were enclosed in a world of their own.

'That's another thing,' she said after a while. 'Where was my mother in all this? She wasn't the shy, retiring type. If she'd suspected for one moment that Adam might have harmed Beth, she'd have been screaming blue murder.'

'Maybe she was, at the time.'

Carrie shook her head. 'Not according to Sean and Evelyn. My mother didn't want to talk about it at all. Even years later, after the inquest, she stayed quiet. And she never, once, breathed a word to me about it.'

'You could turn what you just said inside out,' Mark said, looking at her thoughtfully.

'Like what?'

'Your mother didn't believe that Adam had hurt Beth, therefore she wasn't screaming blue murder. She believed whatever Beth said in her note. She thought it was genuine.'

'So he got away with it all, without anyone suspecting anything.'

'Carrie, we don't know if he got away with anything. We're just guessing a lot of this.'

'I know. It's mad the way you get something in your head and everything can be twisted to suit.' She fell silent again and finished her coffee.

'That's life for you. It's not a jigsaw puzzle where everything fits neatly together. It's more like a whole heap of Lego.'

'Is that what you play with in Bizz? Lego?'

'Not quite. And what I meant was, you can make a dozen different things out of the same pile of bricks.'

'Like what I'm doing.'

'I'm going back in to get some water for us. Do you need anything else or are you okay to go home?' Mark asked, after a while.

'I'm fine, thanks.'

* * *

She sat in silence most of the way back to Dublin. Once again, the music was on low and, every so often, Mark glanced at her and asked if she was okay. A couple of times, he reached across and patted her hands where they rested on her lap, and when she felt the warmth of his hand, she realised how icy cold hers was. She gazed out at sun-dappled farmland, bogs and pastureland, rimmed by blue-grey mountains, letting it all drift in front of her vision as though she was dislocated from it all, while everything spun round in her head coalescing into different pictures.

She deliberately tried to stay on the surface of everything, her eyes fastening on the moving traffic and the road signs sliding by the car window, rather than be sucked down deep, deeper than the dark, night-time woods behind Willow Hill where Seamus said he had seen Beth. Flitting through the woods, all white and pale.

Seamus, she reminded herself, who talked through his whiskey and couldn't be trusted. Seamus, who had clearly loved Molly and her daughters, and who, for some reason, her mother had warned to stay quiet when he talked about Beth. Because he'd be laughed at or locked away? Or could there have been any other reason?

'Are you joining some dots?' Mark said. His eyes were focused on the road ahead, which was now busier with traffic. He changed gears and slowed down a little as the traffic thickened when they passed the on-ramp at Portlaoise.

'I don't know,' she said in a thin voice. 'I could be rewriting history. I was just thinking about what you said and turning it inside out again …'

He reached across and took her hand for a moment.

'Supposing – just supposing, my mother wasn't screaming blue murder because she didn't believe Adam had hurt Beth, because Beth wasn't hurt? Not really. And the note that Beth left was a fake all right, but for a different reason? Seamus said Beth could swim like a fish. She'd have known all about the dangerous currents in the cove. Just like my mum did. She warned me often enough.'

'In other words, Carrie, you think Beth could have faked her own death and is still alive somewhere,' he said bluntly.

'That sounds crazy, doesn't it – but it fits in a funny, crazy way. Especially the way my mum clammed up about Beth and stayed silent all those years.'

'If we've thought of that, then Adam must also have thought of that. And he could have found her by now.'

'People can disappear if they really want to. Then again, maybe he found her and we don't know about it.'

'Do you think Beth would have kept in touch with your mother, somehow?'

'God knows. Mum never had any secrets, as far as I know, but there was something she was going to tell me, before she went off on her trip. She said it would keep until she came home. Even her trip …' Carrie paused and gave a little cry. 'Oh God.' She covered her face with her hands.

'Are you okay? I can pull in if you like.'

'It's okay. I don't want to think anymore. I'm adding two and two together and making a thousand.'

'Like what?'

Her mum ticks off the itinerary on the fingers of one hand, giving her a quick rundown of their homeward journey. 'Brazil, Paris, London, Dublin.'

'My parents have never been to London since their honeymoon,' she babbled. 'I used to tease Mum about it, but she brushed me off.

Before they went off on their trip, I teased them about flying back home through London on the final leg and only seeing the inside of Heathrow. But I found out recently that they'd planned to spend two nights there. She conveniently forgot to tell me that.'

'What does that add up to?'

'Probably nothing. They went off on their great trip, including a stop-off in London, at the same time as Adam Gilmore was out of the country for six months. Working in New York, he told me, but most likely hiding from all the bank fallout.'

'Okay.'

'Next up, my mum had a friend in London who sent her a card every Christmas.' By now Carrie's teeth were chattering. 'I joked about her in the way teenagers do, saying we never heard from her all year round except for Christmas. Mum said she was an old friend from the Irish-speaking college she went to the summer she was sixteen. It was their tradition to exchange cards at Christmas, nothing else, and it had gone on for years. I remember saying they were old-fashioned and should bring their friendship into the twenty-first century. What was wrong with texting or email? Thing is, her friend's name was Anna.'

'Anna? Is that significant?'

'It's the same name as Beth's dead sister. Who was born in England when Molly lived over there in the early 1950s. She was six years older than Beth, but died at the age of twelve after Molly came home.'

By now Mark had pulled into the hard shoulder. 'This all adds up to one helluva story,' he said.

'So fantastic it couldn't have happened.' Carrie folded her arms, hugging herself to try and stop herself from shaking too much.

'I didn't say that.'

'No, you didn't, thank you, but *I'm* saying it.'

'London is huge. Almost nine million people live there. A woman called Anna going over there in 1980 could easily disappear like a needle in a haystack.'

'I know. I don't know. *God.*' She shook her head as if to clear it.

'Carrie, are we really thinking this?'

'No, I'm just making it up as I go along.'

'The Christmas cards … was there a return address on the envelope?'

Carrie laughed. 'I have you as bad as me! No, Mark, I can't remember and Mum never kept the cards or the envelopes. They were always recycled.'

'If there's the slightest truth in any of this and Adam was keeping an eye on you …'

'Well?'

'If he thought you were digging around old history, he could have a problem with it.'

'How so? If Beth's still alive, then he couldn't have killed her.'

'Yes, but he can't be very proud of the fact that his wife ran away. Look at the way it was all covered up, and how he paraded his broken heart all across the media, never mind the profile he's built up over the years. Men in his position wouldn't want the risk of any dirt crawling out of the woodwork.'

'What kind of dirt?'

'Think of it, Carrie. It was practically unheard of in those days for women to walk out of a marriage, unless it was a serious problem with domestic violence. If that was the case, it probably suited him to have her dead.'

'God. We've gone from possible murder to domestic violence,' Carrie said. 'That's what I mean about the circle getting bigger and more fantastic. I can't think anymore.'

'Is it okay if I talk to someone?'

'Like who?'

'We have a department in Bizz that works closely with the cops. We sometimes have to run internet queries for them, or bring unsavoury stuff to their attention, so I see the guys regularly.'

'I didn't know that. So it's not all Lego and primary colours and lounging on hammocks.'

'Not all the time,' he said. 'I can chat to one or two of them off the record, see what they have to say. We'll probably never find out the truth about Beth, if anything nasty did happen, but I don't like the idea that Adam might be keeping tabs on you – for whatever reason.'

'Okay, go ahead, and now I think it's best to get me home before I think up another fantastic story.'

* * *

She asked him in for coffee as they neared Faith Crescent.

'I think I'll pass this time, Carrie,' he said, throwing her an apologetic smile. 'Thanks all the same.'

Pass? Her heart sank. She blinked her eyes. She wasn't going to cry. At least not in front of him.

'Fine, then,' she said, so brightly she thought her voice would crack. 'Could you drop me at the shops on the main road? I need some bread and milk.' *And a bottle of wine.*

It was there again, the same as the other night, a distance, a preoccupation on his part as he pulled in to the kerb.

'See you … around.' She forced a smile, lifted her tote bag and tried to connect with the door handle, horribly let down that the day with Mark was suddenly over. 'Thanks a million for today, it helped to have someone to bounce things off, even if I did sound a bit off the wall.'

'No worries, Carrie, I'll chat to you next week sometime.'

She could hardly feel her legs underneath her as she got out of the car. Somehow she was standing on the pavement as shoppers scurried round her, but she felt utterly alone as she watched his car pull away from the kerb and gradually disappear. She felt even more alone when she walked into the cul de sac ten minutes later with her shopping and the first thing she saw was her house alarm soundlessly flashing.

Chapter Fifty-five

Carrie knew exactly what the police would say – on a Saturday evening, an empty house with a broken alarm is a sitting target and a crime begging to be committed. She let herself in, keying in the code to knock off the light that was flashing outside the house, her shoulders tightening in anticipation of what she might find. Nausea flooded into her throat as she checked the downstairs rooms, leaving the hall door open in case she had to make a dash for it.

She saw it immediately; a small, hard ball, under her kitchen table. She stared at it for a moment as though she couldn't figure out how it got there. Going across to the window, she raised the blind to see a hole smashed in the glass and shards of glass lying on the floor underneath.

It seemed silly to call the police. She hadn't really been broken into, had she? The neighbours' kids had been playing in the church grounds when their ball was hurled in the air and just happened to connect with her window. Carrie tried to imagine the trajectory their ball would have had to take over the high wall in order to impact on her window.

She checked the house hurriedly but everything else seemed undisturbed. There wasn't much of any significance to rob, and yet the creepy feeling that someone had been in her house, invading her space, persisted. She closed the hall door, went back to the kitchen and looked at the distance between the hole in the glass and the handle of the window. She told herself her imagination was running riot when she pictured a hand coming through the jagged hole and reaching up to open the window … stepping into the room and looking around before going upstairs. Then the reverse, stepping back out through the window and closing it carefully.

The house to her right was rented by a young couple who were away on holiday, but a couple in their sixties, Mr and Mrs O'Leary, lived in the house to her left. She knocked on their door, apologising for disturbing their evening, and explained what had happened.

'We didn't hear anything,' Mr O'Leary said. 'It could have been the teenagers farther around the cul de sac, but they're a little far away to have aimed a ball at your back window, unless they had been playing in the church grounds.'

'I know them,' she said. 'I thought they played mostly in the cul de sac.' She didn't bother saying that she didn't think she'd ever seen them playing in the church grounds.

'We had our front window busted before by the kids,' Mr O'Leary said as he gave her the number of a twenty-four-hour window repair firm. 'It's quiet enough around here but you want to feel safe tonight, I guess.'

Safe? She felt shaken by the knowledge that her solid, red-bricked house on Faith Crescent was no longer impregnable. Her perfect sanctuary didn't exist anymore.

Carrie's head was aching by the time she got back to her house. A ball, through her window. Of *course* it was an accident. Not even by the wildest stretch of her imagination could she somehow pin this on Adam Gilmore. She checked the files she'd brought back from Willow Hill but the big lever arch file with her parents' documents was still tucked into the bottom shelf of her bookcase and seemed untouched. Heart thumping, she checked the folder with the photographs, which was resting on top of a row of books. They looked, she thought, as though they'd been rifled through, the order of them slightly different to the way she'd left them. She could have sworn the photographs of her mother's birthday had been on top of the pile, and now they were down beneath other photographs of her parents. She looked at the row of books, her scalp prickling as she tried to figure out if they were lined up the way she fixed them only recently. She thought they didn't sit quite the same, as though they had been taken out and replaced. As though someone had been looking for something that could be tucked into a book. She thought of the way Adam had stood in her hall and intercepted her glance when she'd been unable to stop herself from looking at the bookcase.

Which was why she'd left the folder with some photographs in sight, and slid the envelope with the copy of the inquest report and press clipping along with Beth's wedding photos inside the lining of her tote bag. Just in case.

She went around the house all over again, opening presses and wardrobes, her head pounding as she checked to see if anything had been disturbed. It was impossible to say, beyond the vague feeling that someone had been in her drawers and her wardrobe, and that things weren't exactly as she had left them.

Surely she was adding up two and two and making a hundred again. It was much too fantastic by far. She picked up her mobile and called the emergency repair firm.

* * *

Adam reached into his desk drawer for the bottle of whiskey and poured himself a neat glass. Too much alcohol was not a good idea as it lowered his guard. He sat back in his deep leather chair and swung it around so that it faced the view outside the window. Dublin city was bathed in mellow evening sunlight. The city was revving up again. There were more cranes silhouetted on the horizon, which could only be a good thing because it meant his investments were ripening. The next two years couldn't come quickly enough.

The search of her house had proved fruitless. Or so he'd been told. With a sigh of exasperation, he went to the wall safe. Reaching into the depths, he took out a mobile once more, making sure he had the right one. Interpol would be very interested in the contents of his other mobile, switched off and well secured at the back of his safe. *If they ever got their hands on it.*

Occasionally, a chill went down his spine when he read of dawn raids, the arm of the law swooping down on unsuspecting criminals. He told himself he was safe up here in his citadel of sorts. But one bad mistake and it would all come crashing down. He made a call he didn't really want to make, drawing more attention to himself in a way he preferred not to. He didn't like raising his head above the parapet – every call left some kind of trace.

'You're certain there was nothing in that house, nothing incriminating?'

'Our best man went in there,' the voice at the other end said to him. 'He was so good the police weren't even called. If he found nothing, then there was nothing.'

He'd asked them to look for anything at all with his name on it. Or any unusual photographs. But you couldn't trust anyone. Not really. He'd been foolish to involve them. Supposing they'd found something to incriminate him? Like the photographs Sylvie had talked about all those years ago. Photos of Beth, she'd said, nice ones. What had she meant? He couldn't remember how bruised Beth might have been before she'd gone running down to Cork. Likewise wasn't sure if his collection of images had been disturbed. He could have left himself open to blackmail. He would have to work out how best to deal with Carrie himself, although he still wasn't sure what threat, if any, she posed to his little empire and it was a bit more difficult nowadays to silence a disruptive voice. Difficult, but not impossible.

To hell with her anyway. She was a complication he didn't need at this time in his life. He was still trying to figure out why she had gone to Lucerne at the same time that Luis Meyer was settling his affairs, a Luis Meyer who'd been in Cork, staying by the beach, in 1980. A Luis Meyer who'd been nineteen years of age, and not the young teenager he'd mistakenly assumed. Not that Beth … the idea was preposterous. It was just that he didn't like loose ends, that's if this was a loose end.

His greatest fear, deep down inside, was that because they'd never found the body, he'd never been absolutely sure that Beth was actually dead. She'd done what she'd threatened to do and run into the sea rather than stay married to him. He'd been there, he'd seen her, he'd witnessed it. In a way, he'd forced her into it. She'd run into the sea because she'd been afraid he'd kill her. He probably would have. She'd done him a favour in a way. Sometimes he still heard the roar of the water as he stood by the edge of the sea that night, the cold knowledge that he'd gone too far thudding into his head. He'd not only sent her into the sea, he'd ignored her cries, he hadn't attempted to summon any help, he'd walked away and left her there, driving back to Dublin in a cold fever.

Occasionally, after the inquest, and the way Sylvie Sullivan had looked at him and mentioned the photographs, he'd had nightmares in which Beth was somehow still alive. To his annoyance, he'd once found himself travelling to Manchester and walking the streets in the city where her mother had lived, just in case. By then, of course, any trail out of Cork had gone cold. He'd even googled her name, but nothing of any significance had turned up.

It was a bloody nuisance that so many of his police friends had retired in recent years, taking their accommodating practices with them. Years ago it had been far easier to keep tabs on people in a different way. Like the Cassidys. He'd eventually had to call a halt to having their phone tapped.

The whiskey warmed his stomach and soothed his fears. He relaxed a little as he looked out the window of his fortress at the gulls drifting freely on the early-summer thermals, their wings iridescent against the sun.

Meek and mild Beth would never have had the guts to think about doing something outrageous like fake her own death, let alone have the guts to carry it through. If by some absurd twist of fate she was still alive somewhere and intent on some kind of justice, he'd have heard from her by now.

Wouldn't he?

Chapter Fifty-six

September 1980

'You have to pretend I'm dead,' Beth said.

'I can't do that,' Sylvie said. 'It's impossible.'

'You have to. Because I will be if you don't, or if you give Adam any reason at all to be suspicious.'

'I can't believe this is happening.'

'Neither can I.' Beth stared at her white face in the mirror. White, except for the vivid bruises forming over her eye and cheek, and the cut along the side of her mouth. She was sitting in front of Sylvie's dressing table, a dressing table she'd envied as a teenager, wondering what it would be like to sit there and *be* Sylvie – with her life, and her clothes and her makeup and her good looks. *And* John. She was wrapped in a big blanket for warmth and underneath that, she was wearing Sylvie's clothes, right through to her skin. Her own sodden clothes were squashed into a black plastic sack, ready for disposal. Sylvie had offered to scatter some of them by the tide line down in the cove, but Beth had asked her not to, it was enough that her shoes and cardigan would be found. And the note. She'd told Sylvie exactly where to find that.

She stared in the mirror and watched as if from a distance while

Sylvie cut off her long blonde hair. 'I don't have time to dye it black,' she said.

'Ah sure, you won't be recognised by the time I'm finished with you,' Sylvie said.

'You're crying,' Beth said, looking at her friend's reflection in the mirror.

'I can't help it. God, Beth, what are you doing?'

'I'm getting away from my husband before he kills me.'

'Couldn't you go to one of those shelters or something? There are places, you know, for ...'

'For battered wives? And what do you think Adam and his precious father would do if that happened? There'd be hell to pay. The law is on their side, thanks to their position. The boat to England is my only escape route. I bet Adam is already rehearsing his role as the sorrowful husband. And his father won't want any scandal. He'll be only too glad to have me struck from the Gilmore family tree.'

'I can't not keep in touch with you, I need to know how you're getting on ...'

'No, Sylvie. If Adam ever finds me, I'm already dead. He'd kill me and get away with it.'

'Please, Beth.'

'I can't even phone you. What's the betting he'd have your phone tapped or something? His father has powerful connections, right up to Leinster House. I'm sorry I brought this on you, because he'll be keeping an eye on you. Just in case ...'

'I can deal with him,' Sylvie said staunchly. 'I wish I could lock him up and throw away the key.'

It's funny how life can change, Beth thought. Her friend was deeply unhappy and upset, her face twisted with tears, whereas Beth felt calm and composed. She didn't envy Sylvie any more. Beth was filled up with the love she had shared with Luis, it was a warmth that would stay in her heart forever. Like Luis, she was facing into the unknown, but, in the past week, thanks to him, she had found something she didn't know she'd had, an inner strength, something strong and shining at the very core of her. She thought of her mother, not lying down under the things life had thrown at her, but making the best of what she had.

'Hey, I should have cut my hair years ago,' Beth said, grinning at her elfin reflection in the mirror. 'It suits me.' She got up from the chair, took off the blanket, did a little twirl.

'It does too,' Sylvie smiled through her tears. 'If I'm ever looking for another job …' She let the words trail away as she bent down and gathered long clumps of Beth's hair, shoving them into the black plastic sack on top of Beth's sodden clothes.

'How about …' Sylvie paused. 'Even a card at Christmas? It wouldn't be noticed in all the cards we get. A card from my old friend from Irish-speaking college?'

'Okay. Just once a year.'

'At least I'll know you're still alive.'

'And just supposing Adam starts to cause you trouble, as a last resort, you have the envelope …'

The envelope with the polaroid photos Sylvie had taken of her bruises and welts, before she'd walked out on Adam, along with some photographs of Adam's magazines and illegal images. When Beth had taken off her saturated clothes earlier that night, Sylvie had gasped in shock and taken more photographs for good measure.

'I've hidden it away in the attic here, so well that no one will find it, except me. In case anyone does, it has my name on it and it's marked confidential, so it's perfectly safe. Beth, look, would you not just go to the police with all this? John and I will support you.'

'Who'd believe me? What's the betting it would be covered up? I can't take that chance. I want to start a new life away from all this, forget all about Adam. The envelope is my insurance too. If Adam does happen to turn up at my door, I can threaten him with it. And if my card doesn't arrive some Christmas, try and find out what happened to me.'

'Beth … please …'

'And if you can't find me and anything seems odd, you have my permission to go straight to the police with it. You never know, the law might change in some far-off, distant time. Low-life like Adam might eventually be brought to justice.'

'You're really going ahead with this, aren't you?' Sylvie said, looking sad.

'Absolutely.'

'So will I see you again?'

'Probably not. You'd best keep away from London, just in case. I wouldn't put it past Adam to have you followed.'

'Oh, Beth. He must be some nasty piece of work.'

'He is. Be careful. Now, how does this look?' She struck a pose in front of Sylvie. While they'd been talking, she'd taken a cushion and fastened it around her middle. Now she pulled down Sylvie's smock top over it.

'About six months pregnant, I'd say.'

'Probably a bit late in the day to be taking the boat to England.'

'Aren't you worried about being spotted?'

Beth shook her head. 'Are you joking? Fortunately for me, thanks to this' – she patted her bump – 'people are going to avoid me like the plague, even if things are changing. Getting knocked up isn't quite the sinful disgrace it was ten or twenty years ago, but I bet I won't be the only one like this on the boat. Even my black eye will work in my favour – it'll look like my father clocked me one before he threw me out.'

She picked up a travel bag. It held everything she had in this world: documents belonging to Molly McCann that Sylvie's mother had put away in Willow Hill after the council house had been handed back and clothes and toiletries that Sylvie had got ready for her in anticipation of this moment. No matter that she was travelling light. The most important things she'd be carrying were in her heart.

'Are you ready to go?'

'Beth, I don't think I can do this.' Sylvie started to cry.

'You have to. Of course you can. You'll find out I'm missing later tomorrow, by which time I'll be halfway to Wales, where I'll get the train to London. John will be down to you like a light and you'll have him to lean on.'

'I'll have to tell him everything.'

'That's fine, you'll need his support. You can both grieve over Beth, but just for a short while. Anna McCann needs someone to drive her to the docks in Cork. She's six months pregnant by a married man and needs to be on that early boat out and well gone before anyone knows Beth Gilmore is missing.'

Sylvie mopped her tears. 'Are you sure you have enough money?'

'I have, thanks. Enough to keep me going until I find work as a domestic somewhere. Sorry I can't pay you back.'

'Would you go away out of that,' Sylvie said. 'And you have your documents?'

'I've Anna's original birth cert from Manchester, that's all I need. It'll get me by.'

'Right then. Off we go. If you're sure?'

'On Anna and my mother's grave, I'm sure,' Beth said solemnly.

'The car is parked in the outhouse. Mum is out for the count with all her medication and I can hear Dad snoring his brains out from here. So we should be okay. Come here to me.'

They met in the middle of Sylvie's bedroom and embraced tightly.

'Love you,' Sylvie said, patting her on the back.

'I know. Me too.'

Chapter Fifty-seven

On Monday morning, Carrie was up early. The window company came to fix the temporary repair they'd done on Saturday night and she finally got her alarm fixed. She phoned Maria that afternoon to see how Luis was.

'It won't be too long now,' Maria said. 'Two or three weeks, at the most, they think. Would you like to talk to him?'

Carrie swallowed hard. 'Can I?'

'Of course you can, Carrie,' Maria said. 'He'd love to hear your voice. It would cheer him up.'

A few minutes later, when Carrie had taken several deep steadying breaths, Luis' voice came on the line. 'Hi, Carrie.' His voice was weak and feeble, but she knew by the tone of it that he was smiling.

'Hey, Luis, I hope you're behaving yourself,' she said. 'Maria told me you're giving those nurses a terrible run around.'

'Run around?'

'Keeping them busy, driving them mad.'

'I need them to know I'm still in charge. What are you up to?'

'Lots of things.'

'Did you climb any more mountains?'

'I did, Luis. Did I tell you I've left my job?'

'That is a big mountain all right. You are getting your life back, the life you want.'

'I am. Thanks to you.'

'What did I do?'

'You brought me up to Rigi and pushed me off the edge of a cliff.'

'I did, didn't I?' She heard faint laughter. 'Are you going to come back for more mountain climbing?'

'I've a few things to sort out. I went back to my parents' house and looked at their things. I let myself have a good cry.'

'Good. Anything else?'

'I'm talking to Mark again.'

There was a short silence. Then Luis said, 'I'm very happy to hear that, Carrie. You are giving me lots of brownie points. It makes me feel good.'

'It makes me feel scary and vulnerable.'

'Don't ever be afraid to love, Carrie.'

'I won't.' She took a deep breath. 'I love you, Luis.'

'And I love you, Carrie Cassidy, I hope you will come back to Rigi sometime and go on jumping off cliffs.'

She looked out at the church spire, but it was all wavy and distorted thanks to the tears in her eyes.

After she had said goodbye to Luis, she spoke to Maria. 'You'll let me know?' Her voice was breaking.

'I'll call you myself, Carrie,' Maria said. 'I have a few people to contact before word is officially released. You'll be one of them.'

'Thank you.'

* * *

That evening just after six o'clock, Mark called her.

'Carrie – um – about what we discussed on Saturday ...'

'You've finally decided it should be included in the best fairy tales of Ireland, volume three,' Carrie said, making light of it.

'Not quite.'

There was something sober in Mark's voice that put her on high alert. 'What do you mean?'

'They'd like to talk to you, the guys.'

It took a moment for it to register. 'What guys? You don't mean the cops?'

'I do, actually ...'

'For serious?'

'For serious.'

'Jesus, Mark, you're joking.' She gripped her mobile.

'I wish I was. Look, don't get all worried, I talked to the cops we liaise with, and they passed me on to a couple of detectives who'd like to have a chat.'

'Oh, no, I'm not in the least bit worried, especially when I had to get my alarm fixed this morning as well as my window.'

His voice was terse. 'Run that by me again.'

She knew then, too late, how he'd react. 'I was sort of broken into. Last Saturday evening.'

'*Sort* of?'

'It was a ball through the kitchen window, that's all, and the alarm didn't work properly.'

'Was this after I dropped you off?'

'Yes.' She reproached herself as she gripped the phone, waiting for his explosion.

'For feck's sake, Carrie, why didn't you call me back? I would have helped. Why did you deal with this on your own?'

'It was nothing, just some kids messing.'

'You don't know that for sure. Did you call the police?'

'There was no need. Nothing was taken.'

'Did anything look disturbed?'

'Not really.'

'Not *really*? Carrie Cassidy, if I could get my hands on you right now, I'd … I'd—'

'Mark, look, I thought of calling the police. I imagined Adam Gilmore himself putting his hand in through the jagged hole and opening the window catch, climbing through the window and going through everything in the house. How's that for a great leap of the imagination? The kids around here are fond of playing ball games. That's the reality.'

'Either way, I wish you'd called me.'

Her heart warmed. 'Sorry, yes, I should have.'

'Are you up to talking to the detectives? They could be with you in an hour.'

'You mean now, like this evening?'

'Yes. Don't worry, I'll be with them.'

'What do they want to know? Is it about Beth?'

'I think it's more about Adam.'

* * *

Carrie tried to rise above the cloud of anxiety that engulfed her when Mark arrived with two plain-clothes detectives in tow. She brought them through to her kitchen, full of banal chatter that did nothing to dissipate her nerves. They introduced themselves as Rowan and Brian. They were dressed very casually and she would have passed them by in the street, taking them for off-duty barmen or takeaway delivery guys, until they sat down at her table, showed her their identity cards, and looked at her with eyes she could only describe as forensic. They refused tea or coffee.

'What do you want to know?' she asked.

'We'd like to know in what way you're acquainted with Adam

Gilmore,' Brian said. 'The dealings you've had with him, phone calls, meetings.'

'What's he done?' she couldn't help asking. 'You don't think he killed his wife, do you?'

Brian's face was expressionless. 'Carrie, we're not in a position to discuss Adam with you. From what Mark has said, we gather you've had dealings with him recently and that's what we'd like to hear about.'

Her head swam with a formless kind of panic until Mark smiled reassuringly and suggested she start at the beginning, from the time she'd met Maria, just like she'd done with him the previous week. The detectives listened to her impassively as she ran through the events of the past few weeks, Mark helping to fill in any details she omitted. They didn't show much interest in anything she said, and she was beginning to think it was all a waste of time until she came to the part where she'd visited Adam in his office. Then the questioning began.

'Could you talk us through this, Carrie, right from the time you entered the building, and describe everything that happened. Don't leave out any detail, no matter how small.'

'Carrie, go back to the foyer again, how many lift shafts did you see?'

'Carrie, what happened after you got out of the lift? How many doors did you pass through?'

'What kind of locks were on the doors?'

'What was through the other fire door, do you know?'

'How big was the office, how many windows across?'

'What's all this about?' she asked, throwing her hands up when she was unable to tell them with any kind of certainty exactly what was on Adam Gilmore's walls. 'There were some paintings, there were screens, then again they were everywhere, a couple of big ones on the wall, others inlaid into his desk.'

'Thanks, Carrie, you've been very helpful,' Brian said, his voice devoid of expression. 'One more thing: what happened when you went to leave the office? Did you walk straight out?'

'No, Adam pressed a switch, and I heard the door unlocking.'

'A switch where?'

'It was on his desk – no,' she closed her eyes and tried to remember, 'I think it was a remote control that he'd left on his desk.'

'You said he gave you a card with his private mobile number. Could we see that please?'

'Sure. I left it on the kitchen window sill. Mark?'

Mark obliged, fetching the card and handing it to Rowan.

'Great, thank you. We might need to talk to you again,' Rowan said.

He and Brian exchanged a look.

'You might be able to help us with one more thing.'

When they put their suggestion to her, she refused. 'Go back to the lion's den? I don't think so.'

'I'm not having Carrie upset any further,' Mark said. 'She's told you everything she knows.' Standing behind her, he put his hands on her shoulders. She was amazed at how good it felt.

'This would be a great help to us,' Rowan said. 'We don't think Adam will do anything stupid to Carrie. He watches his step very carefully.'

'So you *are* investigating him,' Carrie said.

'We can't confirm or deny that.'

'But you must be, if you're asking me all these questions and want me to visit him again.'

'There are procedures we have to follow.'

'Procedures?' Carrie said.

'And in all cases, we need factual evidence.'

'There's no factual evidence in Beth's case, is there?' Carrie said.

'No, not from the sound of it.' For the first time that evening, Brian's voice was a little empathetic.

'So you have something else on Adam.'

'We can't say.'

'Something to do with the internet?' She threw out a wild guess.

'Carrie,' Mark said, 'the less you know, the better.'

'So that I won't look as though I'm hiding something if I meet him again?'

'Exactly.'

She turned around and faced him. 'Do you think I should meet him again?'

Mark smiled. 'I think you should do whatever your gut is telling you.'

'You won't be all alone,' Brian said.

'Have you any good reason to see him again?' Rowan asked.

Carrie thought for a moment. 'I have, actually. He seems very keen on seeing some photographs I told him I had of Beth. He even came knocking on my door.'

Once more the detectives exchanged a glance. 'What kind of photographs?'

'What exactly are you looking for?' Carrie asked.

Chapter Fifty-eight

Carrie took great gulps of air and swallowed her panic as she stood outside the offices of Gilcorp on Wednesday evening. She could do it. It was simple really.

Carrie is grabbing Adam Gilmore by the balls.

Metaphorically, of course, she grinned to herself. All she had to do was chat to Adam for a short while and give him some wedding photographs. The detectives had also given her a mobile to put in her bag, which was to be left switched on. It looked ordinary enough to her, she said, but they just smiled. Mark was going to call her on that a few minutes after she'd arrived in Adam's office. She could use it as her excuse to leave.

She gathered from what the detectives had told Mark that very few people had ever been in Adam's private penthouse office. Most of his business was conducted in the boardroom or in a meeting room. Whatever Adam had been up to, she owed this to her mother and Beth, she told herself, and she felt cloaked in a calm determination as she walked up the granite steps. She went through the same signing-in ritual, happy in the knowledge that Mark was waiting with the detectives in a nearby pub. Once more, Michael escorted her up in the lift, Carrie slightly more observant about her surroundings than she'd been the last time.

Adam sat behind his immense desk, his elbows on the table, fingers interlocked. He didn't get up to welcome her this time. In silhouette, with his back to the window, his squat, powerful figure seemed more intimidating.

'Carrie. I was quite surprised when you called me and wanted to see me as soon as possible,' he said smoothly. 'You said something about photographs?'

'You asked me to contact you if I came across any,' she said, relieved to find her voice steady and calm. 'I was down in Willow Hill at the weekend so I brought some back for you.'

'You were down in Willow Hill?'

'Yes, on Saturday,' she said, meeting his gaze.

'And did everything go all right?'

'Everything went fine. There was just a little matter of a break-in when I got home.' She gave him what she hoped was an innocent, self-deprecating smile.

'A break-in? I warned you about that alarm.'

Surely his studied reaction and patronising tone of voice confirmed that he already knew?

'You did, but I'm still not sure what's been taken.'

'Oh, dear, it must be upsetting.'

'Not as upsetting as it must be for you, going through old photographs,' she said, taking out an envelope and putting it on the table.

'What are these?' he asked, his voice stiff.

'It's Beth and you, on your wedding day,' she said, opening the envelope so that half a dozen photos slid out. 'It's hard to believe she was dead six months later.'

Carrie looked at him, but his eyes were on the photos spread across his desk. 'She looks beautiful, doesn't she? Although I hope I'm not dragging up painful memories for you.'

'She was beautiful in a quiet way,' he said, his eyes still fastened on the images in front of him.

'She never grew old,' Carrie said. 'Did you know Beth could swim like a fish?'

Once again, she was treated to a stare from his lizard-like eyes. 'Where did you hear that?' he said coldly.

'When I was down in Willow Hill at the weekend. That's why I can't understand what happened to her,' Carrie said. To hell with it. She was only supposed to engage Adam in light conversation, but she couldn't resist it. There was no factual proof. If he'd done anything out of order with Beth, he'd got away with it. 'I can't help thinking about her,' Carrie said. 'She had everything to live for, I'm sure she had a fantastic life married to you, it seems so strange that it all ended so tragically ... missing, presumed dead.'

There was a terse silence.

'I even saw a newspaper report of the accident,' she said silkily. 'That's what it said. More or less what you told me, Adam. How sad it must have been.'

He sat back and threw her a challenging look. 'You seem very fixated on my wife's untimely demise, Carrie.'

'Yes, I am,' she said. 'Beth's story intrigues me. I can't believe I knew nothing about it until recently. It's a total mystery. Especially the way they never found the body.'

Another loaded silence. This time it was broken by the mobile ringing in Carrie's bag. 'Excuse me,' she said, fishing it out. 'I thought I had turned this to silent.' She pressed the accept button. 'Yes, Mark?'

'Carrie?' he said, as already rehearsed. 'Where are you? I thought we were meeting now?'

'Sorry, Mark, I got delayed,' she said, also as rehearsed. 'I'm in Adam's office, just on North Wall Quay.'

'Have you got the concert tickets?'

'Yes, I'm all set and I have the concert tickets, don't worry.'

'Will you be much longer?'

'I'll be with you in five, ten minutes max.'

She put the mobile away and smiled apologetically at Adam. 'Sorry about that, I'm running a little late and I'd better get going.'

'What's the concert?'

'Damien Rice in Vicar Street,' she said, glad she'd had the foresight to be prepared.

Adam stared at her as though he didn't quite know what to make of her. Then he said, in slow, measured tones, 'You're either very stupid, Carrie Cassidy, or very clever.'

'I'd say it's more of the former, wouldn't you?'

She felt a moment of shock when his hand snaked across the table and grasped her wrist. 'You don't know, do you?'

'Know what?'

'Anything. Life isn't quite the airy-fairy adventure you might believe, full of appealing mystery. Neither is it black or white. Sometimes things are unsolvable. Sometimes people's destinies are cast before they're even born. Infants soak up whatever is around them, and it's often impossible to break free from that conditioning.'

She didn't understand what he was talking about and she didn't particularly care. She'd got what she came for, a fix on the signals in this room. That was all she knew.

'Yes, it is, Adam,' she said. 'You can break free at any time. You just have to draw a line in the sand and make the decision to be responsible for yourself.'

He shook his head. 'The idealism of youth, Carrie. Do you seriously think we're all born equal in this world?'

'I didn't say that. Of course we're not born equal as far as nurturing and environment go, but that doesn't mean we can shun responsibility for our lives. It all comes down to the choices we make.'

He looked at her in that sneering way as though she was being ridiculous.

'If you'll excuse me, my boyfriend is expecting me, so you need to let me out the door.'

'Sure, Carrie. You hardly think I was going to keep you prisoner here.'

'You wouldn't have got away with that,' she said.

'Wouldn't I?' he smiled, but only with his teeth. His blue eyes were cold.

'See you around,' she said, tilting her head as cheekily as she could as she stepped into the lift.

Chapter Fifty-nine

On Friday morning, Carrie texted Mark.

> Some post here for you.

He replied eventually.

> Thanks.

> It's marked urgent.

> Right.

Right? She felt a pang of disappointment. What kind of an answer was that? She hadn't spoken to him since Wednesday evening. After she'd left Adam's office, she'd met Mark and the detectives in a pub on the quays, where she'd handed back the mobile. The detectives had thanked her profusely for her help, but refrained from any further comment. Mark had bought her a drink and then insisted on seeing her home in a taxi, but he'd waited outside and watched her safely inside, refusing to come in for coffee.

He didn't want his heart damaged again, he'd said, standing in her kitchen last week. She'd have to go carefully with him, but take a few risks herself, in showing him in a real way how much he meant to her.

She felt she was climbing another mountain when she opened the door in Faith Crescent that evening and let Mark in.

'You have post for me?'

'Yeah. Coffee?'

'Sure, just coffee,' he said.

She laughed, shrugged, 'That's all I offered.' Her heart beat faster when he pulled a stool over to the counter and sat on it. His soft check shirt was open at the neck and his knobbly wrists protruded from the cuffs.

'How've you been since Wednesday?' he asked.

'Okay. I don't suppose, you know …'

'I know nothing, apart from the obvious. Adam must be under some sort of investigation. As soon as I began to talk about him to the guys in Bizz on Monday, it was like some kind of flag was raised. But these things take time and it might come to nothing, so don't get your hopes up.'

'I'm not hoping anything as far as Adam is concerned. I'm going to forget about him from now, and get on with my own life. I might never find out what happened in Willow Hill but I'll just have to accept that. Right now, I've some very important things to sort out.'

'Like what?'

'Like …' She took a breath. 'I would have liked it if you had come in for coffee last Saturday, or even on Wednesday.'

'I was too nervous to come in either of those days, because I might have done something silly.'

'Something silly like what?'

'Something silly like kiss you.'

'I might have liked that.'

'Carrie … I need to be very sure.'

She turned away. 'Let me get your post.'

She went out into the hall. She stood there for a couple of minutes taking deep breaths, feeling as jittery as she'd felt the moment before she'd paraglided off the mountain. That time she'd jumped off a cliff and soared. She took an envelope out of her bookcase and went back into the kitchen, tingling with a painful excitement as she handed it to him.

He glanced at the address on the envelope and put it down on the counter.

'Aren't you going to open it?'

'Nah. Later.'

'It's marked urgent.'

'So? You needn't worry about that.'

Spots of colour came and went in her face. 'Maybe I want you to open it.'

He looked at her curiously. 'And why would that be?' He picked up the envelope and opened it, taking out a single sheet of paper. It was an image of Iguazú Falls that she'd printed off the internet. Across the top of the sheet she'd written: 'Carrie is happy in South America with Mark.'

He stared at the image and the caption over it. Then his grey eyes searched hers for a long, breathtaking moment. 'Is this— Does it mean what I think it means?'

'I hope so. I can't think of any other way to show you that I want to share my life with you …'

When he kissed her, she felt as if she were overflowing with love and gratitude.

* * *

They agreed to take it more slowly this time. Like, no rushing into bed, certainly not on the first date. Or the second or the third. In fact, Mark said he was going to put it off for as long as possible, because once they went to bed, he wouldn't be able to think straight for a long time, and he needed to think straight to make sure they got it exactly right. He wasn't going to sweep her off her feet this time.

They dated like they were starting over again. They went to the movies, to the beach, up Killiney Hill on a wonderfully bright evening. Little by little, she put Adam Gilmore and his insulting blue eyes out of her head. There was nothing further she could do, Mark said. She laughed when he showed her the letter marked 'private and confidential' that he'd called to collect a couple of weeks earlier, opening the envelope to show her a blank sheet of paper. He'd asked a guy who worked with him to post it to her, so he'd have an excuse to call. Then they went out for a meal with Sam and Fiona, who couldn't keep the told-you-so grins off their faces.

'It's still early days,' Carrie told Fiona out in the ladies.

'Sure it is. Sam was right.'

'How?'

'He told me you'd both be getting laid with your eyes. I didn't know what he meant at first until I saw you both in action tonight.'

'*What?*'

'Staring at each other across the table. It's a wonder it didn't catch fire.'

One night, Mark told her about Rachel, the girl in Singapore, who'd messed him around big time. He hadn't dated anyone for ages until Carrie, which was why he'd come on a bit strong at times. Another night, over a quiet, midweek meal in a restaurant on South William Street, she talked to him about her parents, what it had been like growing up on Waldron Avenue, and how she'd felt in the aftermath of the accident.

'See, some of the problem is that I don't know,' she said to him, opening her heart as they sat together in the booth, finishing the bottle of wine.

'Know what?'

'When the plane went into a dive. How much did they know? Were they scared? What were they thinking of? It's sometimes tortured me.'

'You're going to have to accept that you'll never know, no matter how much you torture yourself, Carrie,' he said, curving his arm around her. 'If I were you, I'd think of the most special moments you all shared and hold on to that as your best memory.' He drained the last of the wine into her glass. 'I think we'd best get going to South America, as soon as possible,' he said. 'If you still want to go.'

She relaxed into his arm. 'I do, very much.'

'Good.' He pushed her hair back behind her ear, kissed her forehead and said, 'Because we'll have to share a room and I'll have no choice then but to sleep with you.'

South America. She'd need him to sleep with her there, she wanted him to sweep her off her feet, and to colour that part of the world with his love.

As Luis told her, time doesn't heal, but love does.

I hope Mum and Dad were okay, calm in that final instant in the way Luis said, or else it happened so fast they knew nothing ...

Chapter Sixty

South America, five years earlier

They almost miss their flight. That morning, everything that can go wrong does go wrong.

First, they sleep it out. When Sylvie wakes up and reaches across to her bedside table, she picks up her mobile to check the time, her face frowning as she tries to recall what happened when she set the alarm the night before, because it didn't set properly. She rolls over in bed, snuggling into the heat of John's body, curling her arm around his waist, holding him tight for a long, precious moment, and she remembers what happened the night before.

'Hey, sexy,' she murmurs, 'the alarm never went off. We'll have to shift ourselves. Double quick.'

'Mmm,' he says sleepily, snaking his arm out behind him and reaching around so that it encloses her and clutches her against him, her breasts pushed against his chest.

'I mean it,' she says, wriggling away out of his reach.

His hand waggles into empty space. 'Spoilsport,' he grumbles good-naturedly.

She slips out of bed and goes across to the window, drawing back the heavy hotel drapes. Morning light presses through the filmy net curtains. 'Nice day for flying,' she says. 'Calm and dry.' She laughs as she goes back to the bed and drags the duvet off John. 'Come on, lazybones, or we'll miss our flight.'

'Lazybones?'

'Sexy lazybones.'

He leaps out of bed and chases her into the bathroom.

They spend the next fifteen minutes playfully dodging each other and darting between the bathroom, the shower and the bedroom, in a muddle of fluffy hotel bathsheets, last-minute packing, checking for phone chargers, adaptors, travel documents and luggage tags. Sylvie puts on a grey tracksuit, dressing comfortably for the flights ahead. She starts to dry her hair then gives up halfway through, shoving the hotel dryer back in the dressing-table drawer.

'I'd rather have time for something to eat than perfect hair.'

'I always knew you were a hungry woman,' John says. 'We'll get everything downstairs, then have a quick breakfast. The airport transfer has been ordered through reception, hasn't it?'

'Yep.' Sylvie briskly rubs damp hair at the back of her head, teasing it into shape. She walks across the room, picking up her sports shoes with her free hand and sitting into a chair. She kicks off her slippers and rolls stripy socks up her feet before putting on her shoes. She tosses her slippers on top of the clothes in her open case that is sprawled across the floor. She flips over the lid.

'All done?' John asks.

'All done.'

He locks the suitcases, wheels them across to the door. Sylvie checks her carry-on bag, then her handbag, and then her face in the mirror, where the reflection of the unmade bed and tossed pillows remind her of the previous night's love-making. A wave of nostalgia washes over her. She wants to be there again, in that perfect moment. The milestone holiday, with its adventure and excitements, will soon be over. They will share it all with Carrie, when they see her again, giving her a running commentary on their videos, she and John no doubt having a friendly disagreement over picky details. Then it will be relegated to their memory bank, titbits of which will be taken out and marvelled over as they head into their golden years.

'Right, missus?'

She takes a final look around the room where they've spent a wonderful week, a sudden lump in her throat. Then she follows John out the door and closes it behind her.

She wonders if they'll end up extending their stay when they go downstairs and she finds out that the hotel has forgotten to order a car for the airport, so that is another delay. Then an accident on the interstate holds them up further. Even when they reach the airport, with just minutes to spare before the flight closes, Sylvie realises that in her haste that morning, she has put the wrong flight confirmations into her bag. The printed e-ticket in her hand is for the final leg of their trip home, and there and then she has to open her carry-on luggage and sift through everything until she locates the plastic folder containing more documentation.

John is laughing.

The airport attendant is not amused.

'I'm beginning to think fate is conspiring against us,' Sylvie laughs. 'We're not supposed to catch this flight.' She and John have to rush all the way to the boarding gate, and they can hear their names already being called from the airport tannoy urging them to board the plane as they run the last few yards. When they get on board, they are met with rows of upturned frowning faces chaffing at the delay. They collapse into their seats, puffing and panting, laughing at their close shave. When they are airborne, John orders champagne to celebrate, heedless of the early hour. They clink glasses and Sylvie finally relaxes, stretching out her feet and wriggling her toes. She looks out the window at the far-off earth, visible through intermittent clouds. For someone who'd been anxious about travelling around the world, her vague fears had never materialised. She'd love to start all over again, from the time they left Dublin. Maybe even from the time they began to plan this holiday.

But it's not quite over yet. They have one more stop, one more visit she's been looking forward to with all her heart. She sits back in her seat as anticipation floods through her. They have so much to talk about and catch up on.

In a heartbeat, everything changes. The aircraft gives a peculiar shudder, stalls and begins to plummet. Her champagne glass slips through her liquid fingers. She stares at John in terror. The cabin is plunged into darkness and a horrible noise shrieks through the plane. Everyone is screaming. She is jerked sideways and cracks her head against the window. Down below, the earth is slanting towards them in a very frightening way.

'John? Jesus, I'm scared.'

As she speaks, John is already fighting against the centrifugal forces and he manages to push up the arm rest so that he can put both of his arms around her, encircling her tightly. 'Don't look out, my darling. Look at me.'

'Oh, my God ... what about Carrie?' she whispers, raising stricken eyes to his.

She wishes she could reach her daughter across time and space. The words of a favourite bedtime story come back to her: *Carrie darling, you'll have to be braver than you believe, and stronger than you seem.*

The aircraft is vibrating wildly as it goes into a spin. Her husband's eyes are perfectly reassuring, and calm, like the tranquillity of the ocean out beyond Willow Hill. 'Carrie will be fine,' he says. 'I love you.'

As their eyes lock, she feels their love for each other pulsing between them; it's a powerful thing, strong like molten steel, vibrant and alive. She knows it's the only thing that matters at that moment; the only thing that matters, whether it lasted a day, a week or a lifetime. With his arms secure around her, John's mouth covers hers in a warm, deep kiss that seems to go on forever.

Chapter Sixty-one

In the cool elegance of her spacious hall, Maria Meyer straightened her shoulders and put a forced smile on her face. Three months, she'd told Carrie in the Merrion Hotel all those weeks ago. It looked like she'd been overly optimistic. She went into the downstairs bedroom where Luis was lying peacefully in bed.

'It's another beautiful summer's evening,' she said as brightly as she could.

A faint smile flitted across Luis' face. 'Tell me ...'

His voice was thin and ragged. She sat down beside the bed, took his hand and, summoning strength from somewhere, began to describe the silvery glimmer of the lake, the blue-grey mountains rising serenely in the distance, and the long shafts of sunshine pouring down like celestial columns through gaps in the clouds, bathing everything they touched in a white light.

'It sounds like heaven,' Luis whispered. 'I'll soon find out if it exists or not.'

'I think somehow you might be finding out before me. Will I read to you?'

'Yes, please.'

'Some poetry?' she said, reaching for the books on the small table beside his bed. 'Or would you like if I read you the letter again?'

'That would be good, thank you.'

Even since Carrie had visited, more fan mail had arrived from all corners of the globe, handwritten cards and letters, messages of hope and best wishes, emails to his website. Luis' trusted secretary continued to open his post and print out emails, passing on any that she thought were particularly special to Maria; because of the volume, it was impossible to read out everything to him.

One letter had stood out. Maria had already read it to Luis, surprised herself by the eloquence of it; it had drawn a long silence from Luis when she'd finished reading. She had put it to one side, placing it between books on the side table, as she knew she'd be reading it to him again. She popped on her reading glasses, picked up the letter, and began to read. It spoke of the beauty of Luis' music and how wonderful it made the writer feel. It told him that his piano notes were alive, fluid and clear, the sparkling sound streaming out like bubbles into the calm, still air. It soothed her heart, the writer said, and it filled her with joy and hope.

Once again, Luis was silent when she finished.

'Where did that letter come from?' he asked. 'It reminds me … I thought …' He stopped, concentrating on his breathing for a few moments. He gave a little sigh and went on, 'There was something about it that brought me back to the time I was in Ireland.'

'It reminded you of Sylvie?'

'Yes.'

'Darling, it shows you have more fans who love you and your music as much as she did,' Maria said. She checked the envelope. 'There's no return address but it's an English stamp and it was written by a woman called Anna.'

He was silent again and after a while he said, 'I love you, Maria, more than anything in the world. Never forget that.'

'Thank you.' She squeezed his hand.

Later that week, on Thursday evening, his breathing changed. It would not be long now, they told her. She sat vigil by his bedside as the lake turned white-gold in the late-evening sun, until it reflected the orange, purple and pinks of the vast sunset. She described it all to him, although he gave no indication that he could hear her. She read the letter to him one more time and then she read some of his favourite poetry. As his breathing grew more shallow, she sat with him as the last of the light ebbed from the sky and night fell, cloaking everything outside the window in a soft darkness. She couldn't pinpoint the moment Luis slipped away, but she sensed his spirit had flown his tired, ailing body long before it gave up the instinctive fight for breath just before dawn.

Then all was quiet.

Chapter Sixty-two

They met at the airport on Thursday evening, Carrie feeling ridiculously shy and nervous when she first spotted Mark waiting for her as they'd planned, close to the lifts in the Departures area. She stalled, watching him, unobserved. Then a rich happiness flooded through her heart. This man in the dark jacket and jeans, with a neat, grey suitcase at his feet, looking relaxed but alert, was here now, waiting for her. She thought of the journey ahead, Dublin to Paris, Paris to Buenos Aires, and then on to Iguazú, and thoughts of sharing it all with him seemed almost too much. He still hadn't seen her, and she paused a little longer, a heady anticipation sweeping through her veins, conscious that she was caught between two worlds: the old, safe, risk-free world of Carrie Cassidy and the sweet possibilities that lay ahead.

Then he scanned the crowds, looking for her; when he saw her, his eyes lit up. She went across to him, wheeling her case, feeling that she was stepping away from the past as though she was shedding it like an old winter coat.

'Are we really doing this?' she asked, unable to stop a silly grin from spreading across her face as she neared him.

Mark bent down and kissed her cheek. 'Yes, we are. You look lovely.'

'I'm dressed for comfort,' she said, gesturing to her navy tracksuit and yellow Skechers, still a little flustered that this was happening at all.

'Comfort is compulsory,' he said. 'How are you feeling?'

'I'm good.'

'No nerves?'

'Oh, loads, but,' she smiled, 'rumour has it the guy I'm travelling with is a whizz at sorting out in-flight nerves.'

It's the other kind I'm finding it hard to handle, she thought in a fizz of expectation; over twenty-four hours in the company of this man in the close confines of an aircraft, including a long, thirteen-hour, overnight flight from Paris to Buenos Aires.

Then a shared hotel bedroom.

'Let's get started then so,' he said, looking so utterly at ease that as she fell into step beside him, it seemed so right and natural that some of her fears melted away.

The next twenty-four hours passed in a bubble of time – busy, noisy airports, where they hung around between flights checking out the shopping outlets, moving together in the queue of passengers shuffling on and off planes, the whole sensation of being with Mark seeping through her veins, whether it was the brush of his fingers as he handed her a drink, their elbows touching, then his fingers gripping hers as the aircraft screamed down the runway in Charles de Gaulle before lifting into the navy-blue vault of sky shortly before midnight. They got as comfortable as they could for the long flight to Buenos Aires, sipping water, picking at airline food, watching the same comedy on their respective television screens, Carrie slightly ahead of Mark so that she teased him with her soft laughter. They drowsed, and she watched him sleep, vulnerable and unguarded, and she wanted to touch his face with her fingertips and kiss his mouth. She slept on his shoulder for some of the journey. Then one more stopover, both of them stiff, sleepy and disorientated in the clamour of Buenos Aires airport, and a final flight to Iguazú.

When they eventually reached their hotel in Puerto Iguazú, Carrie was exhausted and dishevelled. She took one look at the large, king-sized bed before she dumped her case and bag inside the door, yanked off her shoes, and fell on top of it. She was asleep in minutes.

When she woke some two hours later, she was covered by a light quilt. She could see blue skies peeking through the net curtains covering the window. Mark was sitting at the table by the window, reading a guide book. He looked fresh and alert. She lay on the bed studying him for a moment, then he sensed her eyes on him and he looked up and smiled.

'Hey, sleepy head.'

'Hello yourself,' Carrie said, swinging her legs off the bed. 'Didn't you sleep?'

'I did – and I showered and shaved.'

'That's where I'm going next,' she said, opening her case for her toiletries before heading into the bathroom.

She emerged fifteen minutes later swathed in a huge bath towel. 'It would have been handy if I'd brought in a change of clothes,' she said, acutely aware that she was wearing nothing at all under the towel.

Mark's eyes unwrapped the towel from her body as they gazed at her. 'That would probably be advisable. For now.'

She opened her case, heat flooding through her as she tried to gather a selection of clothes, her fingers shaking a little as she fished for underwear. In the end, she grabbed whatever she could and retreated to the bathroom to dress, putting on white trousers and a white cotton vest top and light floral cardi. She slid her feet into flat, sparkly sandals. She came back into the room, suddenly stricken with shyness, covering it up by striking a pose and saying, 'Ta-da!' She picked up her bag and upended it on the bed, putting her passport and travel documents to one side. Then she picked up her mobile.

'It's about time I reconnected with the world,' she said cheerfully, her fingers tapping in her password. 'But I promise, no Twitter.' A minute later, she gasped and her mobile slipped out of her hands onto the bed.

'What time is it in Europe?' she said.

'What's up? They're about five hours ahead of us, so it's around 9 pm.'

She picked up her mobile again. 'I've missed three calls from Maria Meyer,' she said, something thudding into the back of her head.

Luis.

Chapter Sixty-three

He'd never been one hundred per cent, absolutely sure that his fortress was impregnable. Like everything in life, it was only as strong as the weakest link. But this was no dawn raid. It happened as the evening sun was settling into a Dublin skyline swathed with tender streaks of buttercup yellow mixed with marmalade orange and baby pink – colours that reflected off the underside of gulls' wings as they floated freely and soundlessly outside the large picture windows; colours that bounced across the far walls of his office, the office that was a hub of determined activity.

They were good, he had to grant them that. They had disabled the alarm quietly and efficiently. He'd only realised they'd breached his sanctuary when he felt the charge in the air. It rippled around the room like the silent aftershock of a bomb.

There were five of them. They worked cleanly and economically, dismantling his landline with great care, and the row of flat-screen monitors embedded in his desk with an equal dedication.

He sat back in the buttery soft leather chair and calmly sipped his whiskey, relishing every drop. He watched the speck of a plane gleaming like a silvery pin, high up in the sky, drawing behind it the perfectly straight line of a vapour trail. He wondered, idly, where it was headed to. For a moment, he envied the careless holidaymakers their freedom. Far down on the street below, people were milling between pubs and restaurants, out for an evening's entertainment. He thought of the joviality of a busy Dublin pub on a night when summer was in the air and people took their drinks outside and everyone was in good spirits.

The television screens were next to come down, and the contents of the black lacquer cabinets were systematically emptied. He felt like telling them it was a futile exercise. They wouldn't find anything there, but he let them go about their business. He knew that no matter what he said, he wouldn't stop them searching.

He sipped his whiskey, knowing it was only a matter of time before they came across his safe. They wouldn't find the mobiles, though, not now. He'd panicked after Carrie's last visit and, having bundled the phones in what looked like breakfast-roll wrapping, he'd joined the throngs in Stephen's Green one lunch hour and dropped them casually into a waste bin. He'd been so terribly annoyed at the blasted inconvenience of it all, never mind the photographs and videos he'd be losing – a collection spanning many holidays abroad, and a far cry from what had begun in boarding school. Although he'd kept a private note of his circle of valuable contacts.

It didn't seem to bother them, though, that the safe was empty. When they had stripped everything they could from the room, they turned to him. For a moment, he wondered which part of his life had unravelled – Beth and what had happened in Willow Hill or had Interpol finally caught up with him, despite his best efforts to be untraceable?

They escorted him down in his private lift, right down to his underground car park and up to street level where an unmarked car and a van waited. He sat in the back of the car between two detectives young enough to be his sons. He caught glimpses of city streets teeming with life and energy and flashes of glorious, late-evening sunshine as they sped towards the station.

In the dull, airless room with the hard, wooden chair he saw what looked like his mobiles on a side table, in clear cellophane bags. He wondered what, if anything, they had managed to salvage.

One of the detectives followed his gaze and smiled, but it didn't reach his eyes. 'We've been watching your comings and goings for quite a while,' he said.

Interpol then, not Beth.

He wasn't sure if it was the lesser of two evils …

Chapter Sixty-four

After she spoke to Maria, Carrie put her mobile away and turned to Mark.

'Can we go out for some fresh air? I want to walk around for a bit, and then we both need some food that doesn't come out of a plastic container.'

'Sure. I know just where we can go to stretch our legs,' he said, picking up his guide book and shoving it into the pocket of his jacket. 'And I know where to get the best tenderloin steak and a rich glass of Argentinian red.'

'You've been doing your homework,' she laughed softly.

'And then, after that, I think we could both do with an early night,' he said.

'Oh.' Her stomach contracted.

'Tomorrow will be action-packed. It'll take a full day to get around one side of the falls, and there'll be more the day after. And who knows, maybe a helicopter ride?'

'It sounds fab.'

'It will be,' he smiled at her, catching her hand as they went through the door and she knew by his eyes that he wasn't talking about the falls.

* * *

He brought her up through the small town, past tourist shops, market stalls and food outlets, up to a sloping countryside area by the banks of a wide, fast-flowing river, to a tall blue-and-white monument. Another monument close by held both the flags and the emblems of three countries. He asked her to stand to one side of the monument, in a spot overlooking the river, and then he stood close to her and took out his mobile.

'What are you doing?' she asked.

'I'm taking a selfie,' he said. 'We're standing in Argentina. Right across the river banks behind us is Paraguay, and the land across to the other side is Brazil.'

'Oh, wow,' she grinned, 'Really?'

'Yes, really,' he said. 'I might even let you put it out on Twitter.'

They stood for a while in the incandescent afternoon, over by the railings up above the banks, idly watching the flow of the river swirling between three countries.

'Maria was trying to reach me all day,' Carrie eventually told him. 'She was hoping to get to me before the news broke.' She felt Mark's arm going around her and she allowed herself to relax into his embrace. 'It was very peaceful,' she said. 'Luis was in no pain. He just slipped away. I think it must have been around the time I was laughing at a silly movie at thirty thousand feet. Maria said Luis would have loved that.'

'For sure.'

'I told her we were going to the falls tomorrow and she said he'd have loved that too.'

'Good.'

'Then she asked me ...' She was lost for words for a moment.

'Yes? Come on, Carrie ...'

She was still a little hesitant to speak of a future with Mark. 'Well, she wants us to visit, in a few weeks or so … Luis said I'm to bring you paragliding off Rigi. Apparently,' she swallowed, 'it was one of the final things on his wish list.'

She felt warmed when he squeezed her shoulders and said, 'Bring it on, so.'

She took a deep breath and wondered where Luis was now, or if indeed he was anywhere. Not that she imagined he'd be looking over her shoulder, but maybe there was something out there after all, some place his music had come from. Maybe his spirit was swooping and dipping over the lake; or he had soared to the top of Rigi, where the deep stillness of the mountain ranges had found a resonance in her heart.

She scanned the landscape. 'I think my parents were here,' she said presently. 'I think one of their last photographs before they went to the falls was taken around this area.'

'It probably was. You can't stay in Puerto Iguazú and miss this.'

'Not that I'm seeing any butterflies or feeling warm spirits or anything …'

'That's okay.'

'I'm going to do as you said and hold on to my best memories.'

With this man by her side, she could do anything. Images poured through her head – birthdays, Christmases, holidays in the sun – so many good times to choose from.

'There was one I can't help remembering,' she said, laughing gently. 'Mum reading me a Winnie the Pooh bedtime story and telling me that I was braver than I thought.'

Instead of feeling sad with the memory of her mother, Carrie had a sudden glimpse of herself, in some future time, repeating the same words to a small child at bedtime. A little person like Mark, in a bedroom decorated with soft teddies and soft lighting. A bedroom full of warmth and love. She swallowed hard. Could the future hold such boundless joy?

Taking a risk, she said, 'I hope it's a story I'll read to our children in the not too distant future.'

He kissed her forehead and hugged her, filling her with peace. 'I hope so too.'

She stood in the warmth of his hug, her senses brimming over as she absorbed everything about him. Then, hand in hand, they strolled back into the town.

Epilogue

In a busy residential suburb of London close to Highbury Fields, she switched on the television, poured a glass of wine and sat down to watch the 9 o'clock news. Outside, the sky was beginning to sink into twilight, and long shadows cast by the lowering sun slanted across her colourful front garden. Children were playing on the quiet green outside, and the sense of freedom in their raised voices floating across the air spoke of the prospect of long summery evenings ahead.

She'd been half-expecting it, yet still her heart lurched when his face flashed across the television screen and the newscaster announced his death, earlier that morning, in Lake Lucerne. There was a brief video of one of his final appearances on stage in Geneva before they moved on to the sports news. She raised her glass in a silent tribute to the man whose love had warmed her heart and given her the courage to turn her life around.

There had been other men since Luis, but none had compared to him. There had been joy in her life also, but not quite the heights he had taken her to. There were friends, book clubs and hill walking, charity pub quizzes and bridge. And there were children to love and cherish, not her own, never her own, but almost hers – children in the school where she worked as a cook, children in the nearby hospital where she volunteered on the cancer wards.

She sat for a while, absorbing the news of Luis' death, coming to terms with the finality and implications of it all. Since she'd read of his illness, she'd found herself back there again, the memories of September 1980 as fresh as if it were yesterday. She recalled the young woman who'd first met Luis on the beach, the young woman who'd been beside herself with fear and disillusionment and rock bottom self-esteem. The young woman who'd felt invisible and who'd paid a huge price to escape the clutches of an immoral man.

She felt full of joy at the sparkling memories of Luis, but she also felt gripped by a cold anger on behalf of Beth Gilmore. With the chance of having Luis involved in any way in her sorry history now gone, there was nothing to stop her from finally serving some justice to Adam. The laws had changed, thankfully. Money and position didn't talk in the way they used to and past misdeeds now had a chance at catching up with people. Courageous people were coming forward and crimes that had been brushed under the carpet, or wilfully ignored a couple of decades ago, were now being exposed to the full glare of the spotlight and the rigours of the law. It would mean, of course, that she'd be exposed as well for what she'd done in September 1980, but it would be worth it. While Luis was alive, it had been best to let sleeping dogs lie in case there was a chance the Meyers would be called as witnesses.

'It's all quiet here,' Sylvie had said in one of the last Christmas cards she'd sent, which meant that Adam wasn't giving them any trouble. Not that Sylvie gave him any reason to cause trouble, she'd always been very conscious over the years that he was watching them.

'Our mutual friend and I are keeping an eye on each other,' she'd written years ago, tucking a copy of both the inquest report and the much shorter newspaper account into her Christmas card. 'It seems money talks. To all appearances it was simply a terrible accident. Only for Dad knowing the coroner since their schoolyard days, we wouldn't have this report.'

Then, five years ago, she'd had a card out of the blue that had filled her with delight.

'The rat has deserted the sinking Irish economy and is holed up on Wall Street for a few months,' Sylvie had written. 'We're taking the opportunity to spread our wings far and wide and will come home through London.'

But a couple of months later, her delight had changed to grief and devastation at the news of the plane crash, and the loss of Sylvie and John. She'd scoured the newspaper and internet for details, her heart going out to Carrie. Carrie, whose photograph had accompanied each Christmas card so that she'd fondly watched her growing up, year after year.

Luis might be at peace now, and anything she did regarding Adam couldn't touch him any more, but of course there was Carrie to consider – Carrie who knew nothing about Sylvie's help with her disappearance, let alone an envelope with Sylvie's name on it hidden away in the attic in Willow Hill, full of incriminating photographs. It mightn't be all that much of a scandal nowadays, but the exposure would tarnish Adam's name and ridicule his portrayal as a man who'd loved his wife to the exclusion of all others.

She'd have to contact Carrie shortly. She could write care of Willow Hill, or maybe Waldron Avenue. Then again, she could find her through the internet. A young woman like Carrie was bound to be on Facebook or Twitter, something she had scrupulously avoided along with email. She'd need to talk to her first and explain everything, before Beth Gilmore went back to Ireland to settle old scores.

But first, she was going to allow herself a week or so to mourn Luis' passing and celebrate his life. Outside, the summery evening folded into a calm, indigo night. She switched off the television, lit a scented candle and poured another glass of wine. Then she went over to her music centre and the large collection of CDs and, turning on Luis' music, she let it swell around the room.

Acknowledgements

A big thank you to the enthusiastic and hardworking team at Hachette Books Ireland, in particular my talented editor Alison Walsh and the lovely Joanna Smyth, also Breda, Jim, Ruth, Siobhán and Bernard. Congratulations to Ciara Doorley on the birth of her beautiful baby daughter, Elsie. Thanks also for the valuable input of the copyeditor, proofreader and cover designer.

I am grateful to have the warm support and friendship of my agent, Sheila Crowley, of Curtis Brown, London, and thanks are due to Rebecca Ritchie for all her help.

Huge appreciation goes to my circle of family and friends, for love and encouragement and for always being there for me. I feel blessed to have you all in my life, especially Derek, Michelle, Declan, Barbara, Dara, Louise and Colm. I'd like to celebrate the memory of my parents, Lockie and Olive, who left a great legacy in their wake. This book is dedicated to the very precious Cruz, Tom and Lexi, who mean everything to me and who have brought great joy to us all.

And a very special thank you to all the enthusiastic booksellers and the wonderful readers who continue to pick up my books and connect with me on Facebook and Twitter. It really is lovely to hear from you and it makes it all worthwhile. I wouldn't be here without you and I hope you enjoy *A Question of Betrayal*.

Zoë xx

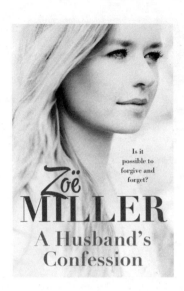

A HUSBAND'S CONFESSION

Is it possible to forgive and forget?

The artisan bakery Ali and Max Kennedy own isn't just a successful business – it's a second home, a dream come true. But when bad luck begins to stalk the couple, Ali worries that her fear of losing it all is becoming a reality.

Across the city, Max's brother Finn and his wife Jo long for the carefree happiness they had when they first met in Australia over twenty years ago. But when Finn loses his high profile TV job and becomes more bitter by the day, Jo starts to suspect that he's hiding something from her.

While both couples navigate their marriages, little do they realise that Max and Ali's daughter Jessica harbours a dark secret which threatens to destroy the whole family.

Then it happens – the accident. And the Kennedys will never be the same again.

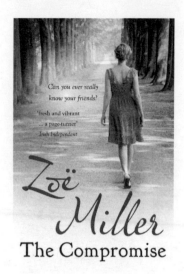

The Compromise

THE COMPROMISE

Can you ever really know your friends?

Childhood friends Juliet, Rebecca, Rose and Matthew grew up in a small village outside Dublin. Now privileged, wealthy and powerful, they appear to have it all. But when Juliet is involved in a suspicious accident and lies trapped between life and death at the bottom of a cliff, a secret that has been hidden for years threatens the seemingly perfect lives of the close-knit group.

For the beautiful, fragile Rose, Juliet's accident brings unwanted attention on the sins of the past. For her husband, the ruthlessly ambitious Matthew, it removes a critical obstacle from the path of his political career. As Rebecca discovers more about what happened to her friend, she begins to wonder if she ever knew the real Juliet Jordan.

Rebecca's troubled young daughter Danielle, hiding out in Rome, knows a truth that can shed light on what happened. But as secrets are revealed, the childhood friends are about to discover that, sometimes, old friends are the ones you know the least.

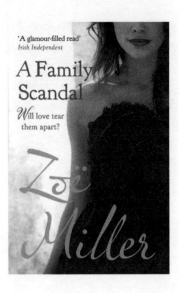

A FAMILY SCANDAL

Will love tear them apart?

The mystery of rock musician Zach Anderson's tragic death has never been solved and now, twenty years on, renewed media interest in his life has thrown the spotlight on his daughter, fashion model Lucy, and her half-sisters Ellie and Miranda.

When the pressures of notoriety and family become too much, Lucy returns to London full of unresolved questions about her father's death while Ellie flees Dublin for the anonymity of New York, and Miranda, desperate to spread her wings away from her family, reclaims her life in Hong Kong.

When their mother falls ill, the sisters return home to face each other and, in doing so, confront the truth about Zach Anderson and what happened all those years ago. But will their love for each other hold them together or tear them apart?

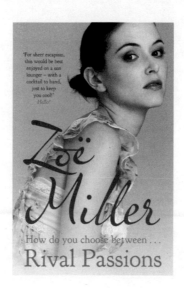

RIVAL PASSIONS

How do you choose between rival passions?

For the beautiful and aloof Serena Devlin, Tamarisk Manor is more than just a family business. It's her life. And her legacy.

For her twin brother, the charming and privileged Jack, the luxury 5-star haven only holds constant reminders of his wife and her tragic death.

But the future of Tamarisk depends on them both and Serena will stop at nothing to protect her legacy.

When Jack leaves for La Mimosa, their sister hotel in France, Serena is left to run the hotel alone, chasing after the coveted Haven of the Year award she so desperately wants, while struggling to cover the cracks appearing in her own marriage.

Then Jack returns home a changed man. As Serena is forced to confront her choices, she discovers just how much she is willing to sacrifice to succeed...